Father's Legacy

I0666656

Thaddeus Nowak

Books by Thaddeus Nowak

Snow Cat Series
Snow Cat's Shadow (Coming 2024)

Heirs of Cothel Series
Mother's Curse
Daughter's Justice
Daughter's Revenge
Daughter's Search
Father's Legacy

Queen of Ista Series
Queen of Ista (Coming 2024)

Bound Series
Bound

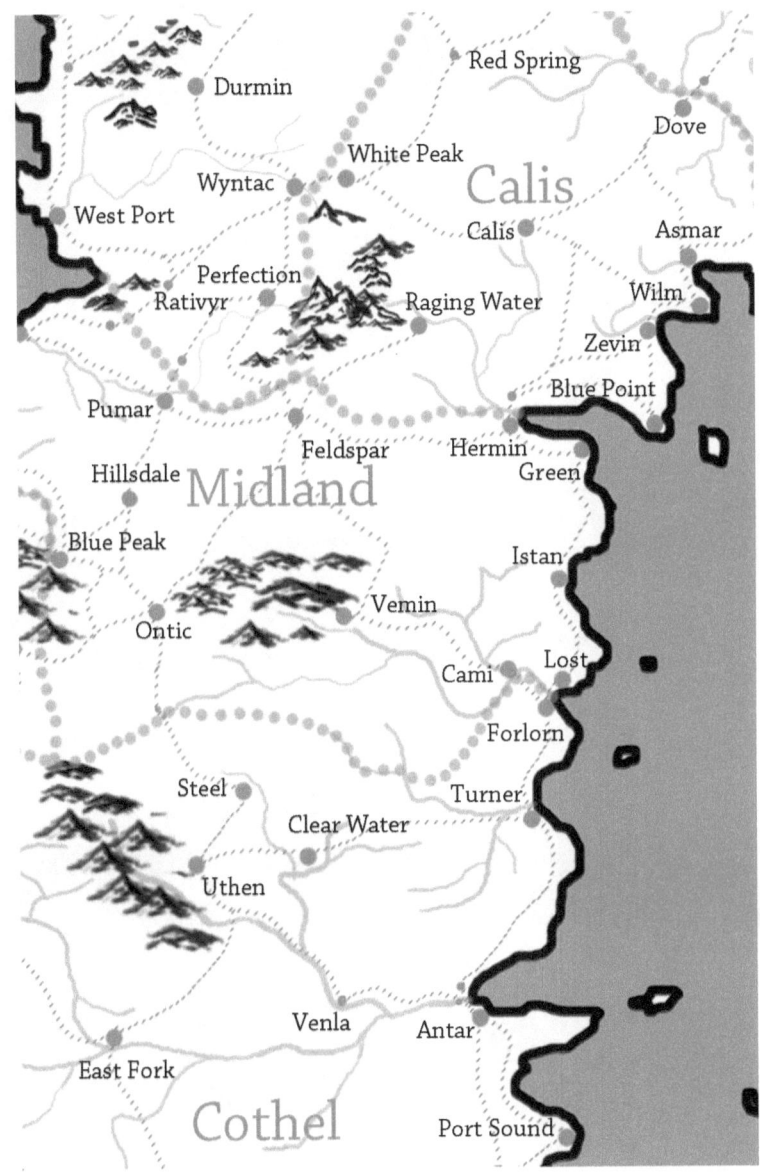

Map of Calis, Midland, and Cothel.

Map of Kynto, Salzen, Uvar, Calis and Midland.

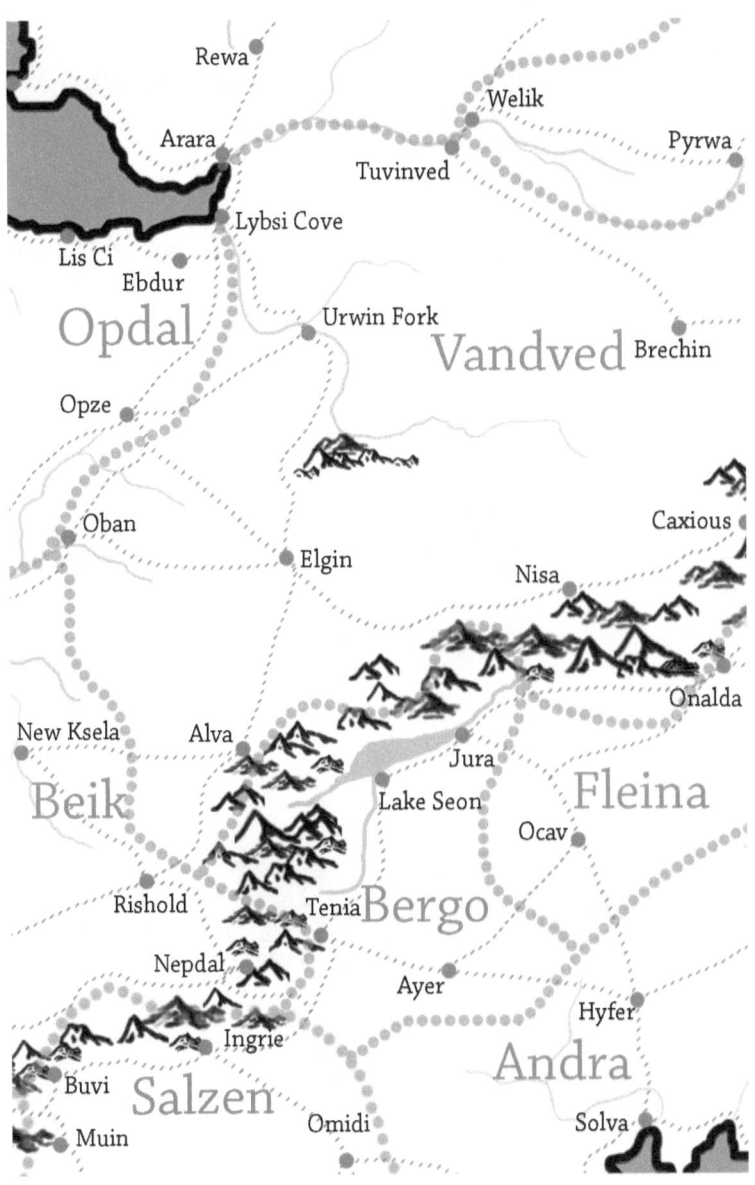

Map of Opdal, Vandvend, Beik, Fleina, Bergo, Salzen, and Andra.

Map of Mestad, Algrem, Garder, Ervik, Jaren, Fleina, and Talset.

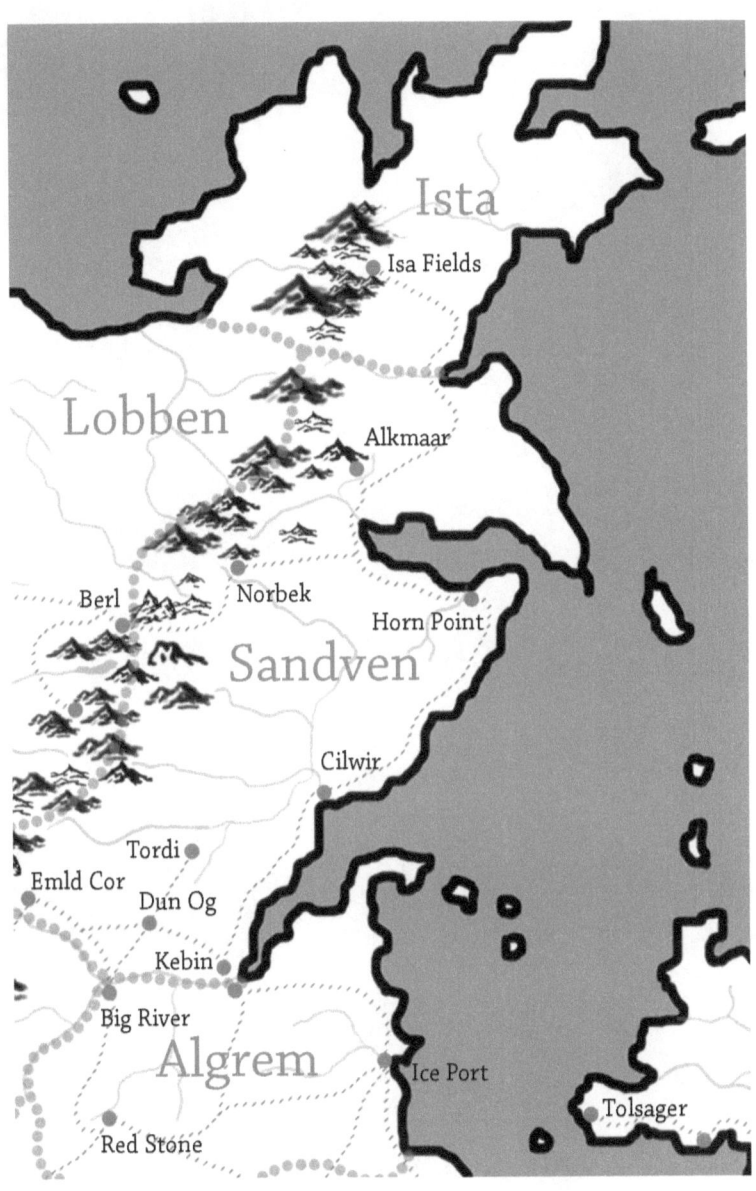

Map of Ista, Lobben, Sandven, and Algrem.

Acknowledgements

I would like to thank the many people who have helped make this work possible. My wife Sherri, my best friend Chad, my brother Joe, my other brothers Dave and Dan and their wives Jenni and Linda, and my parents. I would also like to thank my editor Judy Reveal as well as the others who have inspired and offered advice. Any errors left in the work are entirely mine.

Chapter 1

Stephenie leaned back against the tower's cold crenellation and closed the book on her lap. Neither moon was visible in the star-filled sky, and while it was not too dark for her eyes to read, she had found nothing of use in the old tome. She lacked the will to pick up another book from the pile next to her. Instead, she turned her face into the icy wind that whipped through the mountain valley. Her gaze fell on the keep sitting inside the curtain wall. The square building with its massive walls stood sixty-feet high and had few ornamentations.

After a moment, her gaze to drift to the ground. Her long red hair fell off her shoulder as she leaned to her left and allowed her upper body to hang over the side of the tower. Gravity tugged at her, threatening her balance on the edge of the fifty-foot fall into the rubble-strewn courtyard below her. The rocky debris had once been a section of the outer curtain wall. Such devastation and destruction of old buildings bothered her in general, but in this case, the chaos ate at her all the more because she had unleashed it herself by collapsing part of the wall.

"I didn't come here to kill anyone," she mumbled into the wind. She found it hard to turn her eyes away from the corpses scattered about the rubble. Some of the dead wore armor, but her powerful sight spotted at least three who were clothed in simple garments. Those people had likely come from the town nearly three miles to the south. The men, women, and children had fled their homes for safety, fearing her expected response. However, they had failed to consider the possibility that she would actually take the keep by force. In the aftermath, and consumed by terror, the priests of Mertor had left their dead as they fled. In this, as in all other aspects of these priests' lives, death meant little.

No one hurts my friends, she swore silently and the hostility still burning within her gave her pause. She slowed her breathing and tried to push her rage away, but no matter how much she tried, it continued to simmer under her calm exterior. *I won't lose control. I won't let them drive me to that again.*

She knew her anger had justification. The priests had taken her friends from the town and held them hostage with the threat of torture and death unless she surrendered herself for execution. "They almost killed Douglas and with what they..." She closed her eyes and pushed back against the possessiveness that bubbled up within her. "I will not let this beat me," she swore, wishing that Senzar mage had never invaded her mind all those months ago, awakening a possessive darkness within her that she had to constantly suppress.

She closed her eyes and reminded herself that the majority of those who had made this valley their home had escaped unharmed. *And it was only those trying to kill me that died.* She did her best to ignore the handful of people who had died from stray debris as they ran for cover, but she really could not forget them.

She turned her focus back to the keep, trying to will away the screams echoing in her memory. The structure remained dark. No light shown in any of the narrow windows, but she knew her friends were inside asleep and recovering. She had driven everyone else from the building so they would be safe as they slept.

"As you should be also." Kas' voice floated through the air, commenting on the thoughts of sleep she knew he had picked out of her mind.

Stephenie did not turn toward her friend. She could sense his fear for her safety, not only in his voice, but in the emotional energy that radiated from him. She knew he waited for a response, so she finally spoke. "I can't sleep. I tried, but all I can think about is what they did to Ryia...what I let happen because I wasn't there to stop them."

She lifted her eyes to meet those that Kas luminesced for her. The nearly transparent ghost floated a few feet away from her, hovering high above the ground and directly between her and the keep. His form lacked proper coloration, but Stephenie knew his perfectly combed hair and sharp eyes had been brown when he had a body.

"I expect she will recover with time," Kas offered. "Douglas also has healed well, though I imagine he will remain sore for a number of days, perhaps even some weeks. His body cannot heal as easily as yours. However, he is young and healthy enough that you should not worry yourself."

She glanced down at her left arm. The skin and muscle showed no sign of ever being damaged and stood in a sharp contrast to the remains of her shirt sleeve that no longer existed below her upper arm. The burned edges of cloth were all the evidence that remained of the deadly lightning that had momentarily destroyed all the flesh of her forearm. *And it has never felt stronger,* she admitted to herself, knowing with certainty that the energy she pushed through her body had not only knitted her flesh back together, but had for a brief moment, transformed her physical form.

She turned her head to the north and looked up at Dantborn Peak looming over her. *I need to free those men I left trapped in the cave,* she thought to Kas.

"Even though they fancy themselves as priests of this...stupidity... this fake god Mertor? They would have tried to kill you had they been here."

Stephenie frowned. "Kas, you can't prevent me from going on a murderous rampage yesterday only to tell me today to allow two men to die slowly because I trapped their feet in stone."

He bowed his translucent blue-green head in her direction, but a hardness remained in his expression. *Stephenie, you are incorrect in the belief I cannot tell you that, seeing as I just did so. I will grant that you are correct in the fundamental essence that I have provided you contradictory advice.* He sighed. *I should not seek to cause you to avoid that action entirely. However, I doubt the others would be capable of making the journey to the cave at this time. Therefore, I suspect you will endeavor to free the men on your own and leave me here as guardian of our friends. I fear for your safety if you should go there alone, therefore, I argue for caution.*

Stephenie smiled at Kas. "I'm not that fragile. And it won't take me long to go there and come back."

"And yet you have slept little, despite all you did. That will impede your ability to react effectively."

Stephenie assumed the sounds he made by using his powers to vibrate the air mirrored the sound of his actual voice when he lived. However, she had no way to know for certain and neither did Kas. As a ghost, his energy field felt the disturbance of the sound waves moving through the air and he had long ago learned to translate that into an understanding of words and noises. By sharing a mental link with someone who was alive, he learned to not only hear without his own ears, but to speak without lungs and a mouth.

She closed her eyes again and returned her thoughts to his statement. She had to admit her body did ache for sleep, but as she had told him, her thoughts had not allowed her the comfort of rest. "I can't leave a couple of men to suffer like that. Perhaps when I get back from freeing them I'll be able to sleep."

Kas floated around her and came to rest on the top of the tower. "There should be no need for me to mention it, but Henton would be quite disappointed if you went out there without informing him."

Stephenie's brow wrinkled. "Damn you," she said, but her voice lacked any venom. She knew the truth of Kas' statement and that was not Kas' fault. Henton would indeed be disappointed and that would be worse than any anger from him. "Fine. I'll wait until they are up, but it will not change the fact that I will go alone. I want to get out of this valley. I know yesterday I said we should rest here for a few days, but I can't do it." She frowned and shrugged as she repeated herself. "I just can't stay here and those men can't be expected to survive as I left them."

Kas bowed his head to her. "Of course." He drifted closer to her, though his lower legs and feet did not form as he moved. "What of the books?"

Stephenie looked at the pile she had carried to the top of the tower. "The ones I can read are mostly logs of who these assassins have killed. There are a couple of journals the priests wrote to explain their own sanctimonious justifications as to why they felt obligated to go around killing people. The truth is simple, they were paid to be assassins. We'll leave them; there is nothing of value."

Kas raised his translucent eyebrows. "I never thought I would find you with the desire to damage books."

Stephenie smiled at her friend and then uncrossed her legs to extend them over the edge of the tower. "These aren't books. They are kindling."

She looked toward the eastern ridge of the horseshoe valley and noted the slight brightening of the sky. "Time to wake the others." With an easy shifting of her body, she slid off the tower and plummeted down toward the rubble fifty-feet below her.

Her stomach lurched, but she had come to enjoy the sensation of weightlessness. As she fell, she extended her senses, increasing her awareness of the energy that existed in the air, the stone of the tower, and in the ground that rushed up to meet her. Subconsciously she opened an area of lower potential within her body, and just like water rushing down into a hole, energy flowed into her. It warmed her as it moved through her flesh.

With her mind, she crafted a field around her body to bend the effects of the force Kas called gravity and immediately the attraction of her body to the ground diminished. She adjusted her field subtly without a conscious understanding of how her body could do what it did. She only knew what the fields needed to look like in order for her to fly—and fly she did.

Three-feet from the ground, her body reversed direction and shot upward, flying past Kas and the top of the tower like a ballista bolt. As she rose high into the air, she spread her arms, and lifted her chin so the cold wind could hit her face and whip her long hair about her head.

She dropped her field and allowed her momentum to continue carrying her upward, but without her field, the ground once again pulled at her body and her upward climb slowed. At the apex of her flight, she rotated, turning her back to the ground. She looked up at the star-filled sky above her as she hung motionless in the air. With both moons below the horizon, the sky was a beautiful field of twinkling lights.

However, gravity refused to be ignored and gradually she began to fall. Like a diving falcon, she picked up speed with her head aiming for the top of the keep. She relished the sensation and complete freedom of moving effortlessly through the air. The diversion emptied her mind of concern for the moment. She did not want to think about anything that had happened. She only wanted to exist; to keep flying. However, the top of the keep was closing on her fast and she knew she had responsibilities and she would not—*could not*—ignore them.

She closed her eyes moments before hitting the flat roof, drew in energy, and again built the field around her body. Her mind sensed and calculated the distance to the tower better than her eyes ever could and a heartbeat before her head crashed into solid stone, she poured power into her field. With the grace of a cat, she flipped over as her fall suddenly halted, allowing her to land on her feet with less force than if she had taken a step. To anyone else, the sudden stop would have broken their bones and ruptured their organs, but strengthened by the energy coursing through her body, she hardly noticed the effect.

Kas flew over to join her as she walked toward the door set into the lone structure on the keep's roof. *You should be more careful. I would not like to see you smashed into a jumble of broken bones and torn flesh. Need I remind you yet again that your death would be very unlikely to result in your becoming a ghost? Unless you desire to punish me in an un-life of loneliness, I would rather you did not die.*

Stephenie sent him a mental smile. Kas had died a thousand years ago. The Denarians, who were the ancestors of the current Senzar invasion force, magically sealed him, and many hundreds of others, in their underground city. The magic had been so strong that those trapped inside Arkani had not simply died, instead they had become ghosts as their bodies perished, trapping their energy forever in the city.

Time had weakened the magical seal and it was through a crack in that city's wall that Stephenie had sought refuge from her mother's soldiers. Her life had changed dramatically by her accidental discovery and wakening of Kas from the trance he and the other ghosts had fallen into as result of the passage of time. However, without something as powerful as that seal, she knew her death would be final. She had never expected anything different and Kas' frequent complaints about her safety were now bordering on the edge of becoming a private joke between them.

"Let's get the others up," she said, not wanting to think about anyone, including herself, dying. "They can gather supplies while I free those soldiers."

Stephenie entered the large bedroom on the top floor of the keep. As a mage, her mind constantly generated tiny energy channels that extended outward and allowed her subconscious to feel the world. And just like a spider in the middle of a web, movement and changes in the world around her were immediately obvious.

Most mages could feel movement as well as the energy waves created by thoughts emanating from living minds. However, for reasons Stephenie did not understand, she could see the actual fields with her mind's eye as easily as she could see with her physical eyes. The fields, as well as the energy potentials inside all matter, were obvious to her if she chose to look at them. The information was not so much a wash of color, but simply an innate understanding of the world.

For now, everything in the keep was quiet and still. Even the energy generated from the minds of her three sleeping friends was muted. However, their minds still emitted enough energy that she had felt their presence from the top of the keep through all the stone and wood that had separated them. The familiarity of their minds calmed her and she slowed her pace as she walked through the door and across the pitch black room.

Henton, the marine sergeant who had become one of her closest friends, shifted slightly in the bed and Stephenie felt a subtle change in his mental energy. She could not understand much that came from his mind, even when focusing her attention on him. His mind was much too disciplined from years of being a soldier. However, the twenty-eight-year-old had always been a light sleeper and she knew he would wake the moment she made another sound.

Douglas, Stephenie's other protector, lacked Henton's build, and at six years Henton's junior, lacked some of Henton's composure and confidence. However, Douglas had as much passion as any of them. *You lanky fool, got yourself stabbed in the gut.* Stephenie closed her eyes to fight back the tears that threatened to leak down her face. *I should have been there for you.*

You got there in time and saved his life, Kas said, reading her mind.

Thoughts of Douglas' injury turned Stephenie's attention to Ryia, the sixteen-year-old girl they had added to their small band in Vinerxan, and now slept in the large bed between the two soldiers, her sandy-blond hair a tangled mess around her head.

Of the three of them, Ryia should have woken at Stephenie's approach. The girl had magic, but her sensitivity and raw potential was minimal, which left her vulnerable to more powerful mages.

I should have been there, Kas, Stephenie repeated, turning to face the man she loved. This time she did not bother to fight back the tears.

As I said, Stephenie, she will recover in time. You neutralized most of the poison's effects and her body will heal the rest. Kas expended the effort to luminesce and a frown was visible on his blue-green face. *As for the rest, she said she does not remember what the men had done to her, so I expect it will not scar her. It would not be the first time she had been taken advantage of and she has dealt with her past remarkably well.*

Stephenie pushed down the possessive rage that still boiled in her. "They are my...responsibility," she said, avoiding any wording that would have indicated her true feelings of ownership. She hoped Kas would not sense just how much she felt all of them belonged to her. She knew it was not a sense of ownership as a master and a slave, where she would ever consider forcing them to do anything they did not want, *but anyone who tries to hurt them...*

"Steph," Henton said, his voice pitched low to avoid waking the others. "You say something?"

Stephenie's anxiety fell away at the sound of his strong voice and she could not contain the small sigh that escaped her lips. She smiled, though even with Kas' illumination, there was not enough light for Henton to see her expression. "The sun's starting to brighten the horizon," she said mirroring the pitch of his voice. "The more I thought about it overnight, the more I want to get out of the valley today instead of waiting around until everyone has healed."

Henton slowly slid from the bed, which caused Ryia to stir.

"Henton?" Ryia questioned, her voice so soft Stephenie felt it rather than heard her.

"Try to sleep some more," Henton replied as he straightened.

Stephenie sensed the oil lamp sitting on a side table and poured energy into the wick from where she stood a dozen feet away at the foot of the bed. Flames instantly sprang into existence, bringing light into the room, though she used a second field to turn down the wick, keeping the light from being overwhelming.

"Thanks," Henton said as he started to move to the foot of the bed. While he still remained dressed in his worn shirt and pants, his boots sat on the floor. His short brown-hair stood at odd angles.

Stephenie glanced at Douglas. From his mind, she sensed he had awoken at the noise, but the soldier continued to feign sleep—*or perhaps a hope to fall back asleep,* she decided.

Stephenie moved closer and sat on the end of the bed. "How are you this morning?" She asked Ryia.

The blue-eyed girl shrugged and then scooted backwards in the bed so she could sit against the headboard. "I'm still feeling a bit worn out. My head hurts." The rumble of Ryia's stomach filled the room. "And I'm hungry."

Stephenie smiled at her. "I imagine both you and Douglas will be starving. I pushed a lot of energy into your healing yesterday that will have taxed your bodies. You'll need to eat to replace what was used to heal you." She looked over to Henton who had finished putting on his boots and had also strapped on his sword belt. "I snacked through the night," she admitted to her protector, who undoubtedly wondered why she had not demanded some food as well.

"I'm glad you finally took my advice," he said with a chuckle.

"Only when it makes sense," Stephenie replied even before he had finished speaking, her smile widening. She tugged at Douglas' closest foot. "You aren't sleeping and you should know I can tell when you are pretending."

"Just because you can't let a man rest in peace, doesn't mean I need to get up and chatter with the four of you." Douglas kept his eyes closed a moment longer, then huffed once before slowly rolling onto his side so he could face everyone. "It's still dark in here without the lamp. We should get more rack time."

Stephenie raised her upturned hands and tilted her head as she glanced about the room. "It's an interior room," she demanded, "It's always dark in here."

"My point exactly," Douglas said with a grin. He tried to move into a sitting position, but winced before giving up.

Stephenie patted his leg. She felt the sharp pain that radiated from him and knew he was not faking his wound. "I need to take care of freeing those two men I left stuck in the cave. But while I am gone, I think it would be best if the four of you got us ready to leave the valley."

Douglas perked up and managed to move into a sitting position despite the pain. "What men?" His voice cold and his bearded jaw set. "Some of those bastards? You let them live?"

Stephenie held her immediate reply. She understood Douglas' anger. Locked in the adjacent cell, he had heard everything they had done to the unconscious Ryia. The wound to his gut had been earned in his effort to kill all the men that had hurt their companion.

"Douglas," Henton said before Stephenie could respond. "We're soldiers. We kill if we have to, but we are not murderers. I won't condone killing in cold blood."

"Even after what they did to Ryia?" Douglas demanded.

Henton's lips compressed into a tight line. Stephenie watched Ryia's pained expression as she waited on Henton's reply.

"Yes. Even then," he finally said. "If they resist and die, so be it. But if they surrender, they deserve to be judged and dealt with as appropriate."

Douglas shook his head. "That's just to make you feel better about yourself. They'd kill you in your sleep if they could. The men that hurt her deserved their death and I don't care how they got it, only that it's done."

Stephenie cleared her throat. She knew how Henton would respond. It was the same way she would. "Douglas, it may be just to make us feel better about ourselves, but it also separates us from them. Don't cross me on that point. We fight when there is no choice, but we're not assassins." She softened her expression. "The men in the cave are no threat to me and likely not even a threat to any of you. They didn't harm us, even if they believed in Mertor." She held his gaze. "There was a time all of us believed in Elrin and Felis and the other gods as well and would have died for Felis' causes, so I won't leave them trapped to slowly starve to death because they also believed."

"I never did," Kas declared, having died before people had adopted the belief in the current set of gods.

Douglas bowed his head. "I am sorry. I...I just hate what happened."

Stephenie gave him a small smile. "I understand and I have to fight some of the same fits of rage in myself." She looked over at Ryia who had grown very quiet. She felt a slight panic as well as a withdrawal of the girl's presence. "Ryia, you feeling well enough to search the keep for more money and valuables?" Stephenie raised her eyebrows in expectation of a response. "I'll ask Henton to make the three of you something to eat while Kas keeps watch if you and Douglas can gather up our things and perhaps look for anything else these priests have left for our taking."

Slowly Ryia nodded her head and then offered a forced grin. "Yeah, I'd be willing to fill my pouches with more coin if we can find it."

Stephenie kept herself from sighing in relief. She did not know how to handle this situation, but she knew she did not want Ryia to withdraw into herself and Henton's glance told her he approved of her approach in keeping Ryia active. "Good. I'll head to the cave, free the men, and come back. I'd like to head out of the valley shortly after that."

Kas' voice filled the room, interrupting Henton's intention to speak. "Henton, I will save you the time. I have already pleaded the wisdom of not going alone and Stephenie has determined I am wrong."

"I won't leave the three of you here unprotected." Her voice boomed through the room and she shook her head as she stood. "I won't discuss it anymore, so, Kas, if you want to express some attitude about it, you can wait until I am gone."

Kas bowed his head. "Please forgive me. I worry about you is all."

Stephenie nodded her head. "I love you and I know you worry, but please, I have enough concerns about leaving all of you alone and I don't need more grief."

Henton put one hand on her shoulder, drawing her attention. "Steph, we'll be fine. Go, release the men and come back here. We'll be ready to go when you get back."

She looked up into his brown eyes. "Thank you," she said, hoping he knew how much his lack of protesting her decision meant.

"But," Henton said as she started to turn away, "I want you to take the staff and dagger."

Stephenie glanced over to the desk sitting against the far wall. A steal capped quarter staff lay next to an ornamented dagger. Both items carried dragon motifs as well as the seal of Ista, a country far to the north. She could not pull her attention away from the weapons. The man she believed to have sired her had given those weapons to the priests of Mertor as a means to kill her. Not only had he provided these assassins with the tools to end her life, he had pretended to be the voice of their god and made them believe she was the spawn of Elrin, the imaginary demon god of the elves—*a god he claimed to be when he raped my mother.* She bit her lower lip. *Why do you hate me? What have I done to you?*

"Steph," Henton said softly, "I know what those represent to you, but they are powerful and if you insist on going alone—after what you did yesterday—then I insist you take them for protection."

Stephenie took a deep breath and then slowly walked over to the weapons. She reached out and picked up the dagger with the golden pommel and dark leather sheath. The emblem of Ista stood out clearly on the crossbar. She did not bother to pull the blade to look at the dragons etched on the steel; instead, she loosened her sword belt and started to slide the dagger onto the leather.

The dagger was barely on her belt when she sensed movement behind the desk. She had felt nothing before a large multi-legged creature scurried along the side of the desk. The suddenness of the change forced her back a step. Instinct brought a gravity field into existence and Stephenie flung the creature backward into the wall.

The creature immediately rebounded, pushed itself from the wall with multiple spindly legs, and flew back at her.

She fell back another step as her mind registered more details of what advanced on her. The thing had nine legs, each at least a foot long and an inch thick. The legs propelled a melon sized mass. The whole thing had a raw meat appearance and the legs resembled broken and articulated ribs.

She gripped her sword handle as she tossed the belt and scabbard across the room, effectively drawing the weapon. At the same time, she used her magic to continuously push the creature away.

"Careful, it is not natural," Kas said quickly as he moved beside Stephenie, talking more to the others than her. "It draws energy."

Behind her, she felt Henton draw his own sword. Ryia and Douglas' emotions contracted as the threat focused their attentions. The two of them scrambled from the bed and drew their weapons.

In front of her, the creature resisted her gravity field. It lacked eyes and did not appear to have a mouth. When its limbs moved, the joints clicked and snapped, as if they were made of broken bones. She pushed more power into her field to counter the energy the creature drew. However, her hopes of holding it in place died as the creature's field modulated and allowed it to slip through hers.

Stephenie jumped back again as the creature leapt at her, its rib cage like legs splayed out as it flew through the air. Her sword caught it in midair, severing one limb as the force of her blow sent the mass off to her right where it hit the wall again.

Kas rushed toward it with the intent of freezing it by drawing away energy, but as soon as he reached the creature, he cried out and retreated. "I cannot fight it," he swore, moving back across the room. "It drew power from me instead."

Stephenie did not bother replying, she knew he withdrew so she would not become distracted trying to protect him. Her focus narrowed as the severed limb at her feet flung itself into the air in her direction at the same time the flesh-spider leapt off the wall again.

Instinct driving her, she flooded herself with energy and used her power to rip a section of books from a nearby shelf, hitting the creature in midair. The books and creature hit the floor and tumbled against the far wall. The severed limb she knocked away with her sword, cutting the fragment of rib into two more pieces.

"Pin it with something," Henton cried, moving toward the creature with his sword extended.

"Stay back!" she yelled as she pulled a chest of drawers down on top of it. However, the mass of bloody meat and bones scurried out of the way before the furniture landed on it.

She tried to protect Henton as the flesh-spider raced across the floor at him, but her gravity field simply rolled off the creature. *Damn it,* she swore, moving toward Henton as he swung his sword, smashing his blade into the top of the creature's center mass.

"Kill it!" Ryia shouted, still on the other side of the bed.

Douglas, with one arm holding his side, moved tentatively closer, his sword wobbling slightly in his other hand. "Where'd the damn thing come from?"

Stephenie held her distance and studied it as Henton continued to hold it to the wooden floor with the tip of his sword. The flesh-spider's limbs scraped against the boards as it pushed and pulled against the sword. The effort kept Henton working hard to keep it pinned.

"The damn thing's strong," Henton swore as he retreated a step to keep his distance from the creature's legs.

Stephenie pulled energy from the creature in the hopes of preventing it from having enough power to function. However, even as frost spread over the floor and she gorged herself on the energy, more power kept flowing out of the creature, *just like an augmentation device.*

"I have never seen such a thing," Kas said, still remaining on the other side of the room. "It does not appear to be living. It would seem to be made up of dead body parts."

Henton's struggles increased and he leaned all of his weight into holding the creature against the icy floor. Then suddenly the middle of his sword started to bend and Henton began to fall forward. Stephenie ceased fighting the creature, wrapped Henton in a gravity field, and flung him back toward the bed just as the middle of the sword liquefied. "It can transform matter!" she shouted, moving herself between Henton and the creature that now had the lower part of Henton's sword extending forward from the center of its body.

The spider scurried toward Stephenie again and instinctively, she smashed a gravity field into the creature from above, but her field rolled off the spider and the modified field ended up cutting through the wooden boards like they were pudding. The spider and the section of the floor dropped into the room below, but she felt the creature catch itself after only a couple of feet.

"It is coming back up!" She stepped back and pushed everyone behind her. "It's using a thread of gravity as a web." *What can I do, Kas?* She pleaded, knowing that if the creature was some form of modified augmentation device, it would have more than enough power to defend itself.

I need more time to study it before I can offer a suggestion, Kas said, though his emotions conveyed his own fear and sense of failure in lacking the necessary knowledge.

"Back!" Stephenie growled, her voice suddenly growing cold as the creature climbed through the hole into the room.

She had tried countless ways to destroy augmentation devices, but the objects received their power through an entangled link to a relay. She never discovered a way to block the nonlinear energy path that gave the object an incredible reserve of power.

With time running out, she decided to do one thing she had never attempted with an augmentation device. She tossed aside her sword and opened her mind and body to the energy around her. Not satisfied with simply allowing the energy to flow into her, she devoured everything she could from the stone walls, the wooden floor, and even the air in the room. Power surged into her, burning and destroying her insides as it filled her body and mind.

In less than a single heartbeat, pain radiated through every nerve in her body. Her bones felt as if they had been crushed in a press and her mind ached under pressure that threatened to explode her skull. *Please work,* she begged. Tears vaporized from her eyes as she pulled in more power than she had ever attempted before. She struggled to hold her body together, sensing an imminent failure of her flesh. She began to question herself, but the thought had not fully formed before she unleashed the raw energy from her outstretched arms.

The air exploded into white-hot flames as a cone of energy struck the creature. A blast of air, formed by the suddenness of her attack, blew out windows in adjacent rooms. Then as the flames consumed the oxygen in the room, the wind reversed, pulling a cold draft through the keep from the outside.

Never before had she pushed so much energy in a single instant. She normally allowed the power to build more slowly and released it over a longer period of time. The heat, radiating upward, burned the flesh from her upper arms and charred her face as well as the ceiling of the room. Instinct took over and a moment later, her body protected itself by extruding energy from everything above her waist. Her skin and muscle adjusted, changing as energy flowed through it. The burned flesh mended and took on an iridescent quality. Her eyes that had burned to black regained sight and her vision sharpened so she could see the flesh and bone limbs and body of the creature disintegrate. Dimly, she also had an awareness that the floor in front of her had ceased to exist even before the flesh-spider had started to decay.

She embraced the pain as she continued to pull energy into her body, recycling some of what she had just expended. Her ability to deal with the pain lasted for only another beat of her heart. The toll on her body went beyond reason and while her body had changed, there were limits to what even that could sustain. *Please,* she begged of no one in particular as she continued to stare at the spider, willing it to die completely before she died herself. All of the muscle and bone of the creature no longer existed and what remained was a disk of metal hanging in the air. Mentally blinded by the power she pushed forth, she could not tell if it continued to radiate energy or not.

Suddenly, the disk wilted and sagged, then was blown back through the gaping hole she had burned through the floor of this room and even the floor of the room below that.

Unable to sustain the draw of power, the flames around her died instantly. Blinded by the sudden lack of light and trembling from weakness, as well as the cold, she dropped to the floor.

"Steph?" she heard Ryia's voice squeak, though the girl sounded as though she was in a distant cave.

Stephenie felt someone's warm hands on her arms and she managed to force her eyes open. Henton knelt beside her, his hair and face covered in a dusting of frost. She continued to tremble as he scooped her up in his arms. He stood and moved quickly toward the door.

Overwhelmed from the effects, she could not sense anything around her. "Kas?" she called, fearing she might have injured him in her rapid energy draw. She turned her head from side to side, noting, but not looking at the ice and frost that covered everything in the room. "KAS!"

"I am here," he said, floating through a wall.

Henton angled her through the doorway to avoid hitting her head. "Douglas, get me a blanket that's not frozen." In the hall, he carefully set her down on her feet so he could wrap himself around her naked upper body.

"Steph?" Ryia asked again. "I..."

"She'll be fine," Henton said.

Stephenie met his stare. The frost that had covered his face and head had started to melt away due to his body heat. He continued to look at her and she knew he was searching her eyes for signs she might have damaged her mind. "My head hurts, but I am okay."

"What's coming off her skin?" Ryia asked, taking one step closer.

Stephenie saw the iridescent dusting on Henton's shirt and knew there would be more dust flaking off her upper body. She closed her eyes and leaned into Henton's chest, absorbing his warmth.

"That's right," Henton said to Ryia, "you've not actually seen her do that."

Ryia shook her head and moved another step closer as Douglas brought over a blanket that Henton wrapped around Stephenie.

"I hate spiders," Stephenie managed to say through chattering teeth.

Henton chuckled. "While they never really bothered me before, I think that thing may have changed my opinion." He lifted her chin to look into her eyes. "You are on your feet. How is that possible? You should be unconscious. That seemed more intense than you normally do and you said you had to absorb a lightning blast yesterday."

Stephenie sighed and slipped her chin from Henton's hand so she could rest herself against his chest again. Mumbling into his shirt, she answered him. "I'm not sure why, but each time seems to get easier. It hurts less and I recover quicker."

Kas grumbled. "It is still not a safe thing to do. A fraction of that kind of energy moving through a person would normally be lethal."

She nodded her head, "Yeah, tell that to the pounding in my head." After a moment, she pushed herself away from Henton's chest and turned toward the others, though she continued to keep her hand on Henton and leaned against him to hold herself upright. "Is it dead?"

Kas shrugged tentatively. "When Douglas went for a blanket, I dropped down to take a closer look." Kas' illumination was almost fully opaque. "Whatever the device had been, it appears to be significantly damaged. It would be my hope that it is now destroyed."

"What was it?" Henton asked.

Kas turned his head. "I am uncertain. What remains is a melted lump of metal. Stephenie's fire burned through this floor and the one below; however, because of the angle of her attack, and the location of where the object had been, it fell onto the floor directly below us and not through to the room below that."

"I smell smoke," Ryia said, acting as a support for Douglas.

Kas nodded his head. "The great intensity of Stephenie's fire destroyed most of what the flames encountered; however, the contrasting draw of energy from our surroundings resulted in most of the flames lacking the energy to sustain themselves. There are, however, a few smoldering areas. It is possible they will begin to take hold and spread now that Stephenie is no longer extracting energy from the environment."

Stephenie loved that even with the current events, Kas insisted on being precise. "Is it safe enough for Ryia to go down there and extinguish the flames? I don't want to draw attention to this valley by burning down the castle, but if there are more of those things, I don't want them attacking anyone else."

Kas pursed his lips. "You are by far the most sensitive to energy fields and the most likely one to feel other such creatures."

"Not right now. My head will need time to clear. I'm starting to get some sense back, but...I didn't feel it until it moved. It somehow hid from my sensitivity. It might have been in the room earlier, but it could have come in while the two of us were outside."

Kas bowed his head to her. "At the moment, I felt no power being drawn into the melted metal. Though if it was an augmentation device, as you suggested earlier, it may not need to draw local energy."

Stephenie bit her lower lip. "Whatever it was, it was wrapped in muscle and bone. It looked like ribs ripped out of a person." She felt Henton tense. "It wasn't alive. It used magic to move and it seemed bent on hurting me."

"And it ate the tip of my sword," Henton said. "Was that heat or what you do to stone?"

"It transformed the metal. No heat." She loathed to move away from Henton's warmth and the support his arms provided, but she had already begun to feel her strength returning, so she slowly took a step to the left. "I've no idea where the flesh came from, but I'd guess one of the dead. Probably the High Priest. I might have missed something the priestess carried."

"We'll have to check the body," Douglas said as he moved from Ryia's side to stand on his own. "But if those were the priestess' ribs, the bitch deserved it."

Stephenie did not challenge the statement; the priestess had held her friends hostage under the threat of torture and death. The woman refused to yield and continued to fight when offered a chance to surrender. Stephenie had killed her to protect those she cared for.

"Steph?" Henton asked.

"Sorry, what?"

"You need to rest," Henton repeated. "We can let you sleep and we'll keep watch."

She shook her head. "No. I want out of this valley now more than before. We have no way of knowing what else might be lying in wait."

"You think that was something your fath—sire left?" Douglas asked.

She turned toward Douglas and ignored his slip. "Yes. There is no way these priests created something like that. He left the dagger and staff with them, probably something else as well." She saw Douglas' concern. "It was not tied to Mertor because the trap is dead. I killed the trap. It would have to be tied to a different relay and trap. I am certain it used an entangled power source. I just don't know which one."

Henton put a hand on her shoulder. "Okay, we'll gather our things and get ready to head out. Ryia and I are the least hurt, we'll get everything ready while you and Douglas rest with Kas, then we'll head south and out of the valley."

"I'm getting stronger," she said, her tone overriding Henton without offering offense. "We need to stay together while in the castle. We'll gather our things, put out any fires, and once we are out of the valley, I'll go back and free those men."

"What?" Ryia demanded. "You can't do that. What if there are more of those things? What if the men are already dead?"

Stephenie looked at the young girl and felt the fear coming from her friend despite the numbness of her own mind. "As I said earlier, I'll not leave them to die. I made a promise to them and I will keep it."

Chapter 2

After Ryia put out the small fires burning on the lower floors, Stephenie examined the lump of metal that had been the center of the flesh-spider. "I can't feel anything from it, but I am not going to touch it." The thought that it might somehow reform by coming into contact with a living person ran through her head, and while she expected that was paranoia, she had no intention of risking herself.

"That is a wise choice," Kas said as he also conducted another investigation of the device. "It appears to have become pitted as it started to melt. I would conclude that the protective matrix it generated started to fail and some of the metal vaporized while it remained in the fire. However, there may have been enough residual protection that it managed to fall out of your fire before the protection died completely."

"Or the damn thing is just waiting to rebuild itself," Douglas said from where he stood in the doorway.

"Steph, do you think we are safe for now?" Henton asked, keeping himself between the lump of metal and the others. He held Douglas' sword in his hand, since Douglas was not up to physical combat.

She glanced at Kas who gave her a mental shrug, though his appearance did not visually change. She slowly stood up, her last shirt hanging loosely about her body. She would put a new binding around her chest once she felt certain the others were safe. "We have no way of knowing if there are more of these things waiting for us or not. At the moment, I think this one is deactivated or perhaps even dead. So, we go back upstairs, get the chest of money, the rest of our things, then head down to the kitchens, get some food, find a replacement sword for Henton, and head out of the valley."

Henton straightened. "Ryia, you and I will do the heavy lifting. We're the least injured, but I think it will still take a couple of trips to get everything downstairs." He extended an arm to Stephenie. "I'll let you get the dagger and staff you left upstairs."

Stephenie nodded her head. Henton's thinly veiled jab at her leaving them in the room while they came down to put out the fires and check the device did not deserve a reply. She did not trust either weapon, but at the same time, neither could be discarded. *And if someone should take the risk of handling them, it should be me.*

Are you able to hear me? Kas asked mentally as they made their way to the stairs and up to the bedroom.

Stephenie smiled at him. *Mostly. My head's still throbbing and things feel distant, like when Joshua had gotten me drunk all those years ago.*

Your color and strength are recovering unusually fast, did you do anything differently when you drew upon the energy?

Stephenie shook her head. *I can't explain it. It just keeps getting easier. Still hurts like a bastard, though.* She glanced in his direction. *I know it is risky, the last thing I want is to incapacitate myself, but it feels like I am getting stronger every time I do it.*

I have never felt it wise to push that much power through your body. The first time you did so, you were unconscious for days and nearly died. However, I have decided I will not base any judgments for your abilities on what is true for others. We will just have to see what you are capable of doing.

She smiled at Kas and ignored the look Henton gave her for having a private conversation. *That first time I had caused the mountain top to crumble.* She did not allow herself to think of the thousands that had died as a result. *And thank you for understanding.*

"Ryia, be careful of the floor," Henton said, drawing Stephenie's attention to Ryia's scowl, but the girl had stopped moving. "I know you're not going to trip and fall, but I caught a look at the beams when we were downstairs and Steph managed to burn through at least three major supports. There is a risk the whole floor could collapse."

"Allow me to retrieve the small things from the other side of the room," Kas said as he floated over the hole in the floor. He returned immediately with Stephenie's sword belt and the dagger.

Henton and Ryia moved more cautiously to the bed and the pile of equipment they had gathered the night before. Fortunately, the chest of coins the assassins had accumulated was in easy reach.

"Good thing you didn't incinerate the chest," Douglas said. "Henton and I had too many cold days unloading ships to earn back the money you destroyed on the way to Vinerxan."

"I love you too, Douglas," Stephenie said and stuck her tongue out at him. The friendly banter felt good and gave her hope things could actually return to normal.

After her sword belt was fastened around her waist, she moved around the hole in the floor and crossed to the desk. She stopped for a moment and stared at the staff. The wood had darkened with age, but showed no signs of wear or damage. A magical object would not likely rust, she told herself. With a bit of trepidation, she extended her hand toward the weapon. Her sire had given it to the priests of Mertor to be used to kill her and she had no idea what other traps it might hold.

The staff did not seem to react to her approaching hand, but she knew it could be very destructive. The High Priest of Mertor had used it to unleash massive bolts of lightning, one of which had destroyed her left arm. Additionally, it had created a protective field that had blocked all of Stephenie's magic.

She glanced to her left arm, the sleeve of her last remaining shirt covered her unblemished skin. She had no conscious knowledge of how to rebuild limbs, but somewhere deep in her mind existed the instinct. *And if I can figure it out, perhaps I can rebuild Kas' body.*

The absence of movement behind her made her aware she had stood with her hand inches from the staff for several moments. The others had noticed her hesitation and stopped what they were doing. *I'm being stupid,* she told herself and put her hand on the weapon.

Immediately she felt the staff's presence reach out for her mind. For something to hold power, some amount of intelligence had to be created in the object. The more the object could do, the greater and more sophisticated the intelligence had to be. She had enough experience with people in her head that she knew she did not want to risk the staff taking over her mind, and in turn, controlling her body. *Stay out of my head,* she swore at the intelligence, blocking the weapon's access to her thoughts.

The staff responded by withdrawing and seemingly returning to a dormant state. The first time she picked up the weapon and pushed the intelligence away, it had respected her desire and never tried to reestablish the contact until she put it down and picked it up a second time. The pattern had remained consistent for the handful of times she had picked it up and set it down. However, she was not ready to trust the device to not simply be waiting for her to become complacent and lower her guard.

"I can carry my gear, Sarge," Douglas said, taking the pack Henton had just picked up. Douglas shouldered the weight with minimal outward discomfort.

"You've still got a gut wound that needs time to heal," Henton challenged, ready to take the pack back, though Henton already had Stephenie's and his own pack on his back. The heavy chest of coins still sat on the floor at his feet.

"If it means getting out of here sooner, I'll carry my things, Sarge."

Stephenie moved back around the hole in the floor and joined them. "Yeah, it's funny how much more everyone can carry if it means making a single trip." She picked up the last sack from the floor and slung it over her shoulder. With the staff tucked under her arm, she bent down and picked up the heavy chest, making it look as if it weighed nothing.

Douglas chuckled as he moved slowly toward the door. "With magic, anything can look easy. If we could all carry things like that, we'd need more pack horses to haul all the loot."

A moment of panic filled her. "I locked up Argat and the others in the stables last night. We need to check the horses," she said, moving quickly to the stairs. She did not want to think what one of the flesh-spiders might do to her chestnut gelding.

They crossed the rubble strewn courtyard and made their way to the stables located against the section of the curtain wall that protected the back of the keep. Stephenie could feel the animals inside and none of the horses, rats, or cats making their home in the barn felt fear at the moment. From the horses, she gathered more a sense of boredom and hunger.

"It seems quiet," she said as she approached the large swinging barn door. "Hang on a moment," she told Henton as he moved to open it. "I melted the hinges to make sure no one took Argat or the others." She set down the items she carried and then narrowed her focus on the four iron bands that were wrapped around iron posts and allowed the door to swing. Linking a channel to each, she pushed in energy until the metal became red hot.

With the surrounding wood smoking, she generated a gravity field to force the door to move. Once the opening was wide enough for the horses, she reversed the flow of energy, removing heat from the metal, and preventing the wood of the building from actually catching fire.

"Argat, you ready for breakfast?" she called out as she strode into the barn, walking pasted the odor of charred wood. She quickly looked about for any sign of a threat. She saw and felt nothing unexpected, though she could not completely relax. Several nickers came from the other horses as she entered the barn, but Argat just silently extended his head out over the stall door and glared at her. She shook her head. "Don't give me that look. I fed you in the middle of the night, so you are not starving."

Henton and the others set down their gear next to the door before they followed Stephenie into the building. They each kept an eye out for another flesh-spider as they started taking care of the eleven horses in the barn.

"Are we going to take all of them with us?" Ryia asked as she filled a scoop with grain.

Stephenie looked up and down the aisle while Argat pushed against her back with his nose. "I'll feed you in a moment, Pig," she said to her horse, pushing his nose away. "We'll take the priests' horses out of the keep and into the valley. It's sheltered and there appeared to be plenty of food for the sheep, so I think they should be okay. It would be far too much work to care for the extras as we move north and a herd of eleven animals would draw a lot of attention."

Douglas brought a grain scoop over to her and she in turn dumped the food into Argat's feed bucket. She felt her horse's appreciation.

"We're still heading north after your sire then?" Douglas asked as he waited for her to hand back the empty scoop. "You didn't change your mind overnight? Don't want to go back to Antar to check on the others to make sure the Senzar chasing us didn't do any harm?" Douglas' concern filled the air around him.

Stephenie felt her chest tighten and from the corner of her eye she noticed Henton's faltered step. She wanted everyone back in Antar to be safe, but somehow the Senzar mage had known where they were going, which meant it likely was not. She exhaled, "Henton and Kas were correct when we discovered them following us in Fallen Grove, if that Yreka harmed someone back in Antar, there is nothing we can do." She patted Douglas' arm. "I need to resolve this issue with the red-haired man and put a stop to all the death he is unleashing. It might even be that those Senzar mages following us are somehow associated with him. He manipulated these assassins to slaughter dozens of people in Antar just to draw me out. What will he do now that we've stopped the threat and destroyed what they thought was their god?"

"I'm just making sure," Douglas said. "We don't even know how far it is. You didn't have any accurate maps. And what do you plan to do when you find this Gunnarr Ralok? I mean, based on how powerful you are, he's got to be even stronger."

Stephenie glanced at the other three, all of whom were trying hard not to watch her. She bit her lip and squared her shoulders. "Nothing's changed. We're at the southern edge of the World's Backbone. We just follow the mountains north along the eastern side and we'll eventually get to Ista." The others remained silent, though she felt Kas' support for her. "For the hard part, yeah, the red-haired bastard that raped my mother is likely more powerful than me. My mother had no magic, so everything I can do, I inherited from him and lost whatever potential my mother's blood stole." She looked each of them in the eyes. "I don't have a great plan. One night is not going to change that and I doubt a hundred nights will make any difference either.

"The only thing I can do is find him and ask him to stop trying to kill me. I don't know what I did that he hates me so, but I can't let him continue to harm any of you. You're my family, and a Senzar mage or not, I am hoping I can reason with him. I just want him to leave us alone. That is my only goal at this point...find a way to keep all of you safe. I'll just ask him what I can do to end this." She shrugged. What she would not say aloud, or even acknowledge where Kas could read her thoughts, was that if it took her death to protect those she loved, she would gladly let the man who called himself Gunnarr Ralok kill her. "I'm sorry I don't have anything better to offer."

"We're all in," Henton said as he turned and dumped grain into another horse's bucket. "We've told you that before."

"Yeah," Douglas echoed Henton's statement, "don't take the questions as a desire to be away from you or change your mind. I just wanted to make sure we're still doing this. It may be summer outside the mountains, but I expect we'll still be heading north as the snow starts to fall. Since we are going, I was thinking we might look here for some cold weather gear."

Stephenie pursed her lips and considered the suggestion. After a moment she shook her head. "With the money we took from these assassins, we're all rich. I'll use my share to buy us gear when we get closer. I'd rather limit the weight now and move faster than save the coin." She chuckled. "You counted it last night. Divided five ways, I'll still be rich even paying all the expenses for this trip."

Henton tossed the scoop into the barrel of grain after feeding the last horse. "None of us are concerned about the money. It's nice to have, but we're here to support you." He wiped his dusty hands on his pants. "The horses are eating, let's get people food from the kitchens and any other supplies we might want, load up a spare horses, and be on our way."

Stephenie followed him toward the doors. "I glanced at the bodies along the way here. None of them had their chests ripped open and their ribs removed. However, the High Priestess's body is on top the gatehouse. Plus there are others scattered about the field in front of the keep. We need to check her and the others. Hopefully we'll find the source of that spider-thing."

"And hope there was only one," Ryia mumbled.

"We can definitely hope that is the case," Henton said as he waited for Douglas and Ryia to catch up to them. "But keep watch for anything that seems odd. They are using things even Kas has not seen before."

Kas uncharacteristically remained visible as he roamed a dozen feet ahead of the group. The priests had learned of his presence and so hiding his existence was no longer a priority in this place. "I am hoping that these are just old artifacts that were provided to these worshipers of false gods. The alternative, that the man who provided them had actually created the devices is too frightful of a thought."

Stephenie felt more than saw Ryia shudder at Kas' comment. "We'll deal with it," she offered. Ryia nodded her head but said nothing. "You doing okay?" Stephenie asked.

"Yeah, just a little tired," Ryia said at the ground.

Stephenie decided not to press her. They were walking past a dead woman dressed in skirts and it did not seem right to talk casually. Instead, she continued moving to the narrow steps that led to the top of the gatehouse. Had her destruction been a little wider, those steps would have been destroyed as well.

It is as you suspected, Kas said mentally from his position a dozen feet above her. *The woman's chest is missing. It appears to have been ripped apart. You and the others may not want to come up here. It is not quite as gruesome as what these murderers did to the people in Antar, but her blood and entrails scattered about her body.*

Stephenie closed her eyes and paused on the steps. She did not want to see more death, but she had killed the woman the day before and had searched her body before it had grown cold. The least she could do was check for any signs she had missed something. "Everyone, stay here. Kas said it was just the one body that is ripped apart."

She could see the slight twitch of Henton's cheek before he finally nodded his head. She gave him a weak smile of thanks and continued to the top of the gatehouse. She breathed through her mouth to minimize the iron smell of the dark pool of congealed blood around the body. A group of birds took to the air as she moved closer. They had been feasting on the remains and might be the cause of some of the scattering. However, the birds had not removed the woman's ribs.

Stephenie moved closer. Foot prints from the scavengers crisscrossed the mostly dried blood, but another set of stumpy prints moved from body, through the blood, and continued toward the keep for a dozen feet before the blood on the multi-legged creature had worn off.

"It is indeed the source," Kas said. "I know I am dead, but this does not get any easier for me to look at."

"You're not dead," Stephenie responded automatically. "You are just without a body. Once we find a way to convince the red -haired man to leave me alone, we will find a way to recreate a body for you. As long as I live, I will never stop working to find a way for us to be together."

She turned back to the corpse and extended her tired senses, looking for anything else that might have a telling draw of energy. She did not observe any odd movements of energy on or within the body. She frowned. "I missed that spider thing. I had not even noticed it in the room. There could be dozens more around here."

Kas moved closer. He placed a translucent hand on her shoulder and generated a field that applied pressure as though his hand had actual form. "No one can do everything."

She turned away from the body. "Let's get the rest of what we want to take and get out of this valley."

The valley opened up as they traveled south along the base of the western ridge. There were still large expanses of forest, but when they passed through sections free of trees, they could see mountain grasses swaying in the breeze. Groups of sheep moved through the green grasses, eating their fill and drinking from the lakes and rivers that speckled the protected valley.

It was in one of these wide expanses of grasses that Stephenie turned loose the extra horses from the keep. They allowed a heard of three geldings and two mares to join the sheep. Stephenie kept one of the priests' geldings to act as a second pack animal. The freed horses looked back at her as she removed their halters. With a gentle touch of their minds, she reassured them they could wander away to graze and they quickly complied.

Argat looked perturbed that he was not given permission to roam about the meadow, but Stephenie just rolled her eyes at him. His protest at the treatment was to reach down and grab another big mouth full of grass from next to the trail. "Pig," she scolded playfully. "You've already covered your chin in green foam and you know the bit will be caked in grass." His response was simply to rip the tops off more grass before she could mount him and rein him in.

"They'll be fine," Henton offered as he watched the loose horses move a little further away. They likely wanted to ensure Stephenie did not change her mind and put them back in their halters.

"I hope so," she responded. "But let's get out of here. We've still got several miles before we hit the southern ridge. Then I want to get you guys some place safe where you can rest out of sight of anyone while I free those men."

After traveling another four miles, the trail started to wind back and forth up the ridge line that protected the southern end of the valley. When they had initially made their way into the valley, they had not known that it was inhabited, and so knew nothing of the trail. Their original effort to break ground and climb up the rugged, tree covered ridge had consumed almost a full day. The trail, despite being concealed and infrequently used, provided a much easier path into and out of the mountain range. By mid-day, they had finished descending the ridge and were once again back into a dryer landscape with fewer tall trees and more scrub brush. The lush green of the protected valley's meadows had turned into more of a tan-brown and once they were on the sandy ground, the trail effectively disappeared.

The priests of Mertor had gone to great lengths to limit knowledge of their headquarters; however, the mass exodus of the town in Ranis Valley had left plenty of tracks for people to follow. Stephenie hoped their own tracks would blend into that of the others and conceal their travels. To that end, she led them another mile south until the tracks from those fleeing started to diverge and go in different directions. She then followed one set to the west for a mile before breaking off toward a series of large rock formations that provided concealment.

"I'll eat a quick meal, than fly back to the cave where the men are located," Stephenie said as she dismounted.

"It's got to be at least fifteen miles to the cave," Henton complained, obviously having received some information mentally from Kas.

Stephenie removed Argat's saddle and placed it on a rock. "I can fly fast. I expect I shouldn't be gone more than two turns of the glass."

"And if you are not back in that time?" Douglas asked as Henton helped him from his horse. The gut wound hurt too much for Douglas to lean against the saddle and slide from Pride's back.

Stephenie considered how to reply. She wanted to refuse to let them come for her, but none of them would obey that command. She did not want to have them separate any further, especially with Douglas' wound. He had refused more healing to avoid letting her back into his head. While she could respect the desire, she would rather have Douglas injury free.

Ryia was physically sound, but she had said very little on their journey out of the valley. Stephenie worried if she would be mentally fit to handle a conflict.

Outside of Kas, they would all have to ride back through the valley and the dangers the valley potentially held. She chuckled silently. *Nothing I say will stop them from coming for me.* "If I am not back by a time you feel is too long, send Kas to find me, but make sure you are safe when you send him."

Henton inclined his head toward the staff she had left tied to her saddle. His eyes told her he knew what she was trying to do. "Don't forget to take that."

Chapter 3

Stephenie wrapped herself in an energy field and lifted into the air. She carried the staff in her left hand and she sensed no reaction from it as she used her power. *If this thing kills me, Henton, I'll find a way to haunt you.* Though he had no way to hear her, she suspected he knew what she was thinking.

She turned north, and though she was looking the other way, she could sense the others watching her flight. Kas followed her for a short distance before he stopped and returned to their friends. She had to bite her lip against the fear she might return to find some harm had come to them. *I will trust them to keep safe.*

Wanting to minimize the time she was away from them, her pace increased and the others quickly fell outside her ability to sense them. She continued north, skimming over the tops of the trees and moving faster than Argat could gallop toward a bucket of grain. She hoped staying close to the trees would minimize the chance anyone would see her. The low flight caused several branches to bounce off the field around her legs, but she did not adjust her path or height.

The haze in her mind had cleared over the morning and she kept her senses open for any indications there were people hidden in the woods as she passed overhead. Her precaution revealed only animals, though her range to sense a person mentally remained far less than the potential for someone on the ground to see her visually.

Once she was over the top of the southern edge of the mountains and was back in the valley, she allowed herself to rise another ten feet above the trees and poured more power into her field, which doubled her speed.

The wind whipped against her face and hair causing her eyes to water. She resisted the urge to strengthen the field in front of her face. Instead, she embraced the pleasure of the experience and continued to push even more power into her flight. She angled her body forward to minimize the buffeting of the wind and blew past a flock of startled birds.

The floor of the valley looked beautiful and the aroma of the pine trees filled the air. This vantage point gave the small ponds, lakes, and streams scatted among the meadows, copses of trees, and boulders the appearance of a patchwork quilt. Nearly two days before, when she had searched the mountain for Mertor's trap, she had done so at night and had missed much of the beauty of these mountains.

This time, her speed quickly put the lush valley behind her and she reached the keep faster than she had expected. Still worried about the others, she did not slow. Instead she angled herself to the west side of the tall Dantborn Peak and started to climb above the height of the western ridge so she could circle around to the far side of the snowcapped mountain.

She quickly spotted the priests' trail that led to the cave where the trap had been secured. The worn scar in the ground wound back and forth up the ridge and over the side of the mountain. Concealed for the most part by trees, now that she knew what to look for, she could easily see the subtle gaps in the vegetation that betrayed the trail's presence.

The footpath continued deeper into the mountain range, but Stephenie soon stopped when she reached the place Kas had found the previous day. As she returned to the ground, she immediately noticed what had drawn Kas' attention to the location. The wear of the trail beyond the switchback where she stood diminished, indicating people came this far and stopped. The rocky path to the north simply had less erosion, more grass, more low hanging branches, and a greater number of obstacles than the section of the trail leading back to the valley. *These men got too used to being isolated and lost their discipline.*

Henton had told her of the bickering he and Douglas had overheard from the castle inhabitants during their escape attempt. *No matter how good these priests were at killing people, those not used to working together won't be as effective as those who are.* In her mind, she heard the voice of the man she had grown up thinking was her father, the King of Cothel. *No, he was my father. The red-haired man simply raped my mother. He's nothing more to me than that.*

She put thoughts of the past from her mind and moved around a large boulder that stood more than three times her height. On the other side of the granite rock, she found a two-foot wide and fifteen-foot high opening that had been formed by magic. While disguised to have a rugged appearance that blended into the mountain, the opening was in a solid block of stone and lacked any cracks or fault lines that would have allowed the stone to shift and create the opening naturally.

Already having explored the passage, and sensing nothing threatening in the immediate area, Stephenie slid into the opening without hesitation. The passage quickly opened up around her, spreading out to a width of twenty feet. The nearly perfect vertical walls rose eight-feet before arching over and forming a curved ceiling that peaked twenty-feet over her head.

It took her eyes only a moment to adjust to the ambient light, but the limited light would not provide illumination very far beyond the entrance and even her eyes could not see in complete darkness. However, the energy potentials of stone and air differed greatly, so she opened her senses and used her mind's eye to see the passage through the difference in the energy.

The distance to the men was nearly a mile and she did not feel like taking the time to walk that far. She drew in energy, levitated a foot off the smooth floor, and then flew quickly into the mountain.

The majority of the passage was straight without any bends, but the last few hundred yards before she reached the large chamber had several sharp turns. She slowed only slightly as she made the quick adjustments to her flight. The result was her feet brushing against the walls as inertia flung out her legs in the ninety-degree turns. She wanted to claim it was an attempt to hone her skills, but the risk and thrill of barely avoiding failure plastered a smile across her face.

A moment later, she burst forth from the tunnel into the large chamber. A rush of wind followed her, creating a low pitched whistling.

She immediately slowed and adjusted her flight to avoid the debris that she had left scattered about the room. She exhaled slowly as she hovered in the dark chamber, a slightly pungent odor of men registering on the back of her tongue. The stagnant air unpleasant, but not overwhelming.

The oil lamps that had been burning when she left the men sitting against the wall had burned themselves out. However, the men stood out easily in her mind's eye. The heat from their bodies radiated an energy potential that would be easier to draw upon than the cold stone because it existed in a more excited state.

The men remained huddled together, aware that something had changed in the chamber, but with their feet and lower legs disappearing into the solid stone floor, they were unable to move. The men's arms flailed about for a moment as panic set in and Stephenie had to block out the fear and uncertainty their minds broadcast.

She hesitated a moment more, watching the trickle of energy flow into the men. They both had some limited ability with magic, but their ability was even less than that of Ryia. The augmentation devices these men believed to be holy symbols required some ability with magic to activate, but the priests around the Sea of Tet had killed off everyone they found with significant ability, leaving only minimally skilled mages to become priests. The priests then use the augmentation devices to supply their power and enforce their dominance over others, most never realizing the hypocrisy of their actions.

Stephenie knew that nearly all of the people who worshiped the gods believed that the priests' power came from their gods. However, she also knew some who were aware of the truth. Some of those who knew the truth hid within the ranks of the empowered for safety and to conceal their magic. Others held positions of power and continued to perpetuate the lies and murders for their own gains.

She pushed the politics from her thoughts and looked about the room, searching for any movement or indication there might be another flesh-spider or something worse. Nothing in the room appeared to have changed since she had been there the day before: the remains of the meal she had interrupted remained on the table, the three cots still sat against the far wall, and the crumpled remains of the large iron door she had ripped from the second passage had not moved.

"Who—who's there?" One of the men asked; his voice breaking.

Stephenie sensed a spare oil cask next to the passage she had just come from; it sat under the lamp that hung from the wall. She drifted over to the lamp and lifted it from the hook that was pounded into the stone. She landed, filled the lamp, and returned it to the wall. Turning away from the lamp, she started to float back toward the men as she pushed energy into the wick. Flames caught instantly, bringing a blinding light into the once dark chamber. With the light coming from behind her, and her eyes compensated by magic, the change in brightness did not impact her sight. However, the two men blinked and looked away, even though they sat more than forty-feet from the lamp.

"Demon," the blond-haired man said.

His companion said several things in a language Stephenie did not understand, but she understood the intent of the cursing.

"I told you that if you did not cause me trouble and your friends failed to kill me, I would set you free. I'm here to keep that bargain."

The blond-haired man continued to blink and shield his eyes with his hand. When she had come close enough for him to recognize the staff she carried, his eyes widened despite the light. "You have taken the gift that was given to High Priestess Alci."

"Your High Priestess is dead," Stephenie said, the narrowing of her eyes evident in her voice. "I also told you that my friends had to remain unharmed. While they live and will recover, she did not keep them free of harm."

The blond tried to disappear into the stone behind him. His friend, picking up the increased fear in his companion, struggled to escape, but both men's feet were firmly encased in stone.

"I am not here to kill you. Neither of you were involved with what happened to my friends, but I will give you this warning: never do anything to harm those under my protection. Ever. Cease your practice of being assassins. Your god is dead and there is no one left to protect you from my justice."

The blond nodded his head. "Yes, Demon—"

"I am no demon. I am Stephenie, Princess of Cothel and Prophet of Catheri." She held both of their stares for several moments before nodding her head. "I will free you, but if you do anything stupid, I will end you." She nodded her head to the shorter man who did not speak Pandar, the trade tongue. "Explain it to him as I work."

Stephenie moved closer as the blond spoke to his friend. She set the staff down on the floor and then crouched down so that she could put a hand on the stone that surrounded their feet. Narrowing her focus, she tuned out the sounds of their speech and concentrated on the stone. She no longer saw the stone as a single mass, but instead as an infinite number of small pieces.

The tiny particles of stone were too small to physically see, but she knew these particles were held together by an energy field. With a practiced hand, she injected her own field into the stone. At first nothing happened, but as she adjusted the signature of her field, slowly the natural attraction between the particles of stone started to fade. The effort did not require large amounts of energy, only an enormous amount of concentration. Too much energy would heat the stone and that was not her intent. Even though it would be easier to push in enough energy to melt the stone, doing that would have burned the flesh from these men's feet. What she wanted was to make the stone liquid, with no real change in temperature.

While the effort did not stress her body for energy, the focus made her head throb. Each type of material had different structures and the bonds that held the substance together varied slightly. This stone, however, had long ago been formed and modified, just as she was doing now, and the result was a more uniform block of material. The consistent nature of this stone allowed her to quickly find the right field to break the bonds between the tiny particles.

Once her field reached the proper frequency and form, the stone suddenly lost its attraction to itself and turned into a cool liquid. Stephenie had to continue to adjust her focus and enlarge the area as the men sloshed the material about in their attempt to pull their feet from the one foot-deep trap she had created.

The moment she sensed their feet were free, she dropped her field and allowed her senses to switch back to the macro-world around her. The change in perspective sent shooting pain through her head and she fell back onto her rear.

The shorter man seemed to stumble toward her. She did not know if he meant to attack her or if the night encased in stone had left him unable to stand. Her instincts took over and the man flew back into the stone wall he had sat against the whole night. "Do not think I am vulnerable to you," she growled as she turned her eyes and attention back to the men.

"No! No! We won't harm you!" The blond man cried as he tried to avoid stepping on the area where his feet had been encased. He fell to his hands and knees and bowed his head. "Please, I can barely feel my legs from sitting all night."

Stephenie pushed herself back into a squatting position, grabbed the staff, and then rose to her feet. Her head pounded from the movement, but she would not let it show on her face. She glanced at the floor; the once smooth section of stone now bulged and dipped where the waves of movement froze back into place the moment her field dropped. She could see stone had embedded itself into the leather of their boots and the wool of their pants. Their limited movement had already caused the now very stiff material to crack and split. She spared a momentary thought for how much of the liquid stone might have soaked into their skin. She suspected very little would have made it through their clothing, but having once liquefied a copper bar in her own hands, she knew some might have seeped in and it would take time for that to work its way out of their flesh.

"Go. Take some food and clothing and leave. Leave the valley and do not return. Do not go to the keep. If you happen to see me again, turn and walk away. Because if we meet, you will not enjoy the experience."

She moved away from the men, allowing them enough room to stand without the appearance of invading her space. The two of them did not stop for any supplies, instead, they stumbled directly for the exit and took off into the dark passage without even stopping to grab the lamp for light. Stephenie turned toward the other passage that led further into the mountain. She kept her mind open for the men's presence, but with the bends in the passage, soon there was far too much stone between them for her to sense them. Certain they were not coming back, she entered the passage that had once been restricted to only their High Priest.

The passage went deeper into the mountain and led to a vast circular chamber. A vaulted ceiling rose thirty-feet overhead and had points of magical light that shown down, illuminating the solid stone floor. There were no columns to support the ceiling as one might expect in such a wide space. Instead, where the vaulting came together, the stone extended downward into a curved point bearing the heads of various animals. However, these ended twenty-feet above the floor.

Scattered about the edges of the room were a number of stone tables formed with legs and tops so delicate that only magic could have created them. The alabaster tables appeared alive in the light, their milky forms holding a hint color that shifted as she moved her head. Stephenie noted numerous bins and objects on the tables, but her attention was once again drawn to the center of the room and the round platform that supported a metal column standing seven-feet high and three-feet in diameter. It was all that remained of the trap of Mertor. Unlike the last time she had entered the room, she felt no energy being absorbed by the trap. The power the metal cylinder had drawn, like a parasite from a being in another world, had been cut off and the magical device, created more than a thousand years before her birth, now sat useless deep inside this mountain.

Stephenie felt tears form at the corners of her eyes. Of those she had killed, the intelligence of Mertor—the cursed trap that had been slowly killing some unknown creature—had been her most painful kill. She had removed her own mother's head with her sword, she had hung a friend who had committed treason, but Mertor had simply done what he had been constructed to do. *It was murder,* she told herself. *I asked him to turn himself off and because he viewed me as a creator—because I could see the fields—he obeyed my command.*

She took a deep breath. It had been the right decision and she knew it. This device, like many others, had been crafted to extract magic from another world and make it available to people in this world. When the people of Kas' age had discovered the devices were actually sucking away the life of another being, people's views polarized, both for, and against, their continued use. Kas' people, among others, died trying to put an end to the traps. The people supporting the use of the traps appeared to outlast those that opposed it, but the true nature of the devices were lost to history. *And now people believe these things are links to gods who provide power for the faithful.*

Stephenie felt disgust for those using the traps. "They are hypocrites." She looked at the trap for a moment longer knowing it represented just another way for people to exert power and control over others. It was a device to aid those with power to keep it. "I'm not like that," she whispered.

The man she called her father, the King of Cothel, had ruled honorably. He had tried to protect his people and treat everyone fairly, though she knew not everyone's life was truly held equally, even to her father. She also knew many of her ancestors had fought viciously to keep control of the throne so that in the end, her brother could now rule Cothel. *But I am better than that,* she told herself.

She moved closer to the cylinder and slowly walked around it. Runes and images were carved into the surface, and while she had learned how to read a fair amount of them, much of what was written in the metal lacked any meaning for her. She stopped when she reached the far side of the trap. Four deep gouges were torn into the surface as though a giant claw had slashed it in anger.

She reached out and touched the raised metal and felt the sharp edges. When the trap had been powered, legend had said the metal was indestructible. The holy symbols, or augmentation devices as she knew them, had resisted all of Stephenie's efforts to destroy them because they always had a much larger supply of energy at their command. *Even what I had unleashed earlier today had not completely destroyed that device.*

She continued to stare at the gouges, knowing that the trap was almost infinitely more powerful than the augmentation devices. "So how could he damage the trap when it was active?" Stephenie shook her head. The man who claimed to be her father had used the trap to send a message to all of Mertor's followers, telling them that she was the spawn of Elrin and needed to die. Then he scarred the trap, damaging the area that generated energy fields that acted as a challenge to be answered before one could command the trap. "He knew how to disable it."

Stephenie glanced once to the relay that still sat on the floor where she had left it. The two-foot tall statue of a man had been considered a shrine by any of the god-fearing people around the Sea of Tet. She had managed to use the relay to get around the damage, but only because Mertor, the intelligence that lived in the trap, had violated some of the rules he was supposed to follow.

"Kas, I know it had to be done, but this was hard," she said to no one.

She turned away from the trap and proceeded to examine the other contents in the circular chamber. On the tables, she found what she expected, several wooden boxes with small bits of metal. The small boxes were labeled with symbols. Based on what Mertor had taught her, she knew the values were numbers. On another table sat two additional relays as well as a series of medallions, or augmentation devices.

She picked up one of the metal disks. On the face was a raised image of the man depicted by the statue. "Mertor, I know you never lived, but you were crafted with the personality of a real person. Did that person look like this?"

She turned the disk over and looked at the hollowed out back of the medallion. Glancing to the small boxes with the handful of short metal pieces, she knew that those bits of metal were tied, or entangled as Kas had told her, with a particular relay. For someone to get power from the medallion, one or more bits of metal would be placed in the back of the medallion, then through a special process, the medallion would get activated and fused solid, thereby, forever linking it to one or more relays. As long as the medallion remained within a certain proximity of a relay, that medallion would be able to draw on the power from the relay. Each relay in turn was linked to the trap and provided a conduit for the energy.

Stephenie dropped the medallion back onto the table. There were several dozen empty shells in this room. At one time, she expected there might have been hundreds or even thousands of these augmentation devices.

The tables that circled the edge of the room were set up as workstations. Now most of the tables were simply covered in a layer of dust, the original contents long ago used and distributed.

The first time she had been in the room, she had rushed out because her friends were in imminent danger, now she continued her slow examination. There was beauty in the construction of the room. The ceiling and even the walls were formed with an artistic eye that evoked a feeling of power and purpose. "Did these people know what they were doing when they created this, or did they create it before they learned the truth of the traps?"

She sighed and hoped that people powerful enough to build such magical items and form huge rooms out of the very heart of the mountain would not have done so if they knew the truth. She had felt Mertor's mind and had not felt malice or hate, just a desire to exist. "Did he have the personality of those who created him? Were those people like Kas' people, innocent and simply looking to make people's lives better, or..." She bit her lip. She knew it was naive to think that Kas' Dalish country men would be any more innocent than anyone else. "But they at least fought against the traps."

She looked at the subtle patterns formed into the wall and noticed a section that was a little too smooth. Expanding her senses, she could tell there was a void behind a thin layer of stone. Smiling, she recognized someone's ancient storage bin. It was a trick she had used herself, and if someone ever broke apart a number of stones in her tower in Antar castle, they would find some of what she had hidden.

Leaning over the table, she put her hand on the surface of the stone and narrowed her focus. After several moments, the stone liquefied. Using a gravity field to protect herself, she allowed the stone to slide down the wall and splash onto the table. Once her focus returned and the pounding in her head subsided, she looked into the opening and saw four large books as well as a small statue of a cat sitting on top of a pile of scrolls. Stephenie could feel the slight draw of energy into the statue.

The books, though hidden inside a small stone vault, appeared dry and in excellent condition. "Could that be something to preserve the books?" She asked, looking at the energy fields coming from the cat. "Like Kas' library?" The library in Arkani had dried out her skin and would have eventually preserved her had she stayed there too long. If the device had similar properties, she did not want to risk having her skin suddenly become dried and cracked from touching the statue.

She pulled down the books and carefully opened the first one. The pages contained writing similar to those Mertor had been teaching her. It was a language that the secret sect of Senzar mages also seemed to know.

"I need my notebook," Stephenie mumbled, "but these marks should mean fields and that would mean instructions." She turned several pages and found some illustrations. Two of the other books seemed to contain more of the same, while the last book appeared to be a ledger. "To track relays and augmentation devices?"

Stephenie stacked the books into a pile. She examined the fields around the cat again and confirmed her decision not to touch it. She quickly looked about the room for something she could use to pick up the statue, but found nothing made of flexible material. Giving up on that, she generated a gravity field and levitated it out of the opening. The statue did not appear to react to her magic.

With a final glance about the chamber, she carefully picked up the stack of goods and made her way back to the passage where she planned to put everything into one of the sacks the men had left. "Perhaps these can help us destroy the traps, Kas," she said aloud. "Perhaps this is the beginning of the end of an era."

Chapter 4

Islet ran her hands through her dirty brown hair and winced as her fingers caught several tangles. The grime covering her body reflected eighteen days of hard travel. The last time she bathed had been aboard The Spray on the morning the ship arrived in Wilm. That bath had cleansed her, but the uncomfortably small tub, with a decidedly short supply of fresh water, had not offered relaxation. *Of course, there has been little in the way of relaxation since the Senzar invasion.* She blinked her eyes and pushed the memories of her dead husband out of her thoughts.

Talbit, the flea bitten grey horse beneath her, shuffled his hooves in protest of the continued waiting. A moment later, the gelding reached his head down and snapped at a spot on his chest. Islet saw the horsefly buzz away and then, as if just remembering the constant buzz of the insects around her own head, she resumed the futile swatting that only served to build frustration.

She sighed as she forced her hands to stop before she made herself hotter. An oppressive air hung stagnant over the city and it held an odor stronger than her own. *At least for now.* She stank and she knew it.

Movement down the street drew her attention and she quickly focused on the five men in chain armor moving around the corner of a public house. Her breath caught in her chest and a cold shiver traveled through her body. She barely managed to avoid gasping as the panic of confinement threatened to overwhelm her. *Stephenie freed me,* she repeated to herself as she forced her hands to unclench.

However, it did not push the memories of her near year-long confinement from her mind.

The soldiers passed without comment, but they took careful note of her and the four people sitting on horses behind her. She wanted to nod her head to them, but her body remained solid as stone. She heard them speak quietly to each other, but she could not understand their words, which brought back more memories of the Senzar. For weeks her captors had refused to even acknowledge her, simply speaking their crisp tongue and never even making eye contact with her.

Movement to her left sparked her body to move and she jerked her head around to see Sir Walter proceed Tain out of the inn the two of them had entered earlier. The red-haired Knight's chiseled jaw remained hidden under a beard that had become scraggly over their long ride to the city of Omidi. Although she knew he had to be exhausted, his blue eyes still twinkled, bringing a smile to her face and pushing away the last of the panic that had gripped her.

"Ma'am," Sir Walter said softly. "They have room for all of us and our horses. They also recommended a place we can take Tain's horse to get the shoe put back on. With your permission, I would like to have Tain, D'har, and Mic to take care of the horses as well as pick up supplies. That will leave me and Wilson to protect you and Jerylin."

Islet nodded her head. Sir Walter would have preferred to bring a dozen men to protect her and Jerylin; however, the men he had brought were rather obviously soldiers protecting two women. Had she allowed him to bring any more, there would be no chance anyone would believe their story of her simply being a merchant's daughter being escorted to her intended husband.

Islet longed for the days she had ridden with Stephenie and her sister's party. When she had been part of that small band of misfits, everyone had laughed and giggled and joked. *At least once I got off my high horse and didn't act like a self-important queen.* She let go of the longing for the easy conversations and placed her hand on the Knight's shoulder as he stood next to her horse, gazing up at her. "Walter, that would be fine. You know I'm not as fragile as my brother would have you believe."

Sir Walter nodded his head. "Indeed. You have more than proven yourself on this journey and I have always held you in high regard."

"Then don't be uneasy about me doing my share." Without waiting for his hand to help her down, she slipped from the saddle and dropped easily to the ground. While never as accomplished a rider as Stephenie, Islet had learned to feel confident in the saddle.

"Your brother," he said, dropping his voice further now that he had to look down to meet her eyes, "would see me hanged if anything were to happen to you. I still don't know how you managed to convince him to let you bring warning to your sister."

Islet said nothing. She could not tell Walter the truth. He would not accept Stephenie for what she really was. All they had told him was a Senzar witch was after Stephenie to extract revenge for what Stephenie had done when she freed Islet. *And that is all true.*

Taking the reins from her hand, Walter handed them to Tain, who waited patiently behind the knight. "Please put our horses in the paddock and then take yours to the farrier," he told the soldier.

"Yes, Sir," Tain said, his accent as thick as his arms.

The soldier was a head taller than Islet, but he carried his mass easily. Although she did not know his full history, she knew Tain came from across The Straights and had been born to a family of nomads who lived in the country of Rawner. His build and foreign heritage made him imposing to an enemy, but Tain's honest smile and warm nature also made him easy to engage in conversation. "Thank you, Tain," Islet said, and the smirk on his face let her know of his amusement at Sir Walter's continued formality.

"Ma'am," Sir Walter said, drawing back her attention, "if you and Jerylin will follow me, I will get you situated in your room before arranging for an evening meal."

Islet nodded her head again. *If only I could get Walter to break out of the stoic protector mode.* "Please lead on," she said as Jerylin cautiously approached from behind her.

Islet used the wash basin and a piece of cloth to clean her face and arms, but that small amount of cleaning had left the water brown. *I so want a bath,* she mused again, unable to completely banish the desire.

She knew spending the money would not strain their cover story, but she could not justify the expense if she could not reach Stephenie before her sister turned north.

"Ma'am," Jerylin said softly from behind her. "Is there something you need me to do for you?"

Islet turned around and looked up at the tall woman's freckled face. She ignored the cleaning rags in Jerylin's hands as she reminded herself that although Jerylin was only a year younger than herself, the woman had not grown up near any court and lacked the instinctual knowledge of how to be a lady-in-waiting. The woman was a peasant who had been lucky enough to escape being burned as a witch and just happened to have been kind to Stephenie at one point, which had endeared her to her sister.

"Jerylin, I've managed to do without a maid for a while now and as I've said before, I don't expect you to fill that role in private." Islet did not want to scold Jerylin for offering, but she had made that statement too many times. "What you can do is tell me that we are still on course to finding Stephenie."

"Ma'am," Jerylin said, her teeth catching on her lower lip. "I used the holy symbol to check a day ago and they were still to the northwest, probably about a hundred miles or so. I'm not great at understanding the distance that thing shows me."

Islet squared her shoulders. "I want to confirm where they are now. A lot can change in a day and a half," she added, knowing Jerylin had rounded the time down in her favor. Islet wished she could use the device herself, but Islet was not a mage and the device would never work for her. Instead, she had to rely on Jerylin and the woman's ability to understand what the holy symbol told her and that did not inspire confidence in Islet. *If Stephenie has continued to move, I can at least continue to hope Yreka has not caught her and that she is still safe.*

Jerylin bit her lip again and after a moment, nodded her head. "I just feel...dirty after I use that holy symbol." Jerylin could not take her eyes from the saddle bag that held the device.

Islet wanted to shake Jerylin, but she knew the woman did not understand the truth behind magic. "Stephenie has done it many times. She and Ryia used it to find the priests of Mertor in the first place."

"But she's the Prophet. She can do anything. The gods favor her."

Islet wished that were true, but on their trip back from Ulet, Stephenie had opened Islet's eyes to the world of lies and half-truths that most people believed. "She's very powerful yes, but that has no bearing on your using the holy symbol to find the shrine that Stephenie is carrying." Islet could tell Jerylin wanted to argue some more, but even though Jerylin could use magic and could probably kill her, the woman still feared Islet because Islet was a Royal Princess of Cothel and the disposed Queen of Ipith. The difference in their stations remained an enormous gap that had not eased with time. *If anything, Jerylin has grown more uncomfortable with me.*

Islet wished again for the ease she had felt with Stephenie's friends, but these people with her now had known Islet was a queen from the start. Aside from Henton and Kas, Stephenie's friends had grown to know Stephenie as just a person before they found out who she really was and Islet thought that might have been a factor in their willingness to be open with either of them. *Of course, it might just be Stephenie has been around her friends longer.* Islet still hoped she could convert Walter to a close friend. She did not have her sister's ability to sense emotion and read minds, but she observed the way he looked at her, spoke to her, and moved around her. She knew there was an attraction, *but again, his damn desire to remain proper.*

"Ma'am," Jerylin said, bringing back Islet's attention. The freckle-faced woman had retrieved the holy symbol and now held the circular medallion by the edges and away from her body. The mage feared the contamination she thought she would absorb from it.

"Yes?"

"Ma'am, I cannot get the holy symbol to work." Panic ran under Jerylin's words as she held the metal disk out to Islet, as if Islet would be able to fix the device.

Islet's mouth formed a thin line and she nodded her head in understanding. "It means Stephenie has succeeded in her task."

Jerylin's eyes widened. "She killed a god? Did she really destroy Mertor? I never..."

Islet sighed and then nodded her head. She could not tell the woman the truth. If Islet did, the would-be priestess of Catheri would renounce her as insane, or perhaps worse, a person possessed by the evil demon god of the elves, Elrin. "If the holy symbol is dead, than Stephenie has done her task."

"I never really though...she is the Prophet of Catheri. Stephenie can do anything."

Islet bit her own lip. It would do no good to rush back onto the road this evening, but she would insist that Walter increase their already fast pace first thing in the morning. She did not want Stephenie to turn north in earnest before she had a chance to catch up to her.

"So, will we go back to Antar now?"

Islet turned her head to Jerylin. "No. I know Stephenie's plans and she was not to return to Antar right away. We'll continue heading north. I'll have to consult the maps, but I think we will have to go to Ingrie unless there are smaller roads that will take us more directly north or northeast."

"Ma'am? I thought her mission was to destroy the priests of Mertor. Are you sure she will not head back to Antar? And if she doesn't, I cannot track her anymore." Jerylin still held the holy symbol as though she would catch a disease from it. Realizing it was in her hands, the woman carefully set the medallion down on the table.

Steph, now that I know the truth, I can't see how you survived all those years trying to hide your secret. To Jerylin, Islet said, "As I indicated, I know Stephenie's plans and if she has succeeded in destroying Mertor's powers, she will not return to Antar. I will not say more, except to repeat that we will continue north. I know the route she intended to take and if she has done the deed within the last day, than we may be able to catch up to her because we are east of where she was and she'll head east along the mountains before she can go north."

"Of course, Ma'am."

Islet watched Jerylin bow her head and knew the woman wanted desperately to return to Antar. Jerylin had not wanted to go on this mission, but she had not been able to refuse her High Priest's orders.

The real trouble was Jerylin had barely started learning what Will and Sara were teaching with respect to being a priestess of Catheri. She had just recovered from the purification to 'purge Elrin' from her when she was chosen to join Islet's group. The people who had come with Jerylin from Vinerxan would be well into learning how to use their own powers under the guise of being priests of Catheri. Jerylin fell further behind them with every mile she traveled away from Catheri's temple.

Islet did not have the stomach to walk the dangerous line Will and Sara pursued on a daily basis. If the truth were suspected, they would burn. The only thing that gave them a sense of authority was Stephenie's famed trial of fire in the Grey Mountains. Too many soldiers knew she had been consumed by flames, only to later walk away unscathed and they had convinced the masses that she was the prophet of the long dead god Catheri.

Islet took a step forward and put her hand on Jerylin's shoulder. "Do not worry about falling behind in your studies. When we reach my sister, she'll be able to instruct you like no other. After all, look what she did with Ryia."

Jerylin's eyes lit up at the mention of Stephenie's protégé. Jerylin and Ryia had been in Vinerxan together and it was common knowledge that Ryia lacked any real power, but she had learned a great deal of skill in the short time Stephenie had adopted her and with that had come a sense of self-worth for the girl.

"For now, if you want to do something for me, I could use something to drink."

"Of course, Ma'am," Jerylin said with more gusto as she turned and left the small room they would share for the night.

Islet watched the door close and then sat down on the bed. *Steph, don't stop running. You've never taken it easy before, keep going. You don't want that Yreka to catch you, even if it means we are trailing behind you.* She closed her eyes and hoped she would not be too late. She knew Stephenie would have no idea Islet was rushing after her to bring the warning of danger, so she could only hope that she could reach Stephenie before the Senzar mage did, because she no longer had any gods left to pray to for help.

Chapter 5

Yreka looked up at the ruined curtain wall of the keep and sighed. The carrion birds that circled in the air and hopped across the stones told her of the death and destruction that had been unleashed. It also confirmed what she already knew, her quarry had escaped her yet again. "I am getting tired of this damn chase," she swore.

"Mistress?"

Yreka's lip curled slightly at Daeri's questioning tone. The young man stood four inches taller than her, but was by far the youngest member of her entourage. Had he not been her fifth-great-grandnephew, she would never have agreed to train him.

She turned to face Daeri and looked into the forty-nine year old's grey eyes. He barely looked a day over twenty-four and the fact that he had already started to acquire an apparent age irritated her. It spoke of just how limited a ninth-generation child's power really was. The three others standing next to him had the same apparent age he did, but Olena's soft face and gentle cheeks had lived almost twice as long before acquiring that appearance. She glanced away for a moment. Daeri's aging was not what actually bothered her; it was the changes in her own appearance that scared her most of all. At over three-hundred and sixty years old, she had hoped to have several more decades before she looked as old as Daeri did. Now that her own apparent aging had started, it meant that she had at most another hundred years to live.

She suppressed the shiver that wanted to run down her spine and pushed away her brooding thoughts. She turned back to Daeri and held his gaze until the younger man shifted slightly. None of the four of them were truly worth training. However, he was of her brother's line and as she was the only person left in their family tree older than a sixth generation, she felt some responsibility. *And it is not like anyone of even the seventh or eighth generations would want to subject themselves to a role of servant.* She shook her head. She knew that she would not even bother to learn the names of any of their offspring unless these four became fortunate enough to reproduce with someone more powerful than themselves.

To the others she said, "I know, I started this gambit with more gusto. Based on the cunning this Stephenie exhibited in killing Yvima and Favian, I had looked forward to possibly having a challenge... something I've not had in decades." She shrugged. "I even decided to give her enough of a head start so she could have a chance to establish a position of power. However, all she has done is run away. I grow weary of simply chasing after her. Running away is not cunning, it offers me no challenge, just tedium." Yreka glanced over to Werha. The man's black hair and dark brown eyes were added to his family's line by his grandfather who had mated with her own great-granddaughter. While the man offered no improvement on her line's ability with magic, the mingling had added some attractive physical traits. "You wanted to say something?"

"No, Mistress," Werha said carefully.

Yreka let his emotional slip go. Her own frustration would be obvious to them, so she could hardly scold the slender man for the same fault. She glanced at Tibva and Olena before continuing. "She cannot be more than two or three days ahead of us now, if we hurry, we can return to Antar ahead of her."

"Mistress?" This time it was Olena's soft voice that challenged her.

Yreka raised her eyebrows and questioned the only other female in the group with her eyes.

"Ma'am, do you think she is actually heading back to Antar?"

Yreka pursed her lips. She had learned a lot about Stephenie Marn, Princess of Cothel. The eighteen-year-old had a strong possessive loyalty to her country and her actions remained consistent along that theme. The one thing she had not discovered was just who had fathered her. *The girl can't be more than a fifth-gen child.* She could count the number of fourth-generation mages alive in the world and their number had dropped to under thirty. *Perhaps she could be a fourth-gen like me if Lishan had decided to climb down from his mountain palace.* She knew that remained such a distant possibility as to be impossible. *More likely one of his children decided to slum his way across these northern lands, which means she has less power than me.*

Yreka focused her thoughts again on Olena. "Where else would she go?" Yreka's eyes narrowed as she slipped into Olena's mind. "You think that pointless child from Vinerxan warned Stephenie about us and that she is trying to lure us away from her friends?"

"Mistress," Olena's voice held a trace of anger at the violation. "It is a possibility. I know you said that her High Priest did not have any specific thoughts about the natives that Lord Favian had recruited in Vinerxan, but we had heard rumors that those worthless people had fled to Antar while we pursued Stephenie to where she killed her mother."

Yreka nodded her head. She did not want to admit that she had considered those peasants so far beneath her that she had not bothered to probe William's mind for details on Favian's recruits. *Olena will at least speak her mind. The other three are too anxious to please.* "Then what do you propose? We have no indication of where she went from here. Trying to search for her trail could put us even further behind her."

Yreka did not bother looking at Daeri. She knew the man thought himself superior to the others, and in many respects, Yreka had to admit he acquired skill faster than most, but his raw potential remained limited. His annoying conceit, unsuitable for someone of his standing, irritated her the most and in the ten years he had been her servant, he continued to express desires to learn mundane skills that did not involve magic. With his limited life expectancy of perhaps one-hundred, she had dismissed the suggestions. While she might now wish for someone skilled at tracking to be able to look for physical evidence of Stephenie's passage, she would not give the smug man the satisfaction. *Plus, the magnitude of other people who fled the valley would likely have destroyed any evidence of Stephenie's specific tracks.*

"Mistress," Olena said, "it is likely she could have gone in several directions. If she is trying to lead us away from Antar, she might even have gone north. I know searching for her path would delay us, but I fear going to Antar will not lead us to her. I suspect we could hunt down others that fled the valley and force them to provide us with information."

Yreka pursed her lips. "She is very protective of her brother and Cothel. I can't imagine she would go too far from Antar. Plus, we encountered several groups of people that fled her wrath and none of them saw her leave and none of them saw her after they ran from this valley."

"She went all the way to Ulet," Olena protested. "She's come this far north. She has shown that she will travel great distances from Cothel."

"But, only in the pursuit of something she perceives as a threat to her family." Yreka paused a moment and then pursed her lips. "She is also driven by her desire to rebuild a body for her ghost. But that is not something I see as ever being a realistic possibility. I know it is a personal driver for her, but I cannot see where it will lead her." Yreka looked again at the castle's curtain wall. A section thirty-feet wide and at least ten-feet tall had been ripped out of the wall, pulled into the field, and scattered a long distance. All the stone above that section had collapsed back into the keep's courtyard as rubble. Yreka knew the amount of energy it would take to rip the wall into pieces and based on the distance the large blocks tumbled, she began to reconsider how much power Stephenie might actually command. *Sometimes there are spontaneous jumps in power, people born with more potential than they should have. Just like there are people in the eighth and ninth generations who are born dead to magic. Genetics sometimes produces unexpected results.*

Yreka softened her expression. "What do you suggest Olena?"

"We have the communication stones. We could split up into different groups and cover more ground."

Yreka nodded her head slowly. She knew Olena was as motivated by the chance to be on her own as anything else. The woman was almost one-hundred years old and she had started to gain an apparent age. Yreka estimated she had perhaps another fifty years left to her.

While Olena is a ninth-generation, she might just be a person more powerful than their place of birth would indicate. "And how do you suggest we split up?" Yreka had already decided that they would and who she would send where, but she wanted to hear Olena's analysis.

"Mistress, I would suggest that Tibva and I go north along the mountain range to see if we can find any indication of where she went. Then you could take Daeri and Werha in a different direction."

Yreka kept her expression neutral; it was not a secret among their group that she would bring Werha to her bed on occasion. Olena had done the same with Tibva, the tall blue-eyed and white-haired man twenty-five years Olena's junior. She also noted Olena's choice to not tell her which direction to go, only that Olena would go north. *She is wise enough to express her desire without imposing a decision on me.* "Very well, Olena, you and Tibva can go north, but take Daeri with you." Yreka could feel the twinge of irritation from the other woman. Daeri, while nearly fifty-years-old, still tended toward too many immature behaviors for either of them. *But since I am a fourth-gen and your master, you get to deal with him.* "I will take Werha south along the mountain range and into Kynto. Her activities there are many months old, but I may learn something more from her killing of Yvima." She took a breath and used her powers to tame some of her long hair that started shifting in the wind. "One thing to remember, even though Yvima was not of my line and I don't care about the members of a dying family, he was a sixth gen and she killed him in a direct duel. That should serve as a warning to the three of you, do not attempt to engage her alone. While she undoubtedly lacks training and skill, she does have a lot of raw power and could get lucky."

"Mistress," the three of them responded with a bow of their heads.

"Good." Yreka walked over to her horse and pulled a pair of oval stones about the size of her palm from the saddle bags. She handed Olena and Tibva each a stone. "Do not separate your group unless I approve it, but I will give you a second stone in case that should be necessary. Now, find where she has gone and then contact me."

"Yes, Mistress," Olena said, bowing her head again.

Yreka turned away as Olena motioned for Tibva and Daeri to follow her to their horses. She stared at the keep while three of her servants mounted their horses and turned to leave the valley. "Werha, you have remained quiet."

"Mistress, I worry."

"About?"

Werha inclined his head at the ruined wall. "This girl appears to possess a great potential for destruction. The four of us are hardly a match for someone of your power."

"Are you suggesting she is as powerful as I?"

"No, Mistress," Werha quickly replied. "It would not be possible and her youth would make her an infant to your skill. I only worry that the four of us will be of little use in assisting you. She destroyed a mountain top. Her powers crushed our armies."

Yreka nodded her head. Her four servants were quite limited in raw power. They were the least of those anyone bothered to track genealogically, and some, including herself, had argued there was little point in tracking even those who were seven generations from a source. The raw potential simply started to drop off too quickly with each subsequent breeding.

Ironically, those not identified as being of a particular line often lived happier lives. The unnamed tended to possess similar magical potentials as ninth-generation family members, but their lives were their own. For those caught in the middle, like her four servants, they lacked the power to command respect and found few options beyond servitude to more powerful family members. *But, these four have benefited greatly from my patronage.*

Yreka put aside her musings. "As I have said, do not attempt to engage her directly. While I trust in your training, which for the four of you exceed many seventh-gens, this Stephenie has proven resourceful. And while I would never call Favian a disciplined man—and Yvima's line has been falling apart for years, which means he lacked any significant mentorship—it is important to note that she still killed both of them."

"Of course, Mistress. But the question remains, what do you want us to do?"

Yreka turned toward her horse. "The four of you will engage her friends. Since they belong to her, that will distract her, and as she tries to defend them, she will make herself easy to overcome."

Chapter 6

The light drizzle that had plagued them throughout the day continued to fall as Stephenie finally called a halt to their travels. She did not know their exact location, but she suspected the last four days of riding had put them south of Ingrie. Since they had remained off the roads and away from any settlements, she had no fixed points of reference to compare to the maps. *Of course, I don't even know how accurate the maps are.* All of their maps of this region had been copied from older maps that were themselves copies.

"I said I'm fine." Ryia's voice cut through the light rain, echoing what the girl had repeated countless times since they had left the valley.

"Okay," Henton said, stepping away from Ryia and her horse. Without further comment, Ryia slid from the saddle and led her horse away from Henton. "I was just offering to help," he added under his breath.

Stephenie barely heard the comment and paused in her taking care of Argat. She felt her chest tighten slightly at Henton's loss of his composure. Outwardly, he still appeared in control of himself, but she felt a vague sensation of confusion mixed with frustration from him. It lasted only a moment and she doubted Ryia would have the sensitivity to notice it.

She'll talk when she's ready, Stephenie told herself. It had been an unspoken agreement between everyone that no one would press her until she was ready. *And it's only been four days. Hard to believe that's all.*

She felt Kas quickly approaching their position and immediately reached out to him. He had left the group to scout the area before they had stopped, and while he did not seem agitated, Stephenie hoped they had not camped too close to another group of travelers as they had done the night before.

I found one small farmstead nearly three miles to the north. Those living there appear to have settled in for an evening meal, so I do not expect any trouble from them. There was no one else I detected in the area.

She nodded her head. *Good, I'd guess we have another four days until we are out of Salzen and I'd rather not let anyone see us until then. I worry how much word has already spread from those who fled Ranis Valley.* She knew the priests of Mertor had gone to great lengths to keep their location a secret, but now that the cult had lost their power, those people routed from their home would likely tell others how the evil spawn of Elrin attacked them without cause.

"Steph," Henton said, coming over to her. "I've asked Douglas to prepare something to eat, but if you could heat the pot once he's done, we can have something to eat without trying to scrounge enough brush to get a fire going. There's damn little worth burning as this rocky ground is terrible for anything but weeds."

"Sure," she responded, even though Ryia normally handled those kind of tasks to help her build her strength. "Henton, you want to talk?"

Her tall protector stopped for a moment and then walked closer. "Sorry. I'm..."

She gave him a small smile and lowered her voice. "It will take time. At least that's what Kas keeps telling me. She's been through a lot."

"But you'd think we could do something," he said, worry buried in his eyes.

Kas slowly materialized next to them and spoke in the Old Tongue. "I will never advocate adjusting another person's thoughts. The danger is too great. You may fix one aspect of a person's mind while destroying the very foundation of who the person is. Therefore, as I have told you both, I advocate allowing her time to come to terms with what happened."

Stephenie knew the slight tightening of Henton's lips indicated he felt some disagreement with Kas, but she had experience with her mind being messed with as well as actually destroying another person's mind. Her experiences made her agree wholeheartedly with Kas. "She keeps saying she doesn't remember anything and that she's just tired. I'll see if I can get her to talk later. First, let me help get what is left of the food going while you work on the tent."

"Okay," Henton said. "I'll try to sort through the rest of what we have once I have some place dry to do that. In a few days, we'll have no choice but to stop for grain and food, the pack horses could only carry so much from the keep. But I'll have a better estimate for you later."

She smiled at him knowing he found their progress out of Salzen a bit slow. "Thanks. I know the loose ground is hurting our speed, but I still want to stay off the roads." Across the other side of the camp she noted Douglas had started mixing things into their cast iron pot. She patted Henton's arm as she walked past him, leaving Argat to obey a ground tie.

"You really should let me or Ryia do some more healing," she said quietly when she reached Douglas' side. "You're still stiff in your movements."

Douglas shook his head. "I trust the both of you, but I'd rather not have either of you in my thoughts."

"You have my word, I will never tell anyone about your secrets."

Douglas shrugged. "I'm feeling better."

You cannot fix everything all at once, Kas reminded her.

I hate seeing everyone miserable, Kas. I just want things to go back to the way they were.

"Let me heat this up and then I can get back to the horses." She looked at the pot and pushed energy into the iron as well as the contents. Within a couple moments, the stew was boiling.

"Thanks," Douglas said as he slowly knelt down to add more spices and stir the pot. "You might have to heat it up a couple more times, but that should get things started."

Stephenie watched him for a moment and then walked toward the pack horses. She motioned with her hand for Argat to come over, but the horse just stood there. Stephenie frowned at Argat and then whistled once. The gelding tossed his head, flinging the reins into the air. He then lowered his head and grabbed the loose end from the ground. With the leather in his mouth, he walked over to join Stephenie and the pack horse Henton had just finished unloading.

"You've got Argat better trained than Henton managed with most soldiers," Douglas said from where he was stirring the pot.

Henton just rolled his eyes. Stephenie grinned as she took the two pack horses' lead ropes and led them toward Ryia. Ryia had started a picket line between a larger boulder and a spindly tree. Knowing that picket would not work, Stephenie came up beside her younger companion and tried to put a hand on Ryia's shoulder, but the girl moved away quickly under the guise of trying to draw the rope tighter. "Hey, hold a moment."

Ryia wiped the rain from her face with her arm and continued at her task. Stephenie bit her lip and waited for Ryia to stop, but the girl continued to pull at the wet rope. "Okay. Enough. Stop."

"What?" Ryia demanded, throwing the loose end to the ground. "I'm taking care of the horses."

Stephenie silently asked Kas to give her some privacy as Ryia could sense him. The ghost headed back toward Henton and Douglas. "Ryia, I know you have been through a lot. But—"

"Don't." Ryia's blue eyes stared back at Stephenie. "You can all quit acting like something happened. I'm fine. I don't remember anything."

Stephenie stood taller. "Then what do you think you are doing? It should be obvious that a picket won't work here. There's nothing to secure it. We'll have to stake out the horses on a long lead and let Kas keep an eye on them."

Ryia turned her eyes to the ground at Stephenie's feet. "I just know you don't like doing that."

Stephenie let her anger leave her. "It's okay. These guys are smart enough and Kas will make sure they don't come to harm." She bent down and picked up the end of the rope. "You want to tell me what's on your mind?"

Ryia glanced at Henton and Douglas and then back to Stephenie. "Can't I have a headache without everyone thinking something is wrong? It's wet and miserable and I just want to sleep."

Stephenie did not believe her, but allowed the claim to go unchallenged. "I can take care of the horses if you want to help either Douglas or Henton."

Ryia hesitated for a moment and then walked toward Douglas. Stephenie wanted to knock her on the back side of the head, but she knew it would not help. "Yeah, Argat, I know," she said with a pat on his neck.

Stephenie climbed into the tent and moved past Henton, who was sitting with his legs crossed on his blanket and still smelled of dampness. Of all their supplies, she was most happy about the tent. It was a marked improvement from the small shelter they had used after escaping Vinerxan. That tent had been designed for two people at most. The five of them had slept on top of each other, which during the cold months had offered warmth, but had still been uncomfortable. This tent allowed each of them their own place to sleep and a small area for supplies.

"The pots are as clean as I can make them," she said as she fell back onto her rear so she could remove her boots without getting mud on her blankets.

"Steph," Henton said, setting aside another map he had removed from her pack. "At our current rate of travel—and taking a number of guesses regarding the accuracy of these maps—and where Ista actually is—I can't see us getting there in anything less than two and a half months. It could be as many as three."

She nodded her head, having already come to the same conclusion before they left Antar.

"I know we started with enough funds to handle that long of a journey." He shrugged. "And now we could hire someone to carry us there. The only trouble is, I don't see any way to speed up the trip and we don't know even what is north of this country called Talset, other than some rumored names you got from that Calis Ambassador." He set aside another map and watched as she dropped her boots next to the outer flap. "My concern matches Douglas' from a couple days ago, it will be late autumn when we get there. I've heard stories that if we go far enough north, we'll see snow early in the year. Perhaps even now. Maybe all year around. If they say summer can be bad, winter will be worse."

Stephenie could see his concern. He and Douglas had suffered when they crossed through the mountains east of Vinerxan during the last winter. She, herself, had suffered exhaustion and headaches just trying to keep everyone from freezing. "Henton, it is hard to know what we will encounter. But we have a long way to go and time to adjust if needed. I know I didn't manage to do as good a job as I needed to last winter. I simply wore myself out with the effort. This time, Ryia can help—"

"I'm not that strong," Ryia injected.

Stephenie waited a moment to see if she would say anything else and continued when it was obvious Ryia had nothing more to add. "If the conditions are bad enough, then we can winter in one of the cities we find along the way. With my share of the money, I can rent us someplace nice to stay. Perhaps not as nice as in Calis, but someplace nice. We get far enough north, no one will know anything about us and we won't have to hide in the tent every night."

"Well," Henton said, "as I keep telling you, Steph, we are all in this together. Don't worry about the money. We'll consider what we took from the assassins' communal money until we are done with the journey."

Stephenie nodded her head. He had made the comment several times, though she was more than willing to give up her share. Their first treasure trove she had insisted they turn over to her brother, this one was theirs to keep.

"Henton?" Ryia asked tentatively. "What do you plan to do with your share of the money? When we are done."

Happy to have Ryia's talking at all, Stephenie allowed the change of subject to pass and unbuckle her sword belt, setting her weapons to the side, so she could make herself comfortable.

Henton turned toward the sixteen-year-old. "Well, I've not thought about it that much. I suppose there will be enough to retire on."

"Damn right there is," Douglas offered from where he was lying near the back of the tent. The Corporal rolled over onto his side.

"There's enough there for me to buy a shop and a house and probably never have to work a day."

"What kind of shop?" Ryia asked from where she sat next to Douglas.

"A tailor shop."

"Really?" Ryia's face once again had a trace of the playful challenge Stephenie had grown to love about her. "You know anything about being a tailor?"

Douglas frowned. "Not much, but some things. But I should have enough money to pay someone to teach me."

Stephenie let a chuckle escape her lips. "Well, if your ability to keep clean and avoid ruining your clothes is any indication of potential to be a tailor, then you have a great future ahead of you."

Henton had contained his surprise at Douglas' choice, but Stephenie could see it had not been the answer he expected from the soldier. "As long as you don't start making things that Will likes to wear, I'd consider letting you make me something."

"My first customer." Douglas pushed himself into a sitting position with a little effort. "So Henton, would you be wanting a captain's coat?"

Ryia stiffened at the implication. "A captain's coat? Why would you need that?"

Henton put the maps back into Stephenie's pack. "Oh, I've talked in the past about what I would do if I had as much money as I wanted."

"And he always wanted to buy a ship," Douglas finished for Henton. "Can't say for certain we have enough for that, but if you take some of the earnings from your land grant that Josh gave you, you could probably buy a decent merchant vessel."

"Is that what you'd do?" Ryia asked, not completely able to control her voice.

Stephenie bit her lip. She did not mind sailing and she knew Henton loved the sea, but Ryia—*and her horse*—found the movement debilitating.

Henton nodded his head. "I can't say for certain I would, but it had been one of those things I have always considered." He reached out and patted Ryia's leg. "But don't worry, I'm not going anywhere anytime soon. I'm too busy taking care of Steph and making sure nothing..." He cleared his throat. "I won't be leaving you lot any time soon. What about you, Ryia? Any plans for your sudden wealth?"

Ryia took a deep breath and then looked down at her hands. "I don't know. I..."

Stephenie felt the silent pause grow long and was about to say something when Douglas spoke up. "Steph, what about you? What have you always wanted?"

She looked around at all of them, including Kas, who had been listening, but had not luminesced to make himself visible. Her initial thought was to say she wanted a small cottage away from everyone else where she could live in peace, but that was not truly what she had always wanted. "I've already got what I wanted. There isn't anything special I want to buy." She pushed herself to continue speaking, moving her eyes between her friends and hoping she would not cry. "I grew up fearing everyday might be the day someone would discover I was a witch. Just living to see the next day without getting stoned and burned was what my existence consisted of. I had no one I could truly trust. No one knew my secret—at least no one told me they knew," she added, since her father and brother apparently knew without telling her. "While I had access to things, fancy clothes, weapons, good food, I didn't have friends. What I've always wanted the most was all of you. People I could truly count as friends." She tried to hold back the emotion she felt leaking from her eyes and then used the back of her hand to dry off what broke through. "Look at me, just a wreck."

She felt Henton's arms around her and then Ryia and Douglas joined in the hug. While Kas could not physically touch her, she felt his love for her and she opened her mind to him in return.

It took several moments before everyone released her and they went back to their blankets. "Thank you."

"Hey, Steph, you're family as far as I'm concerned," Douglas said. "I'll always be there for you."

She wiped her eyes again. "Sorry for getting all mushy on you guys. I just want to make sure you know how much you mean to me. You mean more to me than even Josh and Islet."

She glanced at Henton and noticed the internal conflict he tried to keep hidden from everyone. *He knows how I feel about Kas,* she told herself.

"Have you figured out anything with the staff or the dagger?" Henton asked, almost as if he knew where her mind had drifted with regard to him. "You've been pouring through the books you found, but I don't think they, or that preservation statue, is related to either weapon."

Stephenie bit her lip. Although Henton had changed the subject away from her embarrassment, thinking of the red-haired man took the strength from her arms and the heat from her body. Henton had given her four days of avoiding the issue, *but I guess that's all he'll allow.* "I've just had a lot on my mind." She turned her eyes away as Henton silently challenged her lie. Unwilling to look at anyone else, she shifted her gaze to the staff that was wrapped in a blanket she had taken from the keep's stables.

Now that she acknowledged the weapon, she could feel the slight draw of power moving into the staff. The red-haired man was a monster and she feared to think what that made her. *I don't want anything from him except for him to leave me alone. I'd never be able to trust him to help me rebuild a body for Kas. That dream no longer involves him. I'll find another way.*

"They are powerful weapons, Steph," Henton urged. "We might as well make use of them if we have to face more Senzar."

She would not say it aloud, but the staff had intelligence and she could not quite rid herself of the fear that they were just another trap designed to take over her mind. The last thing she ever wanted was to have someone else invade her thoughts and take control again. However, the only way to know the purpose of the staff was to open her mind to the risk.

After some hesitation, she reached out, untied the ropes holding the wool blanket, and then grabbed the steel-capped weapon from within the folds of material. The intelligence of the staff immediately reached out to her and she almost pushed it aside as she had done every previous time she had touched it. This time she sensed what she assumed to be a trace of surprise from the inhuman mind in the metal and wood.

So, what does the red-headed bastard expect from me? Stephenie asked in the Old Tongue, but the staff did not respond. She frowned as she wondered if the staff did not understand the nature of the question or if it was a gap in their languages. *Can you understand me?* She asked again in the Old Tongue. *What about now, can you understand me?* She asked, using the language Mertor and the relay had been crafted to speak.

Stephenie did not hear any words from the staff, but she felt an emotional response that she could only call acceptance. *So, you don't speak words?* More acceptance. *Were you meant to end up in my possession?* This time the staff's response left Stephenie feeling empty. *Does that mean no?* The response changed to leave her feeling slightly rejected. *Did the emptiness mean you don't know?* Acceptance.

Stephenie frowned. "It would help if you could just come right out and say what you know," she said, keeping her words to Mertor's language. The feeling of acceptance drew a subtle grin to her lips. *At least you are self-aware. Do you remember the red-haired man?*

A moment passed before Stephenie felt a tentative acceptance from the staff. The others continued to stare intently at her and she gave them a noncommittal shrug.

She turned her attention back to the staff. She realized she had included a sense of the man's mind she had picked up from Mertor as she had asked her question. However, she lacked any real definition of the man who might have forced himself upon her mother. She knew the staff remembered, but her own uncertainty had limited the staff's response.

Changing her line of questioning, Stephenie envisioned everything she knew about Ista and then directed her thoughts to the staff. *Did you come from Ista?* The acceptance came strongly to her.

With a sigh, she put the staff down and turned her eyes toward Henton. "It seems to communicate using emotions. Fairly simple emotions from what I can tell."

"Is that normal?" Henton asked.

Stephenie shrugged. "The augmentation devices and the relay did not use words. The trap is what spoke to me through the relay."

Kas nodded his head as he luminesced to make himself visible. "Many magical devices understand only a limited number of commands. It becomes increasingly more difficult and arduous to craft a device capable of more complex abilities. Spoken language is not something to expect in anything save for the most robust devices."

Stephenie, having discussed the creation of magical items with Kas before, changed the subject. "The staff did confirm it came from Ista. I got a weaker confirmation that it was the red-haired man that brought it here. I think that is because I had more difficulty forming a mental image of him."

"So, do we continue north then?" Ryia asked, injecting herself into the conversation.

"It changes nothing," Stephenie said quickly. "We will continue north." She hesitated before adding, "And I'll keep working with the staff. I'll try to puzzle out how to get it to do what we know it can do and if it can do anything else. If the bastard did something to it to try and disable me, it wasn't obvious."

"What about the dagger?" Henton asked. His expression lasted for less than a blink of an eye, but Stephenie could see his desire to steer the conversation away from anything negative before he schooled his face.

She nodded her head and drew the dagger from its sheath. "I have never felt any intelligence from it. I know it has power because I can feel the slight draw of energy, so it means there is some intelligence in it, but what it does and how you control it I have no idea."

She closed her eyes and directed several questions to the dagger, using every language she knew, but as she expected, no response came. She could not even detect a change in the energy signature of the dagger during the attempt. Opening her eyes, she looked around at the others and shrugged. "I am certain this also came from Ista, but with the High Priest dead, the only way I'll discover the purpose is through trial and error."

"Well, don't burn the tent down," Douglas said. "Those augmentation devices didn't like what you did to them. These things might not like it either."

Stephenie gave her protector a weak smile. "I'm not trying to destroy these."

Chapter 7

"We need more supplies," Stephenie said. "The horses are out of grain and we can't push them on like we have been if all we can offer is some meager grazing."

Henton nodded his head in reply. "I don't disagree, but you are too noticeable."

"Leave my hair out of it," she said with a warning shake of her head. She liked her red hair long and had no intention of cutting it.

"I am just suggesting that Douglas and Ryia go." Henton said after a moment.

"Why can't I go with you instead?" Ryia asked Henton.

Stephenie watched as he turned to Ryia. "Because, I also tend to stand out. I'm taller than most people and I think my description is getting passed around."

"You're not much taller than Douglas," Ryia challenged.

"And I'm just a nobody," Douglas joked and Stephenie could tell his comment remained in good humor.

"I'm still taller," Henton stated. "Douglas, you are not a nobody, and damn it, I'm in charge here, so consider it an order."

Stephenie cleared her throat. "Well, there is a relative amount of 'in charge'," she said with a smile to Henton. "But you are correct, Douglas and Ryia should be the ones to go into the town. Take your horses plus the pack animals, load up on supplies then come back here. We'll be waiting." *Kas, you go with them as well,* she mentally told her friend.

Douglas nodded his head as he walked over to grab the pack horses' lead ropes. "We'll be back before too long."

Ryia simply turned away and mounted Dark Dancer. She waited for Douglas to mount Tonnie's Pride before urging Dancer to walk, but she did not glance back at any of them as she did.

Once they were out of sight, Henton turned to Stephenie. "I don't get it. I can't seem to say or do anything she likes these days. I'm lost."

"She's been through a lot," Stephenie offered.

"I know that. But..."

Stephenie put her hand on Henton's arm. "I've tried to talk to her...," Stephenie sighed, "I don't want to press it because it just makes her angry." She looked up to meet Henton's eyes. "Aside from allowing her time, I don't know what else to do."

"She's happy one moment, then something sets her off. I hate to ask, but are you getting anything from her head about what's going on? Perhaps there is some—"

"Henton, I stay out of all of your heads as much as I can." Stephenie turned away, she had unintentionally learned secrets from each of her friends and would not violate their trusts. "If it gets worse, I'll try to force a conversation, but she just keeps saying she doesn't remember anything that happened and not to worry."

Henton force a chuckle. "Of course we are going to worry." He signed. "I'll try to find something to keep myself busy while we wait. Furball could use some brushing."

Stephenie smiled. Henton's initial dislike of having the horses had faded on their way to Vinerxan and despite periodic grumblings about the extra expense and effort, she knew he truly cared for them. She glanced back at Argat, *you can use some brushing as well.*

Stephenie tapped Argat's nose with the brush in her hand. His coat was shiny and even his mane and tail were fit for a parade. "I don't have any more treats, you'll have to wait for the others to come back."

Argat snorted, blowing his nose at Stephenie; however, instinct protected her clothing from his snot. Once she was sure Argat was done protesting his face being brushed, she dropped her field. "I wish

I had learned that trick years ago," she mumbled to herself. "It would have kept my shirts cleaner."

The others, they are under attack!

Stephenie could barely hear Kas, but the urgency in his mental communication set her in motion. She dropped the brush and flung herself up and around to land on Argat's bare back. "The others are in trouble," she cried as she squeezed Argat's sides, causing the powerful gelding to leap forward and immediately break into a gallop.

Kas' voice became clear as he closed on her. *They are in the town square. The crowd was building and Ryia sent me to get you. They were recognized.*

Protect Henton and then follow, she told Kas, knowing Henton would not be able to ride quickly without a saddle and bridle. She did not wait for a response as she gave Argat his head and urged him to go faster. Her mind raced with scenarios as she and Argat tore across the ground, but she could not bring herself to imagine the others dead. *I've kept them alive so far, I can't fail now.*

She felt the heat of the energy flowing through her body. Had she and Henton been further from the town, she would have flown from Argat's back and attacked from the air. However, before she could lose patience, Argat charged past the first building of the town, startling a dog that went yelping out of his way. Stephenie sensed the mass of people ahead of them as they moved into a tighter grouping of waddle and daub buildings.

A boy stepped from a door, but she refused to slow even though the boy stood motionless as he stared at Argat. Stephenie used her powers and flung the boy back into the side of the building moments before Argat barreled over him. The crowd ahead of them heard the boy's cry of fright and Argat's hoofs beating against the ground, flinging clumps of dirt behind him.

The crowd of more than sixty shifted and scrambled back as Stephenie mentally commanded Argat to slow, forcing him into a sliding stop. His hot breath came in deep gulps with his nose and chest flaring in the face of a young woman who stood paralyzed with terror.

Someone in the crowd finally cried out and pointed at her. A moment later, the crowd exploded into a screams of fear and anger, all in words Stephenie could not understand. At least a portion of the anger appeared to be directed at her charging into the edge of the crowd.

Stephenie did not care about their indignation. She easily sensed Douglas and Ryia standing back to back near a town well, their weapons drawn. She sensed a weak field around them and could detect at least two priests in the crowd that had been using magic against Ryia's protective barrier.

Stephenie pulled more power through herself and strengthened Ryia's field, even though the priests had appeared to cease their attack. The effort for her to strengthen the field over twenty yards away was more an issue of focus than one of power.

"What is the meaning of this?" Stephenie growled in Pandar, her voice drowning out the noise of the crowd.

The emotions from the crowd quickly shifted from a mix of anger and fear to pure terror. The noise settled, but did not completely die. Out of the masses, a man took a step in her direction as the people around him stepped back. The man, in his early twenties spoke in a strong voice, though his Pandar was accented. "We will not suffer the spawn of Elrin in our town. We are followers of Bermet and we honor his name."

"You are attacking a priest and follower of Catheri." Stephenie hated to propagate the lies, but people refused to believe the truth. Instead, she fell back on Will's story since it was one these people would likely believe. "I," she emphasized, "will tolerate no harm to them."

"You and these two are known to us as followers of Elrin. Your destruction of the priests of Talnar and the ending of Talnar's life is an affront to all that is holy. You killed their High Priestess, tore down their castle, and slew men, women, and children!"

Stephenie looked at the man. She could not yet sense Henton, but hoped he would be joining her shortly. She scoffed. "You were deceived. I do not deny destroying a cabal of assassins. Those that died attacked me and held my friends hostage. But they were not followers of Talnar. They were priests of Mertor who had attacked the people of my country, starting a war with me that they did not win."

"You are Elrin's spawn," shouted another person in the crowd.

Stephenie shook her head. "I am the Prophet of Catheri, Goddess of Justice. She has returned and I am her weapon."

The first man cleared his throat. "Why should we believe you, a foreigner, claiming to be a Prophet of a god we've never heard of, over people from our own lands? People of the mountains?"

Stephenie watched the crowd. The emotions were running too high for her to make much sense of what filled the air. *Terror, fear, and anger,* she thought to herself. *I am so tired of death and killing.*

We are coming, Kas said on the periphery of her mind.

She smiled, happy that Henton would soon join her. To the man and the crowd she raised her voice. "You are in a quandary. You have been told two versions of the truth. I am either the spawn of Elrin, who you have been told just killed a god and destroyed an army of priests and who could easily kill every one of you and eat your souls for angering me by threatening my friends. Or, I am her Royal Highness, Princess Stephenie of Cothel, Defender of Cothel, and Prophet of Catheri, a person who killed a god, destroyed an army of priests and assassins, and could easily kill every one of you for angering me by threatening my friends." She paused a moment to let her words sink in as she felt Henton and Kas close in behind her. "I promise you, I do not intend harm to anyone here. We just came here to buy some supplies and move on. I am who I said I am, a person who believes in justice and am willing to overlook your fear here today. For fear is why you have acted."

The man stood straighter. "There's another possibility. Neither you, nor those others that passed through here, are telling us the truth."

Stephenie gave him a genuine smile and a small chuckle. "That is always a possibility." *And happens to be true.* "But even assuming there are three possible stories, you still only have two choices. Let my friends go unharmed or try to harm them." She watched the man consider her words. "Two of the three possibilities are that I can kill every person in this town. The third one might still be that I can do that." Stephenie slipped from Argat's back and moved toward the man. "None of you here can harm them now that I am here. The only decision is if you want to try and die or walk away and live."

Stephenie stopped in front of the young man. He wore quality clothing, smelled of floral soap, and his hair was nicely trimmed. A look of confidence filled his face under the fear she could now feel from him because she was close enough to separate his emotions from the crowd. "What is your choice?"

The man bowed his head toward her. "When considered through a moment of reason, it would make no sense to oppose you. Based on the word of the others that came through, as well as by your own words, you are reported to have personally destroyed an army of priests—who were possibly even assassins. What could a group of commoners do to you?"

Stephenie bowed her head in return. "I thank you for not pressing this. I've seen too much pain and suffering. We just need supplies and will be on our way." She paused at the low grumblings moving through the crowd. Stephenie assumed it was the local language and while she did not know the words, she could read the tone. "We intend to pay for the supplies; however, based on our current treatment, we will gather the supplies ourselves to avoid anything we don't like getting added." The man before her seemed about to protest. "Me and my friends are in no danger from physical attack, but that does not mean we want upset stomachs."

The man bowed his head again.

"Ryia, Douglas, go with Henton and gather what we need. Bring it out here so everyone can see what we are taking and they can tell us the price." *Kas, please watch them.* She looked toward the crowd that had not moved to allow Douglas or Ryia to escape the circle. With a gentle nudge, she created a field and slowly pushed people aside to make room for her friends to pass. However, she did not drop her own protective fields around them, Henton, or their horses. The effort taxed her concentration.

"Your Highness, my name is Tember. My father was Lord Mayor and I have taken over many of his duties."

Stephenie bowed her head again, turned to face the man, but kept her senses on the others. "I am glad to have found someone with a bit of reason here. I had hoped my friends could make their purchases and everyone would have gone about their day without complaint."

"I expect that is true. However, word of your deeds has spread, including accurate descriptions of you and your horses."

Stephenie nodded her head. *I underestimated just how far word would spread.* "Just so you know, I had not originally intended to engage the priests of Mertor, but they took my friends hostage. I killed the few priests that I did to free my friends."

"We are simple people," Tember said. "But we fear the evil that Elrin spreads. If those people from our land have lied to us and falsely accused you, please forgive us."

Stephenie softened her expression, but she still felt the frustration of the events. If Senzar mages were still pursuing them, then this town would become another point on the map for people to plot her course. *Though two points is not much to go by.* "Tember, I will let you judge us by our behavior." She considered warning him to not talk of her presence to anyone else, but she knew he would not be able to control the whole town and if she asked for silence, it would be that much less likely to happen. "What is the name of your town? It is not on our map."

"This is the town of Benis Hill, as spoken in the trade tongue."

Stephenie looked back at Furball and reached out to him mentally, calling Henton's horse to her side. Next, she reached out to the other horses she sensed on the other side of the crowd. The people had fallen nearly silent and found themselves uncertain of what they should do, so they simply stood in the square and watched, forming a wall between Stephenie and the others.

Her familiarity with the horses gave her greater range to reach their minds, but she also simplified her request to simply join her. The animals bristled at the request, but then they pulled their reins out of the hands of the startled town's people who were holding them. The four horses walked across the square, pushed through the crowd, and stopped directly in front of Stephenie. She reached out and patted Dark Dancer on the cheek. *I've already promised you no more boats,* she told the horse who always seemed to question her on the subject. While the horse's mind did not have human thoughts, the harrowing experience for the gelding had left a lasting uncertainty in him.

After a while, Henton, Douglas, and Ryia each carried an armload of goods out from a couple of shops. They carried them over to where Stephenie had gathered the horses and placed the supplies on the ground. Henton poured the contents of a couple of bags on the top of two sacks of grain for the horses.

Several people came over to Tember and began demanding things in their own language. Stephenie could feel Tember's unease, but the young man kept his face as neutral as possible when he turned to Stephenie.

"I fear the combined price for all of these goods will be twelve Talleys." Tember swallowed. "It is a local coin of the region. If you have Pandaras Crowns or something equivalent, it would convert to six crowns. They are very firm on their price," he added.

Stephenie narrowed her eyes. Even in Cothel, what they had would hardly be more than a full Crown. "I will not cheat you, but I will not be cheated. Catheri is a god of justice. I will give you effectively two Crowns. That is more than twice a fair price."

An older woman who had been quite animated in her demands shook her head. "We demanded six. You come here to rob us?"

Stephenie felt Ryia's anger and put her hand on the girl's arm. "Ma'am, it is you who is trying to rob me. If you don't want any of our money, we can find another town to purchase supplies from." She motioned with her head for Henton and the others to move toward their horses.

"Wait," said another man who had been arguing with Tember. "We will take three crowns." He turned toward the woman and said something rather curt to her in their language and while the woman did not seem happy, she held her protest.

Stephenie looked at the man. She sensed fear, but now it felt more like a fear of losing an opportunity. "It is still robbery on your part, but I will pay Tember the money and let him divide it among you." She walked over to Henton's horse and reached into her saddlebags he had tossed over Furball's withers. She fished around for the leather bag that held part of her share of the money and pulled out a handful of coins. She counted out enough to make three crowns as Henton, Douglas, and Ryia gathered the supplies.

"Here is your absurd fee," she said as she handed the young man the money.

"Ma'am, the goods were not mine to barter. I only passed along the price requested."

Stephenie smiled at the man and then used her magic to lift the second sack of grain from the ground without looking at it. It flew behind her back and carefully came to rest on Stubborn's back next to the first one. Nonplussed, Henton quickly lashed it to the frame that held their supplies.

"We're good, Steph," he said as they stowed the last of what they had purchased.

Ready to put the town behind them, Stephenie turned, grabbed Argat's neck, and swung herself onto his back. *Now we need to backtrack and get my saddle and the other supplies we left behind.* She decided to look on the bright side of the event, *Perhaps it might throw people off the track of which way we are heading.*

"Your Highness," Tember called as she turned Argat to head out of the town. "Please do not hold hatred in your heart. We were only doing what we thought was right."

She smiled back at the man. "You saw reason, so I will not harbor ill will toward you. However, I cannot recommend anyone to come here for supplies and will never look favorably on this town." She knew it was a petty comment, but the merchants' greed annoyed her.

"I am sorry, Steph," Ryia mumbled as they rode on into the late evening. "I should have done better. I'm just not strong enough."

Stephenie leaned off Argat's side and nudged her younger friend with her shoulder. "It wasn't your fault. I should have assumed word would have spread that far."

"You did. You sent Kas to watch us. I'm just not strong enough." Ryia shook her head. "I couldn't protect Douglas. I should never have come."

Stephenie rode next to her silently for a few moments. Henton and Douglas were at least thirty yards ahead of them with Kas. "Ryia, you did protect Douglas and yourself and you had the sense to send

Kas to get me. Had you not been there, no one would have been there to protect Douglas at all."

"But even that little bit I did to protect us from those priests caused me to bleed."

Stephenie had not noticed any blood coming from Ryia's nose in the town, but it was possible she had managed to hide it well enough. Tradition held that witches bleed from their noses and eyes because Elrin's power was meant for the elves and for a human to use the evil would poison them. The truth was far simpler, pulling power through one's body did damage. Since the priests only used a small amount of power and did their work through augmentation devices, they seldom overextended their body's tolerances.

Ryia met Stephenie's eyes. "You all know it too. That's why no one trusts me to do anything anymore."

Stephenie felt Ryia daring her to challenge the statement. She resisted with her seat, bringing Argat to a halt while she sent Dancer a mental command to stop. "Ryia, that is not the case. We all trust you. We're just concerned for you. After what happened—"

"What happened? Really, what happened? Am I less of a person now? Am I so fragile none of you want to touch me?"

"Ryia—"

"No." Ryia turned her head away and tried to get Dancer to walk forward, but the horse continued to obey Stephenie. "I don't want to hear anymore from you. LET Dancer go!"

Stephenie reached out and grabbed the sixteen-year-old's arm. "Stop it Ryia. None of us think any less of you."

"That's not how it feels!"

Stephenie tugged on Ryia's arm, drawing the girl to face her. "Then I am sorry. None of us ever wanted you to feel that way."

"It's not like it was the first time that ever happened to me," she said, tears in her eyes. "Just leave it alone and stop treating me different."

Stephenie nodded her head. She could sense the others had stopped, but none of them had come to investigate the conversation. "We'll let it drop. But that doesn't mean if you ever change your mind and want—"

"That is what I mean! Leave it alone. Please."

"We all love you, Ryia. We all want you here."

Ryia nodded her head. "I know. I'm sorry. I shouldn't have yelled." She wiped her eyes and sniffed back her tears. "Can we just keep going and find a place to camp. The others are watching us."

"Sure," Stephenie said softly. She knew that no matter how much Ryia said she was fine, the girl was not. *I just wish I had an answer.*

Chapter 8

Stephenie kept them in the foothills of the mountains and off the road, though they followed the road's general course as it turned to a more northerly route. The majestic snowcapped peaks of the World's Backbone remained on their left and stood as a constant reminder of what awaited them the further north they went.

Four days after their adventure in the town of Benis Hill, Stephenie found herself looking down a small mountain slope at a large city nestled in a protected valley.

"Based on your maps, I am going to guess that is Tenia," Henton said. "There is no lake, so it can't be Lake Seon."

Stephenie continued to stare at the lamps that illuminated the city streets and the large stone gates that allowed entrance into the walled city. They had avoided contact with all travelers and towns since Benis Hill and she hoped that would give them some protection from discovery. "We are okay for supplies for now," she said. "However, we'll need more grain in a day or two."

She looked back into the sheltered valley behind her where the tent remained hidden from view of the city and road. Argat and the other horses munched on the dry grasses that grew in the sandy soil. *There is just not much here for them to eat.*

"What are your plans?" Henton asked as Douglas allowed a yawn to escape his mouth.

Stephenie shifted her focus back to the city that was still three miles away. "To slip around it, we would have to roam several miles out into the plains. That will take time, maybe burn a whole day.

However, it won't get us any information and we need that. I need maps and trade routes. I don't want to rely on hope that this road goes all the way to Ista."

"It's a big city, but do you think it is big enough to have a library?" Henton's statement was barely a question.

Stephenie shook her head. "There will be lords and wealthy merchants with private libraries and collections, but they won't let the likes of us in to peruse through their documents. We're not locals with rank and privilege and I'm not going to announce myself." She let out a sigh, there was so much knowledge potentially sitting on shelves that she would never have the chance to see. "No, I'll find a guildhall and try to purchase some information. Perhaps the carter or teamster guilds will have maps and information about the roads and countries north of here."

"Even to Ista?" Douglas asked.

She shook her head. "No, I think we are still too far south for information that will go all the way there and I don't want to give away too many details on our travel plans by asking for it either."

"So," Henton asked again, "what are your plans?"

"Tomorrow, I think I will take Douglas and Stubborn into the city, confirm it is Tenia, hopefully find some maps, buy a few supplies, and then rejoin you here. Then we can skirt around the city and continue north." Stephenie noticed Ryia's odd expression. "What?"

"You don't want to also take Kas?"

Stephenie rose to her feet. "No. I would rather have more people stay with the horses and if you are in trouble, Kas can help or come find me faster than anyone else." She clasped the girl on the shoulder. "Hey, let's get some rest for now. We'll end up pushing it tomorrow afternoon and evening to make up for the time I spend in the city."

Ryia frowned, but followed Stephenie back to the tent.

Stephenie awoke from a dream that left her with a desperate sense of loss. She reached out with her senses and realized the source of her unease came from Ryia. The girl trembled as a nightmare played out in her head. Stephenie reached out and gently shook Ryia's shoulder, waking her. It had been the third night in a row that Ryia's dreams had woken her, but this was the first time Stephenie decided to disturb her friend. "You okay?" she whispered.

Ryia looked around for a moment, getting her bearings and gaining control over her emotions. She finally met Stephenie's eyes, though Stephenie knew Ryia's night sight was not as powerful as her own.

"I'm fine." Without saying anything else, Ryia rolled over and turned away, though not before Stephenie had noticed the moisture in Ryia's eyes.

Stephenie sensed that Henton had stirred, but had not fully woken. Ryia, however, sniffed once and continued to try to force her emotions down, which only reduced her control.

"Ryia, you're among friends. We won't abandon you."

"Stay out of my head. I don't need anyone's sympathy." A moment later, Ryia huffed and crawled from her blankets. "I need to use the pot," she said as she left the tent.

Stephenie reached out to Kas, who was barely close enough to hear her, and asked him to keep an eye on Ryia. Henton caught her eye and he raised his eyebrows, though he would not be able to see her expression in return. "Another bad dream," she said as way of explanation. "I get the feeling I am coming off too motherly." *Which is absurd, I'm only a couple years older than her.*

"She'll have to let one of us in at some point," he replied quietly. "Just try to get some sleep yourself, you've got a long day ahead of you tomorrow as well."

Ryia rejoined them just as the sun started to brighten the eastern horizon. Stephenie let Ryia sleep while she gathered Douglas and her gear as quietly as she could. Henton rose with them and started to tend to the camp as they readied Stubborn for the trek into the city.

"You think we need to worry about being recognized?" Douglas asked.

"Well? This is the first big city along the road since Benis Hill. Someone might have spread word here."

He glanced at her hair as she pulled it back and tied a strip of cloth around the loose ends. She had removed the braids the day before to give her scalp a rest and now her hair was a wavy mess. Stephenie sighed. "Go get my cowl. I'll cover my head."

Douglas' look told her he knew he had won the discussion even if he had to retrieve her cowl from the tent. When he returned, she put the wool covering over her head despite the warm morning air. She handed Douglas Stubborn's lead rope and indicated he should start walking with a nod of her head. "The sooner we're back and all that."

They had to travel almost five miles to get from their camp in the foothill to the city gates. The sun was well above the horizon by the time they were able to merge with the small crowd of people making their way into the city. Fortunately, their concern for being noticed nearly disappeared due to very inattentive guards who did not even seem to realize people were entering the city.

"Well, we get at least a few small favors," Douglas mumbled. "Where to now?"

Stephenie came to a stop in a large open area and looked up into Douglas' brown eyes. "You've become rather jaded of late. Something bothering you?" She could see him mulling over what he wanted to say.

"You're often in a bad mood as well."

She pursed her lips and nodded her head. "I'm trying not to be. I guess I need to try harder."

Douglas shook his head. "No, I can't blame you." He looked down the street and at the people moving about their morning errands, then he turned back to her. "A lot's changed since we first met. I've been wondering where all this will lead. We've lost people. We've been betrayed time and again."

"Henton took care of Berman," she replied more sharply than she had intended.

"Yeah, but those priests killed the others before convincing Berman to join them." He sighed. "I just don't know if I'll ever get a chance to rest and settle down and spend that money we got." He looked her in the eyes again. "I really have been thinking about buying a tailor shop."

Stephenie smiled. "I won't stop you. You're my friend and I'll do whatever I can to make you happy."

Douglas looked at his feet. "Girls. You turn men into terrible soldiers. We'd rather take care of you than ourselves."

She felt a little playfulness from Douglas. "So, back to girls should not be soldiers?" she teased, reminding him of what he told her so long ago.

"You make plenty good soldiers," he said, returning his gaze to her face. "Us men make lousy ones. I almost let myself get killed so I could get revenge on those men. Henton's not chewed me out for it, but I know he wants to. The smarter thing would'a been to kill those that were an immediate threat and avoid getting stabbed in the gut. Then kill the others later, when it was safe to do so. Stabbed like that, what good was I to either you or Ryia?"

Stephenie took his hand in hers. She wished getting Ryia to talk would be as easy as this. "Henton hasn't chewed you out because he'd have done the same thing if your positions had been reversed. Look into his eyes sometime and you'll see it." She tugged on his hand, drawing his attention back to her face. "And if you look into my eyes, you'll see the same thing. It's not a man or woman thing. All five of us lose our minds when any of the others are threatened. Kas barely kept me from throwing myself against that priestess in a futile attempt at a direct assault." She turned her attention to the blanket-wrapped staff in her other hand. "We've each faced our own mortality lately and it's left a mark on us."

Douglas shuffled his feet. "You're not disappointed in me?"

She smiled. "Hardly. I love you. You're my friend and you didn't do anything I didn't do myself."

He forced a chuckle. "Then let's find you a guildhall so we can get back on the road. The sooner this is all done, the sooner we're back in Antar and I can retire into the life of luxury."

She let go of his hand and stepped aside so he could lead her down the street. "By all means, the sooner we get back, the better your options are for buildings. You don't want to end up in a second rate district."

"Exactly. The good places are all being snatched up while we're out seeing the world."

Stephenie approached the carter's guildhall and considered her options. The teamsters had flatly refused to help her because she was not a member of the guild. And even had she been, without a local sponsor, they would not even let her into the building. If the carters did as well, she might have to resort to less honest methods of gaining the access she wanted.

She slowed her pace as she climbed the stairs. The carter's guildhall was a stone building like most of the other buildings in Tenia. She had learned the abundant supply of stone was a cheaper source of building materials than the lumber harvested from the mountains or the vast forests that covered the northern and eastern parts of Bergo.

The friezes above the building's lintel depicted numerous manner of carts and wagons being pulled by an equally wide assortment of animals and men. The building, like most of the city, was old and many of the stone carvings had lost some of their perfection from the wind, rain, and ice. However, the paint that brought the images to life was vibrant and showed active care.

Stephenie pulled her eyes from the images thirty feet above her head as she passed between two large stone pillars. The guard positioned beside a pair of doors standing a dozen feet high watched her climb the steps and now moved to block her path. The language he greeted her with was foreign to her, but based on how many other people in the area spoke Pandar, she expected he would as well.

"Good morning, Sir." When his expression showed an understanding of her words, she continued, "I know this may be an unusual request, but I am a traveler making a long journey and hoped I might seek aid from your guildhall. You see, I had a close companion whose family were carters and he always spoke highly of his guild."

The man, who appeared to be in his thirties, moved a step closer, revealing some stiffness in his left leg, though his upper body was nimble and strong. "Is your companion a member of Tenia's guild?"

Stephenie shook her head. "No. We are from countries to the south and sadly he died earlier this year. However, I was hoping I might be able to request some time to inquire about the roads to the north and perhaps look at some maps." She could see the man's hesitation. "I am willing to make a donation to the guildhall as compensation." She stepped closer and tilted her head as Ryia often did when she wanted something from Douglas or Henton. "Please, I am far from home and my husband thinks I am a fool for even trying to ask for help. However, my father was a merchant and he always trusted in our local carter's guild and..." Stephenie wiped her eyes. "Now that he is dead and his brother claimed all of his estate, we are trying to get to a distant cousin of my husband who is a long way to the north."

The man, half a head taller than her, looked over her shoulder and down the steps. "Is that man with the horse your husband?"

Stephenie turned her head and looked at Douglas. He now carried the staff in his hand and wore her sword as well as his own. Stephenie turned back to the guard and nodded her head. "Glenn is a good man, but he doesn't realize I was actually quite useful to my father. I helped with the books all the time and..."

The guard put a hand on her arm. "I think perhaps we may be able to offer you some assistance. Please, let's go inside and speak with a scribe. I will help you plead your case."

Stephenie smiled at the man as he pulled open the door for her. Another guard standing inside the large entryway gave a questioning look and after a brief exchange of words, took the first man's place outside. Three other guards in the entryway simply nodded their heads.

"My name is Pendon."

Stephenie smiled. "Please call me, Tsveta." She refused to use Henton's alias for her.

Pendon led her through another set of doors and into a large chamber where numerous tapestries and symbols of wealth and power sat on display, including a gilded cart. Off to the left, he escorted her into a smaller office with five people sitting behind desks covered with papers.

Pendon approached an older man whose face held a resemblance to the guard, though most of the old man's hair had deserted his head, and what little that remained, was a pale white. The two men spoke at length, before the older man indicated she should sit in the chair before his desk.

"My Grandson tells me you are in need of assistance. That you want to look at maps?"

Stephenie bowed her head to the older man. "Yes, Sir. I am traveling north and would very much like to view some maps of what I might face as well as get some understanding of what the roads might be like."

The man watched her and then leaned forward to cross his arms on his desk. "Where are you heading?"

"I am not exactly sure," Stephenie said, not wanting to be so vague as to lose any assistance, but holding out hope she might be able to gain general access to many maps. "We only have the name of a town and know that it is along the World's Backbone. My husband's cousin was not very specific. He doesn't know we are coming as my father only recently died and my uncle threw us out of what had been our home."

The old man frowned. "This seems a risky journey. Your husband should've looked for work and found you a place to live. Where did you say you were from?"

"Duin Point," she offered easily, having already chosen that port city from her maps. "My husband grew angry with my uncle and words were exchanged." She looked down at her hands. "We feared for his life as my uncle threatened to kill him and sell me to slavers."

The old man's back straightened and after a moment his head nodded. "Pendon tends to be a good judge of character. I'll help you for free." The man stood and extended an arm to usher her from her chair. "If you will follow me, I will help you sort through some of our maps." He waited for her to stand and then he motioned for her to head toward a door in the side wall near his desk. "I can say that all reports we receive of the roads in Bergo are generally good. Lake Seon and Jura are the two main cities north along the mountains." He opened the door for her, revealing a long room with numerous rows of shelves as well as a cluster of tables. Three people looked up from their studies, but quickly went back to reading after they saw the two of them.

"There are a few reports of bandits, but that is more common to hear coming from Fleina." He smiled. "That is the country to our east. King Merdan tends to have a better hold on Bergo than the young pup who has taken over Fleina's crown."

"That is good to know, Sir," Stephenie said, wishing for a brief moment that it would be possible to stay and look through the books. For now she would have to content herself with the musk of old parchment and leather.

"You may call me Pendon. My son named his boy after me."

Stephenie smiled. She gathered the senior Pendon had thought it a bit unoriginal.

"Here we are," the older Pendon said, stopping in front of a large table in the back of the room. The man carefully flipped through several sheets of parchment and then pulled out one that showed the country of Bergo. "I can read the names of the towns and villages to you so that you may hear their names."

"That would be most appreciated," Stephenie said, realizing immediately that she was not familiar with the characters used in their language. "Do you mind if I take notes and make some drawings?"

The older man hesitated for a moment and then nodded his head. "The maps cost us a lot of money to have drawn, but I suppose as long as you only make rough notes, it will not compromise our investment."

Stephenie understood the man's concern. "You have my word, I will not share this information."

Stephenie managed to get the older Pendon to show her a number of maps, each going further and further north. Fleina, which was the country to Bergo's east, followed the mountains as they spread to the northeast. North of Fleina was Talset, a country that was wider than it was tall. Unfortunately, from the maps, it appeared she would have to make a decision in Fleina if she wanted to continue north along the mountains or take a road to the east and then go north along the coast.

The difficulty was that north of Talset was a country called Garder, but other than an indication that the country held a pass through the Backbone, there were no details about cities or roads.

In the searching, they found a crudely drawn nautical map that lacked any countries or cities, but showed the World's Backbone extending northeast through a giant peninsula that jutted far into the Endless Sea. The tip of the land was covered by what the cartographer had marked as the Endless Death. Pendon had trouble reading the notations, but said it referenced a frozen waste. After that last map, Stephenie conceded failure in locating her invented town of Pilantar and said she would simply continue to journey north in the hope of finding it.

She thanked both Pendons for their assistance on the way out and then quickly went back to Douglas, who was still waiting in front of the guildhall.

"It's about time," he said as she came down the steps.

"Quiet. Let's head back to the market square we saw around the block. I need to sit and draw out what I can before I forget everything. Then we'll buy supplies and return to our travels."

Chapter 9

Yreka sat across from Werha and quietly ate the meat from a bird she did not recognize. A sweet seasoning covered everything on her plate and she would rather it had been left off. Something with a bit of heat would have suited her much better, but her requests never seemed to translate successfully. Instead, the meal left her unsatisfied and annoyed. *Just another thing I want and cannot have,* she mused.

It had been ten days since they left the valley and there had been no sign of Stephenie. She and Werha even spent a whole day in the city of Buvi and not one merchant, city guard, or innkeeper they encountered had any memories of the princess or her crew. The only thing that eased her annoyance was that Olena had as little success as she and Werha. *Could the little Bitch have simply disappeared? Perhaps she had gone deeper into the mountains instead of returning to the road.*

Yreka took a small drink of wine and put the mug back on the table. *Perhaps I should just return home.* The thought brought a frown to her lips. Although she cared nothing for Stephenie personally, the mystery of Stephenie's father irritated her. *He must be a man of reasonable power and it was likely he was attempting to consolidate power, as anyone of breeding would. But is it enough of a concern to keep me from my own larger interests?* Yreka's empire had been in the hands of her grandson for more than a year, though the boy did not have complete autonomy. She remained in regular communication with the advisers she appointed to him and so far the reports she received indicated reasonable profits.

A man and a woman at a nearby table drew her attention. The two people giggled at a joke and Yreka tried to puzzle the meaning from their minds, but it turned out to hold little amusement as it appeared to be just a play-on-words requiring an understanding of the local language. The sexual nature of the joke was clear in both of their thoughts and Yreka knew the two young people greatly anticipated an evening of pleasure.

She turned her attention to Werha and slipped easily into the muscular man's thoughts. Yreka had grown up invading people's minds and aside from a dozen people she feared would be able to outmatch her mental skills, she simply went where she pleased.

Yreka's frown deepened. Werha was mentally exhausted from searching for Stephenie and had no desire for sex or any other activities. While she could order him to perform, his mental state had already turned her off the mood.

I hate these northern lands. The thought of giving up the chase once again proposed itself, but she forced it down. Too many people knew Stephenie had killed Favian, a protected descendant of hers. She might have been able to ignore the death had she not been responding to Favian's request for her aid at the time he was murdered. *I should have left the sniveling seventh-gen to his fate. Why did I even bother? Now if Stephenie escapes me, it would show far too much weakness on my part.*

The sense of duty to her empire hardened her expression and she took another drink of the dry wine. The red fluid lacked a richness of flavor, but at least it was not sweet and the alcohol had some bite. She considered finding something stronger and perhaps even finding someone to challenge in a binge drinking match, knowing that her powers would prevent her from becoming impaired.

A change in the energy signature of the communication stone in her pack drew her attention. No one was scheduled to make a report. She pulled out the stone and held it in her lap as she reached out mentally to the device, activating the stone.

The world around Yreka folded in upon her and a second reality merged and overlapped the first. She was both sitting at a table in the public house with Werha beside her and sitting outside in a dry landscape with Olena, Daeri, and Tibva standing before her. Olena's body and the table occupied the same space, cutting the soft-voiced female in half. Tibva and Daeri looked over Yreka's head, oblivious to the fact that Yreka was seated.

"Mistress," Olena said, bowing her head and then raising her eyes to meet Yreka's.

Only Yreka and Olena would be able to hear or see what was occurring around the opposite stones so Yreka turned her body and the stone to face Werha. Olena, Daeri, Tibva, and the sandy landscape around them moved with Yreka's shift and now Olena and Werha occupied the same space. "What do you have to report?" Yreka asked in their native tongue to avoid any of the locals from understanding.

Olena smiled. "We have caught sight of Stephenie."

Yreka nearly stood. "Where?"

"She passed through a small town the locals call Benis Hill. She left after a spectacular display of arrogance. It seems she sent a couple of her people, the girl she took from Vinerxan, Ryia, and Douglas, into the town to buy supplies. However, the town's people tried to capture them and before the two could be subdued, Stephenie charged into the city to rescue them."

"I suspect her ghost summoned her," Daeri injected, though he was still looking over Yreka's head.

Olena's jaw firmed, but she said nothing.

Yreka almost chuckled and was glad to have made Daeri Olena's problem. "How close are you to reaching her? I do not want you to engage her."

Olena frowned. "Mistress, we have ridden our horses hard. However, Stephenie has still made better progress. She passed through the town five days ago."

Olena did not need to tell Yreka they had fallen further behind Stephenie since the valley. Based on what they knew from the people who had fled the valley, Olena should have been at most three days behind Stephenie. "You will need to make better progress. Now that you have found her trail, you will need to press harder."

Olena nodded her head. "We will not have to spend as much time searching, but we are riding the horses to exhaustion even with our healing them."

"Then steal others," Yreka snapped. "Or steal the money to buy others after you wear out the ones you have. You need to make up the time and not lose pace."

"Did you cross into Kynto yet?" Olena asked. "I only inquire so that I might know how long it will be before you will reach us."

Yreka bristled at the tone. Olena had shown great foresight in predicting Stephenie's direction, *but she should take care in reminding me of that fact.* "With a hard press, we are six days from the valley and then I would guess another six or seven behind you. Do you have any further information on Stephenie's destination? Perhaps Werha and I can take a more direct route."

Olena shook her blond head. "No, Mistress. She left Benis Hill going back the way she had come. However, I suspect she had left supplies at a camp. She had ridden into the town bareback and in the thoughts of those I read, her man Henton had extra saddlebags draped over his horse."

"So you expect she is continuing to travel along this long mountain range."

Olena squared her shoulders. "There is a passage through the mountains fairly close. We will have to make sure she does not travel that road to the west through the World's Backbone, but my belief is she will continue along the east side of the mountains."

"Any reason?"

"None that I can articulate, Mistress. I just feel there are more potential destinations on the east side of the range."

Yreka nodded her head. *What is Stephenie's goal?* Yreka could not see it. To Olena she said, "Continue your course and ride the horses into the ground if necessary. I do not want to lose her. We will be following quickly." Without warning, Yreka withdrew her mind from the communication stone and the world around her solidified into a single reality. The man and woman at the other table were looking at her and she knew from their thoughts that they felt it odd she would be having a conversation with the man in front of her and that man would never say a word.

Yreka's lip curled. She did not care what people thought, Olena had uncovered Stephenie's trail and she could finally resolve the issue of Stephenie's insult to her and her family. *Then I will go home.*

Chapter 10

Henton exhaled as he swung his sword, cutting through the air at shoulder height. He stepped forward, flowing into a back swing and thrust. He had grown to accept the feel of the larger sword in his hands; however, he still missed the balance of the blade the flesh-spider had destroyed.

He slid left over the broken ground and released his left hand from the handle to swing the blade in a wide arch with his right arm. Turning, he brought his left hand back to the handle for his recovery swing. He sank lower into a squat before rising with his thrust.

"Do you think they are safe?" Ryia asked as she watched him practice.

He stood fully erect and turned toward Ryia, who had started to cook a small meal for the two of them. "I would hope so. Steph can handle most things."

Ryia seemed to ponder his statement for a moment and then glanced to her left. "Kas, why don't you go scout around to see if she's coming back?"

Henton heard Kas' disembodied voice fill the air. "That would anger Stephenie, as her instructions were for us to remain together."

"Please, Kas. We don't need a nurse-maid."

"I am sorry, Ryia, but I have no intention of leaving."

Ryia frowned and looked away for a moment before turning back to Henton. "You really planning to buy a ship?" she asked as her shoulders slumped slightly. "Wouldn't that get boring? On land, there is so much more to explore. At sea, all you see is water and more water."

Henton wanted to chuckle, but the seriousness of Ryia's expression kept his face neutral. He knew that her debilitating seasickness would keep her from ever willingly setting foot on another ship. Therefore, trying to explain the beauty of the sea and the thrill of pulling into distant ports and seeing new lands would be wasted on her. "I wouldn't worry too much about me sailing off any time soon. I think Douglas has overestimated our funds. We've got coins from countries I've never heard of and getting a fair exchange on some of it will be hard. Plus, ships cost a lot more than you'd think."

Henton slid his sword back into its scabbard. He had intended on also working out with the short sword he had taken from the priest of Mertor, but simply going through the motions was not the same as sparring with a good partner using practice blades. *I wish we had not dumped them to save weight,* he thought. He had always been a good fighter, but Stephenie had greatly improved his techniques. *Though I taught her a few things her land-loving weapons master never knew.*

He focused back on Ryia who was once again biting her lip. "You never got to tell us what you'd do with your share of the coin, Ryia."

She sighed and shrugged. "I don't know. When I was starving on the streets, it would have been to have a castle with an army of servants to bring me food and stoke the fireplaces to keep me warm." She stared off into the past. "A giant bed with down feathers. Gold goblets to drink from. Pretty dresses...with ruffles." She shook herself out of her reprieve and looked back at Henton. "You know, useless things."

He moved away from the flat spot where their tent had been set up and down to the place where she had been using her magic to heat their food. "I don't know. Those things have uses."

"They're not weapons. They won't keep you safe."

Henton squatted down next to the pot and looked inside. His stomach grumbled, but the burned food inside did not look appetizing. "You may have overheated this."

She came over to the pot and swore, then she kicked it over with her foot before swearing some more. After a moment, she looked down. "I'm sorry."

He took a deep breath and stood up. "Well, let's just clean out the pot and we can find something to snack on. I know there is still a good chunk of hard cheese in our supplies."

She started walking away. "I'll get it for you."

Too busy letting her mind wander, he told himself as he carefully picked up the pot. Had it been one of his soldiers who had done that, he would have made sure they never made the same mistake again. *I'm getting soft.* He turned it over, being careful to keep his fingers from getting burned on the hot iron. The burnt remnants remained firmly stuck to the bottom. He was about to hunt for a stick or a rock to scrape it out when Ryia started cursing again.

"Damn you, Argat. You stupid horse! Shut up Kas!"

Henton got to his feet and walked over to where the horses where picketed. One of the bags of grain had been knocked over and Argat was standing protectively over the spilled food. Ryia had pulled him away and he was showing his displeasure at being separated from the feast. Dancer had started to move in to get his own time with the grain.

Henton crossed the ground quickly and the horses turned their ears to him. "Hey, get out of that," he demanded without shouting. Dancer paused, considered the consequences, grabbed a mouthful of food, and backed away.

Henton grabbed up the spilled sack and scooped the loose grain back into the opening. "How much has he eaten?" he asked over his shoulder.

"I'm not sure," Ryia choked out and then swore. "You stupid horse. Damn it, what do you think you're doing?"

Henton stood up with the grain sack in his arms. "He was being a horse. You must have left the grain here after you fed them."

She looked away.

"I am sorry, Henton," Kas said, barely materializing to his right. "I should have paid closer attention to what she had done."

Henton gave Kas a withering look, "This was her responsibility, not yours." He turned his attention back to Ryia. "When did you feed them? How long has he been eating the grain?"

She continued to look at the ground as she held Argat's lead loosely in her hand. "I don't know. I did it while cooking our food. Then I watched you practicing."

Henton shook his head. "If he colics, Steph will kill you. You can't just forget things like this. Damn it, Ryia, you have to be more responsible."

Her shoulders sunk lower.

"Walk him for now and let's hope he doesn't founder or colic."

She mumbled something under her breath in a language Henton did not know, but he was fairly certain it was directed at Argat and not himself. "It's not Argat's fault, it's yours. I'll move the horses away from what's left on the ground and finish getting the camp picked up. Steph should be able to check him out when she gets back."

Henton almost felt sorry for Ryia after Stephenie had returned. The excitement of finding maps had fallen from Stephenie's face only to be replaced with cold anger that left Stephenie silent as she carefully examined Argat. Ryia's apology had brought no reaction from Stephenie and he knew just how powerfully knowing someone was disappointed in you could cut. He had learned to hone that emotion as a means of training his men. He had even used it to try and motivate Stephenie to do things he thought were safer than what she had planned.

In this case, the disappointment was so thick it choked the air from everyone's lungs and hung around them even after Stephenie had declared Argat healthy enough for them to continue their journey. The cloud did not lift until after they stopped again for the night and set up camp beyond the foothills of the mountains in a dense copse of trees.

"I can forgive many things," Stephenie swore as they were getting ready to turn in for the night. "But Argat can't take care of himself the same as the rest of us. None of the horses can, so you damn well better be more careful next time."

"I'm sorry," Ryia said, her head held so low that her chin rested against her chest. "I know I am useless. I don't deserve to be here."

Stephenie tossed her hands in the air and shook her head. "I'm not in the mood for this." Without another word, she walked out of the camp and into the woods.

Henton heard Ryia's quiet sob. He hesitated a moment as Douglas caught his eye giving him a subtle sign that he should talk to the girl. *Like I need you to tell me that.* With quiet footsteps he walked over to Ryia. "Give her time. She's very protective of Argat."

"I know," Ryia swore at him.

"Hey, don't take it out on me. She's got some odd bond with the horse. She's not talked much about it, but after the Senzar mage had messed with her head, I think Argat helped to bring her back to herself." He put his hand on Ryia's shoulder. "Steph will forgive you in time. Let her get over her anger and just make sure you are careful with the horses from now on and—"

"I can't do anything right. I'm weak. My magic is worthless. I can't take care of the horses. I can't get y..." She closed her eyes and turned away.

"Ryia, she doesn't hate you. She's angry, but it will pass. You don't want to know how many times I wanted to strangle Douglas and Will, but they are still my friends. And don't think that I haven't had Stephenie angry at me either. It happens."

She lifted her head and slowly looked up at him. It was dark enough that he could not see the red in her eyes, but the hint of moisture on her cheeks glistened in the moonlight. "What about you? Do you hate me?"

He forced a smile to his face. "Never. But, I do want you to do better next time. Okay?"

She closed her eyes and nodded her head.

"Good. Now get some rest. You've had a long day, but just know that it will all be forgotten in a couple of days."

She walked away and climbed into the tent.

I better talk to Steph. Just in a way that doesn't make her mad at me as well, he added as he headed into the woods.

Chapter 11

Islet put the thoughts of how much farther ahead Stephenie had gone from her mind. When they passed through the small town of Benis Hill, they had been five days behind. They had traveled four days past Tenia before Islet had caught word of Stephenie again, this time in the small village of Cas Tu that was not on her maps. Only now Stephenie had extended her lead to seven days. Islet had ordered everyone to keep going longer into the evenings and rise earlier in the day. Sir Walter had complied, but the horses just could not keep pace with Stephenie and Islet knew it was her sister's magic that helped.

She glanced at Walter who rode ahead of them and felt the gulf that had opened between them ever since he learned that Stephenie had always planned to continue north and Islet had not shared those details with him. Now he only spoke to her when necessary and most of the other men viewed her with a questioning gaze. If they continued to fall further behind, she expected Walter might override her and forcefully escort her back to her brother. And worse, as the accuracy of her maps continued to diminish, her ability to predict her sister's route would also decrease. If her sister continued to cover her trail as she had been, Islet worried she might never find her, let alone catch up to her. *Please, Steph, let me reach you before it's too late.*

"Ma'am," Tain said from her left. The big man rode his horse with an ease and grace people would not expect of him without knowing that his homeland was mostly populated by nomads and horsemen. "Would you like more of this..." He looked at the red fruit in his hand and frowned. "They called them something...I can't remember.

Damn thing looks like a large apple, but too squishy." He shrugged as he softly squeezed the smooth orb in his hand. "It tastes like a strawberry and—"

"A current," she finished for him. Tain was the one exception, the one person who always tried to raise her spirits and offer his support. "Okay, I'll eat another, but this has to be my last one. I'll make myself sick."

He smiled and handed her the heavy fruit. "How come your sister travels so must faster than us?" His question was pitched low so that only she and Jerylin would hear it.

Islet took a large bite of the cal'toran and tried to not let the juice drip from her chin onto her clothing. The back of her hand came away covered with clear fluid as she savored the sweet and slightly tart chunk of fruit in her mouth. After swallowing, she looked over at Tain and his big brown eyes. "She's better at motivating everyone than I am."

"Aww, now that ain't true," Tain said.

Islet shrugged. "She's the Prophet of Catheri." *Likely, she doesn't even realize she's using her powers to keep everyone fresh.* "She's always been good at covering ground quickly."

Tain remained unconvinced. "She's got skills. I never knew her, but I saw her train before the war. You're as good as her."

Islet took another bite of the juicy fruit to hide her smile. The importance of having women learn martial skills and understand battle planning was something her late husband had shown her. Growing up with her mother, only Stephenie and Joshua had managed to get time in those pursuits. Her mother's loathing and contempt for Stephenie meant all of her older sisters had been barred from the pursuits that her father had allowed Stephenie to enjoy.

"Ma'am?" Jerylin's voice had risen an octave, but it came only moments before Walter called out a single word of alarm, bringing everyone in close to protect Islet.

Islet turned her head looking for the threat. The narrow road ran through a section of dense woods and she could not see anything in the trees, but she could hear the sounds of sudden movement. Ahead of Sir Walter, she saw two men move from the trees to take position in the road, one was armed with a crossbow.

Walter and D'har were directly ahead of her with Tain on her right and Jerylin crowding her horse against Talbit's rear. Wilson, Mic, and Carac had started to move around to cover her flank.

"Moving damn fast for a bridal party," the taller man demanded in Pandar. His tunic showed signs of wear, but the crossbow was held with confidence. "Had to steal horses just to keep up with you."

"Clear the road. We don't want any trouble with you," Sir Walter demanded.

The second man, who held a sword, chuckled. He tossed his long blond hair over his shoulder. "If you're lucky, we'll just take the horses and your things. Though a couple of woman may be nice to warm our beds."

"Unless they are worth a pretty ransom," the first man said.

The sound of movement in the woods grew closer and Islet felt Tain's hand on her arm, though she did not look in his direction.

"Get down between the horses, you'll be less likely to get hit with an arrow," he whispered in Cothish. "Walter's about to attack."

Islet noticed the way the Knight was holding out the reins of his horse, his fingers spread. Without waiting any longer, she slipped off the right side of her horse and dropped between Talbit and Tain's roan. A moment later, Tain jumped clear of his horse and ran into the woods as he drew his sword. Seeing Tain's horse start to move, Islet reached out and grabbed the reins.

Outside of her view, she heard the rest of her men jumping from their horses and moving into the trees. She heard the attackers calling out what she could only assume were curses. Then the crossbow was released and the bolt flew over the top of their heads.

"Jerylin, get down here!" Islet shouted as she crouched down. In the woods on her right, she could hear weapons making contact and people yelling, but the yells were not from her people. Her people spoke in crisp sentences, calling out assailants and claiming targets. The number of reported attackers had grown to at least eight.

Islet grabbed Jerylin's wrist and pulled her close. Between the horses' legs, she could see Walter and D'har engaging four men. "Use your powers, help them."

"Stay down," she heard Carac call from her left. He had remained in the road and close to them while all of the others engaged the attackers in the woods.

"I...I don't know how," Jerylin said. "I only know how to draw on Elrin's evil."

From her left and just inside the treeline, she heard Mic grunt in pain and saw Carac leave the road to confront two men moving around some trees. Mic staggered back as the sound of a crossbow discharging rang in her ears. "Do it! But use Catheri's holy symbol as your focus!"

Islet heard another crossbow discharging from her right but did not hear any cries of pain. On her left, Carac continued forward, wielding his sword with a controlled ferocity only a seasoned soldier could manifest.

Islet turned her focus forward. Walter's and D'har's horses had scattered. D'har was down, but Walter now only faced a single man. Beside her, she heard Jerylin pray to Catheri and quickly start chanting.

To her left, a third man that had been coming at Carac flew backward into a tree as Jerylin slammed her right fist into her left palm. There was enough force that a branch tore through the man's gut, spraying the ground with blood. As the man slipped from the branch, he left a trail of entrails pulled tight by the tree.

The remaining assailants, all out of Islet's view, suddenly started shouting, but now in fear. Islet hoped they would not suddenly be accused of harboring a witch. She knew towns and cities would ignore all manner of crimes if the victims could be associated with Elrin.

Several more shouts rang out in the woods and then she heard Walter calling out everyone's name. Islet listened as each person responded: Tain; Wilson; Carac, with a pained voice; herself, and Jerylin. *Where's Mic and D'har?*

"Mic?" Walter called again.

"Sir, he took a hit in the woods," Carac responded through clenched teeth. "I've got a cut...they sunk a damn bolt into my chest."

"I'll get him," Wilson said, coming out of the trees with Tain.

"Tain, you're with him," was Walter's response.

Walter quickly moved to Islet. "Are you injured?"

"No. Are you?" she asked.

Walter brushed aside the question. There was blood on his clothing and his blade, but she could not tell if it was his or his attackers. "Stay here between the horses." Walter moved over to Carac, who had sunk to the ground, though Walter kept his attention on the woods.

"Jerylin, please see to Carac. I need to keep watch and he needs help." Islet saw the nervous shake in Jerylin's arms. "Look at me," Islet demanded. "You can do this. What you were learning in Vinerxan is not far off what you need to know as a priestess of Catheri. Just use your holy symbol as a focus and you and Carac will be safe. You don't need to worry about Elrin or any of his evil working its way into you." Islet held Jerylin's arms and stared into her eyes. "Do you understand? Carac and the others need your abilities."

Jerylin nodded. "Yes, Ma'am. I understand. I just don't want anyone to think I am a witch." She lowered her voice. "I don't want that and I can't see how anything I am doing is any different than when I was using Elrin's evil."

Islet regretted the fact that Jerylin had been ordered to go on this journey. She left before Will had been able to sell her on whatever lie he had come up with to convince people who thought of themselves as witches and warlocks, that they were in fact priestesses and priests of Catheri. *Stephenie never preached it to Ryia, so I never learned Will's angle.* She took a stab at reassuring Jerylin. "Look, Catheri has come back to us through the bones of the world. Through the very rocks. Like the one around your neck. Just like water is purified by flowing through stone, so is magic. And magic..." Islet paused at Jerylin's expression. "Sorry, that's an old word that Stephenie taught me. But the underlying power all the priests wield is based on the same thing. You know how to heal and to fight, use what you know and save Carac's life."

Jerylin nodded her head and then slipped around the back of the horses, leaving Islet to stand alone between her horse and Tain's. *Please, everyone be okay. Please, no one die on me.* Islet ducked down and looked forward between the horses' legs. D'har still had not moved from where he lay on the ground. He had been left there by

Walter, who was now in the woods on the right hand side of the road. Islet blinked back the tears in her eyes; she knew why Walter had left their companion on the road. "I am so sorry, D'har."

"Ow!"

Islet turned to Carac's cry of pain. Between Talbit's legs she watched Jerylin set aside the bolt the woman had pulled from Carac's chest. Carac flailed his arms as his head rolled back and forth on the ground. Blood oozed out of the hole on in his chest. "Jerylin," Islet cried in panic. "You have to stop his bleeding!"

Islet saw Jerylin's jaw tighten, then she placed her left hand on the hole in Carac's chest while she gripped the stone she wore around her neck with her right. Her chanting started slowly and quietly, but increased in speed and volume. After a painfully long time, Carac's movements eased and his breathing slowed.

He sighed and slowly lifted his head. "Thank you," he mumbled, patting Jerylin's bloody hand that remained on his chest. He set his head back on the ground. "I think I might lay here for a moment."

Jerylin let out a whimper of relief and smiled. She looked up and Islet caught her eye and smiled. "You did good." Islet could not bring herself to look down the road to where D'har still lay.

"The woods to the east are clear," Walter said from behind her.

On the western side of the road, Tain and Wilson carried Mic from the woods. The blond man's head was supported against Tain's chest, but his lower abdomen was covered in blood. When Tain saw Walter, the large man shook his head. "We stuffed as much of him back in as we could, but it was too late."

Walter came around the horses as Islet moved out from between them, though she still held their reins. "D'har took a bolt to the eye. He didn't make it."

"Orders?" Tain asked.

"We need to move away from this location," Walter said, surveying the scene. "There are at least six other bodies on the road and in the woods. Several got away. We don't need someone coming upon us with this around us."

"What of D'har and Mic?" Islet asked.

Walter turned to face her. She saw the pain in his eyes and the hardness of his face. "We can't do anything for them." He turned to

Wilson. "Remove anything that could tie them to Cothel and Her Majesty. Take any money and valuables and then place their bodies beside the road. We can't do any more." Walter then turned to Tain. "I see you're wounded, if it can wait, I need you to help search these bastards on the road for anything of value, don't go into the woods alone." He turned to Islet and Jerylin. "Ma'am, you did very well to stay under cover. I appreciate not having to worry. And Jerylin, good work calling on Catheri. We will need you to do some more healing when we find someplace safe. For now, the two of you please continue to care for Carac while I gather the horses up."

Islet nodded her head, unable to find her voice. Though Walter had remained stoic in his posture, she could feel the biting pain that filled his being. *And I feel every bit of the responsibility as well, so please don't fight me when I say we must continue on.*

They did not stop until well after dark. Little had been said during the remainder of the day, but by silent agreement, they continued north with as much haste as they could achieve.

Once Walter found a small clearing off the road, he put Tain and Wilson in charge of setting up the camp, while he cared for the horses and Jerylin tended to Carac. Islet insisted on taking over D'har's normal task of preparing the evening meal. On the road with Stephenie, she had been given equal time at most tasks, but as the daughter of a wealthy merchant, her cover had restricted her usefulness on this journey.

She worked on the fire, but the absence of the short man brought tears to Islet's eyes. She quickly wiped them away. She missed D'har's laugh and while Mic had been more reserved, the blond man had been kind enough. Breathing slowly, she steeled herself against the emotion. As Queen of Ipith, she and her husband had sent friends and advisers into countless dangers, and sometimes even to their death. Only in private had she been allowed to mourn the dead and she would give these soldiers no less honor.

"Ma'am," Sir Walter said quietly as he joined her.

"Yes, Walter?"

"We should talk." He took her hand and helped her rise to her feet. "Over there," he said, inclining his head toward the trees and away from the others.

Islet nodded and followed after the Knight. The loss of two of their number was a heavy blow, but she still had an obligation to warn her sister. *She saved my life and as long as it is likely I can help her, I won't quit.*

"Ma'am—"

"Islet, Walter. Please, call me Islet," she repeated for the countless time.

Walter nodded his head. "Islet, we have to face some serious facts. With only three of us left in fighting condition, we will have a very hard time protecting you."

Islet placed her hand on Walters arm. "Walter, I understand your concern. I really do, but Steph is out there and there is a Senzar witch looking for her. A very powerful one that strode right into Antar without a concern in the world and assaulted Will in his home."

"You won't do any good for your sister if you, or the rest of us, are dead."

"Walter, I understand that, but as long as there is a chance we can make it, I want to try." She glanced back at the large tent that Tain and Wilson were assembling for her and Jerylin. "Perhaps we should change the cover story. We would draw less attention as simply a small band of travelers. I can wear some of Jerylin's clothing and just be a commoner. Perhaps I can simply be your wife."

She felt Walter stiffen. "Ma'am—"

"Islet." She took a deep breath and turned him away from the camp. "Walter, I've hoped for weeks that you might loosen up around me and just talk to me like a person and not some princess or some deposed queen. Please, for my sake, just treat me like a normal person."

Walter looked at her for several moments. She had trouble reading his expression in the moonlight, but she knew he was considering his words.

"Islet, you are a princess and in my opinion, you are still very much a queen. How can I simply toss that aside? I have to set an example for the men. If I don't maintain the discipline, then they will also assume they can take liberties with you."

She knew that was a false excuse. "Damn it, Walter. I spent a year in a small cell and had no privacy. I spent months on the road with Steph and Henton and we literally slept on top of each other because the tent was nowhere near big enough for five people. I enjoyed traveling with her and her friends more than I have on any day since I started this journey." She held his stare. "And the reason was, they all treated me like a friend and we joked and laughed and allowed ourselves to have fun, even when we were running from my mother's guards."

"Islet—"

"No, you will hear me out. If you want me to be a queen, fine, I will start giving orders instead of making request." She softened her expression. "But, I would much rather just talk as equals with everyone."

Walter exhaled. "It doesn't change the fact that we are getting further behind your sister every day and now that Carac is injured, we will fall further yet. What mission is she on that even her brother doesn't know? You want me to treat you like everyone else, you first need to trust me enough to be honest with me."

Islet swallowed. "They are not my secrets to share, Walter. But she is searching for some answers and we believe those answers are at the top of the World's Backbone."

"What?" He shook his head. "I have no idea what is even up that far to the north."

"I memorized a number of maps before I left. I had hoped we'd be able to catch Steph before she got too far, but it didn't happen."

He sighed again. "If you were expecting to potentially go that far north, it would explain why you have been so frugal with our money."

"And I have even more hidden away in my things." She put her hand back on his arm. "We can sell or just get rid of that huge tent. I can sleep in something reasonable and dress as a peasant. We can travel with less pomp and blend in more. That should hopefully avoid some of the people who might think about attacking us."

Walter looked back at the camp. "I will consider it. We can't take this road back to the south, we'd run into whomever decided to attack us in the first place. So for now, we don't have any choice, but I am not sold on staying the course. The further your sister goes, the safer she will be and the less value we bring."

"Until she starts back for home. If the Senzar, this Yreka, decides to wait for her along the way, Stephenie could walk right into a trap and not be aware."

Walter shook his head and stared at her for several moments. "Your brother is going to have my neck."

"Please, Walter. I have no intention of throwing away our lives, but if there is a chance, we have to try."

He sighed again. "We'll do it your way for now. Okay, Islet?"

She smiled at him and brushed her fingers along his muscular arm. "Thank you, Walter."

Chapter 12

Rain had fallen in a relentless assault for almost six days as Stephenie led the others along the southern edge of the expansive Lake Seon. The fifty mile journey from the city of Lake Seon to the city of Jura took them five miserable days of slowly trudging along a road that had turned into a river of slippery mud. The mostly flat ground south of the lake collected water and then refused to allow it to drain away.

The terrible conditions kept them in a perpetual state of uncomfortable wetness that penetrated through their oiled cloaks to their clothing beneath. Despite Stephenie's ministrations, they constantly fought sores and injures. Dark Dancer strained tendons in his left-rear leg twice on rocks that were hidden in the mud. Had Stephenie not been able to heal the damage, Ryia's horse would not have walked again.

Each night they found shelter in small towns crowded with travelers or at farmsteads, where they slept in barns or any building that had some measure of dryness. When they reached the walled city of Jura, after a day where they had managed to travel less than five miles, no one objected to finding shelter inside the city.

Jura, which was the second largest city in the small country of Bergo, sat on the northeastern corner of Lake Seon. It was located at the point where several rivers coming down from the mountains merged together before draining into the lake. With the heavy rains, the rivers were now a wide torrent of water that had swollen their banks and were ripping into the land. The dangerous flood of water exposed buried boulders and shut down the normal barge traffic that took hunters and prospectors to the far shore of the lake.

From the moment they entered the walled city, Stephenie could tell an eclectic group of people called this place home. The various building styles and colors reflected different nationalities and trades. Even with the rain, conflicting aromas from baking bread and frying pork to feces and vomit wafted through the air, drawing reactions between hunger pains and gag responses.

Because of the rains, the normally busy city was overflowing with people waiting for the conditions to improve before continuing their journeys. Fortunately, the city had been built with wide streets to accommodate heavy merchant traffic and that prevented things from coming to a standstill. Unfortunately, the large number of people meant that even with a willingness on Stephenie's part to spend money, it took a very long time before they found an inn and stables with enough room to accommodate them. And when they did find the inn, they rented the rooms even though it had minimal services and no adjoining public house.

Night had fallen before they had finished taking care of the horses and managed to store their gear in their rooms. Starved and exhausted, they found themselves drying out in Elard's Tavern, which was just a short walk down the flooded street. The smell of roasting meat and sweet rolls stoked their hunger and they quickly dove into whatever food was ready.

After several mugs of warm ale, three rounds of food, and a rich dessert, they leaned back to enjoy the dry room and lively music. Douglas and Ryia watched the people who were dancing while Stephenie and Henton pulled out one of the books she had acquired from the trap room and started to study the contents.

"This character," Stephenie said over the music as she drew a curved mark with three small branches in her red journal, "means ownership. The other mark here is the number eight."

Henton nodded his head. "They really look like the same thing."

"I'm going to get something from the bar," Douglas said after he finished his mug of spiced ale and pushed back his chair. "The two of you are boring me to death."

Stephenie reflexively grabbed the staff Douglas had knocked away from the table as he stood. She pulled the blanket-wrapped weapon closer, pushing back the intelligence that now reached out to her even through the material. The intelligence had never become forceful, nor had it done anything she did not like, but she still did not fully trust the weapon.

"This part of the curve is squished more here," she said, indicating the bottom of the mark with the tip of her quill.

Douglas, not having elicited a response, chuckled and walked away. Stephenie noted Henton's quick glance in the direction Douglas had gone and knew that in spite of his outward indifference, Henton would keep an eye on his friend.

"A sloppy writer will make a mess of this language," Henton said.

She knew Kas agreed with Henton's statement, but she had found the logic behind how the language was constructed fascinating. That admiration made her overlook some of the challenges it held. "Then just learn to be neat in your penmanship. Don't be a slouch when holding the pen." Henton's frown brought a smile to her face.

"Henton, want to dance?" Ryia asked and then glanced once to the open area on the other side of the large common room. The small group of musicians had switched to a song with a faster beat and several more people had moved to the floor. The laughter and merriment was loud enough to drown out the sound of the rain.

"Not right now, Ryia. Perhaps later." He looked back at the paper Stephenie had been writing on. "I still don't get how you managed to learn so much of the language so quickly."

Stephenie shrugged. "I guess it is like flying," she continued in Cothish, taking the risk of speaking openly because it was unlikely anyone here spoke their language. "Just like I can feel where I will be well before I arrive at a point in the air, I can almost see the relationships between the characters and words and sentences." She pulled back some loose hair. "I've always had a knack for learning languages. I picked up Kyntian without my mother or her people ever realizing I had learned it."

You are very spatially aware, Kas said mentally. *You just have an innate way of feeling your way through things.*

"Are you sure you don't want to dance? The music is really good. I don't know what this song is, but I like it." Ryia leaned across the table to put her head over the paper they were writing on and looked up at Henton with wide eyes.

"Sorry, Ryia. I really don't feel like it. You could ask one of the men already dancing if you could join them. I'm sure they'd be willing to let you."

Her lips compressed as she leaned back in her chair. She glanced at the men dancing with their partners, then at the rest of the room and shrugged. "Fine. I'm not really in the mood either." She looked toward the door. "I'm done eating, I'm going back to the inn."

"Wait," Henton said, but she had already stood and started for the door. She did not pause to look back at him, only sharing a quick glance with Douglas before she pushed her way through a couple of men who were coming in the front door.

Stephenie bit her lip. *Kas, do you want to watch her?* She felt Kas' hesitation. *What is it?*

She became very angry with me the last time I followed her. She does not like me acting as her keeper. It is not like I can hide my presence from her.

"I don't get her," Henton said. "She'll chat my ear off for a whole day, going on about this, that, and anything really. The next thing I know, I'll say something—or more often not say something she wanted to hear—and she's furious with me and won't say another word for the rest of the day. And the next morning it is like nothing happened. We're past the grain incident. Any idea what's going on now?"

Stephenie set down the quill. "I really work hard to keep out of everyone's mind. I can't tell you what's going on in her head."

"No female insight?"

She raised her eyebrows and dared him to ask the question again.

"You think I was wrong to say no to the dancing?"

Stephenie shook her head. "No. We were talking and you've been wanting to learn more about this language. She could have waited."

"But?" he questioned after a moment of silence.

"I really don't want to get involved," Stephenie said.

Henton nodded his head. "She's been trying to flirt with me." He looked from the book to her eyes. "I know she's just sixteen, but does she have to be so flighty in everything?" He shifted in his seat. "Since I've known you, you've never gotten temperamental with me. You've always been direct and to the point if you want something. Never all this hinting and implying. Always have your head on your shoulders. Why does she have to act like a normal girl and not more like you?"

Stephenie put the stopper on the inkwell. "So I'm not normal?" She raised her hand to stop him. "Stupid question." She turned slightly in her chair. "I don't know what a normal girl is supposed to be like. When we met, the only thing I wanted was to save the life of my father and brother...and get away from my crazy mother." She picked up her mug and drank some more of the ale. "I had a lot of things weighing on my mind. I never got to simply be a girl who liked a guy."

Henton shook his head. "I'm too old for her. She should realize that." He looked down at his own mug. "I'll apologize to her later. I just wish she wouldn't act like everything is the end of the world if she doesn't get what she wants the moment she wants it." He looked up. "You were never like that, even after we rescued Josh. She's just so young sometimes."

Stephenie chuckled. "I'm not that much older than her. Just two and a half years." She leaned closer to him. "I seem to recall a time when you had some strong feelings for me."

"I'll be twenty-nine in just a couple of weeks."

"And I'll only be nineteen a month after that."

"You're...older for your age," he said, looking back into his mug.

"You think I act like an old-maid?" She teased. "Always so serious and never able to have fun?"

He shook his head. "Not an old-maid. You can be serious, but not in a bad way. After what you've been through, how can you not. I think you are just more mature. That's what I meant." He met her eyes again. "I mean, you were raised to rule a country, you had to be more mature than most girls I've known."

"And just who are all these girls you know?" She raised her eyebrows in demand of an answer.

Henton chuckled and shook his head. "Oh, no, I'm not going to be drawn into one of those conversations. I have a younger sister, Melisa, who was a terrible flirt growing up. And I've known a few other women over the years."

"None serious enough to get you off your ship for more than a night or two I'm guessing."

"Now who's acting like a flirt?" Henton glanced over her shoulder. "Kas here to put you back in line?"

I want no part of this conversation, Kas demanded in her mind.

"Put me in line?" Stephenie shook her head at him. "Good thing we managed to get two rooms at the inn, otherwise you might end up in the stall with Furball." She chuckled and then she let the smile fall from her face. "In all seriousness, Ryia's been through a lot. I think you need to talk with her about this."

"I've tried, but she stalks off or moves away if she thinks she won't like what I have to say." Henton pushed his mug across the table. "Boys are pretty simple. I've dealt with several I had to train into soldiers. Their minds are on one thing at a time and if there is nothing to keep them busy, it will be on girls." He looked intently at Stephenie. "What is it girls think about?"

She leaned back in her chair and shook her head. "You think there is an us and a them? I thought you were a little more evolved than that, Henton."

"My younger sister was close to my age. She got very good at manipulating people. She was cunning. She didn't think like me."

Stephenie sighed. "I can't tell you about other girls because I really wasn't around them growing up. My sisters and mother were not friendly. I spent my time with Josh and his friends and my father. I grew up around men. I feared for my life everyday. I kept my feelings hidden and buried. I don't have the context to know what Ryia is feeling." She finished the last of her ale and pushed the mug away from herself. The food had been too good and she had drunk too much. "I really don't want to get in the middle of this and she's still refusing to talk to me about anything she's feeling as well. My getting mad about Argat has made it worse, but, let's just plan to stay in town tomorrow and dry out a little more. I'll take Douglas out again to see if we can find some more maps and I'll ask Kas to leave the two of you alone so you can have a quiet conversation with her."

"And if she gets mad and stalks off?"

"Henton, you've corralled a bunch of rowdy boys, you can't handle one sixteen-year-old girl?"

He raised his eyebrows. "Probably not." He sighed. "I don't want to hurt her. I do like her, but..." He looked away. "I think I can understand what she's feeling." He looked back at Stephenie. "I've had way too much to drink tonight. I don't normally let myself get like this." He pushed back his chair. "I'll go round up Douglas if you've got your books and papers."

Stephenie lifted a saddle bag from the floor and smiled warmly. She understood what Henton was facing, only he had been more rational than what she expected Ryia would be. *Though we never really finished our conversation about that either,* she thought to herself.

Are we heading back to the inn? Kas asked.

Stephenie hoped Kas had not picked up too much of her thoughts, though she knew the ghost accepted the oddness of the situation, she was not fully comfortable discussing the relationship the three of them shared. *Yes,* she told him. *I'll try to prep Ryia for Henton's discussion. I just really don't want to be in the middle of all of it.*

That is wise.

She gathered up the items she had pulled out of the saddlebag earlier and started wrapping them in the waxed cloth and pigskin cover to keep everything safe and dry.

"Where is she?" Henton asked as they stood in the room Ryia was supposed to share with Stephenie.

"I don't know," Stephenie said, panic sending her heart pounding. "I couldn't sense her as we came into the inn."

"Dancer is still in his stall," Kas said, materializing beside her.

"Let me get my other weapons," Henton said. "Someone might have grabbed her on the way back here."

Stephenie raised her hand to halt him. "Her things are gone. She's been back here." Reaching out with her powers, she felt for the bags of coins they hid high in the ceiling where she had formed a cavity near the outer wall. She pulled down four leather bags. "Her money's gone, but ours is here."

"Damn it," Henton swore.

"What do you want me to do?" Douglas asked, looking between the two of them.

She turned to Kas and he quickly spoke. "When I failed to locate her in the stables, I proceeded to check in the immediate area around the inn. Unfortunately, she is not close."

"Kas, can you please check the western gate and outside the walls?" Stephenie levitated the bags of coins back into the hiding spot. "I'll go north and then check the docks." She looked toward Douglas and Henton. "I want the two of you to stay together for safety. Can you work your way east?"

Henton nodded his head. "It's still raining, so I am guessing she'll go for cover. We'll look for any taverns and inns, but it's going to be hard to find her." Henton balled his hands into fists. "Damn it, I should have talked to her sooner."

"I should have said something myself," Douglas said. "I just never expected her to run off."

"Don't beat yourself up." Henton flexed his fingers, trying not to ball his hands into fists again. "Let's go find her."

Stephenie followed her two men out of the room and shut the door behind her.

"Perhaps she'll change her mind and come back," Douglas offered.

"We can hope," Stephenie agreed, "but for now, we just need to find her and talk to her. She's not going to be safe on her own this far from any home she's known." The moment she said it, Stephenie knew the girl had never really called anywhere home. *Except wherever we've been together. Damn it, Ryia.*

Stephenie spread her senses wide and searched for the mental signature that would be her friend as they left the inn. She found no sign of Ryia. "Be safe," she said to Douglas and Henton as they went their separate directions. She resisted using magic to shield herself from the cold rain and resorted to pulling her cowl down to keep the water from hitting her face. *When I find you,* she swore. *Damn it, I had gotten dry.* She pushed the thought away. She just wanted Ryia to be safe and back with them.

*   *   *   *   *

Stephenie raced up and down the streets, working her way north and growing more desperate with each step. The multitude of people she felt made her nauseous. With her mind opened, she could not help but absorb some of the emotional energy. Because it was often contradictory, her own sense of self felt torn and damaged.

Stephenie muscled though the discomfort and continued moving along the edge of the city, trying to cover the streets in such a way that would allow her to not have to walk each one, yet still be able to feel those inside every building. As the night continued to draw out, she reached the docks and paused to give her throbbing mind a rest. *Ryia, where are you?* She pleaded. *Perhaps the others have found her already.* She sighed, she would have no way to let them know if she found Ryia and they would have no way to tell her either.

"You stupid girl," she swore under her breath. Until she had found Ryia or finished searching the whole area she set aside for herself, she would not go back into the inn. Instead, she would endure the wind that whipped the rain about and sent ripples across the flooded streets. Her boots were filled with water and her oiled garments were no longer effective. Even the blanket wrapped around the staff hung unevenly as the weight of the water pulled and tugged at it. *We are going to have a long talk when we find you, Ryia.*

Stephenie's attention narrowed. A man behind her suddenly drew in energy. The amount had been minimal, but the resulting field he crafted unleashed a powerful wave of energy. The wave struck her, knocking her forward, but her instincts had built a field of her own, forcing most of the energy to roll around her body.

"Surrender," came a heavily accented voice yelling in Pandar. A narrow beam of energy appeared less than five feet from her side and struck her, knocking her into the air, but not penetrating her defenses.

Stephenie spun around before her feet hit the ground, orienting herself toward the man as another candlestick-wide beam of energy hit her. This attack ripped into her abdomen. Surprise and pain raced through her, but she pushed it away as she unleashed her own gravity attacks on the man.

The man barely reacted as her fields collapsed without doing any damage. The man retaliated before Stephenie could even understand how he had defeated her attack.

The staff rose up in her mind as did the sense that it wanted her to not force it away. The staff reacted on its own and a gravity pulse that would have ripped through her body struck the staff's field. It dissipated as a momentary blue aura in the dimly lit street. Unlike one of the augmentation devices, Stephenie felt the staff pull energy from the ground to generate the field and she spared a half-thought of thanks that the staff would not be killing something to protect her.

The man had moved closer, but hesitated before attacking again. Stephenie raised her voice. "I don't know you, but it doesn't have to be this way." She expanded her senses, desperately seeking the other Senzar she expected would soon be attacking her.

The man responded with an attack. This one struck the surface of the staff's spherical field, but the man's field suddenly changed, modulated, and penetrated the staff's protection, refracting through the defense to strike her in the leg.

Blood sprayed outward into the rain filled street as she lost her footing. She gorged herself on energy, using some of it to keep her upright, but she held the rest in reserve as protection from the others that had not yet shown themselves. The power crackled within her and slowly burned, but she continued to hold it.

The staff drew her attention and she knew it wanted to retaliate. *Loose your energy,* she told it as she pointed the blanket covered weapon at the man.

Lightning exploded from the tip of the staff and struck the startled man, though most of the energy diverted away, hitting the building to his left. Thunder rumbled through the street shaking the oil lamps and rippling puddles of water.

In the distance she could hear people screaming in surprise, but she continued to search for the other Senzar as fear began to settle into her. *They better not be hurting my friends!*

More energy coursed through her body and her wounds instinctively closed as she stepped toward the man who had attacked her.

The blond-haired man quickly unleashed another series of attacks. They came at her from several angles, two of his attacks broke through, ripping into her arm and leg. However, the staff adjusted its approach and the subsequent gravity blasts rebounded into the night. She sensed the man attempt another set of attacks and she strengthened her own fields inside the staff's sphere just in case he got through the staff's protection. The odd nature of his fields gave her a moment's pause as she tried to see how the man vibrated his fields in a way that would cancel out the effect of the staff.

The man's attacks failed to penetrate the staff and Stephenie winced under the strain of the energy she held. Without the other Senzar attacking her, her fear for her friends grew. Tired of the man, she lowered the staff again, shooting another bolt of lightning. This blinding flash sent him staggering back, but again most of the energy exploded into a building off to his side. She growled and then unleashed her own gravity attacks on the man while she continued to allow the staff to unleash its lightning.

Rolling thunder filled the streets and the noise started to deafen her as the staff grew hot from all the energy coursing through it. The blanket on the end had completely burned away, revealing the ornamented steel cap.

Subconsciously, she repeated the man's own modulation technique with her gravity field and her attack suddenly penetrated his defenses, ripping a hole through his chest. A moment later, the seventh and eighth blast of lightning struck him directly in the head, burning the flesh from his skull.

Stephenie found herself hovering five feet above the street, unaware of when she had drifted into the air. The man's mental presence was gone and she knew the last blast had killed him. Around her, she could feel a multitude of people at their windows and doors. Those who had been in the streets had enough sense to flee, those thinking themselves protected, had decided to watch.

Still unable to sense any other Senzar attackers, she launched herself upward and quickly flew toward the buildings on her left. She skimmed the roof and then flew over the next street as well. Many people were in that street and she hoped none of them had looked upward.

She flew over one more street and another row of buildings before she dropped back to the ground, staying close to the buildings as she descended. She did not sense any sudden spikes of fear from the people milling about and hoped the rain had covered her flight.

I have to find the others, she swore. *Damn it Ryia, where are you?* She shook her head, *You'll have to wait until I make sure everyone else is safe.*

Chapter 13

Stephenie raced back across the city no longer caring how wet she got. She needed to find Henton, Douglas, and Kas to warn them of the threat. She hoped the others might have heard the commotion her fight had caused and sought safety, but on a grand scale, the amount of energy drawn had not been enough for Kas to have felt it unless he was relatively close. *Maybe he'd feel the sound of the thunder.* She could only hope they would understand the danger and not run toward it, but back to the inn. *Please, Ryia keep yourself safe I have to protect the others.*

As she moved through the streets, she could hear Kas' voice reminding her yet again that skill almost always wins out over power. *That man knew things,* she admitted to herself. He wasn't powerful, *but he outclassed me.*

Stephenie turned down the street leading toward the inn and brought herself to an abrupt stop. *Thank you!* She cried out silently and started jogging toward Ryia, who was hurrying toward the inn from the other direction. She reached out with her power, and even with the distance, tapped the girl on the shoulder so she would notice Stephenie coming.

Ryia slowed, saw Stephenie, and started running toward her. "Steph!" The girl called with a tremor in her voice when she drew close. "What happened?"

Stephenie ran into the girl and grabbed her by the shoulders. "Are you hurt?"

Ryia shook her head. "I...I'm, sorry I left. I saw the lightning and heard the thunder. I wasn't sure what was happening."

"You're not hurt?"

She shook her head. "I'm sorry."

Stephenie set her jaw, but she could not hold all the anger back from her voice. "Henton, Douglas, and Kas are somewhere in the city looking for you. I think Yreka's here. A man attacked me and I'm pretty sure it was one of her men. I can only hope the others are at the inn and not hurt."

"I'm sorry."

Stephenie wanted to shake the girl, but she could not waste the time. She turned Ryia around and ushered her toward the inn. "We can talk about it later, we need to leave the city as soon as possible."

"They are not at the inn. I just came from there." The girl slowed and started to cry. "I left again and then changed my mind to come back and wait."

Stephenie slowed, but did not stop. "No more running away."

"We need to find them!"

She took a deep breath and fought against her instinct. She did not want to do the intelligent thing, but Henton had reinforced what she already knew, *keep your head together and think, don't react.* Stephenie leaned close to Ryia's ear. "Look, I want to scour the city, but if any of the others heard what happened, they should be making their way back to the inn. No matter how much I don't want to just wait, it would be worse to go looking for them." *At least for now,* she added, knowing her patience would not last the whole night.

Stephenie led Ryia back inside the inn. The young man who watched the front door and manned a desk looked up at them. "Back again?"

"Yes," Stephenie said more sharply than she wanted. However, she did not apologize. She herded Ryia up the stairs and down the hall to their rooms. Inside, she shed her cowl and outer garments, dropping the soaking wet clothes to the floor. "What do you think you were doing, Ryia?"

The sixteen year-old wiped her eyes and dropped back to sit on the bed. "I...I couldn't stay. I'm spoiled goods and I know I'm not good enough—"

"Ryia," Stephenie almost swore her name, but then moved closer and knelt down in front of the girl. "I've told you before, you're not spoiled goods. Whatever those men did to you is on them, not on you. Don't value yourself by what happened."

Ryia shook her head. "It...it's not me...why does he treat me so differently? He doesn't want me. You all treat me different."

Stephenie let out an exasperated breath. "Ryia, Henton and Douglas aren't looking down upon you, they just don't know how to react. You say you're fine all the time, but then you bite their heads off without warning. They are just guys. The only thing they know how to do is try to fix things and they don't have a clue how to fix what is wrong because you are not telling us what to fix. We don't know what you want us to do."

Tears fell faster down Ryia's face. "I don't know what I want! I don't know what's wrong. I'm angry all the time, but I don't know why. I try to talk...I want to talk about it, but I don't want to either. I...I don't know...I don't..."

"Then how are they supposed to know?" She put her hands on Ryia's knees. "They are trying to do their best. We all are and I'm not blaming you for not knowing what you want, but don't expect them to be able to solve what you can't. It's going to take time, Ryia." Stephenie smiled, hoping to lift Ryia's spirits. "Just work with us."

Ryia nodded her head slowly.

Stephenie removed some dry clothing from her pack and quickly dressed. "And," Stephenie held up her hand, "if you ever plan to leave, we won't stop you, but please, at least tell us you are going. Don't just slip away. We won't force you to stay if you don't want to, but we will try to talk you out of it, because we'd rather you stayed with us then go."

Ryia slid off the bed and into Stephenie's arms, placing her head on Stephenie's shoulder. "I don't want to go, but it hurts. It just hurts so much."

"What hurts?" Stephenie asked, holding Ryia's soaked body close to hers, once again making her wet.

"No matter what I do, I can't seem to make Henton love me."

Stephenie held back the initial thought that came to her mind. After a moment, she helped Ryia back up to sit on the bed. "Henton does care for you, we all do."

"But I love him."

"And he is quite a bit older than you."

Ryia shook her head. "I don't care. Why should it matter? Is it beca—"

"It is not because of what happened to you." Stephenie frowned and sat down next to Ryia. *Am I really that much more mature?* "Henton is almost twenty-nine and you've just recently turned sixteen."

"Your sister was married at fourteen to the King of Ipith and he was older than Henton." The defiance in Ryia's voice slowed her tears.

"And she had no choice in the matter because it was political. I didn't realize why at the time, but I could feel how uncertain Islet was and I knew she did not want to be sold off to some man whom she didn't know."

"I know Henton."

Stephenie felt her back straighten. "Henton is used to how we do things in Cothel, where people tend to marry those closer to their own age. Outside of wealthy families, many people choose their own partners and for him, your difference in age is going to be an issue."

"It shouldn't be a problem if it is not a problem for me. I don't care what others think. He should like being able to brag about a young..."

"I would agree with not living your life for others, but he's almost twice as old as you and he's not one to brag about things like that."

Ryia closed her eyes for a moment. "That's not the problem. The problem is Henton loves you, not me. Nothing I do will compare to you."

Stephenie felt Ryia's desperation. "Henton knows that I care for Kas."

Ryia shook her head. "I can see how he looks at you. It's all a lost cause. You love Kas, Henton loves you, I love Henton." Ryia wiped tears from her face. "And Kas doesn't have a body, so no one will be happy."

Stephenie felt her own chest tighten. "Ryia, I cannot say what the future will bring. Magic cannot predict what's going to happen. But, I would suggest you talk with Henton. No games. No simply hoping he'll notice what you want. Tell him how you feel."

Ryia shook her head again. "What if he..."

"Ryia, he is not a man who likes people who play games. He prefers to deal with people directly. Be honest and open and he'll be honest back. You can't fear being embarrassed or hurt." She smiled at Ryia. "First of all, he would never try to hurt you and if you don't actually talk to him, you can't expect him to know how you feel." She raised her hand to keep Ryia from speaking. "But, I can't say he will do what you want. His feelings are his own. It might take a couple of years before he feels you are old enough."

"I'm old enough now. Why shouldn't he think I am old enough for him?"

"You'd have to talk to him. Just understand, no matter what he says or does, it is not the end of the world. Don't think that it is, even if he tells you he just wants to remain friends."

Ryia sniffled back her tears. "But I love him."

"And if it doesn't work out for you, you still have a chance to find someone else."

Ryia raised a defiant eyebrow.

"I'm serious. I know what you are thinking, but despite all the years of brainwashing from priests, we've found several people who know what we are and accept us for it without fear. I am certain we'll meet many more in time."

Ryia nodded her head. "I suppose."

"I know so," Stephenie said, a smile spreading across her face as she shook with relief. "I can feel Henton and Douglas coming up the stairs."

Stephenie jumped to her feet and went to the door, opening it just before they reached it. "Ryia's back, have you seen Kas?"

Henton shook his head as he quickly pushed pasted Stephenie into the room. Seeing Ryia, he moved quickly to the bed as she slowly rose to her feet. "Are you okay?" he asked, taking in her appearance. "Injured?"

"No. I'm..."

Henton shook his head. "I'm sorry for not dancing with you, but please, do not ever run off like that ever again."

"At least take your horse," Douglas said from where he stood next to Stephenie.

"I didn't want to be accused of being a horse thief," Ryia mumbled.

Stephenie crossed the room pulling Douglas with her. "He's yours if you ever do decide to leave, but that's beside the point. We've got bigger problems."

"What happened earlier?" Henton asked. "There are guards running all about and we heard a lot of thunder and we saw a lot of lightning flashes."

"I'm fairly certain one of Yreka's mages saw me looking for Ryia. I think he wanted to capture me more than kill me...at least at first. I ended up using the staff quite a bit because I was expecting Yreka and the other three to show up as well. When they didn't, I feared they had gone after you." Her fingers clenched into fists. "I just hope they haven't found Kas. I want to be out there looking for him, but I'm also a bit scared they might know about the inn. The problem is, until he returns, we can't go anywhere, not that there is anywhere in the city with room." She swallowed. "But I won't wait much longer before I do go hunting for him."

Henton glanced once to Ryia and Douglas before looking back at Stephenie. "Staying here is the wisest course. If Kas was still searching outside the city, he might not have seen or heard the lightning. You already know it's not wise to send people out to search until it is clear that needs to happen."

Stephenie wiped her face of the water that had run from her hair. "Yes, I said the same to Ryia earlier." She unclenched her hands. "I've been trying not to worry, but I can't help it."

"What's the plan?" Douglas asked. "Do we fight them?"

Stephenie slowed her pacing and paused for a moment. "The little bastard that attacked me from behind wasn't very powerful. At least he didn't draw lots of energy, but I wasn't even close to being in his class skill wise. He did things I had never seen before."

"Then we need to get out of the city without them seeing us," Henton decided. "The trouble is, will they expect us to flee tonight and be watching for us or will they wait and watch the gates in the morning. My guess is they would rather not engage in a fight in broad daylight. They might be powerful, but that just brings too much attention."

Stephenie pursed her lips and nodded her head. "I had wanted to flee tonight, but you raise a good point. Plus, the guards will be watching for anything unusual after the commotion. We try to leave in the middle of the night during a torrential downpour and that will not go unnoticed." She watched Henton's face for a clue as to his thoughts, but he seemed conflicted as well.

She took a step to the right. *There was only one of them, since no one has come at us here, could it have been he just stumbled upon me?* Stephenie glanced again at Henton and then Douglas and Ryia. *Kas, where are you?* She hesitated a moment longer and then made up her mind. "We can't go anywhere until Kas is back. So we might as well stay here for the rest of the night. Hopefully, Yreka doesn't know where we are, though we need to keep a close watch through the rest of the night. We leave like normal in the morning, heading back out the western gate, then we'll circle south and cut back north after a day or so. Hopefully it will keep them from being able to follow us." She picked up the staff and started to remove the burned blanket. "And if Kas is not back soon, I'll go looking for him." The determination in her eyes kept anyone from questioning the statement. "He can move fast. He shouldn't be gone this long."

Chapter 14

"Kas, what took you so damn long?" Stephenie demanded, wishing yet again that she could actually wrap her arms around him. "Henton was about to lose an arm trying to keep me in this room."

Kas bowed his translucent head. He never altered the appearance of his clothing to match the environment when he luminesced, he simply displayed lightweight garments throughout the year. Although from time to time, he would project a different style of shirt. "I encountered two people who sensed my presence. Unlike most, they seemed to recognize what I was immediately and started to pursue me. Not wanting to lead them in your direction, I went further from the city."

"I think Yreka is in Jura. I killed someone who sounded like a Senzar mage. His accent was like those from Vinerxan and he was very skilled."

Kas' expression tightened. "Am I correct then in expecting that would account for the thunder and lightning I sensed coming from the northern section of the town? That display was a direct result of your duel?"

Stephenie glanced toward the staff sitting on the bed; she had cut away the burned section of the blanket and wrapped it again. "The staff generated most of the show. My real concern is that I only saw one person. If Yreka is here, I would have expected all of her people to have attacked me."

"I was pursued by a woman and a man. I could move faster than they, but they were able to cut the angle on me and that prevented me from easily moving around them and back into the city where they could not detect me."

"That would leave two more unaccounted for," Henton said. "What we heard from the man in Fallen Grove was that Yreka had four people with her, three men and a woman."

Kas nodded his head toward Henton. "I continued to sense the same two. Once the thunder and lightning had died away and it was obvious the city guards had been summoned, my two pursuers broke away and I was able to circle around and return. I waited for a period of time to make certain no one followed me."

Stephenie exhaled and then sat down on the bed. As the tension from not knowing Kas' fate left her, so did the energy that kept her standing. "Then we should assume there are at least four Senzar still in the city. They could split up and watch the gates to see when we leave."

"It's still raining," Douglas said. "Not as hard as earlier, but perhaps it will be raining tomorrow as well and we can still slip out without getting noticed. Unless you want to change plans and leave now."

"Rain may give us cover," Henton said, "but these people have done a good job in following us to find us here. Even if we slip out of the city, we have to assume they will continue to track us."

"We've left enough of a trail," Stephenie said. "It may be more our fault than any skill of theirs. I was hoping we'd come far enough that we could just stay on the main roads. Obviously not."

"Your maps don't show a lot of other options," Henton said with his arms crossed. "We either travel along the edge of the mountains or go several hundred miles out of our way."

Stephenie looked up. "I know that." She sighed. She knew there were two options, leave immediately or leave after a period of time. *But how long to wait?* She let her thoughts run aloud. "Assuming the four others are watching the gates for us to leave, we could disrupt that by not leaving first thing in the morning. We could wait until later. Perhaps even wait a couple of days. If the rains let up, then we could even cross the lake. If we factor the docks back in, then they'd have three places to watch with just four people."

"I don't know that we want to try the horses in the mountains," Henton challenged.

"Dancer hates water," Ryia whispered.

Stephenie held her tongue; she wanted to yell at Ryia to stop being meek. Instead, she extended her hand and caught the saddlebag that flew across the room. She pulled out the leather map case and removed her stack of maps.

"It may be possible for me to search for them," Kas said. "Perhaps I can draw them to the wrong gate."

"That might work," Douglas offered. "Then you can loop back to join us later."

Stephenie shook her head as she set aside several of the maps. Once she had finished looking at the papers, she set the remaining items down on the bed. "We have two choices going north. Stay along the mountains, or as Henton said, head east and go an extra few hundred miles out of our way." She picked up one of the maps she had initially set aside. "I had originally planned to head east at this place called Elk Valley. I don't have a lot of information about what is north of that, but what I learned in Tenia indicated the roads were better closer to the coast. And based on the other map I saw without country names, it looks like the end of the Backbone is quite a way to the east, so while it might be more miles, the travel might be easier."

"For whatever it is worth," Henton said. "There are lots of roads and towns we've found that were not on those old maps you made copies of."

"I know. But, if Yreka has looked at any maps and figured out our travel plans from Islet..." Stephenie closed her eyes, *please, not my sister.* "...then she might expect us to head east. That's what I was planning on."

"So we head east now instead of later. There are a lot of different routes," Douglas said.

Stephenie disagreed. "No. I don't want to go the predictable way. What we'll do is drop off the main road now, but we continue to head north and just follow the Backbone all the way to Ista. We skip going east for as long as possible."

"We'll go slower if we have to cut across country and hunt for food," Henton said.

"I can hunt with magic," she challenged. "But, yes, we'll need to find places with grain for the horses. I can't imagine that there won't be towns and villages."

Douglas shook his head. "And will anyone speak Pandar? Too far off the main roads, we'll have a harder time. We've already been to places where some of the people didn't speak the trade tongue."

Stephenie knew Douglas was not entirely wrong. The influence of Pandaras, the huge city-state, could not spread absolutely everywhere, *but it has spread far.* "I think we'll manage to explain what we want in the places we'll be forced to stop."

Kas floated across the room. "That still does not answer how you intend to leave the city. We first need to get outside the walls before you can take us off the main roads."

"And what will we do when we get out?" Douglas pulled his wet shirt off and wrung it out over the chamber pot. "I'd almost rather fight them than keep running and waiting and looking over my shoulder."

"Part of me agrees, Douglas." Stephenie let out a long breath. She wanted this Yreka to pay for possibly hurting those she cared for, but she would not give into the possessive rage. "The trouble is, we don't know what we might be facing. Remember the flesh-spider? Dealing with that one thing drained me. If we face something like that plus skilled mages, I don't think we'd survive." She glanced to the floor. The duel with the man had scared her. "The one good thing is that the man I killed tonight might have taught me something new. I just need to think about it."

"And I'm useless," Ryia said. "If someone could hurt you, I'd be dead within an instant."

Stephenie glanced at Douglas and Henton. Henton remained stoic, but she did not need her powers to know Douglas felt uncomfortable about facing Yreka and her people, despite his declaration of wanting the conflict over. "I've seen what the staff can do and it is not impervious, but it learned to adapt to the man tonight. Ryia, I think you should carry it."

"What?"

Stephenie pushed the staff to the girl. "I've not liked the idea of the weapon because of who gave it to the priests, but I can't find anything about it that is threatening. It just seems like it obeys my desires. It obviously worked for the priestess of Mertor, I think it will work for you as well."

"There is a strong potential it may work for Henton and Douglas also," Kas injected. "Most magical devices I have seen did not restrict access simply to those with magic."

Ryia's eyes widened. "But it is so powerful."

"Which is why I want you to carry it. If they have to deal with magic from two sources, it will give us a better chance. Besides, I am getting tired of carrying it and so now it will be your problem to keep track of." Stephenie felt her shoulders loosen as a small smile made its way to Ryia's face.

"Back to the problem at hand." Henton moved to the only chair in the room and sat down. "How do we get out of the city without them seeing us?"

"There are two gates and the docks. Let's rule out the docks for obvious reasons." Stephenie wished she had a better understanding where the Senzar might be hiding in the city and what their plans would be. "Leaving before sunrise will draw attention from the guards and might also draw Yreka's notice. Plus, we can use more supplies."

"So we leave mid-day tomorrow at the earliest," Henton agreed.

"There could be some value in waiting for a few days," Douglas said. "Make them think we already left."

"Or give them time to find us," Henton challenged.

"Yes, four people with six horses won't be uncommon in this city, but Jura is not as large as Antar and I don't want to fight them in the city. Too much chance someone will get hurt." Stephenie drummed her fingers on her thigh. "I dread the idea, but we might be best served by breaking up the group. We'd be less obvious to someone watching."

"I don't like the idea of splitting up," Henton said.

Stephenie turned to face him. "Nor do I, but what if we hire some men to help lead the horses out of the city. Tell them we plan to meet up with a wagon train that won't come into Jura...or really anything. We don't need overly honest people, just four or five men who will work for money and lead the horses out of the city."

"And whoever is with them will be at risk of them betraying us." Henton shook his head. "I don't like it."

"If I go with the horses, the risk will be minimal. I'll pull back my hair and cover my head." She looked toward Ryia and Douglas. "I'll work with Ryia tonight to get her comfortable with the staff. That will offer you protection. And the three of you, plus Kas, should hopefully be able to walk out without being noticed, since they would be looking for a group of four people on horses."

"I still don't like it."

"You got a better idea?" She asked Henton.

He sat for a moment and then shook his head. "I agree, we don't want to wait in the city for too long. Too many innocents could get hurt."

"Okay, I'll work with Ryia for a short while. The staff is not hard to learn. In the morning, Henton, you and Ryia stay here to protect our things. I'll take a pack horse and Douglas to get supplies. Kas can stay with the rest of the horses and make sure nothing happens to them. Once we get back, we'll head for the southern gate, go back the way we came, then circle around the city and head north."

"Sounds easy," Douglas teased.

Chapter 15

Henton waited for Ryia to wash her face for the third time. Stephenie, Douglas, and Kas had already left the room and she had been avoiding him as much as possible. He knew Stephenie would have preferred to keep everyone together, but working out Ryia's troubles was now more important.

"Ryia, w—"

"Please don't," she said, keeping her back toward him. "Please."

"Ryia, we need to talk."

She shook her head. "I can't. I don't want...please."

"Ryia, you ran off last night."

"Please, just let it be. I don't want to hear...please."

He stood up and moved from the bed over to her, but she moved away as he reached out to touch her shoulder. She retreated across the room, kept her back to him, and shook her head.

"Ryia, look at me." He watched her swallow and wipe her eyes on her sleeve. "Please, Ryia. I know you have feelings for me. We can just put that out in the open."

She turned slowly, but kept her gaze on the floor. "It doesn't mean anything. You don't feel the same."

He closed the distance and stood next to her. The top of her head only reached his chin. "Ryia, I care for you. I do."

She shook her head. "Not the way I want, but I understand. I'm no good. I'm damaged."

Henton kept himself from challenging her statement. He stood there for a moment looking at the top of her head. Stephenie had tried time and again to convince her what happened was not her fault, but so far it had not worked. After several moments of silence she raised her face and looked up at him, confusion and perhaps a little fear in her eyes.

"What do you want me to say?" He asked. "You are damaged." Shock kept her from saying anything. "You keep repeating that and we keep saying you're not, but you keep repeating it. I guess the rest of us are wrong. You're damaged."

She closed her eyes and turned away from him.

"But that has nothing to do with how I feel about you."

She stopped and turned back to him. "Then why don't you love me? What is wrong with me?"

Henton took her forearm in his hand and moved her gently to the bed, had her sit, and then he sat next to her. "Ryia, I'm nearly twenty-nine years old. I'm almost twice your age."

"I don't care. Why should it bother you? Most men would love that."

"Perhaps, but you might regret it later. You're a mage. You're likely to live longer than I am and you'll age slower."

She shook her head. "I'm not like Steph. She might live a couple hundred years Kas said. I barely have any power, so I won't live any longer than anyone else."

Henton gave her a single nod of his head. "That may be so, but you'll age better than I. Do you really want to be taking care of a wrinkly old man when you are still in the prime of your life?"

She closed her eyes as tears leaked out. "I love you, so yes. That won't matter to me."

Henton paused a moment, trying to think of a way to get through to her. Although he had finally got past Ryia's initial stubborn wall of silence, he knew this would be an even greater challenge to overcome. "What you want today and what you want tomorrow can change."

She shook her head violently. "You think I am just a stupid girl." She stopped her crying and met his eyes. "I know what I want, and yes, perhaps someday that may change, but that doesn't mean I don't know what is in my heart. If only you would look past my age and see me. See who I am. Why won't you even try? What are you afraid of?" She reached out and touched his face. "You know what I am and it doesn't scare you. Who else will love me, for me?"

Henton took her hand in his and moved it back to her side. "Ryia, don't look at me as the last person around who might love you. Douglas knows what you and Steph are. We have others—from Cothel even, a place rather set in its belief in Felis—who accepted Steph for herself. I rather think there are more people out there than you might realize."

"I'm not Douglas' type and you're not Steph's." She turned her head away. "What's wrong with living in the moment? We might all be dead tomorrow. We have Senzar mages chasing us. We'd be burned as witches if caught by any powerful priests in these lands. And we've got no idea why Steph's father has been trying to kill her, and us as well. Why should we be unhappy if we can find a moment of love now?"

Henton watched as a section of Ryia's hair fell off her shoulder and across the side of her face. For a moment, he wondered why he should hesitate at embracing life as Ryia suggested. He understood a lot of what tormented her. However, a part of his mind knew that she had lived on her own from an early age. To survive, she had to learn how to manipulate people and situations. Now that she was older, she had other means of influencing men. *And she might not even be aware of it, but I'd bet her powers could sway thoughts just like the priests have done for years to reinforce their message.* He looked at her sitting hunched over. She projected an innocent vulnerability that tugged at him, but he had spent too many years as a soldier to take things at face value.

He bit his lip. He knew she was not trying to deceive him and that she truly felt the feelings she claimed, *but how much is just youthful emotion?* "Ryia, I understand and even agree with you, but right now is not the time. Right now we—"

"So it is hopeless," she said. "I love you, you love Steph, she loves Kas, he doesn't have a body. We're all to die miserable." She looked at him. Her eyes were red, but no tears fell. "I still don't understand why you won't just give it a try. You might find you like me more than you think. We could be dead tomorrow and you might die never knowing. I might die never having the touch of someone who actually cares for me."

"Ryia, I know that rushing to embrace things makes sense to you right now. Believe me, at one point in my life, I used to do the same thing." He sighed. "But I've seen the mess rushing into things can leave and I'd rather not risk destroying the relationships we have as a group." He raised a hand. "What happens if it doesn't work between us? What happens if it gets ugly? Then what will Steph and Douglas do? They'd be forced to pick sides and that would likely drive one or more of us away. Do you want to risk having that happen?"

She shook her head. "It wouldn't be that way. I don't understand why you are so fearful. You don't make any sense."

Henton smiled. "I know. And perhaps that is something that separates us and is a reason for caution here." He turned her face to him. "I do care for you very much, but my perspective is one that comes from age. I've lived life and made mistakes you have not yet made. I know you'll say that you should have a chance to make your own mistakes and I won't disagree, but that doesn't mean I want to repeat my own mistakes."

She frowned and looked down at her hands. "So you're saying our differences on this are the reason we shouldn't be together. It just seems like a convenient excuse. You might lose a lifetime of happiness because you're afraid to take a risk."

She's just sixteen, he reminded himself. "Ryia, I have—"

"And you don't have a problem with how young Steph is. You still wanted her."

"Are you trying to read my mind?"

She shook her head. "I wish I could, but no, I heard it in the sound of your voice: 'She's just a girl.'"

Henton let out a deep breath. "Ryia, I won't deny that you're attractive. I won't deny that I do have feelings for you, but in Ranis Valley, when that High Priestess came for us, my duty should have been to prevent any of us from being taken alive. I knew the moment they came that they intended to use us against Stephenie, and for her safety, it would have been better for us to have died. I was weak. I couldn't stand to let them hurt you and that put Stephenie at risk and...you still got hurt." He raised a hand. "Let me finish. I swore an oath to protect Steph and while she is getting more powerful every day, she still needs our help. I can't say when this is done how I will feel about you. I am still so much older than you, but until Steph no longer needs us, you really cannot ask me to divide my loyalties any more than they already are."

Ryia sighed. "So your obligation to Steph is why you don't want to risk something with me."

"It is not that simple." He glanced at his hands. "I wish I could explain it better. I wish I could make you understand. I have a duty and that is who I am."

She nodded her head. "I'm sorry I've made such a mess of things."

Henton could see a change in her demeanor and hoped he had actually made some progress. "I don't want to lead you on, but I don't want you hating me either. There is nothing wrong with you and nothing in your past would prevent me from loving you. However, I have my own issues and—"

"And for now, neither of us get what we want." She forced a small smile to her face. "I'll try to grow up."

"Hey," he said, "I'm not telling you to give up on everything fun. But, when something is really bothering you, just talk to me or Steph or even Kas. He's actually quite good to talk to and often can bring a different perspective."

"Do you think she'll ever be able to find a way to rebuild his body?"

Henton shrugged and then nodded his head. "When she sets her mind to something, it normally happens. And with regard to that, sometimes I would say that Kas is a bigger priority for her than even protecting Cothel."

"You don't hope she'll give up so she might fall in love with you?"

Henton turned a little more toward Ryia. "You keep assuming that I expect one day she might choose me over Kas. I know that she thinks of me as an older brother. No one wants to be someone else's second choice. Plus, all the arguments I have offered you hold true for her. Perhaps more so. If she really might live a couple hundred years looking as she does, why would I want to subject her to taking care of an old man in just a handful of years?" Henton shook his head. "No,

Ryia, not even to simply gain a few moments of pleasure, do I want to have her suffer a lifetime of pain."

"It should be her decision," she mumbled so quietly that Henton decided to ignore she said it.

"Let's finish getting things ready. When Steph gets back, she'll want to leave right away."

They left Jura just as Stephenie had planned and they saw no sign of Yreka or the other Senzar mages. The men Stephenie hired to help her lead the horses were slightly perplexed by her actions, but walked away with coin in their hands and did not look back.

Instead of backtracking to the southwest, Stephenie led them down the southeast road, which she understood headed to Solva, a large port city in the country of Andra. Even with the muddy conditions, she pushed them hard, working both the horses and themselves to put as much distance between their position and Yreka.

As the afternoon turned into evening, she looked over at Henton. "I've been thinking," she said.

"That's trouble," Douglas remarked from where he sat on Pride's back.

"What have you been thinking about?" Henton asked.

"Yreka and her people." She turned sideways in her saddle to look at those beside and behind her. "What do we know about them?"

"They want to kill us," Ryia said, a hint of her old confidence returning.

"Jerylin told me that Yreka wanted to kill me for having killed Favian because he was a relative of hers. I had thought for a while that perhaps the red-haired bastard might have sent her as well, but what if revenge is truly her only motivation? What if that is what this is all about?"

"Then she's quite determined," Henton said. "She's followed us all over the damn world."

"I've been thinking about that as well. At the time, I had considered she might have been involved in all the murders back in Antar, but once we found the priests of Mertor were responsible, I put her out of my thoughts."

"Those false priests were sent by your sire," Kas' disembodied voice floated between them.

"Yes, but the more I think about it, the less I think she's associated with the bastard."

"So," Henton started, "where are your thoughts leading you?"

"Well, we didn't know she was following us until she got ahead of us and we almost ran into her at Fallen Grove."

"Which was due to our problems on the ship," Douglas added.

"And the side trip into Calis," Stephenie confirmed. "It is quite possible that she might have simply followed us out of Antar. Our leaving was rather public. I had been afraid she had harmed someone in Antar. Perhaps even Islet. But it's quite possible she simply hired or forced a ship to follow us to where we were supposed to go. Then she could have just headed north..."

Henton shook his head. "We didn't advertise anything beyond throwing the shrine into the sea."

Stephenie frowned. "That is true. And if she did find the sailors from The Swift, they would have told her we were put off west of Blue Point."

"While accurate," Kas said, "it is also a fact that the sailors were aware our original heading was for Wilm and that we had no intention of returning home with them. That would indicate a northerly journey of some type. Perhaps this Denarian woman made some assumptions about you and concluded you were getting revenge upon the assassins. Assuming she had a general idea of their location, Fallen Grove was a logical place for you to pass through."

"But we've been hiding our trail pretty well as we've come further north since then," Ryia said. "Other than my failure in Benis Hill."

Stephenie ignored her added comment. "That's just it. We haven't really been hiding our trail. I assumed we lost Yreka because we had not encountered them after we destroyed the trap. But, Jerylin said Yreka read her mind. I think ripped the thoughts from her head is perhaps more accurate to the way she described it. All Yreka has to do is stop in each town and read people's minds to see if any of the four of us had come through. Stop in the public houses, the inns, the market, ..." Stephenie shrugged. "It would be easy for her to find our trail because, while we've limited our exposure, we've not eliminated it."

"Okay, so this woman is going to keep coming, what do you propose to do about it?" Henton asked.

"Well, we have to decide if she knows why I am heading north and where I am going. If she doesn't know and is just catching sight of us, she's got to wonder what the heck we are doing going further from Antar."

"And if she does know?" Douglas asked.

"Well, then we're in trouble and Islet has been harmed because she was the only one who knew."

Henton rubbed the stubble on his chin as he considered the options. "It would have been hard to get to Islet and Yreka would have no reason to know Islet would know where you are going. I have an easier time believing she got to Will or Sara, who did know we were going to destroy the trap and generally where the trap was, but nothing about your sire or that we are heading to Ista."

She felt Kas' agreement before he spoke. "I concur with Henton's assessment. She likely read William's mind. Because, while she managed to get ahead of us in the most plausible location for us to have passed through on a northerly journey from Wilm, her doing so does presuppose she had expected our northerly journey in the first place. Without that knowledge, we could have just as easily been intending to go to Kynto, since Wilm is the port we sailed from after liberating the gold your mother stole from Cothel. It indicates to me some knowledge of your plans."

"Okay, so that means three of us think she doesn't know about Ista."

Douglas shrugged. "I'm torn, but I'd say it is less likely than likely."

"Same," Ryia said.

"Then I have an idea. We just need to have a plausible reason for us to have traveled away from Cothel after destroying Mertor's trap."

"Another trap?" Douglas offered.

Henton shook his head. "She would have to understand Kas' history and we need something obvious, not subtle. Give me the maps. I want to take a look at what's around here."

Stephenie rifled through her saddle bag, and pulled out the maps for Henton. He unwrapped them and carefully flipped through the sheets of parchment as Furball trudged along under him. After reviewing the stack, he wrapped them back up and handed them to Stephenie.

"Solva is a decent port city, but we'd not have had a reason to go this far north if that was our destination. We'd have cut south sooner."

"Then you're thinking our destination is Pandaras as well?" Stephenie asked. "Not reading your mind, it's just where I was thinking."

"Yeah, I was. There appears to be a coastal route, but it is longer because it follows the coast. However, there's another route that cuts across a number of countries before heading back south to Tet and Pandaras. It's the biggest city state on Tet's waters and a massive shipping power. If you can't buy it in Pandaras, it doesn't exist."

"Or so they say," Douglas corrected.

"Then I have an idea," Stephenie said with a grin. "We need to ride hard to get to the next town, whatever it happens to be. Then we'll make use of Yreka's mind reading to lead her astray."

"How do you mean?" Douglas inquired.

"Oh, you'll see."

With their late start, it was well into the evening when they arrived in the small town of Nicsir. Only a dozen buildings made up the center of the town. The rest of the population lived on a few farmsteads carved out of the forest that covered the land.

Stephenie had Henton, Kas, and Ryia ride around the town to avoid changing their pattern. With Douglas in tow, she stopped at the village shop. The inside of the small building contained a wide variety of items anyone in the small town might need, including sacks of grain.

"Sir," she said in Pandar. "I am hoping you can help me."

The middle-aged man dusted his hands together and walked around the barrels of oats in the middle of the floor. "Ma'am, what do you need?"

"I need a sack of oats for my horse."

"I have some sacks over there," he said, pointing toward the wall. "Is that all?"

"I could also use some information." She waited for him to nod his head. "Can you tell me if the southerly road will eventually lead to Pandaras?"

The man wrinkled his brow. "I am not sure. That place is a long, long way from here. I imagine the coastal road will eventually lead there. I do know this road leads to Solva. I'd say you could find a ship to take you to Pandaras."

Stephenie frowned. "My husband gets deathly ill on the water. I can't take a ship. We had hoped to cut across the north of the country, through Fleina and then go south to Pandaras."

"Well, Jura is not more than half a day north of here." He chuckled. "At least when the roads are not mud. I would suggest that route if you know it already."

She nodded her head. "My father is searching for us. He didn't approve of my choice of husband." She saw the disapproval in the man's eyes and felt it in his emotions. *So not like Pendon,* she decided. "My father intended to sell me to men from Uvar," she said, knowing Uvar was still rumored to trade in slaves. "The men will put me to work...servicing...men." She felt the merchant's indignation. "So I ran away with my brother's wife's brother and we are desperate to get to Pandaras. He has a distant cousin there who we hope will take us in."

The merchant shook his head. "We do not tolerate slaves in Bergo. This is reprehensible behavior. Where are you from?"

"Kynto. It is a country a long way to the west."

He put his hand on her arm. "I have not heard of that country, but I have heard of Uvar and do not like them. Unfortunately, I cannot say much about the roads to Pandaras. The farthest I have ever traveled is to Jura. We could ask Alard in the tavern to see if he knows the answer."

Stephenie shook her head. "Thank you, but we must get on the road. I fear they are catching us up. I will continue south. If nothing, the coastal road should take us there."

"Well, there is Hyfer, which is a major trade city in Andra. You may find an easterly road there."

Stephenie let her eyes light up. "Thank you." She reached into her pouch and began to pull out some coins. "How much...can I ask you another favor?"

"What is it?"

"If anyone comes asking, can you tell them we headed north through the woods? Perhaps even have your friend in the tavern say the same thing?" She pulled out two crowns worth of coins. "It would mean a lot if we could get them going the wrong direction."

The man took the coins. "I will. I saw you head north into the woods."

"Thank you." She turned to Douglas. "Glenn, would you grab a sack of oats. We need to get going before they catch up to us."

Douglas bit his lip to keep from grinning, grabbed a sack of oats, and followed Stephenie out the door. He put the sack on Stubborn's already loaded back, tied it down, mounted Pride, and followed Stephenie south out of the town as the merchant stood in the door watching.

After they were outside the city, Douglas leaned close to her. "So, you tell him to lie, she reads his mind to see you heading south after telling him to tell her you went north, and so she ignores the north because you'd never tell him to tell her where you were actually going."

Stephenie shrugged. "Let's hope it works."

Chapter 16

Yreka opened her eyes and rolled out of the worn bed. She sensed the sun rising over the horizon, even though the shutters to her room were closed. She almost never slept past sunrise, even if she had stayed up late the previous night. Many of her servants despised that aspect of her personality, but their approval had never concerned her.

She ran her hand through her long hair, using a little energy to break and then reattach the strands of hair where it had become tangled in her sleep. Some people considered her vain in the attention she gave her hair, but no one would think that when they were close enough that she could read those thoughts. *However, more than one person had intentionally recalled conversations with others who said insulting things when they were certain I would overhear the memories.* All of it was a game, but she knew it was a game that needed to be played.

She dressed without ceremony and then retrieved the oval communication stone from her pack. The thin device's smooth surface had no markings, just small flecks of green and pink mixed into tan base color. However, anyone sensitive enough to magical fields would sense the slight draw of energy the device used to power itself.

Reaching out with her mind, she activated the device and called Olena's name. She repeated herself three times, feeling her irritation grow with every unanswered attempt to summon her follower to respond.

"Olena," she said aloud, the steel in her voice growing cold. But no response came from the device.

Yreka took a deep breath and closed her eyes. She reached out to the device and commanded it to tell her where the companion devices were located. She felt a tug pulling her toward the northeast and determined that the communication stone was still about two-hundred miles away. The second one she had given to Olena was in the same location. A third stone, entangled to the one she carried, sat many thousands of miles to the south. *Damn my foolishness for thinking Stephenie would have gone west. But, Olena, your lack of response eats away at my respect for your foresight.*

Giving up on her servant obeying her demand for a report, Yreka gathered her belongings and left her room. Werha, likely having sensed her waking, joined her in the hall with his own saddlebags and gear.

"Mistress," he said with a bow of his head.

"Let us find out what constitutes food in this town and be on the road. That damn Stephenie has kept the others constantly moving and if we are not careful, the last few days of progress will be wasted."

Werha bowed his head again. "Olena had reported to you the weather had been moving south along the mountains. I have looked out the window and I suspect we will be dealing with it ourselves."

"Which is even more reason to get on the road."

Yreka had kept the drizzle off her body through the morning, but she could not do much to improve the roads. The ground had started firm under a thin layer of moist dirt, but that changed by the late morning and had grown worse as the day turned into the late evening. *Had I listened to Olena, I would have had Stephenie by now.* Yreka hated the constant traveling, but she was willing to concede the time away from her family interests had been a pleasant break. She now knew that she could allow others to manage more of the day-to-day affairs, which she would continue when she did return. *At least if I assume the reports are honest. Of course, few can manage to lie to me and if I ever caught them, they would regret it.*

Her musings were interrupted by a change in the energy signature of her communication stone. The change was slight and had her sensitivity to energy fields been less, she would not have noticed the stone while it was in her saddlebag.

Without stopping, she used her magic to pull open the bag sitting behind her and extracted the stone, flying it around to land in her hand. The stone emitted a slight pulsing warmth, indicating a request for contact. Reaching out with her mind, she activated the stone.

Mistress, Olena's voice echoed in her head.

The world around Yreka folded in on itself and the horse and road she traveled along merged with another outdoor scene in the middle of dense woods. However, the overlaid image remained fixed as the real world continued to shift around Yreka. For Yreka, Olena, with her blond hair blowing in the wind, continued to slide across the underlying ground. However, Olena saw the opposite, Yreka constantly moving toward her. The disconcerting imagery projected directly into their minds caused Olena to swallow sharply and shift her body.

Yreka held her composure, easily separating the visual disconnection in her mind. For a brief moment, she considered stopping for Olena's benefit, but dismissed the thought. *Had she answered this morning, I would have been stationary.* Instead, Yreka turned her attention to what was around Olena and noticed Tibva standing at Olena's side. He held the reins of three horses whose rear-ends faded away into non-existence as they extended beyond the range of the stone.

"You are very late with your report," Yreka said aloud, drawing Werha's attention from where he rode ahead of her. "What is your situation? What has changed in the last two, and now almost three, days?"

"Mistress, we are outside the city of Jura and have headed southeast. Jura is the large city on the northwest point of the lake we have spoken of. We allowed Stephenie and her party to leave ahead of us in the early afternoon."

Yreka wanted to smile at the news Stephenie was that close, but the emotional energy she picked up from Olena through the stones spoke of fear. "What has happened? Where is Daeri? I do not see him."

"Mistress," Olena said calmly, though her words came slowly, "he was killed by the woman."

Yreka's jaw tightened, but she gave no other betrayal of her anger. "I told you not to engage her."

"Ma'am, we did not intend to do so." Olena swallowed. "We are not exactly certain of what happened. Daeri was out purchasing some supplies and was asking after her. Tibva was with me in another part of the city doing the same thing so we could cover more ground. Jura is not as large as some of the others cities, but it is substantial enough."

Yreka doubted Olena and Tibva had sent Daeri on his own for purely that reason. She would have expected all three of them to act independently in order to reduce the time it took to find word of Stephenie. "How did he die?"

"We assume he accidentally encountered her and she attacked him on sight. We were not present for the duel, but we saw and heard many lightning bolts and crashing thunder exchanged inside the city. At first we wondered if it was the storm, as it was raining hard, but the concentration was far too great." Olena bowed her head. "We had no expectation of encountering her. We had assumed she had continued to move further ahead of us. The rains had hampered our travels greatly."

Yreka kept her lip from curling, but she doubted Olena's assumption that Daeri was the one surprised. She knew that Olena was simply trying to protect Daeri's name. *The stupid boy had skills, more than even Olena...and an ego to match it, even if he lacked power.* "I am not sure how many days I am behind you based on the weather that appears to be coming our way. However, it is critical you do not engage her again. It is highly unfortunate that she is now aware we are pursuing her...what?"

"Ma'am, her behavior so far leads me to believe she had some awareness there was pursuit all along. Tibva and I encountered a ghost. At first we were uncertain it belonged to Stephenie, but the ghost tried very hard to avoid us while attempting to get back into the city. We tried to follow it, but we had to brake off pursuit when the lightning strikes occurred."

Yreka pursed her lips. "A coordinated attack perhaps? The ghost keeping you busy while Daeri was isolated and killed?"

Olena faltered before she spoke. "It is a possibility. They would have had to know we were in the city and that we had separated, but if they did, it is possible."

Yreka felt Olena's doubt. "Do not agree with me just because I proposed the suggestion. If I wanted puppets, I would not have any of you around."

"Of course not, Mistress."

"However, there are also the other facts you have relayed before that supports your belief in her awareness. Such as her trying to cover her tracks by avoiding towns. What troubles me is that you have indicated that has been inconsistent." Yreka looked into Olena's eyes. "You must now assume she is certain we are following her and will behave accordingly. I just wonder if she was aware specifically of being followed or just generally covering her trail?"

"I do not know."

"I was speculating aloud," Yreka said.

"What do you wish us to do? We concealed ourselves and watched the gates. Tibva saw Stephenie leave through the western gate, not the northern one. She separated the group, disguised herself and the others, hired a number of men to lead her horses from the city, then she joined up with the others."

"If she took such precautions, then she definitely knows she is being pursued." Yreka considered the possibilities. "What did she do outside the city?"

"We held back. However, we found the men she had hired and questioned them. They considered her actions odd. Being paid to lead the horses out of the city and then leave her there. They did observe the others join her. They said she rode southeast and we have followed her from a considerable distance. There is a town just ahead of us."

Yreka pursed her lips. In front of her, she watched as a group of people moved to the south along the road she was traveling. The small group would be upon her soon and she did not wish to draw attention to herself. "Werha, ride next to me so we can pretend to talk." To Olena she continued to muse aloud in Denarian, which would keep the conversation secret. "Stephenie has been heading north. We do not know the reason, but I would not expect her to change to a southerly course. It is likely a ruse. Assume she will travel south for a while and then double back to go north when she feels she has lost you." Yreka paused a moment and considered Stephenie's actions. "Wait, there is another possibility. My maps are old, but it may be that she always intended to cut to the east at some point. There are some significant cities in that direction. Perhaps you forced her hand early and have caused only a slight change in her path."

"Mistress, we will do our best."

"Stay back and allow her to think she has lost you. Do not enter the town tonight, wait until morning and then learn what you can. Contact me immediately after you learn something and we will decide what to do. She may grow sloppy again if she thinks she lost you. Based on my memory of the maps, there is a significant trade route to the south that runs east from the road I am assuming you are on."

"Mistress, perhaps it would be wise to try and get ahead of them and be in that city before they arrive? We could then watch to see which way they go?"

Yreka toyed with the idea. However, she suspected they had gotten ahead of Stephenie before Stephenie had destroyed the trap. Because they had not anticipated her movements correctly, they had lost her path over the sea voyage. "No. I want you to follow behind her. Continue to look for signs. We will double our efforts to make progress. Hopefully, most of the rain from that storm drained out on your heads and will not delay us as much as it slowed you down."

"As you command, Mistress."

Yreka ordered the stone to break the connection and she allowed the snarl she had been withholding to surface. "The damn fool. He should be glad he died at her hand and not mine."

"Mistress?"

"Daeri likely tried to capture Stephenie on his own. He's dead." Yreka allowed herself to calm. "Perhaps this will once again turn into a hunt worthy of my time."

Chapter 17

Stephenie pushed them late into the night, traveling several miles south of Nicsir. She allowed Kas to scout ahead of them while she used her powers to watch for hazards on the dark road. Eventually, Kas found a small path that disappeared into the trees on the east side of the main road. When he returned to tell Stephenie, the group was still about a mile away.

After a quick discussion, they agreed to take the path. However, Stephenie insisted that she build a complex gravity field under their feet and the horses' hooves. The field separated them from the ground by a few inches and prevented them from leaving a trail in the muddy ground.

The field required a great deal of concentration as she worked to keep the surface textured, providing needed traction. With Henton's help to guide her own movements, they traveled the mile along the main road before turning onto the narrow path.

Even on the path, Stephenie continued to maintain the field despite the throbbing headache beat behind her eyes. They followed the path for more than a mile before Kas directed them toward a small forest glade that would conceal them for the night.

Stephenie groaned from the pain, but she carefully elongated the field and stretched it into the dense woods, providing a route that led over fallen trees and around larger obstacles. After another quarter mile of covering their passage, she finally ceased generating her field and let them all return to the ground.

When they reached the fire-burned clearing, she hurried to set up the tent and then collapsed onto her blankets, leaving the care of the campsite to the others. She had not physically overextended herself, but the intense concentration had drained her.

In the morning, Kas climbed high into the sky, going beyond Stephenie's ability to sense him. He then drifted back toward the road to act as a rear guard, too high for someone to sense, but within his range to see the ground. Stephenie did not like the separation, but she agreed with Kas and Henton in the wisdom of doing so.

The rest of them rode hard for the whole day and Kas caught up to them in the early evening. He reported no one followed the side path or entered the woods, and while numerous groups of people traveled the main road; unfortunately, he had remained too far away to know if any of them had been Yreka and the Senzar mages with her.

Kas' repeated his watching from the sky for the next four days, but he saw no sign of pursuit and Stephenie had found herself relaxing enough to resume studying the last of the books she had taken from Mertor's trap room. However, the material in the book was not easy to understand.

After studying a page three times, she sighed and wiped her face with her hand. The book in her lap continued to frustrate her and no matter how many times she tried to read it, it did not make sense.

Can I offer some assistance? Kas asked from where he hovered in an invisible and nebulous form in their tent.

She rolled her shoulders. *I don't know. I can read the words. I'm getting better at that, but I can't make sense of what these large sections are trying to tell me. The words around the sections make it sound like they are trying to prove something, but they assume I understand the rest. It's a lot of numbers and special symbols, which I know mean something with the numbers, but I don't know what to make of it. It's like another language. If only I had a book that explains that language.*

Kas moved to her shoulder and contracted his energy into a more human form. *I do not know the symbols in the language of the traps, but I would say they represent the same concepts my people had. If so, the symbols describe a way to express how the universe works using numbers and formulas. It is a valuable skill to have.*

She turned her head toward him. Of late, he had been expressing himself less and less and she suspected some of that was due to how much time he spent invisible and ignored by everyone else. To counter his disconnectedness, she continued to make more of an effort to treat him as though he had a physical presence. She patted the blanket next to her, indicating he should sit. *Can you teach me this skill?*

She felt his uncertainty. *It has been a long time since I practiced advanced mathematics—which is the name of this skill. You are already good at knowing how to calculate many things, including your own self-proclamation at being an expert at calculating the weight and angle needed to accurately fire a trebuchet.*

"That just made sense to me." She patted the open area on the blanket again. "Sit. Tell me about mathematics."

Kas obliged and even luminesced. "As I said, it has been a very long time. I am not sure I still retain all the memories of how the formulas work. Your innate knowledge and understanding may exceed what I can show you."

She sighed. *It's just that I feel so helpless and useless in trying to rebuild your body. This is the last book from the trap room and I am guessing even this won't be useful for that.* She bit her lower lip. *I was even considering cutting off a finger or toe and trying to regrow it just so I can see if I can learn the secret of how I seem to just do it.*

Kas shook his head. *Please do not do that. I would not want to see you suffer the pain and disfigurement.*

Every time I've pushed massive energy through myself, everything has healed back to normal. Even old scars have disappeared. She did not mention the blackened hand print he had left over her left breast when he tried to freeze her heart. That change to her body never faded, if anything, it had grown darker and more prominent. *The trouble is, I can't push that kind of energy through you. And when I push it through myself, I can't see what's happening because I get blind to the fields. It's like staring at the sun. It overwhelms my senses. I need to watch something rebuild slowly.*

"I would advise against that course of action," Kas repeated.

Stephenie did not really want to cut off any part of her body, so she did not press the issue. However, if there was more than just the slightest chance it would provide her the knowledge she needed, she would do it without hesitation.

"Can we shoot lightning tonight?" Ryia asked with the staff in her lap. She had asked it every night since they had taken to the woods.

"I know we have not seen anyone," Stephenie said, certain of what Ryia's next statement would be, "but that doesn't mean we want to draw attention by having a light show. Plus you might catch the trees on fire, and as I've mentioned each night, the noise will carry."

Ryia's chin moved from side-to-side and the strain in her neck broadcast her irritation just as loud as her mind did. "How'm I ever going to learn to use the staff if you won't let me?"

"It's not safe yet," Henton said. "We need to wait a while longer."

"When will it ever be safe? Or are you wanting to just keep me useless?"

"That's not what we are doing," Henton demanded.

"It sure seems like it. I need to learn to use the staff's powers!" She shook her head. "Of course you'd take her side," she mumbled at her feet, though she was loud enough that everyone heard her.

"Ryia—" Henton started, but Stephenie cut him off.

"I told you last night, practice with some of the defensive abilities or with creating fields for attack. Nothing that makes noise or draws attention." She could feel Douglas' unease at the hardness of her voice but she did not care. "Get out of the tent, Ryia. Have Henton attack you with a sword or throw rocks or other things at you. But no lightning."

Ryia scrambled to her feet and tore out of the tent sending the whole structure swaying.

"What?" Stephenie asked the others. "I won't have her talk to you like that, no matter what's she's been through. And she won't shut up about using lightning. She's like a dog with a stick. That's only one of the things the staff can do."

"We know," Henton said. "I'll talk to her."

Stephenie watched him follow after Ryia, who had already moved far enough away from the tent that any quiet conversation would not likely be heard by the other group. An awkward silence filled the tent and then Stephenie shut the book and tossed it onto the saddlebag that held her other books. "She can be disappointed, but I won't have her treating Henton like that."

"Speaking of Henton," Douglas said slowly, "if my tracking of the days is correct, today is the twenty-fifth. Henton's birthday is the ninth of next month. Will we be near any city?"

Stephenie shrugged and allowed the change of subject. "That's hard to say. The maps don't show everything and we're moving over rough ground, some days we do better than others. However, even at my best estimate, I don't think we'll be to Elk Valley by that time. I could try to push the horses harder, but all the healing I am doing to ease the strain on their bodies means they are eating a lot and I don't think I should push any more than I am."

"Perhaps there will be a small town along the way. I'm sure he'd not mind an ale and an easy night in a bed for his birthday. It's still supposed to be summer, but these nights are getting cooler. The north is really messed up. It shouldn't be this cold yet."

Stephenie sensed the rock before she heard Ryia's cry of alarm. She reached out with her mind through the tent and grabbed the fist-sized stone out of the air, preventing it from striking the fabric sides. Stephenie dropped it to the ground without even moving to look in the direction the projectile had come from.

"I didn't mean for it to fly in that direction," Ryia said. "Honest."

"It was a bad throw on my part," Henton called out.

"We're good," Stephenie yelled. "Just make sure you continue to stay away from the horses." Stephenie raised her eyebrows at Douglas. "We will need to find a place where she can actually practice with lightning. I don't want her hitting one of us by accident."

"I still can't get over her having that much power at her disposal," Douglas said. "It's helped her confidence."

Stephenie agreed with his assessment. "I just need to find a small trove of magical weapons to share with you and Henton now."

Douglas smiled. "That would help me sleep better. As long as nothing takes over my mind."

Kas shrugged. "That always remains a distinct possibility depending on the nature of the magical item."

Stephenie thought about the handful of magical items they carried with them, including the dagger at her waist. "Other than the trap,

I've not felt any item with a strong personality. I'm more worried about what damage people could do to us."

"Like the Senzar chasing us," Douglas offered. "You still don't think they are tied to your sire...that Gunnarr Ralok?"

She shrugged. "It is hard to say for certain. I guess they could be. I don't know all that he's done to try to kill me and those people seem to all know each other. It would be a scary thought to have to deal with a lot of them at one time. The man I fought in Jura had a lot of training."

"Which," Kas said, "is something I have repeatedly reminded you: skill beats raw power."

"I understand that. Believe me, I do. I practice all the time. But I only have so much time and it is easier for me to see something done and repeat the effect than to read about it. I've picked up a couple of things from the man in Jura. I just don't have anyone to try it out on."

"Well, I still suggest we throw Henton a small party on his birthday. Even if it is just a mug of ale."

Stephenie nodded her head. "We'll see. I don't want to leave a trail, but we will need some more supplies for ourselves soon. However, if you want to keep your plans a secret, you better stop talking about it. They're coming back to the tent."

"I saw lightning to the east," Ryia said from behind Henton as he ducked into the tent. "Can't I shoot some?"

"We've said no," Henton growled, holding the flap opened for her.

Stephenie stood up and used her head to motion Ryia back out into the night causing the girl to panic. "You are so desperate to push your ability with the staff, well I want to try something the man in Jura did to me to see if the staff remembers how to protect against that attack or not."

Ryia did not move from the opening.

"Out," Stephenie demanded. "I'm irritated with you, but let's put that to good use."

"Please don't blow holes in me. I don't heal as well as you do."

Stephenie put her hand on Ryia arm. "I'd never hurt you...even if you asked me one more damn time about shooting lightning tonight.

But that doesn't mean you're getting off without suffering some consequences."

Stephenie had been pleased with the staff's response. Although she had not generated any powerful forces, the staff blocked her attempts to refract an energy pulse through the shield. It gave her hope that should Ryia encounter one of the Senzar, they would not be able to harm Ryia like the man in Jura had harmed her.

In the morning, they departed early and continued cutting through the forest. When they were getting ready to stop for the night, Kas found a small settlement less than two miles away. Taking advantage of the nearness, once full darkness fell, Stephenie and Kas checked out the settlement, found a barn with a large stockpile of grain, and stole several sacks of food. She left ample coins from the country of Bergo in their place, covering more than the costs of replacing the supplies.

Two nights later, they camped near a larger village and Stephenie quietly robbed the village store, taking more grain as well as jerky, hard cheese, fresh bread, and other supplies for the rest of them. Again, she left local coins as way of payment. As a result of those thefts, they managed eight days of travel where as far as Stephenie could tell, no one had actually seen them.

Chapter 18

Islet wiped her chin; the juicy meat tasted as good as anything she had eaten in Antar or Reol Cove, the capital of Ipith. Of course, endless days of trail food cooked by her own hand could make anything taste like a meal fit for royalty, even roasted chicken at a small inn in a tiny town.

She glanced at the single window in the back room as the wind and rain pounded the fragile shutters. They had several dry days after the last rains and she hoped this night's storm would pass quickly. She hated the cost of staying in an inn, but sometimes safety and comfort overrode that consideration and the men had worked hard enough to deserve one decent night. The private dinner in a small room off the main common room was her way of rewarding them for not insisting that she turn around and head south at Lake Seon. *And would hopefully prevent that request when we reach Jura.*

Carac put down the bone he had cleaned and leaned back in his chair. Islet smiled at the black-haired man. Jerylin's healing had done a lot, though it had left him in a near constant state of hunger. Tonight was the first night in several days that she saw a satisfied look on his face.

"You're looking happy tonight," Tain said, drawing Islet's attention to the big man.

"I'm just glad we are out of the rain and have something warm to eat," she replied, though her eyes drifted to Walter at the other end of the table. The Knight had lost some of his formality since their discussion and Islet thought he looked a bit calmer. *And as dashing as ever.*

"Even this kind of meal must seem like peasant fare," Tain said, a twinkle in his eye daring her to challenge him.

"It is quite good," she responded. "Actually, you'd be surprised by how mundane most of my meals were. Even in Ipith, unless there was a state dinner or something, we did not eat fancy meals."

"Well," Wilson challenged, "when I was growing up, we'd have a meal like this one," he spread his hands to take in the table, "only once every couple of years. My parents signed me up for the army to make some money and so they wouldn't have to feed me."

Islet nodded her head. "I won't claim to have suffered when I lived in a royal household." Wilson was the youngest of Sir Walter's soldiers. He had just turned nineteen on their journey to find Stephenie. She knew her brother had continued the long standing practice of recruiting second and third sons from families. The tax savings for a year of service enticed many families to enlist their children. The long term employment and reasonable pay kept many of those second and third sons in the military instead of returning to the role of a spare at home.

"But," Sir Walter said, "your time in a cell was beyond the suffering of any of us."

"What was it like in Ipith?" Tain asked. "I grew up in the plains and didn't see a big city until I joined a mercenary band that later went to Antar."

Islet scratched the back of her head. Memories of her late husband and their castle came unbidden into her thoughts. Painful memories of the day the Senzar torn through their castle, killing servants and guards, as they took her and her husband hostage. She could still smell the blood and fear.

"Tell us something fun. Something embarrassing," Tain offered.

Islet let out the breath that had caught in her chest. She wondered if he knew where her thoughts had drifted and she allowed herself to chuckle instead of cry. She did not want to remember the bad. "I guess the most embarrassing thing was something that happened when I first arrived in Reol Cove. I had not been there very long, but I was determined to learn to speak Ipish. I insisted on not speaking

Pandar and thought I could handle it. After all, I was fourteen and knew everything." The statement brought smiles to a couple of faces.

"I had a number of maids. I wasn't allowed to do anything by myself. Dress, undress, draw a bath, brush my hair. Any of it." She shrugged. "So the first night I was there, I told them I liked a hot bath. I said, caro udem'ar. Well, when I was escorted to the bath, the water was milky white and it smelled funny. Thinking it was some odd local custom, I was too afraid to question them and simply climbed in."

"What was in the water?" Carac asked.

"Sheep's milk," Isle responded. "I didn't know it at the time. I was alone in a foreign country more than a month's journey from home and standing naked in a circle of woman who were older than me." She smiled at the memory. "I even thought perhaps it was something to do with them preparing me for my husband, since I really didn't know what that involved." She looked at the table, staring into the past for a moment before lifting her eyes. "The trouble was the milk kept the water from being hot, so every day I repeated caro udem'ar, and every evening the bath got whiter and whiter."

"You probably smelled funny after that," Tain said, chuckling. "What an odd custom."

"Only it wasn't one of their customs. I was literally saying bath and sheep's milk. The maids thought I was some crazy girl from the east so they wouldn't question my command. They'd talk about me when I wasn't around, but they'd never once ask to confirm I knew what I was asking for. What I had meant to say was caro udim'ar, with the emphasis on the first part of the word, not the last. That means bath, hot."

"How long did that go on?" Sir Walter asked.

"Six days. My husband decided to surprise me one evening and came in while I was stepping into the bath. He was aghast by what he saw and demanded an explanation for why I was wasting milk." She shook her head. "I broke down into tears and explained it to him in Pandar."

"What happened?" Tain demanded.

"He laughed and the maids that were standing by all started giggling until he gave them a stern look. He wrapped me in a robe and took me off to his chambers to use his bath, since mine had to be thoroughly cleaned." Islet looked around at the others. "After that, my baths were nice and warm and just had water. I let them all know I had no hard feelings, but even years later, I'd hear someone say sheep's milk under their breath and knew they were telling someone about those first few days."

Tain could not keep the smile from his face. "Good thing you asked for milk instead of something much worse."

"Well, a year or two later, I actually heard that in some places a milk bath is not unheard of. But, I will say that I learned to always question something that didn't seem right. I'd rather be embarrassed by asking a question than spending a week bathing in milk."

Islet's smile grew. "I told you something about me, now I want to hear your stories."

"Sir Walter has never been embarrassed," Wilson said. "Always so serious."

Islet nodded her head and looked toward Sir Walter. "When you and Josh were younger, I do remember you were serious most of the time, but you have to have done something that embarrassed you."

Sir Walter frowned, though Islet could barely see it under his beard. Eventually he spoke. "Being a favored companion of His Majesty was an incredible honor for me and for my family. However, my family did not have enough status that I could engage in reckless behavior, so I always strove to remain respectable. Your brother was not always as honorable as I in his activities."

Islet laughed. "He's five years older than me and I remember some of his more famous escapades."

"Well," Walter continued, "he would nag me about being too proper and would always try to get me into trouble. I would refuse as best as I could, but if he asked that I accompany him somewhere, I generally had to do so.

"There was one day he said he planned to skip a banquet we were supposed to attend, as he preferred instead to hunt for berries in the brambles around the castle. He told me to change and meet him outside the kitchens. Not wanting to ruin my good clothing in the brush, I dressed in my worst boots and pants and even a shirt that was stained and torn."

"Let me guess," Islet said, "he didn't plan to skip the banquet."

"Correct," Walter said with a bow of his head. "When he arrived at the kitchens, he was dressed in his best coat and shirt. I promptly refused to accompany him to the banquet until I could change, but he swore to me that the banquet was to honor me and we were already late. He said your father—rest his soul—was already waiting for us and it would be an insult to not attend upon him immediately."

"Wow, King Joshua did that to you?" Wilson asked.

Walter turned to the young man. "He was just a prince at the time and it was many years ago." Walter met everyone's eyes around the table to reinforce his statement. "His Majesty has matured much since then."

"What happened?" Carac asked.

"I followed then Prince Joshua into the banquet, and as I expected, I was immediately disgraced. The King demanded to know why I would choose to insult him in such a manner. I could not surrender Joshua to his father and retain my honor, so I merely bowed my head and begged forgiveness."

"Josh should have been whipped for that," Islet said.

"Your brother, seeing what had happened, immediately stepped forward and confessed what he had done." Walter bowed his head slightly toward Islet. "While he enjoyed causing mischief, he would not let anyone suffer for his folly. His father asked me for my forgiveness and immediately berated Joshua for the insult he had done to me. I feared after that verbal lashing that your brother might choose to cast me out, but he truly felt bad and did everything he could to make it up to me. It actually helped to cement our friendship and His Majesty never did anything like that again."

Islet shook her head. "He still should have been whipped. The gall of him sometimes." Knowing the room had taken on a somber feel, she looked over to Tain. "Your turn. Regale us all with something silly you've done."

Tain smirked. "Dear Lady, you do not wish to know the terrible deeds of Tain the Slayer of Dreams. For I am nearly as old as Sir Walter, but I was never proper." He leaned forward and put his elbow on the table as he turned his gaze on each person. "You see, I have always been fond of horses and one night—"

Jerylin's gasp interrupted Tain's story. Even in the limited lamp light, Islet could see the blood had drained from the woman's face. "What is it?" she asked quietly.

Jerylin moved her head slowly, but could not bring herself to look toward the door that led to the common room. "I felt her. Just now."

"Who?" Islet asked as Walter pushed his chair back from the table.

"Yreka," Jerylin whispered. "She's in the common room."

Islet's hands and feet suddenly grew cold. The panic of confinement started to build in the back of her mind. She wanted to run to the corner and hide, but she could feel the others watching her. She took a moment to steady herself. "Everyone keep calm. Steph has told me many times that strong emotions stand out. If we don't panic, we still might get out of this." *Don't panic,* she repeated to herself. "Jerylin," she spoke the woman's name to hopefully lend the woman strength. "Is the Senzar coming toward us?"

Jerylin concentrated for a moment and then shook her head.

Islet wished Jerylin had spoken, instead of only gesturing. Having to vocalize would help focus the woman's mind and give her less time to build her fear. "It is simple then, there is a chance that we will go unnoticed. We're just a group of people traveling through town and no reason to be of interest."

"But if Jerylin felt her, couldn't the Senzar feel Jerylin?" Wilson whispered.

Islet nodded her head. "Recognizing a mind is something Steph or Jerylin or even that Senzar can do. The difference is, for Jerylin, this woman left a lasting impression." Islet glanced at her would-be priestess. "No offense, but you're not that powerful in comparison. So the Senzar will have less of a reason to remember you over anyone else she's met." Islet hoped what she was saying was true.

"Even so, Ma'am," Walter said, his hand on his sword, "remaining in the same inn is a risky proposition."

"Agreed. We need to wait until they leave the common room. Then any of us who might be recognized, myself, Jerylin, even Walter, will head to the barn and ready our horses. Carac, Wilson, and Tain, the three of you will go to our rooms, grab our gear, and then come to the barn. We'll ride out of town and keep going into the night."

"In the rain?" Wilson asked.

"Don't question your orders," Walter said. "It is a sound plan. We'll leave the road and hold up somewhere until they pass us."

"If they've caught up to us," Jerylin wrung her hands as she spoke and looked between Islet and Walter, "then there's no way we can warn the Princess and so we should just head back to Antar."

Islet hated to hear the words. Jerylin's terror was palpable. However, the girl's statement had merit. "Heading back the way we came may be the safest choice in the short term. However, a final decision on what we will do will come later. For now, let's just remain calm, don't panic, continue eating until they go upstairs, and then we can leave."

"Agreed," Walter said. He paced a couple more steps and then sat back down. He looked at Jerylin, "Whatever protections you can summon from Catheri, do so in a manner than does not draw their attention."

Chapter 19

Islet had felt her resolution wavering long before Jerylin finally said the Senzar witch had gone upstairs. Because Jerylin's skill and sensitivity were not as great as Stephenie's, she had not been able to tell how many had been in Yreka's party, only that Yreka had retired for the night.

Tain was the first to leave the room, he came back after a short time with another mug of ale. "There's no one out there that looks anything like the people Jerylin described."

Islet nodded her understanding. "Tain, you, Carac, and Wilson go get our things from our rooms and meet the rest of us in the barn."

Tain glanced to Walter and the Knight confirmed the order. "Be quick about it, but keep your emotions in check. Don't panic."

Islet spoke as they started to walk toward the door. "Steph always said soldiers tended to be hard to read because your minds are more disciplined. Just remember that."

The three men smiled at her and then left the small room. Islet watched as Walter put his hand on her shoulder. "We'll be okay," he said with a smile. "We'll just walk calmly out the front door and make our way around back."

She returned his smile even though she saw the concern in his eyes. She knew he needed her reassurance as much as she needed his. "Let's go."

The common room held a handful of people, most of which appeared to be locals who had been there when they arrived. The people were still engaged in what was likely a regular evening pastime of drinking and talking. Several heads turned as the three of them made their way to the front door and went outside into the rain, but Islet did not think anyone did more than look. *Just let the others get our things and we can be on our way.*

Outside, the rain fell at a sharp angle, blown sideways by the wind. While the air was not cold, the rain itself gave her an immediate shiver. Their protective cloaks remained upstairs in their rooms and the three of them had become soaked even before they reached the corner of the inn. By the time they pulled open the barn door and ran inside, not an inch of them remained dry.

"This weather will kill us," Jerylin swore. "I should never have come. I shouldn't have. That Senzar…"

"Easy, Jerylin," Walter said as he walked to the lamp hanging from a support post. The wick had been turned low and he turned it up, bringing a flickering light to the long aisle. "Keep yourself together. The witch went upstairs. She's no reason to suspect the others. Let's just get the horses ready and be on our way. We'll dry out easy enough when the rain stops."

Islet moved to the stalls at the end of the barn. The horses looked at her with expecting eyes, hoping for a treat or a scoop full of grain. *Maybe later,* she thought to Talbit. After a long day of being ridden, she knew he was not going to be happy about continuing the adventure into the wet night.

"We may have to walk the horses," Sir Walter said over the sound of the rain beating against the barn. "The road will be too slick for us to ride them."

Islet nodded her understanding. "I'll get Talbit saddled, but I'll leave the girth loose."

Jerylin dropped the saddle she was carrying and started to shake.

"Why would anyone want to ride in this rain?" Came an accented voice from the barn's door. The lamp illuminated a short woman with long blond hair. The rain, which splashed in through the open door, did not touch her. "It is ever so rude of you to leave before we had a chance to talk."

Sir Walter's sword was drawn before the woman had finished speaking. However, he only managed a single step before he crumpled to the ground.

Jerylin sobbed and covered her face with her hands.

Islet stepped away from the stall, the saddle still in her hands. "We've done nothing to you. Leave us be."

The woman walked down the aisle toward Islet. "Oh, Your Majesty, I dare say that when I sensed Jerylin, I had thought perhaps I had somehow stumbled upon your sister. However, it took me just a few moments to realize you were not her."

"We've done nothing to you. Leave my sister alone."

The woman's eyes narrowed and Islet felt a humming in her head that made it hard for her to focus. "Your sister has killed protected members of my family. For that, she will answer for her crimes."

"Who?" Islet demanded, fighting to keep her thoughts from wandering. The one thing she knew was that if she was going to die, she would not do it sniveling and begging.

"My great-grandson, Favian." The woman continued closer. "You were familiar with him. She also killed Daeri, a distant relation, but a personal assistant to myself and so protected. She's killed Yvima Orthas Corha—not of my blood, but a sixth generation Lord of his own right. I won't judge her for his death as it is not my right."

"She killed those men to protect her family!" Islet insisted. The woman's olive complexion glowed when she stopped five feet in front of Islet. Islet did not spare a glance to the crying Jerylin, but she did look toward Sir Walter, who still lay on the ground.

"My family is protected." Yreka's words were spoken softly and without a trace of emotion. "She should never have harmed any of them."

"Your people attacked us first! What of our protection? What of my sister's right to protect me and our brother?"

Yreka raised one eyebrow. "That is the question I have been wondering. I came to judge your sister and execute her for her crimes. To do that, I need to know her family. I have not been able to determine who her father is." Yreka smiled. "I see neither of you know for certain. Interesting, you suspect it to be some Gunnarr Ralok that took your mother in an unpleasant way." Yreka's left cheek rose in contemplation. "Someone from the top of the world in Ista? That is improbable."

"Stay out of my head," Islet forced the words from her mouth. The very act of speaking had become difficult.

"Oh, you cunning little bitch," Yreka said, but Islet knew she was not speaking to her. Yreka chuckled and then looked deep into Islet's eyes. "I see what your sister must have done. She's a clever little thing. She would have known we would read their minds. She must have expected we would. Counted on it. She knew we'd see the lie in those men's minds and that we'd ignore the north in favor of her apparent route to Pandaras. It wasted days of their travel." Yreka shrugged. "It won't help her. Now that we know the reason for her travels and her real destination, my people will catch up to her."

Yreka glanced to the horses and then back to Islet. "I'm not familiar with any verified bloodlines that include a Ralok, especially none that would live that far from society at the top of the world. I've never even heard of Ista." Yreka shook her head. "No, her family is insignificant and therefore she is guilty."

Islet felt her mind clear. "She didn't know your great-grandson was protected. She was simply trying to recover me, a queen, a protected person, that your people kidnapped and locked up."

The woman's gaze held no compassion and Islet's blood froze. "Ignorance of our traditions will not protect her. And you? You are of less significance than that sniveling child that won't stop crying. You have no power and no one of consequence would ever have learned any of your names. Your sister had a chance to declare herself to Favian as she should have. She chose not to. Instead, she destroyed Favian's mind and left him to die."

"Please. If you are to kill me, let the others go. They've done nothing to you."

Yreka grinned. "While you are insignificant to me, Stephenie considers you hers. We have rules. I must first judge her, find her guilty, and then you can be executed along with your sister."

"Just let the others go."

"This Jerylin also has some meaning for your sister and I sensed from you that Sir Walter, the paltry knight stupid enough to think he had a chance to harm me, also carries favor with your sister. The three of you will come with me. We will go to Ista, find your sister, find her father, and all of you shall be judged and executed."

Islet felt tears falling from her eyes. "Please, just let the others go."

"They are already dead. I found nothing of interest in their minds."

"What?"

Yreka turned away from Islet, but Islet found she could not move. "It is nothing personal. They offered no value and would have become troublesome to bring with us. The moment I confirmed they had no value, I scrambled their brains. They died instantly and felt no pain." Yreka glanced back over her shoulder. "I am not a cruel person. I do not torment small animals."

Islet's tears rolled off her chin. "You shouldn't have harmed them. They were no threat to you. And doing that is tormenting me."

"That is your sister's fault. Had she stayed out of it..."

"I'd still be locked in a cell!" Islet shouted.

Yreka smiled. "I said I was not a cruel person. I do not vouch for anyone else in my family and their pastimes."

Islet had been helpless to resist when Yreka took the three of them into an empty stall, dragging and binding them with her mind alone. Islet had attempted to escape when the Senzar witch walked away, but that only resulted in her flying into the back wall of the stall and having the wind knocked from her.

Yreka returned quickly. The metal rim of a wagon wheel floated in the air over her shoulder. Jerylin screamed until Yreka knocked her unconscious. The would-be priestess fell roughly to the ground next to Sir Walter, who appeared to have a broken knee. Without ceremony, the metal rim twisted and writhed as it floated in the air before breaking into multiple sections. Two sections flew at Jerylin and wrapped themselves around her ankles and wrists, binding her with the thick metal. Another two sections of the rim wrapped themselves around Walter's ankles and wrists. The Knight's face radiated pain at having his legs slammed together, but he did not reward the witch by crying out.

Islet regained her feet and stood defiantly as the metal slammed into her body. She grimaced as it wrapped itself tightly in place, cutting into her flesh. Her feet were locked so closely together that she tipped forward. She twisted as she fell, hitting the straw bedding with her shoulder.

Yreka said nothing further before she left.

Once Islet thought they were alone again, she spoke. "Walter, are you okay?"

The Knight grimaced as he tried to move his legs so they did not bind against his knee. "No," he whimpered. "My knee." He took a deep breath to steady himself. "I have never been so helpless. I won't walk again on that leg."

Islet knew he wanted to cry from the agony, but admired him as he managed to hold back the tears. "We'll get Jerylin to heal you." Islet closed her eyes. *Please have lied about the others,* she begged. She knew deep down that Yreka had not, but she did not want to consider Tain and the others destroyed in such a manner.

"You lied to me. You lied to all of us," Jerylin said, slowly opening her eyes. "I should kill you."

"When did I lie?" Islet demanded, not used to hearing such a strong tone from the younger woman.

"Your sister is no prophet. She's not a priestess of Catheri. She's a Senzar witch, just like Yreka and the others." Jerylin shook her head. "Now you've killed me." A stray tear fell from her left eye. "I should have known. You are one of Elrin's agents just as your sister. The god of lies has me and I'll never be free."

"You are wrong," Islet demanded. "None of us are agents of Elrin."

"The others, in Vinerxan, who had gone to bring you and your sister back after your escape, they told us Stephenie had claimed there were no gods and that she was only pretending." Jerylin shook her head. "We didn't believe them. We thought they were lying to keep us from following her, but it's true. There is no Catheri. That is why you had me cast spells like I always had. That is why I felt nothing from your holy symbols no matter how much I tried to feel something. You are brainwashing the others, but our powers come from Elrin."

"Jerylin, you are wrong. There is no Elrin. There never has been." Islet closed her eyes. *I am sorry, Walter. I had hoped we might come out of this without you despising me.* She opened her mouth and spoke the words she knew would damn herself. "But you are correct, there is also no Catheri. The idea of Catheri was not Stephenie's. In fact, she tried to get people to stop spreading it, but everyone wanted an explanation for how she had lived and they believed it no matter what she said."

Tears flowed down Jerylin's face. "Just like me and those that came with me."

"Yes. But Stephenie is not a Senzar."

"That woman," Sir Walter said, his voice filled with an undertone of pain, "said Stephenie is looking for her father. She's not the King's daughter? Is that true?"

Islet nodded in the dimly lit stall. "I will not deny it. Her mother was my mother, but my mother was raped by a mage, which is the term Stephenie uses instead of warlock or witch." She did not want to reveal any more, but having started, Islet knew she had to finish. "We don't know much about him, only that we believe he lives to the north."

"That woman spoke of bloodlines," Walter asked. "What is going on, Islet? Who is your sister, if not a Senzar? Are you telling me these Senzar don't worship Elrin?"

"A long time ago, elves ruled these lands. Humans were here, but the lands and the Sea of Tet belonged to the elves. We all know the elves fought a bloody civil war between different factions and humans took advantage of their weakness and were able to drive them into the Rim Mountains and beyond. However, what you don't know was that the primary force that drove them away were a group of people calling themselves Denarians. They came from lands in the south. To combat the stronger power of the elves, they made use of devices that pulled power from another world into ours, giving these Denarians more strength. Stephenie would call these magical devices... augmentation devices." Islet scooted into a sitting position and then moved against the wall of the stall.

"The humans that originally lived peacefully with the elves fought these Denarians because it was discovered they were getting their power by essentially bleeding a creature in another world to death." Islet swallowed, unable to read either Jerylin's or Walter's expressions. "We don't know all the details, but the original humans lost their fight and the Denarians, who are the ancestors of these current Senzar invaders, took over. However, something happened. We don't know why, but after a period of time, the most powerful Denarians fled, returning home to the south, leaving their weaker countrymen behind.

"It was these weaker countrymen who continued to use the augmentation devices to maintain order, but we suspect they feared being overrun by other mages and so the devices became holy symbols. Each group of devices, which are now grouped to a particular god, are in fact tied to a specific trap—which is what draws the energy into our world. The witches and warlocks that controlled the augmentation devices became priests. They fought a war against those that did not bend to their will; who did not obey those who claimed to get their power from these new gods."

Walter shifted and Islet paused, waiting for a comment, but none came.

"These priests," Islet emphasized, "invented Elrin. They claimed Elrin was a god of the elves, which people still feared. These priests turned the population against those who had challenged them. People like you, Jerylin. People like my sister." Islet continued despite the heat that had entered her voice. She did not know how Stephenie could always manage to maintain any personal distance from the facts when she spoke of this subject. "Time buried the truth and now all those priests that burn you and threaten you, they are just like you, though most don't know it.

"They are witches and warlocks. To use the augmentation devices, or holy symbols if you want to call them that, requires that you have magic. It was built into the devices to keep power out of the hands of those who could not use magic. They wanted to make sure they kept control of the power.

"Walter, did you ever wonder how those Senzar mages that captured our priests—in the war my sister ended—so easily managed to use the holy symbols they took?"

Islet turned toward Jerylin. "You don't sense anything from that rock because it doesn't have any power. Everything you do, you do because you were born with the ability, just like my sister. That doesn't make you evil. Only your actions would. We have to pretend to believe in Catheri to keep people from turning against us. But the hope is one day, perhaps not in our lifetime, but one day, people would not be killed for who they are."

Sir Walter let a small moan escape his lips as he tried to move again. After a slight change in position, he gave up. "How do we know this is not all some part of Elrin's plan to poison our minds? He is the demon of lies."

Islet bit her lip and closed her eyes against the tears of frustration that threatened to erupt. She knew what Kas would say. "You either trust that I am telling the truth and not trying to lead you astray or you don't. If you are unwilling to even consider I am telling the truth and think about it logically, than you're stuck in a circular argument where no matter what I say, you'll just challenge it as 'How can I believe that, Elrin is the god of lies?' And if that is the case, then there is no point to discussing it."

Sir Walter hesitated before speaking. "I don't know what to think. This is too much to take in all at once."

Islet nodded her head. She did not care that her disappointment showed. "I understand."

"However, Jerylin, if you would be willing to help my knee, I would be willing to accept the risk."

The younger woman bit her lip. "I don't want my soul consumed by Elrin. But I don't want to die either." She let out the breath she had held. "I'll heal your knee as much as I can because I'll need you able to walk if I am to have any hope of getting out of this."

Chapter 20

Islet collapsed onto the small bed. It was the first time in several days that they had stopped in a town for the night. Most nights, she shared a small tent with Sir Walter and Jerylin.

Initially, Islet had been surprised that neither Yreka, nor her darkly complexioned companion, had bothered to try and keep them from speaking to each other in Cothish or any other language. However, the Senzar mage's ability to read minds, from her horse or across the room, made plotting an escape impossible. Other than insisting on the fast pace and the threat of great pain should any of them try to escape, Yreka had mostly ignored them. Had things been different, Islet would have enjoyed watching the mountains as they made their way along the World's Backbone. She would have noted the changing smells of the tree species that made up the forests they rode through day after day. She would have listened to the changing of the bird song. She would have written about the subtle difference in the people and the buildings.

However, all she could think about now was becoming a pawn in Yreka's bid to torture and kill her sister. Escape was not possible. Yreka knew her feelings for Sir Walter and she had made it clear Islet's purpose was to control Stephenie and Walter and Jerylin's purposes were more to control her, than for their relationship to her sister. Any bad behavior on her part would result in their punishment.

What surprised Islet the most was that beyond the threats, Yreka remained civil. While the Senzar did not consider any of them to be her equal in any sense, she made sure Werha looked after their basic needs and kept them moderately comfortable, even going as far as fully healing Walter's knee.

Islet kept her eyes closed as she heard the others escorted into her room by Werha. Her body ached from the faster pace Yreka had forced them to undergo and she just wanted to sleep before they would start again in the morning. She tried to ignore the others and hoped they would soon go to sleep as well.

"We need to escape and return to Antar," Sir Walter said, drawing open Islet's eyes.

"What?" Jerylin demanded, making him repeat what he said in Pandar.

"You know we'd never make it," Jerylin responded once she understood his statement. "She probably already knows you planned to say that tonight."

The Knight kept his focus on Islet. She swallowed and then finally she shook her head. "I'm sorry, Walter, but Jerylin is right. I can feel the woman rummaging around in my head every once in a while. I know because I suddenly find it hard to concentrate and then as suddenly as it occurred, it passes."

"She's in my head too," Walter said. "But we can't simply allow them to take us north to be executed. I would rather die escaping than be her tool. There is nothing left for us to do."

"You'd abandon our mission?" Islet demanded, her voice growing louder than she wanted.

"You're sister is one of them," Jerylin demanded. "She's no prophet. She's just a Senzar witch. Another one of Elrin's demons."

Islet sat up abruptly causing Jerylin to flinch and take a step backward. "Listen to the two of you. You find out something isn't what you believed and now you want to turn your back."

"We've been lied to," Walter said. "This is different."

Islet turn her focus on the Knight. "Stephenie has bled for Cothel. She's defended it against these Senzar. She's saved thousands and thousands of people and you're mad that she concealed the fact that she's a witch because the foolish priests would burn her for being one." She turned toward Jerylin. "You. You are a witch just like her. You were born one and will die one. Stephenie has been trying to protect you and slowly work to convince people that you're not evil, because you are not."

Islet took a breath but no one spoke. "You have two choices, Jerylin. Either I am wrong and there is a demon god or I am right and there isn't. If I am wrong, then we should burn you now because you can't be converted into a priestess. Or I am right and you should be allowed to live. You have every reason to support Stephenie and what she is trying to do."

Islet turned back to Walter, but he spoke first. "Your sister is a bastard child of a Senzar warlock. She should not be considered a princess. His Majesty declared your mother a traitor and so Stephenie can't even claim any ties to Cothel through her."

"You've known Stephenie for years, is she evil? Did you get to pick your parents? She's been far more loyal to Cothel than most of the nobles who call themselves Dukes or Barons."

"But she is not royalty."

Islet forced her hands to relax. "Walter, Stephenie has never wanted the throne. She rescued you and Josh from the Grey Mountains. She just wants to protect her country."

"And find her father," he challenged. "And she's drawn powerful enemies to her. How many people have suffered because of that?"

"Walter, she's fought against all of them. She can't control the fact that some man raped our mother." Islet shook her head. "If you want to secure Cothel against invaders, who better to do that? You learn something you don't like and you'd willingly throw away everything you know about who she really is, what she's done for you and the country, just so you can claim to be true to a belief that is itself a lie. You know what my sister's done, now answer me, do you really think she is evil?"

Sir Walter took a deep breath. "No."

Islet let herself begin to hope again. "She truly wants to help people, not harm them. She's a good person."

Walter looked away and then back. "Then what do you want us to do? You know Yreka is going to use us against your sister. We'd be better off dying or escaping than allowing her to take us as prisoners to your sister."

Islet noticed Jerylin tense. "I know, but there is no way we'd be able to escape. How can you plan something if your own mind and memories will betray you?"

"Then perhaps I should kill you and myself."

Islet shook her head. "You'd never succeed." Islet moved closer so she could lower her voice. "When I was a prisoner, the Senzar leader had another captive. He was a man from their lands, not a mage. No, Orlan was different. He was very good at manipulating people's minds. Even minds of witches and warlocks. In the process of planning our escape, Orlan ended up teaching Stephenie several things about controlling other people and he came with us when we escaped. Some of the stories he told me chilled my blood." She swallowed. "Right now, Yreka is merely reading our minds. However, if we try to escape or kill ourselves, she is likely to start influencing our thoughts in such a way as to make it impossible for any of us to hurt each other. In the process, it would likely destroy who we are. She'd fundamentally change us and we'd become mindless hunks of flesh." Islet could see Jerylin's hands trembling while Walter had grown unusually still. "I saw Stephenie take control of Favian's body. She found a way into the man's head and ripped control of his body from his mind. She left the man standing in the courtyard unable to do anything for himself."

"Lord Favian starved to death," Jerylin whispered. "He was dead long before his body died."

"If we actively oppose Yreka, she has the ability to do that to us. Our only chance of making it out of this is for Stephenie to defeat Yreka."

"Do you think that is even possible?" Walter asked.

Islet nodded her head. "It is the only choice I have left."

Chapter 21

Stephenie led them another eight days through the back woods and wild grasslands before they neared the city of Sand Peak. They avoided the large city that sat just over the border in the country of Talset. The large Talsetian military presence that patrolled the border forced them to travel half a day southeast before they made a quiet entry into Talset. However, a day later, they made for the northerly road to improve their speed. Once they reached the road, Stephenie pushed them and the horses as hard as she could because the easy access to supplies allowed everyone more to eat each night.

Three days north of Sand Peak, and still about a day and a half outside the city of Elk Valley, they stopped in the small town of Corac's Hill to celebrate Henton's birthday. Douglas did not get his wish for an easy day of relaxation, but they did stop for a midday dink and a meal.

"Based on your map without names, we're not even halfway to the end," Henton complained. "And the worst part of the journey is still to go. We don't need to waste time at this pub."

"Shut up and enjoy your ale," Stephenie said. "I never said we'd stay here for the night."

Henton smiled and took a drink of the cold ale. As Douglas had described it, it was a strange blend of sweet flavors with a hint of pine mixed in, not necessarily for good effect. "As it gets later in the year, we'll have to find a way to carry more grain for the horses. I didn't see many fields around this town or the one we passed by last night. Nor have I seen many large animals in pens. We've no idea what to expect further north, but if that is a trend, it might become hard to find grain."

"I know," Stephenie agreed. "We could use another couple pack animals, but then we'd have to carry even more food for them." She waited for the comment suggesting they sell the horses, but no one raised it. *They know me too well.* "We could potentially replace the saddles with pack harnesses and walk. It would allow the horses to carry more supplies. Plus, if we are walking, it will keep us warmer than just riding."

"It's why I want fur lined boots like I saw on that one man," Douglas said, tipping back his mug of ale. He scrunched up his nose and shuddered as he put the still half-full mug on the table. Foam clung to his mustache and started dripping into his beard. He grabbed a large piece of roasted meat from his plate and quickly ate it. "The meat tastes terrible, but it's still better than the ale."

Ryia tried to hide her smile. She had a smaller mug of spiced wine in her hands, having refused to drink the ale after her first sip.

Stephenie grinned as Kas laughed in her head at their folly. For the first time in days she allowed herself to relax and live in the moment while she contemplated ways to quietly dispose of the ale. She knew Kas would betray her if she did, as they had all agreed to a dare to finish the foul beverage. Wrinkling her own nose, she picked up her mug and took a long drink, willing the nasty fluid to hurry down her throat. After a quick thought, she formed a repulsive field over her tongue, preventing the liquid from making contact with her taste buds.

Three-quarters done, she set the mug down and felt her stomach start to rebel against her choice. Henton and Douglas raised their eyebrows. A moment later, she burped and her face paled as the flavor was even worse coming back up. Everyone laughed.

"I declare Steph the winner," Henton said as he pushed his half-full mug to the center of the table.

"Hey, no fair. I'm likely to be sick all over the floor after that."

"And I won't risk doing that myself," Henton said. "I've had enough of that stuff. If you do throw up, do it in Douglas' direction. It's my birthday after all."

Ryia carefully sipped her wine and smiled.

Stephenie grabbed some of the meat from Douglas' plate. The burp's after effect was getting worse and whatever mountain animal was cooked for their midday meal had to taste better.

Henton laugh as Stephenie forced the meat down her throat. He then looked over at Douglas who still had foam in his beard. "You know you look like a fool with that wild hair all over your face."

Douglas shrugged. "My face stays warm at night. Laugh now, but once we get to where it will be really cold, I'll be ready and you'll be wishing you had stopped shaving sooner."

Ryia raised her eyes, but said nothing. Stephenie was rather glad Kas did not project his image with a beard. Her father had one for as long as she had known him and she hated the way it felt when he would give her a kiss.

"Well, my face won't itch right now and I won't carry that ale around with me." Douglas wiped his face and shrugged causing Henton to chuckle again. "Alright, Douglas, let's you and me go get the supplies from next door while Stephenie finishes the last of the ale. I don't know what she did to cheat, but that's the only way someone could drink that much of that stuff." He smiled at her. "And I thank you for that. Kept me from finishing it."

She smiled. "It was my gift to you." *Kas, will you watch them?*

Of course.

Stephenie pushed the mug away from herself as Henton, Douglas, and Kas left the public house. Ryia noticed that she was being watched and took another drink of her wine.

"How are you doing?" Stephenie asked.

Ryia nodded her head softly and set the mug down. "Better."

"You look better." Stephenie had allowed her to shoot lightning from the staff two days ago and Ryia had been grinning ever since. "The staff helping?"

Ryia glanced to the weapon that leaned against her chair. The blanket had become somewhat tattered and stained, but it concealed the nature of the ornate weapon. "That, and I talked to Kas."

Stephenie's own eyebrows rose. "Really. Mind if I ask what you talked about?" She pushed down a possessive urge that came out of nowhere, reminding herself that the more Kas interacted with everyone, the less distracted he became. She doubted he would fall back into the 'boredom' trance that the ghosts of Arkani had fallen into after years and years of isolation, but she did notice his thoughts would grow a little random each morning after a long night awake by himself.

Ryia picked up her mug and took another sip of wine. "Well, we talked about a number of things. But mostly he shared his thoughts with me and showed me how I've looked to the rest of you lately."

Stephenie worked again to keep the sense of possessiveness from her emotions and voice. However, she knew she would ask him later just how many mental links he had been sharing with people.

Ryia looked up. "He showed me that I've been acting like a spoiled little victim." She looked back into her mug. "I know you asked me to talk about what happened and what was going on in my head. You told me to be strong, but for whatever reason, I just couldn't. I don't know why." She took a deep breath and met Stephenie's eyes. "But when Kas showed me...shared his mind with me so I could really see what everyone else saw...I couldn't believe how stupid I looked."

Stephenie wondered if he might have adjusted her mind as well, despite his warning against doing that. "And so what now? Do you want to talk about what happened?"

Ryia bit her lip and shook her head. "No. I still don't remember any of it. So it really doesn't feel like it happened, but I had feared what Henton would think of me. Kas showed me that Henton likes strong people. He doesn't want a kid who's complaining about things not being fair." She nodded her head. "I know, you've said that to me, but it's different hearing someone say it and feeling their mind show you."

"I understand, Kas and I have shared a number of things. It's the little bit of intimacy we have."

Ryia straightened. "I didn't mean to intrude on..."

"Peace, Ryia. I didn't know he had done that with you, but I know he was just trying to help."

Ryia's shoulders eased and she relaxed back into the chair. "It's not easy. I still get frustrated and I still hurt from loneliness sometimes, but I won't whine and throw a fit and run off."

Stephenie was glad to sense the calm that filled Ryia. The girl had suddenly matured, *perhaps with a little help from Kas*. "I'll try and take a lesson from you then and put some of my own issues with the red-haired man out of my mind. Of course, being on the road for months at a time can help temper one's rage and anger. I'll just have to hope that when we find him, we can reason with him and put an end to whatever is causing him to hate me so much."

"And find a way to help Kas," Ryia said.

Stephenie silently agreed, although she doubted she would be able to trust the man that sired her enough to seek his help in that regard.

"Where you two heading?" the village shop keeper asked Henton as they collected some sweetmeats from a wooden tray.

"North."

"Going past Elk Valley?" The older man raised his eyebrows knowingly. "The soldiers there will put on a show, but Garder doesn't have more than a handful of people watching the border. People cross over all the time. No one is really stopped. All those soldiers are just a waste of time and money."

"Why are they there? What's Garder like?" Henton asked, knowing he did not need all the candies he had picked up, but decided he would buy them anyway.

"Garder is poor country with little of value. But Queen Delain of Garder is our King Vance's aunt and King Vance's mother won't let him invade Garder, so he orders his soldiers to march back and forth at our borders. Nothing will happen and Garder is not going to do anything. It's barely got any people at all." The shop keeper looked at Douglas to make sure nothing was stolen. "Heck, Garder really ought to be two countries. The western side has the pass through the mountains and so it has some money. The east is scrub land."

"What's the pass like?" Henton asked, trying to offer a possible misdirection should anyone come through looking for them.

"Well, if you hurry, you might make it to Durlton before the snows fill the pass. I've never been through it, so I can't say how hard it is, but they bring lots of wagons through, so it can't be too hard." The man's eyes narrowed. "Where to in the north are you going?

There's nothing north of Durlton. Perhaps one small outpost, but no one goes there."

"Well, we're heading to Elk Valley," Henton said, not liking the man's tone.

"I guess you could go east from there. That's the last road away from the mountains."

"How much for these skins?" Douglas asked, holding up a large fur blanket made from the hides of several animals.

"Oh, I'll take five stones for it. But if you want more than one, I might take off half a stone. They'd charge you eight for the same thing in Elk Valley."

Henton was not sure of the exchange rate, but if they were in Cothel, he expected it could cost a Cothish crown or two in equivalent money. "You say the road also goes east from Elk Valley. What's that part of the country like?"

"Well, that leads you to the country of Ervik. They are an odd people. The people on the coast are large and hairy and I've heard stories that they harbor pirates that sail the Endless Sea. Inland, they are rude and irksome men that tax the trade routes." The man looked back at Douglas. "Really, if you're interested, I can do four and a half stones. You won't talk them lower than seven in Elk Valley."

Henton glanced at the candies he had picked up and wondered just how much the man would charge him for them.

"If you are traveling north, or even east, it's going to get cold. I can sell you a number of things real cheap. My brother is a tanner. He's got even more furs and things. Things to cover your horses. If you're not heading south, you'll need them soon. I can make sure you get a good deal from him."

Henton was certain the old man could make a great deal, for himself and his brother. The look in Douglas' eye told him that his Corporal was not considering it.

"You'll want to avoid buying things in Elk Valley. Lots of trade going east means the King wants a cut. We're small enough here, he doesn't bother us."

"Well," Henton said, not convinced at all, "that all depends on how much our coin is worth. We don't have any of your local coin."

"I can make you a good deal."

Chapter 22

They reached Elk Valley a day and a half later. An early snow that fell during the night covered the ground, but melted before noon. However, that gave Douglas reason to continue talking about his need of fur-lined boots.

The city was as the shop keeper had eventually described to Henton, a fortified outpost. The walled enclosure bustled with people moving through the coal-smoke filled air, all under the watchful eye of soldiers.

Despite the merchant's warnings, Henton managed to find most of the supplies they expected to need for a reasonable price: lots of food, blankets for the horses and themselves, a heavier tent and clothing, as well as wood and leather masks with a small slit to see through. Their days trudging through the snow covered mountains near Vinerxan after they freed Islet had taught them the value of the masks.

With Stephenie's blessing, he sold their riding saddles in exchange for pack harnesses. The change would allow them to stock up on grain and make it easier for the horses to carry the supplies. While they would be forced to remain on foot for the rest of the journey, their pace riding was about the same as their pace walking, so the change would not slow them much.

Stephenie let Henton and the others deal with the supplies as she tried to gain access to one of the guildhalls in Elk Valley. Unlike her success in Tenia, the three guilds she tried turned her away without a spare glance or consideration. However, because she had always planned to stay the night in the city, after darkness fell, she simply broke into the carter's guildhall, stole the maps she desired, and left without anyone realizing she had been there.

Based on the new maps, she plotted a course north to the city of Snow Fields. In what the maps described as a meager outpost, they would turn away from the mountain range and cut across open country toward the coast so they could find a ready source of supplies. Her plan was to aim for a city called Big River, which sat on the southern border of Sandven, the country directly south of Ista. In Sandven, they would take the coastal road north, which would lead to the trading post that Ista used to establish every summer. She even found an old map of Ista in the stack she stole that showed a single road in the country leading to a single city called Isa Fields. That map lacked any notations, but it gave her a target destination.

The following morning they awoke with the dawn and were out of the city before anyone in the guildhall could realize there had been a theft. Stephenie pushed hard and after a couple of miles, they left behind the handful of merchants and travelers who had also risen with the dawn.

Each day, they continued to hit the road early and travel late into the evening. They restocked supplies in every town or village they passed through, even if the supplies were not absolutely necessary.

The road to Durlton was well maintained and heavily traveled. It took them only four days to reach that city, which was the last major stop on the road.

Durlton sat at the base of a valley that extended deep into the mountains. A massive wall surrounded the city and protected the entrance into the pass. Or more correctly, protected the country's ability to tax merchants using the pass. The city itself was small in size, though a sizable castle left no doubt that this city had a primarily military purpose.

After purchasing more supplies, they continued north, traveling upon what could barely be called a road. Snow fell again on their second day beyond Durlton and this time it survived on the ground until the following day.

The day after, they arrived in the small outpost of Snow Fields. The collection of buildings could barely be called a town. It was more a place where trappers would collect as they gathered and processed various animal hides, leaving a heavy odor of decay and urine in the air.

As predicted by the maps, the road ended with the outpost. The cost of the grain and supplies was excessive, but knowing there would be few other settlements for many days, they purchased as much as the horses could carry before setting off to the northeast.

Days turned into weeks as they continued their relentless march across the frozen ground. Gradually any signs of forests thinned to small clumps of short spruce trees and eventually, even those gave way to shrubs and brush as the landscape turned into a vast open expanse stretching for as far as any of them could see.

They managed to blaze their own trail to the city of Big River and then joined the road to Dun Og which led them to Kebin before the road finally turned to a more northerly direction along the coast.

The travel was brutal, with bitter winds blowing off the Endless Sea and snow and sleet pelting them regularly. A deep snow had fallen even before they had reached Cilwir and it was only due to the tall standing stones marking the road that they were able to trudge through the deep drifts and remain heading in the proper direction.

Stephenie quickly remembered the pain and exhaustion she faced in the mountains east of Vinerxan as she constantly pushed a trickle of energy into Henton, Douglas, and the horses. Ryia managed her powers well enough to keep herself warm, but would quickly overextend herself if she tried to warm any of the others, which left the work to Stephenie.

The further north they traveled, the smaller and further spaced out each of the towns became. Out in the sea, they saw giant chunks of ice that first appeared as if they were thousands of small islands, but a careful eye noted their gradual southerly movement.

The local people also grew more reserved and watched them pass with suspicion and weary apprehension. Only in the larger towns were any of the heavily dressed locals willing to admit to even knowing Pandar.

The cost of grain and other supplies grew exponentially with each new town and had they not found the money of the priests of Mertor, they would have run out of funds.

Stephenie celebrated her nineteenth birthday looking out across the snow covered land and a sea more full of ice than not. They celebrated by Stephenie using her magic to hunt a large deer-like creature with a thick coat of hair. It was the first fresh meat they had eaten in weeks and everyone relished the change, even if the tough meat lacked seasoning.

When they finally reached Horn Point, they found the port frozen solid with ice. Numerous small mounds of snow dotted the shoreline. After a quick investigation, they realized the mounds were boats that had been pulled ashore until the waters thawed. Although it was still only fall back in Cothel, everything around them claimed it was the dead of winter, including the dramatic shortening of the days.

The next one hundred and fifty miles of their journey north led them to Alkmaar, which was the farthest north anyone in Sandven lived. It took them ten days of bitter travel to cover the distance and they saw no other people on the road that entire time. At night and during the day, the white landscape was filled with various creatures always remaining far enough away to not be an immediate threat, but close enough that the horses and people felt they were being stalked. Stephenie had no idea how the animals survived, but these larger animals managed to eke out some kind of living in the snow covered land.

Alkmaar was nestled at the base of a small mountain peak. The mountain and city were covered in snow, but Stephenie could tell that the city was likely built in that location for the ready supply of stone. The protective outer walls and buildings were mad of stacks of ice-covered dark-grey stones and turf roofs which peeked out where the snow had fallen free or been blown away. Nothing stood very tall and it was clear that most of the living space was set below ground level.

Inside the city, people stared and watched as they passed. They saw only a few shingles above a handful of doors and judging by the state of repair, and number of chimneys with smoke, better than half the town was abandoned.

Stephenie had to talk to almost a dozen people before she found someone who actually understood Pandar. "Is there a place where we can find a room for the night?" She finally got to ask.

The heavily bundled man who acknowledged them stared for several long moments. He looked between them and their six horses as if he was not sure they were real. "You not...here...local," he said, trying to recall a language he did not appear to use often. "Why here?"

"We are exploring. We just want to purchase supplies and find someplace warm for the night."

The man's eyes narrowed. "Ista...death. You no want."

Stephenie moistened her chapped lips with her tongue. "We just want to explore the area. Why would you think we'd go there?"

"In winter? You freeze. Nothing here foreigner, just Ista."

Stephenie understood the man's skepticism. Had she not had magic to keep herself warm, she would be shivering. "Please, we just want to find someplace warm before it gets dark."

The man nodded his head and then glanced at the horses again. "Come."

Stephenie followed the man through the streets. In a few places, she could see stone cobbles through the layer of packed ice and snow. There even appeared to be gutters and drains to carry away water, although if the gutters had fallen into the same disrepair as other parts of the city, Stephenie doubted they would work effectively.

After crossing half the city, the man led them to a large building with a ramp leading down to a pair of weathered doors. The man carefully descended the ramp, which had lines of raised rocks to offer traction. At the bottom, he opened the doors and motioned them inside. He spoke in a choppy dialect to someone else inside the building and then motioned again for Stephenie to follow him. "Horses here."

Inside the building Stephenie found a dark room that was filled with the strong odor of animals. With her magic, she could sense a multitude of deer-like creatures similar to the one they had feasted on for her birthday.

"Oonad'na," the man said, inclining his head to the animals. He hunted for a word and finally found it. "Milk. Meat." He then pointed to their horses and then to a large pen inside the building. "Put in pen."

Stephenie nodded her head and led the horses past a young woman who stood next to the open gate. Once the horses were inside, she helped Henton and the others quickly remove their gear and supplies. To the man, she asked the question that was at the forefront of her mind. "Do you have grain we can buy?" When he looked slightly confused, she lifted one of the sacks of grain and pointed inside. They still had several day's worth of food for the horses, but she wanted to acquire a full supply before setting out further north.

The man nodded his head. "Much cost."

"We'll pay," she replied as she finished tending to Argat. *You be a good boy and watch over the others,* she told her gelding. He snorted and bobbed his head up and down before nosing the bags of grain she had removed from his back.

"I'll feed the horses," Henton said. "You finish the negotiations."

Stephenie walked back to the man and closed the gate behind her.

"You...things there." The man pointed to a raised stone platform outside the pens. "Jella watch and protect."

Stephenie glanced to the young woman who stood watching Henton and the others tend to the horses. The building, although lacking any fire for warmth, was actually fairly warm due to the body heat from all the animals. Three oil lamps provided a small amount of illumination and the limited light revealed the building was clean and well cared for.

"What do we owe you for putting the horses here?"

The man and Jella had a quick exchange of words and the man turned back to Stephenie. "Local coin?"

She nodded her head. "Some." Having anticipated people not wanting to deal with foreign money, she had exchanged a number of coins in the various Sandvenian cities they had passed through to get as much local currency as she could.

"Six," the man said, holding up seven fingers.

"Seven," she corrected and he nodded, repeating her word.

She knew Sandven had a primary coin which they physically cut in pieces for smaller exchanges, she pulled seven ingots from her pouch. The long, flat and narrow, bits of copper had various groves in them that allowed them to be easily broken or cut. The man indicated she should hand the money to Jella.

"What about the four of us? Is there some place to stay where we can get some food?"

"You stay me. I have good place. Four," the man said, holding up four fingers and nodding his head to her pouch.

Stephenie smiled. Judging on how many coins it took to exchange for each ingot, she should expect a manor house for the eleven coins she had given up already. She handed them over and the man smiled back at her. "Can I ask what happened here? Why is the city deserted?"

The man nodded his head as he slowly processed her question. "Ista...closed. No go there. Die if try. People have no...reason come." He raised a gloved finger. "It winter. Cold. People go south."

Just us crazy people coming north at this time of the year, she told Kas. *If the weather is good in the morning, we'll get back on the road.*

There would be little reason to stay any longer than necessary, he said. *While it looks as though they likely have enough supplies, presumably restocked during the summer, I do not understand why they would remain here in the winter.*

Maintain ownership of their homes I would expect. To the man she said. "What should we call you?"

"Name Lamikaden. You Lami."

"Thank you for taking us in, Lami."

Lami's home lacked many of the creature comforts that they might expect to see in even the most modest of inns. However, he had a ready supply of coal he used for heating and cooking, which meant the sizable single room building was warm.

They ate a filling, if not exactly tasty, meal. They talked a little about the lands they had passed through, but avoided describing anything south of Elk Valley. For beds, they were offered a large pile of animal hides placed on the floor next to the fire pit. The pile of hides did an excellent job of keeping the cold from seeping up from the ground and for the first time in weeks, they all managed to sleep easily through the night.

In the morning, they were woken by the sound of someone knocking on the door. Stephenie picked herself up from the floor as two men helped a third man into the Lami's home. She could sense the third man was in a bit of agony and the bloody bandage around his hand gave away the wound.

The men spoke with Lami and shared a few glances toward her and the others, but then they simply helped the injured man to a table and slowly unwrapped the bloody cloth. Stephenie had a hard time seeing exactly how bad it was, but the man appeared ready to pass out and based on the amount of blood, it would be bad.

She moved closer, ready to offer her services, but Lami suddenly drew energy into himself. She watched as he closed his eyes and placed his hands over the bloody mess. Since healing tended to be more internal than anything else, she was not able to see exactly what Lami did, but she could tell energy flowed from the healer into the injured man. After an uncomfortably long silence, the man's complexion darkened from the snow-white it had been and Stephenie could tell the erratic beating of his heart returned to a more normal pace.

Lami straightened slowly, obviously having to adjust his perception to being just back in his own head. He looked at her and tightened his jaw. "I know you gods different. They...they more vicious. If you not want stay, you go. Do not think to insult the Goddess."

Stephenie raised her hands. "No. We would not do that. I am not familiar with your Goddess, but we would not insult her or yourself."

The tension left Lami's shoulders. "You pray many gods, but we only two. The Goddess and Dalkin...bringer of night. The Goddess bring life, Dalkin takes. Must have both. No idols. No special..." He fumbled with the clothing at his chest.

"Holy symbol?" Stephenie offered.

"Yes, no holy symbol. Just Chosen of Goddess."

"Does Dalkin have priests as well?" Henton asked, moving closer.

Lami shook his head. "Dalkin is. That all. Exists. Not to pray to. He breath...breathes in all summer. Hold air. Then when Goddess sleep, he blow ice and snow. He fight the Goddess. But she wake and push him back to sea."

Stephenie translated the man's broken Pandar to Kas as Lami spoke and Kas responded to her. *I am not familiar with this legend, but there are similarities to the belief systems of the elves of my time. The idea of a duality of nature. This concept was not foreign to my people, but it was only followed by a few.*

"Thank you for sharing the story, Lami." Stephenie looked toward the injured man. He still looked weak, but was growing more coherent. "Is he well? Will his hand be whole again?"

Lami bowed his head to her. "He cut hand cutting bear meat. It take time. I heal slow. Make whole again." He turned back to the men who had brought in the injured man and spoke with them at length. The men would shift their attention to Stephenie and nod their heads. Eventually, they smiled at her. After a few more head nods, they helped the injured man to his feet and walked him out of Lami's home. "They home to rest."

Stephenie's mind raced with questions, but her limitation in not knowing the local language would make a long conversation difficult. "May I ask you more about Ista?"

Lami sighed and then sat. He indicated she should sit across from him as he moved the bloody clothing from the table. "Not safe. Ista bring death."

"Why? What happened there?"

He paused and considered his words. "Many years. I still young. You very young. They stop come to border to trade. No summer trade. No one ever allowed in Ista. Any go not return. The silent guardians."

"What do you mean by silent guardians?" she asked.

He shrugged. "None see them. But some see deep prints near border. No animal make. Silent guardians."

"Has anyone tried to go there recently?"

He shook his head and then reached out and put his blood stained hands on hers. "Go, die. Don't go, live. Stay here."

She took a deep breath. "Lami, I wish it was that simple." She motioned to Henton to grab the saddle bag, which he picked up and brought to her. She pulled out the ornamented dagger, removed it from its sheath, and set the dragon etched blade on the table. "A man—a red-haired man—that we believe recently came from Ista, gave this to some people. We believe the man...sired me."

Lami looked confused by her choice of words but then he looked down at the weapon. He picked it up and examined the markings in the limited light inside his home. He quickly set the blade down and looked up to meet Stephenie's eyes. "What mean sired?"

"I believe the man was my father. A man who came from Ista."

Lami mumbled several things in his own language and shook his head. "No one go. No one come from Ista. We never...know about those live there. No one go return."

"Even if they avoid the road and the summer camp?"

"On ice, Dalkin take you. His icy breath. His white breath of death. They hunt the ice. Not safe."

Stephenie nodded her head. "I am going anyway."

Lami sighed. "Then follow road. Buildings at border. Place stay if need. Though you summer wait."

"Thank you, Lami."

"No thank. It...five...ten times miles. Long time on horse."

"Based on the maps, I estimated one hundred and fifty miles. But we actually travel rather quickly."

"Yes. One hundred-fifty." He shook his head. "No with horse. Road not cared for. Go faster use dogs and sled."

Stephenie felt her chest tighten. The thought of leaving Argat behind terrified her. She was about to protest when Lami continued speaking.

"Leave here. We care for. Let you borrow dogs for fee. Bring back dogs, give back horse. Save days travel."

Stephenie pursed her lips and noticed a slight shift in Henton's posture. The idea that something might happen to Argat on the plains scared her, but the idea someone might take him from her was just as terrifying and threatened to raise her possessive urges.

"What's involved with sleds and dogs?" Henton asked. "We've seen several near Horn Point and Cilwir as we made our way north. It looks complicated."

Lami shrugged. "Not hard. Can teach. Day...two for learn. Two teams. Good teams. Two day to camp."

Henton raised his eyebrows and Stephenie had to admit the idea of covering that distance in only a couple of days was intriguing. *What do you think, Kas?*

She felt Kas' uncertainty, but it was an uncertainty of her reaction to leaving Argat behind. *It would be advantageous to limit your time out in the snow. I believe Henton would be in favor of it.*

She sighed. "Will our horses be safe here?"

Lami nodded his head. "I give word. You give same for dogs."

"Of course. We'd not harm the animals."

"You no return, we sell horse next spring."

Stephenie swung her head toward Henton. She searched his eyes for a confirmation that this was the best course of action.

He spoke in Cothish, "If we die out there, at least they will still have a chance to live. We don't know what we'll find. But if we can get to the border in two days and perhaps on to Isa Fields in another two, then, assuming they let us leave again, we can come back and make sure nothing happens to the horses. Though you have to wonder, with all the talk of people never returning, is this going to be a one way journey?"

Douglas cleared his throat and spoke in Cothish as well. "It is fairly ominous. We know the man to be a bastard and should probably be slowly ripped apart for what he's done. But, I've said it before, I'm with you to the end. If there is anyone that can put him in his place, it would be you."

Stephenie glanced to Ryia. "If Henton and Douglas are going, don't think to leave me behind. It's damn cold here and the last thing I want to do is sit around shivering." She forced her shoulders back. "Just don't get me killed or locked up. I'll be pissed at you if you do."

Stephenie chuckled and then turned back to Lami. "Alright, we'll leave the horses with you and take dog sleds. Just teach us what we need to know...and don't let anything happen to the horses."

Chapter 23

Lami escorted them to the edge of the walled city where a sizable area had been set aside for kennels. Because Lami had revealed himself to have magic, Kas had continued to envelope Stephenie in the hopes of minimizing the mage's ability to sense him. Lami had not shown any awareness of the ghost, but the thin man might have decided to conceal his knowledge.

They stopped and Lami called out to a wiry man who was playing with one of the numerous large dogs tied to individual shelters. The man strode over and spoke with Lami at length in their local language before the two of them turned to Stephenie. "This Perain. He take care you."

The thin man had no beard and his wax coated lips spread into a wide smile. "As Lami said, I am Perain. It is a pleasure to meet you. I understand you need two dog teams."

Stephenie smiled. Perain's Pandar was as good as anyone she met on their journey north. "Yes, indeed. We will be out on the snow and ice for a number of days. At least eight or nine days, maybe ten."

Lami bowed his head. "I leave. Perain help. Come back house when done."

Perain smiled and said a couple more things in his language as Lami walked back toward his house. Perain turned to Stephenie. "Lami never travels. His..." Perain shrugged. "I won't speak ill of such a good man, but..." He chuckled, "Lami's ability to speak Pandar is rather limited. Better than most here, but not the greatest."

"He did very well," Stephenie said. "We really didn't have trouble understanding him. Sometimes it just took a little longer to puzzle out a meaning."

Perain nodded his head. "Then let me be perfectly clear. I owe Lami a favor—or three—and so I will lend you some dogs and sleds for a reasonable fee. However, I will only do so once I am certain you are able to care for and manage the dogs. I won't have you killing them because you don't know what you're doing."

"Agreed," Stephenie said. "I would not want to take them out without knowing what we are doing."

Perain smiled. "Good. A sled is not hard to use, but it is work. Don't expect to just sit back and do nothing. You'll be pushing and pulling and helping the dogs. You'll be taking care of the dogs and making sure none of them gets over hot or..."

"Hot out there?" Ryia interrupted, then looked down as she realized she spoke aloud.

"Yes," Perain said, a touch of wariness in his voice. "The dogs have thick coats and work hard. They get hot even out there. And so will you." He looked back to Stephenie. "Come, let me see how good you are with some of the dogs."

Stephenie followed quickly behind Perain, her boots crunching through the hard surface of the snow. As they neared several dogs, the large animals jumped up and started barking, which cascaded through the pack. Perain stopped in front of a brown and tan dog whose shoulders came to his hips, but as the dog jumped and pulled against the rope that tied it to the shelter, its head rose equal to his.

"This is Uteg," Perain said, trying to get close enough to grab the dog's harness. He shouted to be heard over the noise. "Uteg is my judge of people. If she likes you, then we go further."

Stephenie nodded her head and calmed herself. The animals around her were all very excited and she knew she did not want to add more energy to the current chaos. The majority of the dogs were now on their feet and barking, but she also heard some growls and snarls mixed into the noise. Perain did not seem phased by the more angry animals.

Kas, just in case the dogs can sense you somehow, you might move back just a bit.

Of course, Kas said as he moved near Henton.

Stephenie stepped forward and the dog continued to try to jump out of Perain's grasp. She felt the animal's excitement, but also felt a bit of uncertainty mixed in. She reached out with her mind and touched the dog's thoughts. Immediately, she became overwhelmed with the smells around her. There was dog, and people, and smoke, and something else that confused her for a moment. She pulled her senses back a little and recognized the smell as Argat. The other three also smelled of horse and Stephenie smiled. *Easy,* she told the dog and repeated it aloud. She stepped forward, held out her hand, and projected a sense of calm into the dogs mind. "Hi, Uteg. I'm Stephenie."

The brown and tan dog dropped down to all four paws and started sniffing her hand. Then the dog's nose moved to Stephenie's legs and boots and ran up and down her body as its furry tail wagged back and forth.

"Damn," Perain said taking a step back after releasing his grip of her harness. "She likes you. I've never seen her take so easily to someone. You wouldn't be one of the Goddess Chosen, would you?"

Stephenie turned to face Perain as the dog continued to sniff her. "Not that I know of. Perhaps she smells our horses."

The man chuckled. "Well, that or Lami gave you some tasty food for your pouch." Perain stood straighter and yelled a series of words several times. Shortly afterward, the dogs started to settle down and the barking dropped to a reasonable level. "Can't think when they make so much noise. Anyway, we'll go over all the details of the sleds. Once you understand how all that works, I'll put together a small team and we'll work on drills for the rest of the day. I want all of you to know what you are doing. Then tomorrow we can put together a bigger team and if you manage them, I'll let you take some sleds mid-morning."

"Thank you," Stephenie said.

"Don't thank me yet. You'll find yourself worn out before I am done with you."

*   *   *   *   *

They worked with Perain through the morning to learn about the sleds, harnesses, and ropes. In the afternoon, he taught them the command words for the dogs, and then they each practiced controlling a moving sled until the sun dropped below the horizon. Once the warmth of the day was dying away, Perain made them take care of the dogs as they would have to out on the ice.

Stephenie found the work invigorating, but she knew her magic helped to considerably lighten her load and keep her body temperature consistent. The others had to constantly work to avoid sweating, otherwise they would freeze once they stopped moving.

"How'd you learn to speak Pandar so well?" Stephenie asked as they brought the last of the dogs back into the city and to Perain's kennels.

He laughed. "I travel a lot. I go to Horn Point at least a couple of times a month." He leaned closer to her. "We hate the name. A foreigner gave it that name a long time ago."

"Really? What was its name before?"

Perain shrugged. "No idea, but I like to think it was called Kutdirveld Denkarilma. It means 'Home of the Bloody-Ass, Damn-Cold Wind on a Beautiful Shore' or something close to that."

Stephenie laughed. "That sounds like a good name for it."

Perain gently shouldered her in agreement. "You've got real talent with the dogs. Not unheard of, but they really like you. I don't know what you are looking for out on the snow, but I will warn you against the hot springs. You might feel like you're frozen and the water might look inviting, but some of that water is boiling and you'd cook yourself. Then comes the problem of getting out. You'll freeze being wet in the wind. So don't get the idea to go swimming and make sure you keep the dogs away from the springs. The water isn't good to drink."

Stephenie nodded her head. "We'll try to avoid them. Where might we run into something like that?"

"Mostly near the mountains. But there are a few places out in the snow fields. If you see a place without snow, avoid it. The springs will normally be close to those bare areas." Perain tied the last dog's harness to its shelter and glanced back to Henton and the others who were standing a number of feet away, all of them, including Henton looked exhausted. "Do you think you can find your way to Lami's on your own or do you need me to take you there?"

"I think we can manage. Thank you again, Perain."

"Well, tomorrow, bring your money and be ready to prove yourself capable with a larger team. Then I'll let you go. I'll have enough food and supplies ready. You said you plan on being gone eight to ten days, I'll make sure you have fifteen days of supplies in case you get snowed in with a blizzard. Nothing worse than being stuck in the cold and being hungry at the same time."

"Thank you."

When they returned to Lami's home, Lami had a dinner ready for them. "Hope day well."

"It did go well," Stephenie replied as she sat down at the table. The thick soup waiting for them smelled of fish, but Stephenie was hungry enough that she expected to find it very good regardless of the taste. "Perain is very good with his dogs. And very protective of them."

Lami nodded his head. "He good man." Lami filled their bowls with the soup and sat to join them at the table. They talked a little between each spoonful, but even Ryia did not complain about the choice of food. A day working hard in the biting wind left them all eager to eat.

When they finished, Lami cleared away the bowls and brought out an exquisite bottle with a dark red liquid and a set of delicate glasses. Even in her father's private collection, Stephenie had never seen something so finely crafted. Lami poured a small amount of the red fluid into a glass for each of them.

Stephenie picked up the glass she was offered. "This is a beautiful set," she remarked as she examined the glass with delicate cuts and patterns etched over the surface.

"In family long time," Lami said as he took a small sip of the liquid. "Came from Ista."

She let her sight lose focus and noticed a uniformity in the potential energy of the material that she had learned to associate with materials that had been manipulated and formed into a specific shape by magic. Stephenie pulled back her sight and took a small sip. The strong alcohol gave her a shudder as she swallowed the sweet beverage that held a slightly fruity taste.

"I watch. You do good with dogs. Natural. Perain let you go, I sure."

"Even with my getting dragged today?" Henton asked.

Lami chuckled. "That happen everyone. You no let go. That important."

"It made me laugh," Douglas said as he took a second sip of his drink.

"I want to thank you, Lami," Stephenie said. "You have been very kind and helpful."

Lami shrugged. "I like help." He set his glass down and his smile faded. "They say, water touch Ista never thaw. The Goddess no drive Dalkin from land. Even summer, Dalkin come from north. Walk from sea ice. Freeze men dead." He looked directly at Stephenie. "Even if blessed from Goddess, she no power in Ista. Dalkin rule that land. Even if father from Ista, beg not cross border. Dalkin take you. None come back."

Stephenie nodded her head as she set down her glass; the drink was far sweeter than she liked. "I understand your concern and we will be very careful. We don't intend to be reckless, but I need some answers and unless I am prevented from making it to Isa Fields, I will go there."

Lami bowed his head to her. "Then finish drink. It Blood of Goddess. Make from meadow flower. Means life, rebirth." They all obliged the man and resumed sipping their drinks. "Recommend follow road. It not...maintained. But, markers show road. Lead old camp. Buildings there. Find shelter."

In the morning they gathered on the snow pack as Perain assembled two teams of twenty dogs. "That's a lot of dogs," Henton whispered to Stephenie.

"Well, the sleds are larger," she said with a glance to the heavily laden craft. "Plus one person will be riding while the other drives. And we're going further."

"I know. It's still a lot of dogs."

Douglas and Ryia stepped closer to add to the conversation. "You know, I've kind of liked sleeping in a coal heated house," Douglas said. "Don't suppose they packed one in the extra gear?"

Stephenie shook her head. She had been keeping everyone as warm as she could reasonably do. The last day had actually been a nice break from the constant use of energy and she had to admit she had not realized just how tired it had made her. "If we are two days from the camp, we won't have to endure too much time exposed to the wind and cold and without having to warm the horses, I can do a better job with the two of you. But..."

Henton shook his head. "You won't talk us into staying here while you go it alone. We're in it together."

Stephenie smiled. "It is scary how easily you read my mind. Too bad you don't listen to what I want you to do."

"Yeah, well, that's your punishment, always having to put up with us," Henton said, matching her grin.

Perain tested them on how they handled the larger sleds and dogs. He corrected a number of small details, then questioned them on the care of the animals three times before he let them head off into the white expanse on their own. His parting wisdom was to avoid going too far north for fear of accidentally crossing Ista's border—and another reminder to avoid the hot springs.

Stephenie and Henton took their places as the first set of dog drivers, while Ryia and Douglas snuggled into bundles of hides on the sleds to keep warm. After the dim sun crossed a third of the sky, Douglas took over for Henton on the second sled while Stephenie pressed on. Ryia finished off the day, taking over for Douglas as Stephenie insisted she was capable of remaining a driver.

The snow pack was firm, allowing the two teams of twenty dogs to easily eat up the miles. They avoided the snow covered road and the drifts that accumulated around the marker stones. Instead they rode to the west of the toothy mounds of snow that made the trail easy enough to follow.

They took frequent breaks to keep the dogs from overheating and wearing out. Although Perain had given her specific signs and behaviors to watch for, Stephenie found herself maintaining an empathic link to the dogs that gave her a much better insight into their condition and when they needed to stop.

The first night on the snow fields with the dogs was restless. The minds of the edgy animals kept Stephenie awake, even after she touched their minds to urge them to settle down and sleep. In the morning, they resumed their journey before the sun rose and were many miles further north when the sun finally crossed the horizon.

They came upon the buildings suddenly. Covered in snow, the mounds that hid the summer camp blended into the background of the fading afternoon light. Henton had to crush his weight down on the break to slow the dogs and avoid running past the small cluster of buildings. Stephenie had a slightly easier time, she reached out mentally to her dogs and urged them all to a graceful stop. The effort saved Douglas from the bouncing and twisting that Ryia and Henton endured. After setting the hooks, and turning the sleds over to add weight to the anchor, the five of them carefully set off to explore the remains of the permanent encampment.

"Looks like half a dozen buildings," Henton said, brushing fresh snow from his fur-lined pants. With the mask on his face, he looked like a monster created by stitching together numerous pieces of various creatures.

Stephenie used her mind to examine the area and found six sizable buildings under the snow. She sensed nothing alive in the area, just frozen buildings covered in white. She turned her head and squinted against the brightness. To the north the road markers continued three hundred yards toward a depression in the ground that ran east to west. What appeared to be a bridge stretched over what she assumed to be a summertime river. On the other side of the river, she noticed a long row of small mounds that looked like the road markers. These mounds followed the river and stretched for as far as she could see to the east and the west. Beyond the bridge and border markers,

Stephenie thought she could see more road markers heading north as they climbed a rise in the ground and then disappeared over a hill.

"Is that the sea?" Ryia asked, pointing to the east.

The land appeared to stretch past the horizon, but a quarter mile away the rougher terrain dropped away toward a flatness that could only be caused by frozen water. Large mounds dotted the landscape and appeared to be massive chunks of ice heaved up from below.

Stephenie nodded her head in agreement. "Based on the maps, there should be some type of cove near this encampment."

Douglas rubbed his mittens on his arms for warmth. "Let's check out these buildings and get out of the wind."

Kas luminesced, though in the glare coming off the snow, he still appeared nearly transparent. "The smaller building due west has the appearance of being a storehouse. The interior has remnants of animal carcasses, but the roof has partially collapsed." Kas rotated his body to face the southwest. "The structure just ahead has many beds and several fire pits. The appearance is that it might have been a traveler's way station. I found another building," Kas pointed to the one southeast of them, "which has a sizable quantity of coal."

Douglas perked up at Kas' comments, but his beard hid any potential smile. "I'll get a bucket of coal. Steph, Ryia, want to light it so we can get warm?"

Stephenie nodded her approval to Douglas and he walked away to get the coal. "Any place for the dogs?" She asked Kas.

"I believe there were a large number of external shelters to the west. They are similar to what Perain uses. However, most of them are covered in snow and many look to have collapsed. Of the other three buildings, two appear to have been residences for a small group of people and one might have been administrative. There are a number of wooden tables and desks."

Henton raised his eyebrows. "That's a long way to bring wood."

Kas turned toward Henton. "As we have seen in Alkmaar and Horn Point, most of the construction here is with stone. However, there are always some wooden parts. I will admit the desks seem unusual."

Stephenie looked over as Douglas was working to pull snow away from the building Kas had indicated contained a store of coal. She extended her senses and located the door, which was a dozen feet from where Douglas was looking. With a gravitational tug, she cleared the snow from the door, drawing an appreciative nod from Douglas.

"Are you planning to stay here for the night?" Henton asked.

"Yes, please," Ryia added, she stood with her shoulders scrunched up and her arms wrapped around herself, cold despite her powers.

"Yes, we'll stay the night. I want to check the border for these guardians that we've been told about before we cross. Best to do that slowly and without the dogs." Stephenie started walking toward the way station. She reached out, found the door, and cleared it of snow. "Based on what we find, we can resume our journey to Isa Fields tomorrow. If our destination is just another day and a half, then including the return trip, we have nine days of buffer in our supplies." She glanced to the smaller mounds that Kas had pointed out further to the west. "Let me clear the snow from those and we can give the dogs some shelter for the night."

"Sounds good to me," Henton said as he grabbed Ryia to help him care for the dogs.

The sunlight had faded and the temperature had dropped by the time the dogs were cared for. Henton, Stephenie, and Ryia gladly retreated from the cold wind to join Douglas in the now warm building. Douglas had fixed a small meal and laid out their fur blankets around the fire pits he had stoked with mounds of coal. However, despite the comfort of the building, once they were done eating, Stephenie coaxed them back into the cold and headed toward the border. She led then down and across the rocky riverbed toward the standing stones that lined the far side.

She slowed their pace as they neared the boundary markers. With her mind's eye, she looked below the snow and tried to appraise the five-foot high stones hidden from sight. What she felt caused her to stop and hold out her arms to keep anyone else from approaching further. No one spoke as she narrowed her focus and looked at the energy fields that emanated from the nearest stone. They extended outward and linked this stone to its neighbors ten yards to the left and right. The energy fields arched outward in tiny threads. *Just like a mind reaching out to sense the world.*

She expanded her search and found hundreds of channels running from stone to stone like rope between fence posts. However, she also felt a multitude of fields that looped outward into the air in a series of tiny arches.

"The stones are empowered," she said, sensing the questions building in her friends.

"Magical?" Henton asked. "Are they a threat?"

Kas hovered next to her. "I can sense their potential energy, which seems high considering the cold, but I do not sense anything else."

"There are small threads of energy running between the stones. They extend outward. The farthest reaching spots are between the stones, perhaps fifteen feet high as well as out in front of the line. I also feel smaller loops that blossom around each stone. They don't stretch from stone to stone, they just fill the gap at the stone. It's not as high, perhaps ten feet, but it's there."

"Like the fields around a load stone?" Kas asked.

"What do they do?" Ryia asked, the staff in one hand and the other on Henton's arm.

"It's like the threads a mind uses to feel the world."

"A magical sentry?" Henton asked.

Stephenie shrugged. "If I had to guess, that is what I would say."

"Have we crossed any?" Henton asked, his gloved hand on his sword.

Stephenie shook her head. "Close, but I think we've avoided them. Unless they have some so faint I can't see them."

"I don't like this," Ryia said to Douglas, who immediately agreed.

"What if we head inland a few miles?" Henton asked, turning toward the west. "We could see if these boundary stones continue or if there are gaps."

"Or, we could go out to sea and cut back inland," Kas said. "Assuming the ice here melts in the summer, it would be an impossibility for the people who placed the stones to position the sentry points out past the edge of the land."

"They could have some along the coast," Henton challenged. "But they can't stretch the whole border of the country. How much effort and time would it take to make all these?"

"What about the ones along the road?" Ryia asked. "Have we set them off as well?"

Stephenie continued to stare at the stones that marked the edge of Ista. *You can't keep me out with just a line of stones. I won't be put off that easily.* To Ryia, she said, "These stones are different. The ones along the road so far are not magical. Plus, under the snow, these are nearly perfectly square and are covered in runes."

"And the road markers are more random in size and don't have marks," Ryia mumbled, having cleared the snow from several the day before.

"What about at the bridge?" Douglas asked.

Stephenie turned her attention to the east and the wide gap of nearly thirty yards between the stones. She carefully made her way to the bridge, watching for any stray fields as they pushed through the powdery snow. When she got close enough to sense the area she stopped and shook her head. "There are channels of energy there as well, though they seem more spread out because of the distance between the stones."

"It would be easy to fly over these if they are only fifteen feet high," Kas said. "You could fly everyone and all of our gear over this fence without much effort."

She nodded her head. "I can. It just worries me that someone has gone to this much trouble."

Henton reached out and put a hand on her shoulder. "We should wait until tomorrow. We can try going out to sea or going further inland. I'd guess we'd see an end to the stones after a few miles, if they even go that far."

She looked up into Henton's eyes and saw concern under his calm exterior. This kind of magic in such a desolate and foreign place was taking a toll on him. She forced a smile to her face. "Let me fly us over these marker stones. While the stones could do something, my guess is they are a warning system." She glanced back to the buildings of the encampment and the smoke coming from the chimney where they left the fire burning. "Someone at some point would have to have crossed the border by accident or on a dare. You won't have a group of people sitting here for very long before someone gets drunk enough to see what would happen. If the stones were what killed people, then there would be stories of that in Alkmaar. My guess is they have some form of entangled link, like the augmentation devices, and when someone crosses the border, someone finds out about it."

"That's rather powerful magic to watch a border," Henton said.

"You've seen the outer walls of Arkani where I found Kas," she said in the Old Tongue, still unwilling to share that secret even with Douglas and Ryia just in case anyone ever read their minds. "What exists under everyone's feet back home is positively incredible. A whole city underground with a dome so high you can't see it in the dark. The library there..."

Henton raised his hands and spoke in Cothish. "I understand, the man who built this was likely very powerful and Ista has been here a long time, so they could use ancient knowledge. I concede your point, we fly over and avoid announcing ourselves."

Stephenie turned to Douglas and Ryia. "If the two of you would rather stay, I can go ahead with Henton and Kas."

Douglas snorted. "I'd rather stay near you personally."

"I've got my staff," Ryia said, holding the blanket wrapped weapon up for her to see.

Stephenie smiled, drew energy into herself, and lifted them all high into the sky and over the line of stones. She was careful to avoid the fields and landed three hundred yards over the border along the road. From the air, she could see much further than she could from the ground. The snow covered stones stretched for as far as was visible, both inland and along the shoreline.

"You know, those deer-like things that roam the land and the small fox and other animals would undoubtedly cross the border," Henton said. "If the stones warned of every crossing that occurred, it would keep people very busy dealing with false alarms."

Stephenie directed her thought to Kas. *I suspect the stones would likely also be sensitive to mental activity and would be able to differentiate between humans and other animals. What do you think?*

I would advise caution. However, we have come this far. Without something more substantial to go by, I would say that fence should not prevent us from proceeding.

Stephenie gave Kas a mental hug and started making her way along the road. "I saw no buildings on this side of the border when we were in the air. Just the border markers and the ones along the road, but those along the road don't have any fields around them."

"We don't know exactly where Isa Fields is located," Henton cautioned. "Unless someone who had been there drew a map or spoke of it, the maps you found would be someone's guess."

Stephenie slowed and stopped. She closed her eyes and let her mind see the world around them. After a moment, she chuckled. "The road on this side has been flattened and packed. I'd almost say it was cobblestones, but it is not quite that good. I wonder if it is just for show for those that had come here, or if it goes all the way to the city like that."

Henton shrugged. "Implied power or real power. Do you want to walk a little ways down the road or do we go back?"

"Let's walk a short distance. I can always fly us back so we don't have to fight through the snow. I just want to get a sense of things and see if there is anything else to worry about."

Stephenie took the lead with Kas roaming thirty yards ahead of her. Henton, Douglas, and Ryia trailed ten yards behind her. As they moved along the road, Stephenie continued to spread her senses out. She slowed to a stop as she realized several large stones just off the sides of the road and hidden under a blanket of snow held great potential energy. A series of threads erupted from each of the stones the moment she stopped.

Without warning, snow flew in all directions as these massive stones moved and shifted, leaping into the air. The four pony sized creatures charged toward Henton, Douglas, and Ryia. It took her a moment to realize they had the appearance of a massive winged, cat-like creature.

Stephenie threw a gravity wall at the four stone beings, blocking their path toward her friends. The field knocked the attackers back into the snow with a resounding thud. However, the stone beasts recovered nimbly, sending up another spray of snow as they charged forward again.

Ryia anchored her back foot and held the staff before her, ready to strike as Henton and Douglas loosed their swords.

Stephenie threw out a channel, linking herself to the creature closest to her friends. She unloaded energy down the path, filling the air with lightning and rolling thunder. The stone creature showed no reaction.

Ryia unleashed lightning from the staff, striking the same creature, but it only swerved to angle its approach and to move around Ryia.

Stephenie tried to lift the others into the air, but her field rolled off the shield the staff generated. *Damn it!*

The four creatures circled around the back side of Ryia and the staff's shield, silently growling and snarling at Henton and Douglas.

"I can't lift you with the staff's shield active," Stephenie shouted as she moved closer.

"I'm not lowering it with them this close!" Ryia shouted back as the creatures stalked back and forth. Their stone muscles flexing as they moved. Their wings furling and unfurling.

Stephenie sensed the fields that shifted within each creature, allowing the stone to move as a fluid where necessary to achieve the appearance of life. "I'll try to draw them off," she called as she slowly walked toward them with Kas invisible at her side.

"They have a massive reserve of power," Kas said softly. "It was concealed before they started to move. I think they are entangled with a remote power source."

As Stephenie closed the distance, the creatures looked in her direction, but had no interest. "Hey, you pieces of stone crap, leave them alone. Come at me!"

Ryia waved the staff at one that came near Henton and it backed away, avoiding the staff, only to circle around toward Henton again as he moved behind Ryia.

Henton turned toward Stephenie. "Steph, I am ready to admit I am a bit uncomfortable with our current situation."

"Damn it," she swore as she continued forward. The stone beasts moved away from her, but continued to circle around the outside of the shield the staff generated. "Go on, get." Stephenie used her sword to usher the nearest creature away. The scale like texture on the surface of the stone gave its skin a more lizard than cat-like appearance, though the face, body shape, and clawed paws were definitely feline.

She turned her attention to the others. All three of them radiated fear, though it had diminished from the initial encounter.

Kas luminesced near one, but the creature ignored him. "I am not significant to it," he remarked.

Stephenie watched as the one she hit with lightning walked within three feet of her. She followed the beast's stone eyes and slowly pulled out the dagger she had taken from the High Priest of Mertor. The creature eyed it and continued walking.

"Ryia, put Henton and Douglas between you and me. Then drop the shield when they are walking around the front of you. I'll fly us up as soon as you do it."

"What?" Ryia demanded. "The shield is keeping them back."

Stephenie shook her head. "It's the staff, not the shield."

"I think you are right," Henton said slowly.

After a moment of hesitation from Ryia, Stephenie felt the shield drop and she launched the four of them high into the air. The four creatures leaped after Henton and Douglas, extending their wings and snapping their fang filled mouths.

Stephenie felt her concern grow as the four massive stone creatures generated fields around themselves to fly after them, but her field had more strength and it took only a few heart beats for them to fly back over the border. She rotated in the air, flying backwards to watch the creatures break off pursuit just before the frozen river.

With her heart racing, she set everyone down near the cluster of buildings. The four stone beasts landed at the edge of the bridge. Two of them sat down on their haunches, while the other two laid all the way down in the snow like a cat. The four guardians kept their focus on Henton and Douglas.

"Well, I think the story of guardians is real," Douglas said as he sheathed his sword.

Chapter 24

"**Y**ou can't be serious." Henton's hands clenched in his lap.

Stephenie blocked out the emotions around her; Henton had dropped his reserve and she did not want to feel his fear. "The guardians somehow recognize the staff and the dagger. They simply ignored me and it appeared they ignored Ryia. However, they seemed quite intent on you and Douglas."

"I'd rather not get ripped apart by their stone teeth, thank you very much," Douglas said. "I had a good look at their mouths. It didn't look like they had a throat, but they had fangs."

"And claws," Ryia added.

Stephenie looked at all of them. "I have to do this. I need him to stop hunting me and trying to have me killed." She would not admit that she still held out a slim hope of learning how to rebuild a body for Kas for fear Kas would see it in her thoughts.

"You still think he's trying to kill you?" Ryia asked. She lifted the staff from her lap. "Perhaps he meant for you to have the staff and dagger."

Stephenie frowned. That idea was almost worse than him trying to kill her. If he wanted something from her, she doubted she would want anything to do with it. "Look, I will keep the dagger with me. Ryia will keep the staff and the three of you will remain here with the dogs. You have shelter and they don't seem interested in crossing the border."

"And how are you going to make it to Isa Fields?" Henton asked. "Those things might leave the dogs alone, but they might not."

"Kas and I can fly. We can cover a lot of ground in the air. I'll take supplies and a tent, but I'll leave the sled and the dogs here."

Henton shook his head. "I don't like it."

Stephenie did not like splitting up either, she would rather be present to protect her friends than leave them on their own; however, if the man that raped her mother had plans for her or would try to kill her in person, then she would rather none of them were with her.

"What if he kills you or captures you?" Henton demanded. "How are we to know? How are we to rescue you?"

Stephenie frowned at how easily Henton knew her thoughts. "Look, those things are not going to let you cross the border. If something happens to me, I don't think there will be anything you can do to help." She reached out and put her hand on his. "Henton, I'll be okay. I'll have Kas with me. I won't be alone."

He sighed. "At least think about it overnight. If in the morning you still want to go...I won't stop you."

"You have my word. Though, you do understand, this is something that has to be done. I have to get him to stop sending people to hurt those I care about and those I am supposed to protect."

"I know," he replied quietly.

In the morning she helped take care of the dogs, gathered her gear, said tearful goodbyes, and took to the air. There were still only four guardians on the bridge, but as she flew north over the road, she noticed several that were partially exposed and tracks in the snow leading to others who were sitting on their haunches. They were spread across the area and simply waiting. The fact that the stone creatures turned their heads as she flew above them did not escape her notice.

These are much more powerful than that flesh-spider, Kas said. *The spider just required gravitational fields to move the stolen body parts. These stone guardians loosen the bond in the stone so that a gravity field or some other mechanism allows them to move in a lifelike manner.*

Additionally, they are able to generate a field with significant power to enable them to fly.

It does pose a concern.

Kas moved ahead of her. *Any single one, which seemed unaffected by your lightning blast yesterday, would be a concern. The fact that there are so many along the road is terrifying.*

Stephenie slowed and looked at Kas. *Do you want to turn back?*

This man has incredible power. I do not think it would be possible for you to ever engage him in combat and survive.

Stephenie gave Kas a mental smile. *I came to that conclusion myself...a while ago. I don't intend to challenge him to a battle; I just want to talk to him.* She sensed he would not ask her to return to the encampment and so she resumed her forward flight. *I'm sure you've sensed it by now, but I'll do whatever is necessary to protect you and the others.*

I know that and many times I have wished you would run away from this. However, I also know doing that is not in your nature. We will face this together.

She gave him a mental hug and continued moving north. They both knew the other would sacrifice himself or herself if that was the only way to divert her sire's attacks.

It was not long before she could no longer see the camp at the border and as she moved away from the coast, she was once again in a world of dull white. The wind swept away the fresh snow, digging down to a layer of ice frozen long ago and made dirty by the passage of time. A few dark rocks stood exposed in the wide expanse of ground that spread in all directions, but Stephenie wondered if these might actually be guardians that were scattered across the bleak landscape.

Initially, she chatted with Kas, but as the miles passed beneath her and the weight of the food and equipment on her back took its toll, she grew quiet. They stopped every ten to twenty miles for her to rest, eat, or drink, but nothing approached her on the ground. After a while, the monotony of the landscape left her wondering just how anyone could survive in such a desolate environment with so few resources. She could see no way for crops to grow and the further she moved away from the frozen sea, the fewer signs of life appeared.

By the time late afternoon arrived, the sun was already well on its way to the horizon. In the distant southwest, the jagged peaks of the World's Backbone were backlit by a sun that seemed to have forsaken this northern country. She continued onward, following the trace of a road that did not appear to have been cleared in years. However, as the sun moved further below the mountains, she felt a biting wind nipping at her body. Her magic kept her warm enough, but as the short day waned and the temperatures dropped, the amount of energy she needed to draw through her to remain warm increased.

Stephenie, I believe there are buildings ahead of us, Kas said.

Stephenie narrowed her focus and looked back toward the ground. She could see several dark masses that resolved into low structures. She continued to close on them and once she was near enough to sense the buildings, she realized a good deal of heat radiated from the walls and roof. Immediately, she dropped out of the sky and landed on the snow covered road. *If there is heat, we should expect people. I don't want to show off by flying.*

Kas gave his silent agreement. Stephenie adjusted the pack on her back and started walking toward the group of buildings a quarter-mile ahead of them. As she pushed her way through the deep drifts, she noted that there did not appear to be any other tracks in the snow. *Perhaps they only travel from here to the north.* She thought to Kas. She walked past a stone guardian whose feline face did not bother shifting, though the energy massed in the creature let her know it was active.

When they came within a hundred yards of the buildings, Stephenie paused. *No sound except for the relentless wind.* She had yet to sense anyone and the small dog shelters to her left appeared abandoned.

Do you want me to scout ahead? Kas asked.

Stephenie shook her head. *We stay together.* She resumed walking, but at a slightly slower pace. There were five stone buildings ahead of her. Each with steeply pitched roofs. The construction was not unlike that of the camp where Henton and the others waited. *Please stay safe,* she thought to herself, willing her friends to come to no harm.

Before she even reached the first building, she became certain no living human was in the area. "Completely deserted," she said over the wind.

"I concur with that assessment," Kas said, drifting a little further from her. "Our journey started late, leaving after the sun had risen, but my estimation is that this would perhaps be about as far as one would take a team of dogs in a day."

Stephenie nodded her head. She approached the door to the nearest building where she felt the warmth emanating from the building and even the snow had receded away from the stone walls and roof. "What is keeping it so warm though?" She let her mind see the energy fields on the other side of the door and sensed the flow of power moving up from the ground. She pushed open the door and looked into the dark building. The stone floor radiated heat from the very center of the building. The warm air flowing out through the doorway was almost overwhelming.

From the fields, she could tell most of the energy came from a raised area in the center of the room. "It almost looks like a fire pit, but it's not burning coal. It's using magic to make heat." She walked inside the single room building. Raised beds covered in furs lined the outer wall and several stone tables and benches sat around the central pit.

Stephenie took her time, looking at the flow of energy in the room, wanting to make sure she did not miss anything. In doing so, she noted a number of personal items scattered about, including bone combs, blankets, bowls, and clothing.

"Stephenie, I believe there is a body over here," Kas said aloud.

She concentrated her focus and nodded her head as she felt what could only be a skeleton.

"The warmth in the building, assuming the heat has been going for some time, would have accelerated the decomposition of the body," Kas said, all emotion detached from his voice.

Stephenie walked past a stone pillar that helped to support the weight of the roof and noted a small draw of energy flowing into what appeared to be a crystal resting in a brass sconce. She placed a hand on the crystal and spoke to it mentally using the secret language of the Senzar and the traps. *Light, illuminate, bright, turn on, shine—*

The room brightened as that crystal, and five more on the other pillars, flared to life.

She looked over to Kas and returned the smile that covered his translucent face. "I remember things," she said as she approached the remains. The bones were scattered somewhat, and other than a dark stain on the floor, the flesh was gone and most of the clothing was ripped and chewed. "I would say some small animals have managed to get in here and pick the body clean." Stephenie looked around and noted other signs of animal presence where jars and containers that sat on tables were knocked over and empty.

Kas bowed his head to her. "I would still expect this person to have been dead for a while. However, you are correct, estimating a time frame will be hard with the other activity that has occurred here. It is possible that the person has only been dead since earlier this year. However, it is equally possible that the person may have died long before that." He drifted closer. "I would like to make a check of the other buildings."

Stephenie gave Kas her silent agreement and he quickly departed. She looked back to the bones on the floor and knelt down to get a closer look. Several of the smaller ones appeared to have been cracked open by an animal. The larger ones showed scratches and bite marks. However, she saw no other bodies in the building and she could not say there were any signs of a large struggle. She wiped her fingers across the floor and noticed a covering of dust that had settled. "What happened here?"

She stood up as Kas returned.

"My review of the buildings was hasty, though there was little of specific interest. However, worth noting is the fact that there are bodies of a number of dogs in the kennels outside."

Stephenie pursed her lips. "So, perhaps a traveler died from something near the end of the traveling season and no one has found the body and taken care of it?" She shook her head. "I'm not thinking that is likely."

"What do you wish to do? It is already dark. Do you want to continue on?"

Stephenie shook her head. "I'm a bit tired from the flying and it was getting cold out there. We can stay here for the night and leave before dawn."

Kas glanced toward the remains and then back to Stephenie. "There is another building almost identical to this one, save for the body. Would you rather stay there?"

"Yes, I think I would."

Chapter 25

The next morning, after a wonderfully warm night and a hot meal, Stephenie and Kas set out, again flying over the hint of the road. The massive mountains in the distance continued to grow closer and closer and at one point, when they were above high ground, Stephenie even thought she could see what appeared to be the distant city of Isa Fields.

Reluctant to be seen from afar, she continued to fly close to the ground, staying just a few feet over the blanket of dirty snow that covered the rolling hills. She stopped regularly to eat and rest, not wanting to reach the city exhausted and vulnerable.

As they moved further toward the northwest, and the mountain range that had grown very close, occasionally she felt a warm breeze cross her path, but then the winds would shift and the icy cold gale would continue to strip heat from her body. The random fluctuations of temperature left her wondering if they might be approaching some of the hot springs Perain had warned them away from. However, they had not come across anything that fit Perain's descriptions as they traveled along the road.

Stephenie crested another hill and came to a stop. The base of the closest peak was now only ten miles away and in the dwindling afternoon light she saw a castle standing proudly on the slope. There was no snow around the grey building and she saw hints of a city in the valley below the castle, though the valley was concealed by the hills between her and the castle.

She dropped from the sky and again sunk her feet into the drifts that covered the road. "I think we should walk the next couple of miles. It might be presumptuous to fly."

Kas, invisible beside her, spoke softly. "I do not detect smoke from any coal fires. I would consider it likely they all use magic like we found in those buildings along the road to heat their homes and cook their food. It would greatly reduce their dependence on outside supplies."

Stephenie grinned. "Henton would have tried to find a way to rip out that stone pit and take it back to Antar with us."

"My people used similar techniques in Arkani. It is unwise to burn all of your air when you are underground."

Stephenie started walking forward. "If they are using this much magic today and in this part of the world, it is not a surprise that they wanted to keep everyone out. I know some of the people we've met in Alkmaar don't appear to worship the gods like the people in Cothel do, but we saw priests like we have at home in the southern parts of Sandven. They are not completely free of the menace even here."

Kas gave her a mental nod of his head. "That is true and a likely explanation for why these people are isolationist."

"Still doesn't explain why we've not seen any signs of people," she said. "Those guardians have obviously seen us and would have reported our presence."

Kas had no reply.

They walked down another small hill and started up the next, which she hoped would be the last one before they reached the city. As they walked, she thought she caught the scent of grass on one of the warm breezes that blew past them. She wondered at that while at the same time she noticed the snow under her feet had thinned and become damper. She sensed Kas' desire to fly out ahead of her, but he kept pace at her side. "Almost to the top of the ridge, Kas," she said. His anticipation flowed over their link and she did not chastise him as he drifted slightly higher.

I am at a loss for words.

Stephenie wanted to demand he share his observations with her, but instead, she pulled extra energy through herself and hastened up the last part of the hill. As she crested the top, the large bowl shaped valley before her came into view. Cut into the side of the mountain, the valley was an island of color in a sea of white. Green grass covered the ground, filling the spaces between pinkish-grey stone buildings. She even saw patches of blue and violet where wild flowers found places to thrive in this arctic world of cold and ice.

At the top of the valley, and on the slope of the mountain, stood the castle Stephenie had seen earlier. The structure looked more like a palace than a fortress. She observed larger clumps of tall trees growing in the grounds around the castle as well as in a handful of groves scattered about the valley. A mix of aromatic scents fill the air and seamed out of place for the surroundings.

Are those fields? Kas asked, his attention pointing her toward the eastern side of the valley.

Stephenie turned her head and looked to the other end of the nearly ten-mile long valley. Long swaths of green grew between walls of stone. With the distance, she could not determine what type of plants might be growing there, and while some sections bent uniformly in the wind, the fields no longer had the appearance of order.

I do not see anyone, Kas said, echoing her thoughts.

"I can only hear the wind," she whispered just above the drone of the cold gale.

She started walking forward again, slowly at first, then her pace took on more purpose. On the downward side of the valley's ridge, the snow became a thin layer of slush and thirty-feet ahead of her marked the border between ice and green growth. A line of obsidian obelisks, standing only three feet above the ground and twenty-feet apart, stretched along the border of the snow.

Scattered about the valley she noticed a number of larger obelisks reaching perhaps forty-feet into the air and placed in a geometric pattern.

"Kas, have you ever seen anything like this?" she asked. Her mind's eye watched as the energy flowed from these stone markers, into the ground and the air. "They are heating the whole of the valley."

He landed next to her, but remained invisible. "Arkani made use of many types of magic. The walls, the lights, the preservative nature of the library. The scale of my people's city inspired awe in any of those who saw it and drove fear into our enemies. These people have done things to adapt their environment to their needs. While it is different in execution, it is not different in general function."

Stephenie continued to look across the large city. With closer study it became obvious that the grass covering the ground had become wild and scattered into places the original designers had not likely intended. She could even see what appeared to be a small tree growing up in the middle of the road a quarter of a mile into the city. "Kas, I can see plenty of those stone guardians, but I have yet to see anyone alive here. The whole place looks abandoned."

He turned his attention to her. "What do you wish to do? You had hoped to find your sire and convince him to leave you and our friends alone. If he is not here, should we return to the others now?"

Stephenie shook her head. "We're here, we'll look around... assuming the guardians continue to let us pass."

"Should I explore ahead?"

She shook her head before he had finished asking. "No. Just because it looks abandoned, doesn't mean it is. Perhaps the red-haired bastard went crazy and killed everyone. Even if he didn't, it's possible he's still here."

Kas nodded his invisible head and Stephenie smiled at him. "Perhaps there is a library here? We're dealing with powerful magic. The others won't expect us back for several days, so as long as it is safe, I think we should explore."

"That is something I can embrace with pleasure. Lead on."

Stephenie stayed on the ground, walking slowly toward the boundary markers. The obsidian stones gave off a subtle, but powerful magic. In addition to warming the ground, the energy fields appeared to offer a limited amount of shielding against the wind, which would help keep the worst of the gales from constantly stealing away the heat. *But it still lets in some air,* she thought remembering how the staff had protected Mertor's high priest.

Kas remained at her side as she moved across the boundary. She let out a small sigh when nothing adverse seemed to happen to either of them.

"It would be obvious," Kas said, "but if maintained year-round, by heating the ground, there would be no snow and ice accumulating, which would allow the darker land to absorb more of the sun's heat, further helping to maintain the warmth, and reduce the energy needed to pass through the stones. The warm ground would warm the air and people would live comfortably." He paused in his movement. "Did I ever tell you about the people who used to build stone buildings that had open cavities beneath stone floors? They would light fires in the opening and that would heat the floor which heated the building."

Stephenie smiled. "What happens when someone lets the fire get out of control?"

"These people were not as primitive as you might expect. However, the old stories of that practice is supposedly what led my ancestors to create magic in their floors that would provide warmth. Since heat rises, it would heat the whole room." Mentally, he motioned to the whole valley. "The people who settled here, simply took the idea to a much grander scale. The work is impressive."

"And based on that and the scaly guard cats," she nodded toward a pair of stone guardians along the cobbled road, "we could be facing a great deal of danger." The guardians' heads shifted ever so slightly to track her movement. She patted the dagger still worn on her hip. "Let's hope this will keep them at bay."

The guardians made no move to follow them, so they continued walking toward the buildings that appeared to start about a half-mile past the boundary markers.

As she walked, she noted the grass growing between the paving stones, indicating few people had traveled over the road in a long time. Even before she reached the first building, she found indications of what might have happened.

She knelt down to examine a section of the road that had melted into a large single mass. "It spread for, what, twenty-feet and takes up half the road. Ten-feet across at the widest part." She rose to her feet. "It's oval in shape and comes to a point here." She walked from where the melt pattern started in the middle of the road and followed it off into the wild grass on her right. She moved carefully, picking her way through the plants. "The rocks in the dirt here appear melt—"

She turned back to face Kas as she moved around a mound of melted stone on the ground. "This appears to be one of the guardians. There's not much left of it."

She felt Kas drift further from the road. "It is hard to tell from the ground, but it appears there is a ragged edge of melt that had spread out in a wider arch." He stopped and hovered over a spot on the ground beyond the melt. "I believe I have found parts of a body."

Stephenie crossed over to where Kas hovered. The ground here was softer with less remnants of melted sand and rock. Below him, she saw a couple of ribs, some longer bones, and a skull. The remains were not bleached white, but had a darker coloration.

"I would assume," Kas said, "that the body had been out here for a while and slowly decomposed. Perhaps birds or other scavengers ate most of the flesh. At least one of the longer bones shows signs of teeth marks."

Stephenie took his word for the description and did not examine the remains any closer. She turned around, slowly taking in the valley that still stretched out below her position. She looked back up at the edge of the ridge, which was beyond the obelisks and remained covered in white. She finally stopped turning and looked toward where Kas hovered. "This country died off twenty-years ago. All contact ended. No word from anyone here." She extended her arm toward the body without looking at it. "This body was left to rot on the ground." She looked back toward the melted road. "The stones liquefied and I'd go with heat on that one. Fire like what I can create."

"This body was not likely caught in the fire that melted the street," Kas challenged.

"Why do you say that?" Stephenie asked.

Kas bowed his head slightly. "Because heat intense enough to have melted the street and the guardian would have caused the bones to have been burned away. These look mostly intact, just exposed to the weather."

Stephenie nodded her head. "Do you know that from your time in Arkani?"

Kas looked away a moment. "Yes. When people initially started to die, we tried to get rid of the bodies by burning them, but the unpleasantness of the effort was too much. After that, we started to store them in the library. And when that effort seemed pointless, many of the others, like myself, were left to rot where we eventually died."

Stephenie looked back at the buildings a short distance away. "In Arkani, you were trapped, sealed in by magic. Here," she said raising her arms, "the people were not bound to this one place."

"What are you suggesting?" Kas asked.

"Someone came through this city and killed most—or probably everyone—who lived here. The man with the red hair had this dagger," she pulled the weapon from the sheath, "which the guardians respond to. Just as they do the staff. That man came from here and he has been seen in the last year, so he didn't die here."

"You think he killed everyone?"

Stephenie bit her lip. The idea terrified her. *If he can do this, then he is beyond reason. He's truly a monster.* She wanted to hope it was something else. Her mother had been cruel and sick, she knew her sire was as well, but mass murder would take the evil to a new level. "Either he survived an attack and left without burying anyone or he did it himself."

Kas moved closer to her. "My Love, we can leave if it will make you more comfortable."

She shook her head. "No. We look around. I need to know what happened here. We need to understand." *I need to know what I am made of.*

They continued along the road, following it into the city of stone buildings and slate roofs. The stonework, while not perfect, showed great care as well as an artistic touch. Decorative beading and creative stone patterns were augmented by blocks with animal carvings and geometric designs. Each building they passed, although not identical, did show similarities, as if a single person or group of persons had constructed every building.

"A city planner," Kas offered. "As we descended into the valley, I observed a consistency in the layout of the streets. Now that we are closer, the nature of these buildings further implies a central control."

Stephenie looked at the building on her right. The front door was missing and the surrounding stone was blackened, though not melted as badly as the street had been. She opened her mind further and allowed her senses to feel the inside of the home. She could not make out all of the objects, but she could feel the general form of a skeleton.

She turned away from the building and continued down the street. Her feet landed on the stone pavers, avoiding the tall grasses and weeds that had taken root in the cracks. After several blocks, they both stopped. The devastation before them was massive. The buildings in this section of the city were toppled over and smashed. Stone pavers in the road were ripped up and tossed about as if something huge flailed about leaving total annihilation in its path.

Stephenie came to a stop in the middle of the destruction. Stone blocks from the buildings lay scattered about, roofs were caved in, and among the debris were decaying bits of everyday life. Tattered bits of cloth, bowls, broken beds, and even faded and ruined paintings.

"What could have done this?" she asked as she crouched down beside a three-foot by five-foot block of stone torn from a building and discarded in the middle of the street. In addition to the cracked and damaged edges of the block, a series of long gouges had been ripped into the otherwise smooth surface of the grey stone. Stephenie spread her fingers apart, but each of the marks were separated by nearly a foot.

"The marks are much bigger and not as uniform as what you saw done to the trap," Kas offered, standing next to her.

She rose to her feet and looked at the long furrows dug into the street, revealing the underlying gravel and soil. The depressions had filled in somewhat by erosion, but they were still several feet deep. "Something fought with a number of the guardians here." She used her head to point out the remains of several stone statues. "Some of these gouges in the ground might have been caused by pushing the guardians back with magic. The others look like large feet clawing up the ground."

"That is a possibility."

"What is it, Kas?" She asked, turning to give him her full attention.

"I am uncertain. But the way the buildings and street are damaged, I would say it looks more like a large animal had struggled and fought a battle."

Stephenie bit her lower lip. "When I was younger, Josh would take me hunting sometimes. I've seen places where the large-eared deer had fought each other during the rut. The ground would be torn up like this, just without the claw gouges." She shook her head. "But what is large enough to do this? It would have to be massive." She did not want to mention what was etched on the dagger at her hip. *They don't exist.*

"My Love, I know of nothing alive that would be this large. It may be possible that there are creatures that live out in the northern reaches of the Endless Sea. Perhaps there are things neither of us have seen that could get this large. But even going back to my grandparents' time, there was nothing in these lands that exceeded the size of a bear." Kas materialized a visible form, "You still have bears, yes?"

Stephenie smiled. It had been a while since Kas had asked her a question about what still existed in the world, though in this case, she knew it was to distract her.

He returned her smile. "The only things larger in my day were some sea creatures, but those never left the water."

"Whatever did this has not been seen by anyone else. We would have heard stories if there was a giant creature destroying cities and killing people. The people in Alkmaar would surely have said something." She looked around again and wondered why such a beautiful city full of life—people simply living their daily lives, should have been attacked. *Why is there always so much death and destruction?*

"What do you wish to do now?" Kas asked. "Do you wish to start searching the buildings?"

"Perhaps, but let's head toward the castle. I would rather start there instead of rooting through a bunch of people's personal items."

They encountered more destruction and remains as they crossed the city. However, Stephenie also observed ornamented gutters, fountains, and various statues that were likely more decorative than protective. There were also empty spots in larger sculptures and fountains where a guardian might have existed. These included open sections of walls.

Once they moved out of the tightly packed buildings and climbed a series of steps, they emerged onto a large open plaza made of white marble with a fountain that stood over thirty-feet high and sixty-feet in diameter. The faint scent of lavender mixed with a cool spray from the fresh water that cascaded down the seven layers of pools and finally collected in a large oval basin that encircled the whole sculpture. The scene was a mix of animals, including horses, large cats, and fish, as well as people lounging about a rocky-forest glade. The fountain and sculpture were made of the same white stone as the plaza.

"Stephenie," Kas said, floating up and into the sculpture, "This is a carving of an elf. You can see the face is ever so slightly more slender and longer than the other figures that appear human. Also, in the elf's face, her eyes are larger, but not overly large."

Stephenie came closer, climbing onto the edge of the large oval pool. She looked up at the pair of figures Kas had pointed out to her. "The stone hair covers her ears. Would they be pointed?"

"Yes. And her stature would be shorter than a human." Kas floated back down to Stephenie. "It is very interesting to see such a depiction so prominently displayed here. I noticed several other elves in the sculpture. Although Dalar supported a small faction of elves in my time, many people were at odds with them. For instance, your people, or more correctly your ancestors, were actively trying to destroy them or at least drive them into the Rim Mountains after the end of the Elvin Wars."

"So why have them here? Could an elf do the damage we saw here?"

Kas shook his head. "Elves are more powerful than most humans. They can pull more energy and with their longer lifespans, they tend to have far more skill. As I understood it, they were also more sensitive to magic. Perhaps having abilities similar to your being able to visualize the energy fields. Not in every elf of course, but on average they had a greater command of power than humans. However, the amount of destruction here would require a sizable number of elves."

Stephenie stepped down from the fountain and looked up the hundred yard wide stairs at the far side of the plaza. The stairs climbed forty-feet to a courtyard and the front of the castle. Even from where she stood, she could see numerous guardians on and around the castle. "I've not heard of any elves living along the World's Backbone, but that doesn't mean it isn't possible."

"This fountain would lead me to believe the elves were friendly with the humans here, if there are indeed elves in this part of the world."

Stephenie started walking toward the stairs. "Unless they had a falling out."

She felt Kas' silent doubt and she could not say he was incorrect. The events had occurred two decades earlier. *And the red-haired man was never described as an elf.* She bit her lip as she started up the stairs. She hated the man who had raped her mother and caused so much pain and death in his attempts to kill her. She knew it colored her opinion, but perhaps it was too soon to jump to the conclusion that he had been responsible for these deaths. *Perhaps he simply came here after everyone was already dead. I don't want to have the blood of someone who could do this in me.*

"Stephenie, your mind has grown very quiet. Are you okay?"

She turned and smiled at Kas. "Just thinking terrible thoughts and didn't want to share them." When she reached the top of the steps, she stopped to look around the courtyard. Trees and stone planters decorated the area around the castle. There was no curtain wall, no protective moat, just a massive building with windows and graceful walls.

Another large set of stairs led up to a pair of double doors that were thirty-feet high and twenty-feet wide. One of the doors remained closed while the other was knocked off the upper hinges and now lay half in and half out of the doorway. Stephenie's initial opinion was that the door was blown outward from the inside.

Aside from the door, she could not see any other damage to the castle's exterior. There were fragments of guardians, but the ground and building looked intact.

She narrowed her focus and moved closer to the castle. "I just noticed the outer walls are a single, solid piece of stone...and are filled with magic. I can see the energy flowing into the building." She looked down at her feet. "Even the courtyard. It is preventing me from seeing through the walls to the inside."

"Is the energy in the courtyard separate from what is heating the land?"

Stephenie looked at the patterns she saw and slowly nodded her head. "There is so much energy flying around it is easy to get distracted, but yes, it is almost like there is a subtle protection field in the stone." She looked up at the slate roof tiles that hung more than seventy-feet over her head. "Even the roof is drawing power. The whole damn castle is magic."

"What of the guardians?"

Stephenie nodded her head. "I count at least twenty-five that I can see from here. All of them look active."

"And none of them have reacted to our presence, even though I am now emitting a visible appearance."

Stephenie chuckled. "Unless they are waiting to spring a trap on us." She grew serious. "I didn't have the heart to dig through anyone's remains, but we might look to see if they carried anything to mark them as belonging to the valley."

"That is a wise suggestion. If tokens are what identifies residents, we could potentially bring the others here. The more I see, the more I suspect it is unlikely that your sire continues to reside here."

Stephenie took a deep breath. "Let's go inside and confirm it before we make that assumption." Without any further hesitation, she started up the steps and climbed over the door that had been partially torn off its hinges.

Chapter 26

The main entrance hall of the castle rose forty-feet over their heads. Crystal chandeliers shaped like a swarm of flying lizards hung down from the vaulted ceiling. Each taloned foot held a faintly glowing stone. High above the lights, the ceiling was a wash of color. Complex geometric designs swirled over the arched stone. The vivid reds and blues and greens glowed high above them, casting the room in eerie shadows. Stephenie tried to like the pattern, but the colors did not seem to blend together with a precise harmony.

The floor was a patchwork of marble under the remains of multiple shattered guardians. At first Stephenie thought the inlaid colors were more random swirls, but as she took in more of the vast space, she realized the darker stone formed a large word that spanned the entire eighty-foot length of the hall. "It has the mark," Stephenie whispered to Kas, taking in and trying to memorize the strokes laid out in stone.

"Perhaps a name?" Kas offered, still remaining at Stephenie's side.

She nodded her head. *A name,* she thought to herself. She looked over to the walls that at one time were covered in massive tapestries, most of which were now crumpled on the floor. The three that still hung from their rods showed signs of being burned.

"Kas, can you feel the energy here? The floor, the walls, the ceiling. The whole thing feels like it is alive. I can almost sense an intelligence."

Kas slowly shook his head. "I can sense a lot of potential; however, I have not sensed an intelligence. Nor am I able to see through the interior walls. The protection the outer walls have appears to carry on to the inside of the castle as well."

"The intelligence feels subtle," she said as she continued to look around, letting her mind's eye examine the building. She did not think the stone was actually so dense as to block her senses, but it was the field inside the walls.

"Oh my," she said as she looked at the ceiling again. Now paying attention to the fields as well as the color, the ceiling took on a whole new perspective. Instead of just a random pattern, a scene emerged of a spellbinding landscape filled with mountains and trees and a massive flying beast gliding effortlessly through the air. "Can you see this?" Stephenie asked, sharing her vision of the ceiling with Kas.

It is amazing. The artistry of the fields and color from the ceiling combining. He turned to face her. *This was only meant to be seen by someone with your abilities.*

She loosened her coat, suddenly feeling warm. The air temperature inside the building felt like a mild spring evening in Cothel, mixed with the energy she had drawn in and held, she was now sweating. "We should keep moving."

She turned toward the far end of the hall and the pair of massive closed double doors covered in gold; across both doors was emblazoned a large raised image of Ista's crest with a dragon prowling around the back side of the crest, leaving only its head and tail visible.

To her left and right, midway along the walls, a pair of smaller doors stood opposite each other. The smaller doors appeared utilitarian to her. *The ones at the far end demonstrate power.* "Let's see where the big ones lead," Stephenie said, walking carefully over the fine rubble and the layer of dust that had accumulated. "Perhaps there is a library or some clues in the offices beyond the public spaces."

She paused at the doors. She could not hear any sounds coming from inside the castle and while she could sense the nearly half an inch of gold that covered each of the two ten-foot tall and five-foot wide doors, she could not see through the raised surface.

"I am growing uncomfortable with all the dragon symbolism," Kas said. "Dragons have been gone from this world for a very long time. There was no evidence of them for hundreds of years before even I was born." He looked at Stephenie. "However, because of the fear and apprehension that lingered long after they were gone, few people ever overcame the visceral reluctance to decorate anything with an image of a dragon. When dragons did live, they were fearsome creatures that no one wanted to anger."

Stephenie's immediate thoughts turned to the tapestries that had hung in the Square Keep of Antar castle until her mother had stolen them. One of them depicted the famous image of Lord Devon riding a dragon. Her great hall had even been decorated with a ridge line of copper dragons and horses. *Something else that changed over time. I wonder if Josh's workers have finished the repairs on the great hall yet.*

She turned to Kas. "Something very large appeared to have destroyed the city out there. Do you think it could be something like a dragon?"

Kas shook his head. "It would be impossible. They are all gone." He turned to her and Stephenie could feel his unease. "If this is the home of a dragon, then we are as good as dead."

Stephenie opened her senses, but no matter how hard she tried, she could feel nothing through the walls. She turned to Kas. "It was people that built Arkani, correct? People?"

Kas nodded his head. "Yes. Humans and elves worked together to build it. Many powerful masters of their skills formed the stone and crafted the magic of the city."

She let out the breath she was holding. "Then people, or perhaps elves," she added with a tilt of her head, "could have created all of this as well."

Kas bowed his head to her. "Based on the skills present during my life, yes. I have not seen anything here we could not have built."

She hoped he could not sense the slight trembling of her arms, but she knew the hope was in vain. "We can't find out the truth just standing here." She put her hands to the right-hand door and pushed. The massive door moved with an ease that could only come from magic. On the other side, lights spread across the ceiling came alive, shining down a brilliant radiance that fully illuminated a throne room. White stone, with blue and green accents covered most surfaces. The walls lined with fluted columns reached up to the ceiling twenty feet over their heads. A dais covered the width of the far wall. The tapestries that once covered the wall behind it were shredded and only fragments hung from the rods that had held them. A small door centered in the wall stood partially ajar. Two stone guardians sat on either side of the door while other guardians lay smashed and scattered about the room. A gold throne, appeared to have been tossed to the side and lay crumpled and broken against the left wall.

"I get the feeling someone was very angry," Kas said.

Stephenie glanced at the right-hand wall. A section of the floor and wall showed signs of a fire, but neither had melted as the road outside had. In the middle of the burned section were fragments of bones. "I still don't feel anyone. If someone lives here, they would have buried these people."

She continued across the forty-foot long room, stepped onto the dais, and approached the door. The two stone guardians did not change positions, but Stephenie felt their eyes, or more correctly, their magic, watching her closely.

She reached out and touched the handle of the door, waiting to see if the large stone cats with wings would react. Neither did. Slowly she pushed the door open and then gasped at the same time Kas swore.

The room on the other side of the door was already lit. The square room spanned forty-feet on each wall, but the only thing Stephenie saw was the giant lizard lying dead on the floor.

"This is not possible," Kas said as he followed Stephenie into the room.

She moved around the creature, whose headless neck pointed in her direction. From the end of its severed neck to the tip of its tail, she guessed it to be at least thirty-feet long. The body and wings were massive, though heavily decayed. Large bluish-grey scales covered the whole body, and through the dust on the body, the scales still held a trace of iridescence.

Stephenie felt her chest tighten and it became hard for her to breathe as she slowly moved around the creature. She observed numerous cuts and gashes throughout the dried and decayed skin and scales. On the far side of the corpse, tossed against a blackened wall, lay the charred head. Horns and long rows of sharp teeth protruded from the skull giving it an eerie, angry appearance.

She slowly turned to take in the rest of the room. Everything was smashed, burned, and destroyed. Below her feet, shallow gouges in the stone floor spoke of a terrible fight that had destroyed the room. "Like two cats fighting," Stephenie mumbled as she noticed more scrapes and scratches in the walls and even the ceiling.

She stepped over what at one time might have been part of a desk. The smashed bodies of multiple guardians mixed into the mundane debris of chairs and tables. She stopped next to the half-foot long claws on the dragon's front hands.

"This is not possible," Kas repeated.

Stephenie closed her eyes to fight back tears that threatened. "The gouges dug into to the trap..." she choked out. "What am I? My skin gets that tone when I push too much energy. I've breathed fire. My abilities constantly surprise you. What am I?"

Kas hovered a few feet away from her. "This is not possible. Dragons..."

Stephenie wiped away the tears with her arm. "We have one sitting right here!" Her voice had turned cold as she pointed at the body. "This thing's not been dead thousands of years. It's been dead... twenty."

"Stephenie, you do not understand the implications. Only a dragon can kill another dragon."

She glared at Kas. "I understand that implication just fine. What of the more important one?" Her body trembled. "It means I'm not human. It..." She turned her head to indicate the three normal doors in the room. "How did this damn thing get in here?"

Kas said nothing for several moments. "I do not know much, but dragons are reported to be creatures of magic. They were—are—the ultimate predator. Cunning. Intelligent. Ancient." He turned back to Stephenie and bowed his head. "They could change form." He raised his hands. "I am at a loss. None of it makes sense. Why would they all pretend to have been killed or to have left our world?"

Stephenie took a deep breath. "Ista was not my sire's land. Whoever lived here...whoever that was," she pointed to the body. "They took pride in this city. They built something of beauty. They would not have run away if they had killed an invader. But the red-haired man..." she shook her head. "He doesn't seem to me to be someone who would build this place; someone who would care."

"Stephenie—"

"What kind of monster am I, Kas? I've felt a dark rage boiling up in me. With my power, I could kill...I've felt the fear people have of me." She closed her eyes. "I'm not...who would want me?"

She felt Kas move next to her. His voice lost the panic she had felt from him a moment earlier. "Stephenie, you are who you are. You are not defined by this. You are good."

She opened her eyes and looked at him. "I'm not human. My mother was, but..." She pointed at the decayed body again.

Kas smiled at her. "I am hardly an expert on dragons. I know stories and exaggerations, not facts. Your heritage, whatever it may be, does not matter to me. I have no body, so what am I?" He put a translucent hand on her shoulder. "In my time, while not common, we had people who shared human and elf ancestry. Look into my thoughts. Please know that I will not leave you over this. I do not think less of you."

Stephenie felt his concern and love for her and she sobbed as tears streamed down her face. She knew he would not leave her. "I'm a fool to worry about losing you." She wiped the tears falling from her eyes. "I just don't know what to do about this."

"This is a shock to me as well." Kas tried to smile, but his gaze went to the blackened head of the dragon and repeated. "This is not supposed to be possible. The implications are staggering."

Stephenie turned to follow his gaze. The horn-covered head was three-feet wide and more than six-feet long. "It must have been terrifying to be around it."

Kas shrugged. "Dragons were feared when they lived, but at the same time, there are stories that indicate at least some dragons and humans and elves cooperated; that even friendships existed. I had always thought those to be tales. However, the fact that he is here and there was a city of humans, and perhaps elves, living near him, would indicate that part of those stories might have been true."

"Or were they his slaves? They were not allowed to leave, if you believe some of what we've heard."

Kas shrugged. "It may be hard to say. With the guardians, the dragon could have kept the people in-line. However, if that was the case, I would expect that at some point, eventually someone would successfully escape and leak news of what was happening here. If there was no knowledge of the truth, perhaps the people desired to live here."

Stephenie sighed. She felt utterly exhausted. She needed time to think. Time to decide what she was going to do. "It was starting to grow dark when we arrived. It's got to be full night by now. Do we want to stay in the castle, go back into the town, or camp out in the snow?"

Kas shrugged. "They are about the same for me. What is your preference?"

She was glad Kas allowed her to change the subject. "Let's look around the castle's upper rooms. Perhaps there is a guest room we can use. I'd prefer not to have to set up the tent."

The castle was deceptively large because the magically reinforced walls did not need to be as thick as normal castle walls. This allowed for more rooms on each floor, though the extra space meant more remains. As Stephenie and Kas made their way through a number of rooms, they encountered skeletons mixed with bits of dried flesh and clothing. In some places, fabrics and wood structures were burned, others smashed and overturned. However, valuables, including coins and jewelry, were left where they had fallen.

The trail of death, years old, had a methodical feel, as if whoever had destroyed the dragon had then move through the rest of the building searching for people who had hoped to hide. Rooms where there were no bodies did not appear to have any disturbance. The memory of her own relentless search through the keep the priests of Mertor had called home filled her thoughts. *But I didn't kill everyone. I drove people away and only fought those that tried to kill me.*

At first, Stephenie had avoided the remains, but as she moved through the rooms, she found the idea of leaving them scattered and forgotten too much. When they left Ranis Valley, she could not forget that she had shown the dead the same level of disregard as the killer who had destroyed these people. She wondered if her, more limited and perhaps more justified, killing spree would look the same to someone else in twenty years.

Not wanting to think about that, she grabbed sheets, blankets, tapestries, or anything that was handy, and carefully wrapped the bones. *If there is time, one day I will bury these people and even go back and bury those damn priests.*

She only managed to tend to two dozen bodies before she found the effort more taxing than she had strength to handle. She returned to one of the destruction-free bedrooms and quickly climbed into bed. But even then, Stephenie had a hard time falling asleep. A sense of loneliness and remorse permeated her very being. The weight of unspecified loss felt almost crushing, even with Kas' presence within touching distance.

Sleep eventually came, but too much of the day and the imagined scenes of death and destruction filled her mind. She never fully awoke during the night, but in her dreams, she remembered wondering if she might have been better off sleeping out in the snow fields.

Chapter 27

"Henton," Ryia pleaded, actually on her knees. "We've sat here doing nothing for two days and nights, let's do something. Please."

"We have done things and will do more. For instance, the dogs need to be watered and fed." Henton knew both Ryia's and Douglas' restless energy had built to a dangerous level. After weeks of hard traveling, two days of sitting mostly idle and worrying about Stephenie and Kas were taking a toll on all of them. Feeling a little mercy for Ryia's desire to be active, he pursed his lips. "What do you have in mind?"

The smile that blossomed on Ryia's face was contagious. She jumped to her feet. "We can take the staff out and try blowing up chunks of ice. The guardians moved away from the border yesterday morning, so it should be perfectly safe. I wonder if we could blast a hole in the ice and find sea water. We could..."

"We don't want to spook the dogs," Henton said. "A bunch of thunder and lightning is going to be heard for a long ways."

"And it's cold outside," Douglas complained.

Ryia ignored Douglas. "We can go down to the shore. It's almost half a mile and there are rocks and snow dunes to help shield the noise. Plus, it's not like there is anyone around that'll hear." She grinned. "I'll even let you go first and then give Douglas a go." She tossed the staff at him, the dirty blanket still wrapped tightly around it.

Henton glanced at Douglas hoping to get support, but the chance to have a go with the staff had piqued Douglas' interest. Henton hefted the weapon. He had carried it a few times and he could feel the staff at the edges of his mind. *At least I don't have to have magic to use you,* he told it. "Fine. We can blow up some ice. But just a couple each, then we need to take care of the dogs and wait quietly for Steph to come back."

Douglas shrugged. "Even assuming just one day there and one day back, I'd guess she'll spend at least two or three days in the city. And if it takes a couple days for her to fly all the way there, then we might be here five or six more days before we see her again."

Henton nodded his head. None of them wanted to consider a possibility where Stephenie's father would not let her come back at all, so it would not be said. "Okay, but we don't want to destroy too much." Ryia's grin told him she was already planning to try to extend their time with the staff, but he intended to keep them all to two shots each. *Three,* he amended, *but that's all. Perhaps four shots.*

They bundled up in their clothing and went out into the cold. The wind blew from the northeast and they had to walk directly into it, the loose snow and cold burning any exposed skin. But the sun was high in the clear sky and warmed their dark clothing. Ryia ran out ahead as Henton walked next to Douglas. "You've been quiet these last couple of days."

Douglas shrugged. "Just been thinking."

"Anything specific?"

"Quite a few things actually."

"Like?"

"What will happen if Steph doesn't come back? What will happen if she does? What will she do if she can't find a way to rebuild Kas' body? What will happen if she does?"

Henton chuckled; it did not surprise him that Douglas would be the first to break their mutually unspoken agreement of silence. "Yeah, just the small things."

Douglas nodded his head. "I'll stay with her as long as she wants or needs me, but how much longer is that going to be?" Douglas waved to Ryia, who was urging them to hurry, making her more frustrated by his perceived lack of understanding her desire. "I was serious about becoming a tailor."

Henton curled his lips into his mouth to moisten them and protect them from the wind. He put his right hand under his arm, pulled off the mitten he was wearing, and removed the small pouch of ointment from his shoulder bag. "I don't have an answer for you." He put some ointment on his fingers and then rubbed it on his lips before putting it away and putting his mitten back on. "I don't know where all this will take us."

"What about Ryia? You two worked things out?"

With the size and closeness of their group, secrets did not remain so for long. "She's too young for me, Douglas. She'd be better with someone her own age. Someone with magic."

Douglas raised his hands. "None of my business. I just wonder if those are good reasons or just excuses to keep you from moving on."

Henton did not want to have this conversation with Douglas. The group's dynamic was already difficult enough some days, Kas had his ideas of what he thought Henton should do and now Douglas wanted to add more.

He looked up as Ryia froze in place and suddenly turned toward the frozen sea, which was now only thirty-yards away. Suddenly she cried out as the white snow around her exploded into a shower of red. Henton could not tell exactly what happened, but Ryia collapsed to the ground.

The staff activated on its own, building a shimmering field around him and Douglas. Henton felt, through the staff, two people moving out from behind cover near the shore.

Henton grabbed Douglas' arm and held him close as the sphere shimmered around them again.

"She's hurt!"

Henton did not respond to Douglas. He leveled the staff at the closer of the two people and commanded the staff to unleash lightning. The weapon throbbed as energy erupted from the end and flashed across the thirty-yards to the man. The blinding energy crackled around him, but the man stayed on his feet.

"She's bleeding out!"

Henton commanded the staff to release lightning again and a third time as he continued toward Ryia. "You're no use to her dead," Henton swore as snow and ice smashed into the sphere around them. Still sensing the two people, Henton unleashed more lightning in a constant stream of energy. The blanket around the staff burst into flames, but he did not relent until he sensed the man had fallen.

The woman screamed something, but started moving away. Henton increased his speed, closing in on Ryia. The cloud of snow that had been kicked into the air was blown clear by the wind and he unleashed more attacks on the woman who was running toward the jagged shore. Lightning struck her in the back. She spun around and flung rocks and boulders at him. He flinched as the debris bounced off the energy field the staff generated around them.

Douglas dropped down next to Ryia and the massive pool of blood that covered the snow. Rage burned in Henton as hot as the staff, which was now causing his gloves to smoke. He commanded the staff to continue and blinding light arced through the air, striking the woman again and again. Like her companion, initially she deflected the lightning, sending it into the ground or sky, but suddenly she became overwhelmed and the full force of the staff's power blew a hole into her chest. Henton did not relent until her head had blackened and she had fallen to the rocky ground, which had become exposed where the heat from the lightning melted the snow.

"Help me!" Douglas shouted from behind him and Henton realized he had moved several feet ahead of Ryia and Douglas.

Henton could sense the two assailants were dead. He used the staff to try to feel for others, but he could sense no one else nearby. He dropped the staff, which had almost completely burned through the blanket. It landed with a hiss in the snow, immediately melting and sinking into the ice.

He rushed to Ryia's side. Her right arm was gone at the elbow, bloody strands of flesh and bone were scattered about. Her hand lay six feet away, free of her mitten.

"I need help!" Douglas shouted again.

Henton came back to himself. He had dealt with severe injuries and the loss of limbs before. Ripping off his own smoldering mittens, he shed his coat and drew his dagger. Douglas had already cut away Ryia's coat and exposed the bleeding stump of her arm.

Moving recklessly fast, he cut a strip of material from his shirt and tossed it to Douglas. Douglas immediately wrapped the material around her arm and cinched it tight. Henton cut off more strips and then pulled his outer shirt off, leaving the two under-layers on to protect himself from the biting wind. He cut the shirt into pieces, balling up a section of the cleanest material to jam against the shredded stump on her arm.

He closed his eyes as he pulled at the ragged strips of skin and muscle that were still attached. Cutting quickly, he removed the remnants and tossed them aside. Douglas wrapped a larger piece of cloth over the wadded mass already darkening with blood. He pulled the ends up over what was left of her arm and Henton tied it down tightly with more strips of his shirt.

"She's still breathing," Douglas said. "How could they do that to her?"

Henton looked at Ryia's face. All color had left it save for the specks of blood and flesh that had sprayed across it. He wanted to wake her, but that might just make her panic. He glanced to the north and the thick clouds moving toward them and then looked toward the camp. "Get the sleds ready. We're heading to Alkmaar now. Leave whatever is not necessary for us to get back."

Douglas' eyes questioned for a moment, then he jumped to his feet and started running back toward the camp. Henton watched him for a moment, then quickly grabbed his coat and mittens from the snow. The wind had already started to make him shiver. "Damn it. Damn it. Damn it." He picked up the staff. The weapon had melted its way a foot through the snow and ice until it had hit the rocky ground. He knocked off the last remnants of the blanket and went to Ryia's side. "I promise. I'll get you to the healer in time. Just hang in there. You're strong. Use your powers to heal yourself." He knelt down and very carefully lifted her in his arms while still holding onto the staff. He then ran back toward the camp as fast as he could carry her, keeping the stump of her arm against him to protect it.

*　　*　　*　　*　　*

Islet shivered on the back of her horse. Talbit shivered underneath Islet. The howling wind and blinding snow had reduced their progress to a crawl and the bitter and endless cold made Islet willing to let Yreka kill her.

Every part of Islet's body ached and she knew she would never be warm ever again. There would not be enough wood and coal in the world to build a fire large enough or hot enough to thaw out her hands and toes. The only good thought was that their slow pace meant Stephenie was getting further and further away from them and that might allow her to escape from Yreka. Only, she had no idea where they were or how many days had passed since they were captured.

Islet heard Yreka's curse as the wind blew the Senzar's words to her. She wanted to laugh, but her lips were so cracked and split that it would only make her face bleed.

Suddenly, Yreka turned her horse and was in Islet's face. "Laugh all you want, when I spoke with my people this morning, they were watching your friends. It seems your darling sister has left them all alone at the border for the last two days. Perhaps tonight I should have them captured and brought south to join us."

Islet's face burned from the wind, but she refused to shield it in order that she could meet Yreka's eyes with her unmasked hatred. "You do that and Steph will find your people and kill them."

"Don't get smug with your thoughts girl. I'm not nearly half as cold as you and your friends are. If you make me angry, I'll simply push on through this storm and let you lose a few fingers and toes as we've been warned will happen." Yreka nodded her head. "Yes, I can feel your willingness to stop in this town. I should make you give me something in payment."

"You've already taken my dignity and hope," Islet spit out, tasting the blood on her lips from even those couple sentences.

"Your dignity yes, but I think not all of your hope. I know you still long for Stephenie to save you. A hope I will see dashed."

Sir Walter pushed his horse forward and put a protective hand on Islet's arm. "Leave her alone. If you want to torment someone, abuse me."

Yreka rolled her eyes. "Oh, will you just get over your guilt and your perceived betrayal of her brother and just bed her already. You both want it and it's not like you will live to see your King again to ask for permission to court her, so you should try to get some pleasure out of your last days." Yreka turned to Werha. "Arrange for a place at whatever inn they have here, I won't have the horses freeze in the storm."

Chapter 28

Stephenie pushed herself out of the musty bed despite how thick her head felt. Throughout the night, she had dreamed about being watched, but the dreams never rose to a level that woken her. Now even the memory of them was fading. "Kas," she called aloud as her mind reached out to find him.

"I am here," he replied, luminescing near the door. "I looked around some more while you slept." He placed his hand against the wall. "I have discovered that I am unable to pass through any of the castle structures that contain the field that is blocking our ability to sense through them." He glanced toward her pack after her stomach growled. "You should eat."

She nodded her head and her pack flew to her hand. "Find anything interesting in your searches? Any troves of knowledge this dragon left? Anything that would help us rebuild a body for you or explain why my sire attacked this place?"

He shrugged. "There are many sections of the castle that are mundane. Kitchens, bedrooms, store rooms, and their like. Those all appeared to be similar to those in other castles or manor houses we have visited. The vast majority of those areas had no blocking field and I could pass through the walls and doors. In some of the protected areas, I found a handful of doors that I was able to open or they were already open. However, there are still many places I could not enter." He drifted toward her. "I did find a series of offices with papers and books; however, those offices had an air of administrative planning and tracking. They would not likely yield information specific to rebuilding my body. They may offer other explanations, though it may be a long and tedious process to search through mundane papers." He grinned. "However, I did find a library."

Stephenie chewed the dried meat in her mouth faster. *You bastard,* she thought at him, matching his playful tone. *You wait to tell me that last when I'm starting to think there might not be much here. Did you look through the books?*

"You are aware that even in your mental communication there is a sense of your chewing, yes?"

Stephenie opened her mouth to chew loudly.

Kas smiled as he drifted to a chest of drawers that sat against the wall. He opened the top drawer and lifted out an undergarment, which he dropped back into place before turning back toward her. "I did look through some of the books. They appeared to be written in a number of languages. Including the language you were learning from the traps."

She swallowed. "I love libraries."

"They are one of the best things in life," Kas agreed. "What do you want to do first? There are rooms on the first floor we did not examine and many other doors that I found were locked. There is also the library and the administrative offices."

Stephenie scratched at her scalp and wrinkled her nose at the odor coming from her body. Between driving the dog sleds and flying from the border, she had sweated heavily several times since she had last bathed. "I need to finish eating, get cleaned up, perhaps check out the bathing room we saw, and change into something cleaner. Then let's go back and examine the throne room and the dragon. If we don't find anything there, we'll go to the library."

Kas nodded his head. They had found a communal bathing room on the floor below them. "It is not a certainty; however, based upon the magic lights, heated floors, and fire-less cooking surfaces, I would expect the water there may be heated. If you would like, I could try to find you some fresh clothing while you clean up."

Stephenie glanced around the room. The personal affects that were present indicated a woman of some standing had been in this room before her. Stephenie shook her head. "I don't want to steal from the dead. The woman's bones are likely somewhere in the castle."

*   *   *   *   *

The bath chamber was a large room with several stone tubs positioned around the edge of the room, all facing inward. The flat bottom tubs sat directly on the stone floor. The front and back of the two-foot tall tubs flared outward to give the bather a softer angle to lounge against. Pipes dropped from the ceiling and ended just above the rolled lip of the tubs. All the stone in the room radiated energy and was warm to the touch.

"I still cannot get over a communal bath," Stephenie said. "There's got to be a dozen tubs in here, all in plain sight of each other."

"I thought it a touch unusual myself." He drifted ahead of her. "Do not forget the tub against the far wall. It is large enough to hold ten people."

Stephenie raised her left eyebrow at the playful thoughts Kas let slip. "I never got the idea you were into that," she teased. Setting down her gear, she went to the closest tub and looked inside. A stone stopper sat next to an opening that drained into the floor. She walked around to the end where two taps extended from the metal pipes. She turned the lever and greenish water splashed out of the pipe to strike the back of the off-white tub. She frowned at the coppery odor.

Kas came to her side. "I imagine it has been sitting for a while."

Stephenie nodded her head. She itched, but smelling of copper would not be an improvement. "If all the water in the city is like this, I may need to go back out to the snow fields and melt some ice to have something to drink."

"You might let the water run for a while. Perhaps it will clear. The fountain in the courtyard did not have the appearance of contamination."

Stephenie looked at the water and watched it run down the drain at the other end of the tub. "Perhaps." She turned away and went back to her pack. "I'm guessing there is a cistern somewhere in the castle that collected rain or snow. If it's been sitting for twenty years, it might all need to be drained. Let's go check out the lower floors again. I'll let this run."

*   *   *   *   *

They went back to the ground level and examined the throne room in more detail. The doors on the side walls led to grand hallways, which opened on a large dining room, a sitting room, a game room, servant's quarters, and guest rooms. From the room with the dragon's body, Stephenie used her power to force open the door on the left wall and they found a series of private rooms. The first was a sitting room with numerous portraits hanging on the walls. A life sized image of a man dressed in blue with a chiseled chin and haunting eyes hung prominently in the center of one wall. Slightly smaller images of three other people filled the wall on either side of the main painting. One painting depicted a woman in her thirties laughing at something only she could see. Another painting portrayed the same woman falling backwards through what appeared to be clouds, her hair and clothing blowing as she fell. Her face filled with pleasure, not fear. A third painting with the woman had her standing next to a beautiful dragon with blue-grey scales.

Stephenie could not help but stare into the eyes of the dragon. The creature held beauty and power in its gaze. Its leathery wings were folded back against its muscular body, not unlike the wings of the stone guardians. *Is that the kind of blood that beats in me?* She continued to look into the creature's face. It was not a face that held malice. *Not that one's blood. No, I've got the blood of the monster that killed that one and everyone else here. There is no other possibility. The red-haired man did this.*

"Stephenie?"

She broke free of her thoughts and turned to the other paintings, ignoring Kas' silent plea for her to reveal her thoughts. Other paintings on the wall were of two men in their twenties. Both men showed a remarkable resemblance to the central man. Each image placing the men next to the woman and depicting scenes scattered across the world. One was on top of a snow covered mountain. Another showed a warm sea. Two other images showed a sandy location with red mountains in the distance.

"It's the same man," Stephenie said after a moment. "His eyes." She reached out and touched the canvas. "The height is different, the cheek bones don't match, and tone of their skin changes, but the eyes are the same. As are their expressions." She turned to look at the larger one containing the woman. "The look on her face is the same in each of them. She loves the man...dragon. Not as a mother, but as something far more intimate." Stephenie met Kas' glowing eyes. "That is what the dragon looked like? Could he have had so many faces?"

Kas drifted closer and slowly nodded his head. "I believe you are correct, they are all the same being." He reached out and touched his hand to her arm. "Stephenie, dragons are magic. There are many stories of them transforming. I had never considered it before, but it is not surprising that they might choose many different forms."

Stephenie wiped away the coating of dust that had amassed on the frame. "There are dates here. And names. Carved into the wood."

"I cannot read the language," Kas said.

Stephenie bit her lip. "I have no way to translate the names. But the dates, this one in the middle says three thousand six hundred and twenty." She moved from picture to picture checking the dates. She stopped at one near the corner of the wall. It showed an image of the woman looking older. "This one is three thousand nine hundred and two." She turned to Kas. "If I read these correctly, the woman had to be over three hundred years older here than in that one."

"I cannot confirm or deny your estimations."

Stephenie looked to the opposite wall. It held many smaller portraits and showed many different people. She hurried over and quickly looked at the faces, but none of those people appeared to be images of the two people on the first wall. She crossed the sitting room and examined the frames of the smaller paintings. "I hope I am reading these correctly. I think this says four, six, two, one." She turned back to Kas. "How long do dragons live?"

Kas shrugged. "They had been gone for hundreds of years before I was born. I never met a person who had direct knowledge of them. At least not that I am aware of." He raised an arm toward the dead dragon. "Though, my world view has taken a violent shift."

She exhaled. "Why did this happen to me? I just wanted to be a normal person. I grew up thinking I was cursed with Elrin's evil. This is worse. At least before I knew what I was. Now...am I human or a monster?"

Kas moved to stand in front of her. "I am not going to leave you, regardless of your sire. I do not believe the others would either."

"I know," she said slowly. "It is just a lot to take in." She turned to the door on the wall that stood opposite the one they entered through. After a moment, she spoke, "Let's see what else is here."

The next room was a small office. Her eyes cleared slightly at the sight of the bookshelves that lined one wall. Display cases, globes, and maps covered the other walls. Another door went further into the castle; through that open door, Stephenie saw a bedroom. She did not enter. Instead, she walked around a table on one side of the office. A miniature of the city covered the surface. She examined the intricately carved details. There even was a clear substance mimicking the water of the fountain in front of the castle. The fields around the edge of the city had thousands of tiny wires sticking up to represent some type of grain.

After she took in the whole of the city, she moved to the ornate desk that sat in front of the bookshelves. Papers lay stacked on the top as though the owner would shortly return.

She sat down at the desk and looked at what was spread over the surface. The flowing handwriting that filled the finely crafted sheet of paper looked mundane to her. *This might have been written by a dragon.* She looked down at the chair she sat in, *I am sitting where a dragon might have sat.* She sighed. *Though, everywhere I ever sat may be where a dragon—or a half-breed—sat.*

She pushed the thoughts from her mind and examined the words on the paper. The markings were familiar, but it took a moment to work out the scripted letters. She chuckled. "It is a letter telling someone—can't put sounds to the name—they are invited to dinner." She struggled with several symbols. "I am guessing it is a day of the week, but don't know. It was signed with the same mark that is on the entrance hall floor."

"The Dragon," Kas said. "I cannot imagine anyone else being lord of this land. It would explain the abundance of magical artifacts."

She looked up at him. "The numbers on those frames. Do those numbers correspond to any calendar you know of?"

Kas shook his head. "We do not have any frame of reference to know how they relate to Cothel's current calendar, which from what you said, tracks back to when your country was formed."

"Well, legend says four hundred and thirty six years ago, the people in my part of the world overthrew their overlords and took control of the lands. So it is a starting point for a number of countries." She looked back to the stacks of paper. There were no obvious dates on the documents. "Of course, most people don't care about the actual year. They just count season to season. It's only scholars and people who want to make sure taxes are collected that really care."

Kas laughed. "That was even partially true in my day, though I think a few more people of my era paid attention to the dates." He settled so that he appeared to sit on the edge of the desk. "How long do you plan to stay here before returning to the others?"

Stephenie set aside what appeared to be a ledger tracking supplies. "A day or two more. I can fly back in one day if I push it. I went slow on the way here because I didn't know what to expect." She glanced behind her. "This is likely his personal library. I would like to go through it, but I doubt we will find what I want to know here. If he was as powerful as you think—and based on what we've seen, I would agree—than there would be little need for him to write down what I want to find." She pulled open a drawer to find several ink wells, pens, and blank paper. "What did the other library look like? Did it have more books than this? Did it look like a personal library or one that people visiting the castle might use?"

"It held at least ten times the number of books and based on where it is located in the castle, I would expect its purpose is to be used by other residents of the castle. It is located on the top floor."

"Okay. We'll look through the rest of these rooms here, then check out that library. There might also be another library in the city. We should look for that."

"Even if you stayed here for a year, I do not think you will learn a fraction of the knowledge contained in this city."

Stephenie agreed. "I didn't see anything consistently on the bones we've wrapped up to indicate how the guardians identify a resident from an intruder. Did you see anything overnight?"

Kas shook his head. "I will keep an eye out and while you look over this room, I will check the other library. Perhaps I will find something."

"Be careful."

"You as well."

The sun had set before she had finished going through the dragon's office, bed chambers, and private belongings. The initial examination of the other library had intrigued her, but Kas reminded her of the water she left running in the bathing chamber and so after eating some food and drinking the last of the water in her water skin, she went back to check on the water in the tub. Seeing it was running clear and the copper odor was gone, she set the stopper, stripped out of her clothes, grabbed some soap from a nearby shelf, and sank into the stone tub as the water began to fill the large basin.

"I examined every skeleton I could find," Kas said. "I found no indication that these people carried anything that acts as a talisman for the guardians. Perhaps it was some other form of magic. Some connection to the dragon himself."

Stephenie nodded her head. "I found a few weapons in his offices, but nothing that was as ornate as the dagger or the staff. Nothing like you'd see even in the homes of most barons or dukes. Nothing that screamed *I am a dangerous warrior, fear me.*"

"He was a dragon," Kas said, sitting on the edge of the tub with his booted feet disappearing into the warm water. "For anyone that knew that fact, there would be no need to brandish weapons about in a display of force."

Stephenie splashed some water at him, but it passed through his body and much of it went outside the tub. She then splashed water on her own face and scrubbed at the grime that had built-up. "I did find two interesting things," she said as she picked up the bar of soap from the bottom of the tub.

"What did you find?" Kas asked after several moments of waiting.

"The first was in one of the ledgers. I think the dragon died in the year five thousand and twenty-one. That would make those paintings very old."

Kas pursed his lips. "I have been dead for perhaps a thousand years. "Could those paintings have survived that many years?"

Stephenie shrugged. "The books in your library in Arkani were in good shape because magic preserved them. Perhaps he did something similar with the paintings."

"That is very plausible."

"The second item of interest," Stephenie said as she lathered soap over her body, "are a series of letters. They appeared to be from a woman. I couldn't make out much of what was written. Even knowing what I know of the language, it is still hard to read some people's writing. What I could translate seemed fairly mundane, and only one half of what looked like a back and forth conversation. A personal connection. Even some playfulness."

"From the dragon's lady?"

Stephenie splashed more water against her face to wash away the soap. "Perhaps. Maybe a new one. I compared the names and it was not the woman in the pictures. But the letters seem to span hundreds and hundreds of years. I actually only found a couple of dates in the letters, but they were a long time apart and there were a large number of letters."

"Think of the knowledge one could obtain over such a long life," Kas mused. "It is a shame that such lives were destroyed."

"I'm not sure they all were." She leaned back against the warm stone of the tube and stretched her legs out, but they did not touch the far end. The water had risen to her chest and she reached up and turned the lever to shut off the flow of water. "I found a letter from him on the top of the desk. It was addressed to her on the inside, but the outside of the letter had a different set of markings. These were in Pandar. They indicated the letter was from someone in Horn Point. A man named Domgur. The instructions on the letter were to take it to someone named Caridelis in a place called Sudhold." Stephenie slid under the water and soaked her hair. She surfaced and shook her head. "From the maps in the offices, it looks like a city in Lobben, which is west of Sandven, on the other side of the World's Backbone."

"What do you propose by that?"

Stephenie wiped the water from her face and grabbed the soap to scrub at her tangled hair. "That she might be alive. Perhaps she's like me, a half-bread. I got the feeling there was an intimacy between them, but not exactly sexual."

"Are you thinking to go there next then? What of the red-haired man? Can I hope you have given up on pursuing him?"

She dropped the soap into the water. "You said it yourself, dragons are not something people can kill. Everything points to the red-hair man killing the dragon we found here, which means he's a dragon himself. That makes me a bastard half-breed." She shook her head. "No. He's not something to reason with...not if he slaughtered everyone here before going south to rape Queen Eayn and then on to rape my mother, all the while claiming to be Elrin, the demon god. Could it be he's really a god? Could we have been wrong all this time?"

"There was no hint or rumor of anything or anyone calling themselves Elrin when I lived. I do not think he is a god."

"Then what's his purpose? Why do all that?" Stephenie looked away. "Eayn killed herself before her child was born. My mother was too much a coward." She turned back to Kas. "So if he wanted me alive, why after nineteen years is he trying to arrange for people to kill me with weapons he stole from Ista. Why not just kill me himself?"

"Do you really think he is tied to the Senzar invasion or those that have been pursuing us? Is he supporting them?"

She turned her head to rinse the soap from her hair. "The head Senzar seem to speak the same language as the dragons and they are obsessed with this concept of generations. Before, we could not understand what they were a generation from, but what if that Yreka is also descendant from a dragon? Perhaps from my sire? Or maybe a different one?"

Kas turned his head toward the door. "It is possible. However, Favian did not recognize you in Vinerxan. Neither did Yvima, who was a sixth generation man, based on what you told me he said."

"And Yvima was not related to Favian." Stephenie dunked her head under the water again and shook it to agitate out the rest of the soap. She continued shaking her head as she lifted it from the water, spraying droplets about the room. "It may be that the Senzar invasion has nothing to do with the red-hair bastard. The trouble is why is he trying to kill me? Why create me and then have others try to kill me?"

"Stephenie, we need to avoid this man at all costs. There is nothing you can do to him and he would be able to slay all of us without effort."

"You know that for certain? I thought you only knew legends and tales."

Kas slipped from the end of the tub and sat down so he was facing her. "Stephenie, the red-haired man destroyed a dragon and a city full of people. Even if you have inherited his powers, I fear it would not be enough to survive him, let alone defeat him." He reached out and placed his translucent hands on her arms. "Please, for me, give up the search for this man...this creature."

Stephenie felt every bit of Kas' desperation. "Kas, I have already decided I don't want to meet him. I just want to know why." She smiled at him. "We'll find another way to get your body back. Perhaps a book in the library. Perhaps that woman, Caridelis. She was friendly with this dragon and lived outside of Ista. If she's still alive, I would like to at least deliver his last letter to her."

Kas frowned. "We know nothing of her. If she was friends, or related to the dead dragon, she may not like who your sire is."

Stephenie nodded her head. "Well, we don't open with that little detail. We simply tell her what we found here, deliver the letter, and then see if she's willing to talk with us." She leaned back against the tub. "I think she had a sense of humor based on what I understood from the letters and delivering the letter is the least we can do after what the red-haired bastard did here."

Kas reluctantly nodded his acceptance. "Do you expect to find her in the same location? She might have fled for her own safety."

"If so, then it might be a dead end. However, the letters that made references to the same mountain valley all the way back to the earliest ones. A valley made warm and fertile by what she seemed to joke as warm springs. My hope is she is still there. Possibly wondering what happened."

"And if you find her?"

"I'll give her the letter. And if she seems trustworthy, I'll ask her to help us."

Chapter 29

Henton could barely see from the exhaustion; his body begged him to rest. The sameness of the landscape that went on forever had not helped. Neither had the periods when they had rested the dogs and he was no longer forced to move, though he knew those breaks had been too few and too short for the dogs. He hoped the animals would forgive him the abuse.

The snow storm that plagued them overnight had passed and the sun was well into the sky when he saw Alkmaar on the horizon. Even though the dogs did not deserve it after running throughout the prior day and night, he shouted the command for them to speed up. Douglas trailed behind him and the gap between them grew, but Ryia was on his sled and that was all that mattered now.

Henton charged through the open gates of the city, barreling down the snow packed streets as people yelled and shouted at his reckless behavior. He yelled back for them to get out of the way as his sled bounced into buildings and slid around corners. Realizing the abuse might harm Ryia, he called on the dogs to slow and perhaps they recognized the danger or were so exhausted they willingly obeyed.

Henton missed a turn he wanted to make, but managed to bend the dogs around and drive them back toward Lami's home. *Just hang in there Ryia. We're almost there.* Time seemed to drag forever as he rode past building after building. Then finally seeing Lami's modest home, he smashed his weight down on the break and ordered the dogs to stop. They growled and yipped, but came to a stop with minimal noise.

Henton threw down the anchor and rushed around to start unbundling Ryia from the sled. He first tried to untie the ropes, but his fingers could not get the knot free. Not having the patience to continue fighting the bindings, he pulled his dagger and cut the ropes. He tossed off the fur hides as Lami came out of his house to investigate the noise.

"What problem? Why here?"

"She's hurt," Henton yelled as he picked Ryia up from the sled. He could hear Douglas' dogs coming down another street on the opposite side of Lami's house and assumed Douglas had missed more turns then he had. Without waiting for Lami or Douglas, Henton moved toward the open door behind Lami. "Heal her! Her arm's been ripped off!"

"Goddess," Lami said as Henton pushed his way into the warm building.

Henton rushed to the furs laying on the floor next to the fire pit and set Ryia down. "Please be alive," he begged. He pulled open her coat and checked Ryia's chest to see if she was still breathing. Henton looked up, searching for Lami. When he saw the man coming up behind him, he yelled again. "She breathes, but she needs help!"

Lami came around Henton and knelt on Ryia's right side. He carefully looked at the stump of her arm. "How long?"

"It happened yesterday about this time. We've run the dogs through the day and night to get here."

Lami nodded his head and Henton noticed the man's eyes lose focus. He wanted to demand he start healing her, but he had seen Stephenie and Ryia do the same thing when they were examining the situation and he did not want to disturb the man.

Outside he could hear more barking and some shouting. Henton would allow Douglas to deal with the trouble while he watched over Ryia. Then behind him, he heard the door open and slam shut.

"I should have you gutted for risking my dogs like that!" Perain shouted.

Lami had not moved or reacted to Perain so Henton stood to make sure that did not change. "Ryia's lost an arm. I had to get her here as quickly as possible. I am sorry for pushing the dogs and will compensate you, but don't press me on this."

Perain looked behind himself as Douglas came down the step into Lami's house carrying their personal effects. Perain seemed to search the room with his eyes and then turned his focus to Henton. "Where is Stephenie?"

Henton turned back to Lami who looked up at him and then looked to Perain. Lami spoke quickly in his native language.

"He said she is near death. Trying to heal her will sap her strength and could kill her. Where is Stephenie?" Perain repeated.

"Heal her," Henton said to Lami. "She's strong. Ryia, do you hear me, fight!"

"Stephenie?"

Douglas moved around Perain, the staff in his hand. "She's not with us."

Perain said several clipped words in his own language. "Lami, you swore this had nothing to do with Ista." Perain pointed to the steel caps on the staff. "You lied."

Henton pointed at Ryia. "Heal her."

Lami nodded his head and put his hands on her injured arm. "Arm not return."

"Keep her alive." Henton stood up and turned to face Perain who had moved closer. "This," he said pointing at Ryia who lay behind him, "has nothing to do with Ista. We were attacked by people. Steph is still out there. We had to get Ryia to Lami."

Perain nodded his head. Two other men came into Lami's home and said something in their language. Perain replied and they went back outside. "They will tend the dogs." Perain moved closer and knelt beside Ryia.

Henton remained on his feet a moment more and knelt down himself. Ryia's body trembled as Lami poured energy into it, forcing her body to heal.

Perain looked at him. "You should not have left Stephenie's body in the snow fields."

"She's not dead."

"What?" Perain stood up. "We have to send some sleds to find her. You can't expect someone to survive on the waste alone. Not someone from the south like her. How could you have done that?"

Lami sat back on his rear. His face was drawn. "She..." He spoke quickly to Perain.

"She still weak, but he thinks she will live. She will need to be cleaned up and her clothes removed. Lami has some female friends who help him from time to time, he will get them. But we will need to wake her so she can eat and drink at some point."

Henton rubbed his face. His exhaustion physically hurt. "Thank you," he said to Lami.

The man nodded his head. "Welcome. I get Jenasa. She clean."

Henton clasped Lami's hand as the man walked toward his front door. Then Henton turned toward Perain. "I am sorry for what we did to your dogs, but Ryia had her arm ripped off."

Perain licked his lips. "Who did this? With that staff, I don't believe you that this has nothing to do with Ista."

Henton felt the weariness in his bones. Douglas had dropped to a seated position on the furs next to Ryia and Henton knew his friend was as ready to fall asleep as he was. "There were two people that attacked us. We killed them, but only after Ryia was injured."

"And Stephenie? Why did she not return with you?"

"She was away at the time. We could not wait for her return, so we left most of the supplies and rushed back."

Perain's gaze took measure of Henton. "You are hiding much. You were at the border, were you not? She crossed over into Ista. There is no other place anyone would go on their own. No sensible reason to separate. No reason to take both sleds and leave her behind. Not unless you wanted her to die or she was already dead or already lost forever."

"We'd never harm one of our own." Henton reached down and picked up Ryia's left hand. He held it in his and patted the top of it.

"There was a ghost sled that Guter saw late in the day that you left. We all thought he had been into his drink again."

Henton raised his eyebrows waiting for Perain to continue. "Ghost sled?"

"No dogs. Just a person, perhaps two, on a sled. A person can push one, but not fast and not far. Not like a team can pull one. This sled had stayed away from Alkmaar and had gone north after you had left." Perain shrugged. "Unless Dalkin was driving the sled, Guter must have been mad. That's what we thought."

That would explain how they got there, Henton pondered, now able to think about it for the first time since the attack without being obsessed with getting Ryia to Lami. He caught Douglas' eye and he knew Douglas had come to the same conclusion, *the Senzar had likely used their magic to push the sled. We should have searched the bodies and looked for where they had camped.* "Could there have been more than two people?"

Perain appraised Henton again. "Guter only said he saw the one sled. Of course it's snowed every night for days and Guter only said something the next day, so there were no tracks to confirm his story."

"Any one but us come into Alkmaar since we arrived?"

Pertain chuckled. "The four of you are the only foreigners dumb enough to come here in winter...or at all anymore. The few that go to Ista never return and we never let them use our dogs or sleds." Perain shook his head. "I don't know why Lami lied for you, but my slate with him is now clean because of it."

"Do not be angry at Lami. If you want to be angry at someone, let it be me. I deserve it for what I let happen to Ryia." Henton pushed back his emotions. "But if anyone else comes into Alkmaar, know that they may be very dangerous."

"And what of Stephenie? Are you to just leave her out there? No concern for her at all? Or has she really gone into Ista?"

Henton glanced down at Ryia. *Had it really been just one day and night since the attack?* "It may be a day or two more before she returns to where we had camped. She will likely come back here on her own. We left her a note."

"A hundred and fifty miles across the waste on foot? Unless she's one of the Chosen, she'd never make it." Perain shook his head. "Of course, if she's crossed into Ista...well, you probably did the right thing in leaving."

Henton watched Ryia's chest rise and fall. She seemed to breathe more easily now. Lami had removed the bloody bandage they had fashioned from his shirt. The end of her arm was red and abused with sharp protrusions pressing against the pink skin that had newly formed, but it was skin covering the end of her arm. *I'm so sorry, Ryia.*

Henton heard Perain get up and walk to the door. He glanced over at Douglas, but Douglas had fallen asleep holding the staff. Henton sighed. He would watch over Ryia until Lami came back.

Chapter 30

The sun had settled below the horizon and the numerous crystals that were scattered about the library had brightened to compensate for the light that no longer filled the large room. Magnificent windows that stood five feet tall filled the top third of the south and east walls. They rose above the stacks that lined the walls and spread out across the floor. Although too high to provide a view to the outside, Stephenie had spent the better part of the day basking in the natural light that had shone through the glass. Now the warm glow of the crystals had changed the tone of the large wooden tables and upholstered chairs so that Stephenie wanted to curl her feet under her and sit back with a warm drink.

During the day, she had lost all sense of time as she poured over piles of maps and drawings that depicted the countries around the Sea of Tet with amazing detail. The maps included the names of small towns and villages that never made it on to most of the maps she had encountered on her way north. She even found several maps of Cothel and when she compared the details to her memory of the maps her father had, she found these maps to be very accurate.

The books in the room were written in numerous languages and many showed a great deal of age as well as care. There were tomes written in Denarian, Pandar, the language of the dragons, and many old languages Kas had only seen once or twice and never learned. There were also many books containing languages neither of them had encountered before.

With night settling in and a strong desire for a sweet drink, Stephenie realized she was famished. Between her obsession with the library and Kas' lack of a body—which often meant he forgot physical concerns—neither of them remembered to have her eat during the day. She put aside the book that contained numerous drawings of a fountain system powered by magic, got up, and left the library.

They returned to the bedroom she had secured, grabbed some trail food and headed back down to the first floor. "For isolationists, they seem to have some very current maps," she told Kas. "There are even maps of places south of the Rim Mountains, where I think the Senzar came from."

"It is likely the ruler of this land had agents that traveled broadly. There was the obvious exchange of letters with the woman named Caridelis, so it is reasonable to assume there are other routes of entry into Ista that our southern friends either are not aware of or have concealed from us."

Stephenie nodded her head and chewed on the dried meat in her hand as they made their way back to the Dragon's private rooms. "I want to look through his rooms one more time to see if we can get a better feel for him."

"You still do not plan to take anything back?"

She shook her head. "Perhaps a book or two and maybe a couple of maps. I just can't bring myself to rob these people. Not with my ties to the bastard that killed them."

"A reasonable decision."

She started with the office again, but this time she ignored the papers and documents. Instead, she focused on the objects left after everyone had been killed. The pens had gold nibs with subtle etchings of animals. Their stems were made of a light, but sturdy wood. The chair was elegant, but crafted for comfort and hours of sitting. A few large crystals sat on the desk, holding down papers or standing on end, but they still appeared more decorative than utilitarian.

On the bookshelves, small wire figures were sculpted to form galloping horses, birds in flight, and even people. She found five wooden boxes acting as bookends. Four were empty, though they were art in themselves with delicate inlays and graceful lines. The fifth one had a few pieces of mismatched jewelry that held a definite feminine quality.

In his bedroom she found simple clothing of impeccable construction. The colors were mostly blues, greens, and greys, but none of it screamed wealth and power. A few more items of decoration adorned the bedroom, including a gold statue of a dragon in flight on a marble pedestal. Stephenie could not say exactly why, but the two foot long dragon did not look male.

"There is nothing here that is morbid. No skulls. No animal heads. No images of sacrifice. This man had an air of peace."

"Can you sense anything in the walls?" Kas asked. "These rooms appear even more resistant to my ability to pass through them than other rooms."

Stephenie closed her eyes and extended her senses. She had begun to grow accustomed to having her mind blocked by the castle. However, Kas was correct, the bedroom seemed to be completely isolated from the rest of the world. She shook her head. "Whatever they did to the walls, floor, and ceiling, even the door, it is like it hardly exists beyond my eye. At first, it felt odd, but being cut off from anything outside my sight is not bothering me as much now." She moved over to the fireplace and peeked up the flue. Without thinking, she put her hand up through the field that extended over the opening. It tingled slightly, but nothing seemed to happen. "Odd, there even seems to be a field up there to block my senses. Why would they do that? I would imagine the smoke could escape as easily as my hand passed through it, but why block my ability to sense things."

"You might want to show more caution." Kas' frown faded slowly as he pondered the question for a moment. "You seem more limited in your ability to read people's minds than many other mages. In my time, those overly sensitive to mental distractions would avoid places with other people to keep from becoming overwhelmed. Perhaps this Dragon suffered from being overly sensitive and this was his way to have a place without distraction."

Stephenie found the explanation reasonable. "I'd never admit it to the others, but it is nice to not have their thoughts floating about..." She narrowed her focus to a slight gap between the wall and a decorative column set against the wall near the fireplace. The fluted column was cut in half lengthwise, with the flat side against the wall, but the small gap was protected by the field. "Why would the field be in the decoration and not just the wall?"

She stepped over to the column. It extended a foot into the room and spanned a width of three feet against the wall. She placed her fingers on the edge of the column and pulled. She stepped back as the decorative wall piece rotated out into the room on a hidden hinge.

"Again with expressing some caution," Kas suggested. "What did you find?" he asked after a moment.

Stephenie shook her head. The opening behind the column was dark and the field that blocked her senses had now expanded to cover the wider opening. She moved to get a better look into the corridor that descended downward at a sharp pitch. After five feet, the narrow passage widened to perhaps fifteen-feet and along both sides of the dark passage were two rows of guardians, all of them had turned their heads to look at her.

Stephenie felt for the dagger at her side. She shifted her hip to show the weapon to the guardians. She could not get a good count of the stone protectors as the end of the passage was concealed in total darkness.

"It is hard for me to make out what is down there," Kas said. "The field over the opening has restricted what I can sense. I am not sure I could even pass through it."

"It is blocking my senses as well, but I can see through it with my eyes." She moved her hand into the field. She felt a slight tingle like the fireplace, but nothing blocked her.

"Be careful," Kas pleaded.

Stephenie put her hand all the way through and paused. After a moment, she followed with the rest of her body. Kas and the bedroom disappeared from her awareness, but she sensed a strong intelligence awaken. It was not fixed, but seemed to come from all around her. The two closest guardians stepped forward, their stone teeth exposed in a silent snarl. She showed them the dagger, but they did not retreat.

She swallowed as the intelligence began to push at her mind. She struggled, but like the trap, there was too much power behind it. She stumbled backward, her hands on her temples as she fought against the mind that tried to enter hers.

"Are you harmed," she heard Kas yell.

She had passed back through the barrier field, but the intelligence continued to surround her. It was in the walls, the floor, the ceiling. "The castle...it's trying to get into my head."

Kas pulled her to the center of the room as several guardians emerged from the passage. The door to the office swung all the way open as several more guardians entered, blocking off their retreat.

Their stone paws clanged against the stone floor, but Stephenie could not hear anything beyond the intelligence. She shook her head violently; however, the intelligence had gained a foothold in her mind and would not let go. *Leave me alone!* She felt the intelligence stop pushing deeper and her senses cleared.

"Stephenie, what has happened?"

She slowly opened her eyes. Five guardians now stood by the exit to the bedroom and four stood in front of the hidden passage. She pulled out the dagger and held it before her with the blade up so the guardians could see it. They made no move to look at it. Their gaze simply remained on her face, staring into her eyes like any cat who might challenge another for dominance.

She slid the dagger back into its sheath. *Do I challenge them or look away?* She wondered to herself. She knew cats that would attack when stared at. *Are these the same?*

She directed her anger at being violated to the intelligence, *Get out.* Unlike the staff, this intelligence did not obey her. She growled, trying to warn it away as she pulled more and more energy into herself. She glared back at the closest guardian. *Go ahead, you look away first, because I'm tired of it.*

The stone lips of the cat curled a little, at first into a snarl, but then into something Stephenie viewed as more of a smile than anything else. The other guardians shifted and then sat down on their haunches.

"Stephenie, have you done something?"

She felt the intelligence pressing on her mind again, but this time the pressure was less intense and more of a request instead of a demand.

"Stephenie?"

"Give me a moment, Kas." *What do you want?* She thought to the intelligence.

The response brought Stephenie to her knees and Kas cried out in alarm. She felt despair and uselessness. She felt bone aching loneliness. She felt a lack of purpose and aimless frustration. Then she knew at once these emotions were not hers, but those of the castle.

"You want me to fix that?" she managed to choke out and the response was immediate.

Stephenie fell back on her rear. The pain of having failed at her purpose overwhelmed her. But it was not Stephenie's failure nor was it Stephenie's purpose.

"Stephenie! Can you hear me?"

Stephenie waved Kas away and shook her head. She pushed back on the intelligence, begging it to not overwhelm her. Pleading for a chance to think.

The blinding wave of emotion stopped and Stephenie opened her eyes. Kas hovered directly over her. The guardians had not moved. She put her head back onto the floor and took several deep breaths. Tears had fallen from her eyes. She felt total exhaustion. The mental bombardment had taken her strength.

"Kas, the castle. It's alive."

"Are you injured? Has it taken over your mind?"

She rolled her head back and forth. "Damn." She took another deep breath. "The staff and dagger won't protect us."

"Ryia and the others?"

Stephenie looked at him. "The border guardians were confused. They recognized the staff and dagger as belonging to the Lord Mayor. So they didn't attack us and chose not to pursue us across the border. When we crossed the border a second time and headed north, the castle wanted to find out how we acquired the weapons and what our purpose was. Now she thinks I may be capable of giving her purpose again."

"What? Does it have that much intelligence?"

Stephenie forced a laugh. "You can't imagine. I'm still sorting out all the emotions it put into my head." Stephenie pushed herself into a seated position. The guardians were all watching her with interest, but none of them displayed any hostility. "Its master is dead. All of the people it had been created to protect are dead. She has no purpose."

"The castle is female?"

Stephenie shrugged. "Yeah, the castle is a she. That's how she was constructed."

"Is she aware of who you are?"

Stephenie thought about it and then slowly nodded her head. "Yes. She's understood everything we've been saying. More by reading our thoughts and intentions than anything else. But she knows the Dalish language, so nothing we've said was private." Stephenie rolled to her side. "Oh gods, she's been around for ages. I can't even fathom how long."

"What does she want?" Kas asked, each word coming slower than the last.

Stephenie moved her feet under her body and stood. She wobbled slightly and then moved to the bed. None of the guardians moved to stop her. "She wants someone to live here. Someone to serve and protect." Stephenie looked up to meet Kas' eyes. "She watched what we did for the dead. It made her sad that she had not thought to do that herself. I think she's pulled the idea of burying them from my thoughts." Stephenie shook her head to clear it. "She thinks that I am compatible with her. Similar in mind and temperament."

Stephenie looked toward the hidden passage. "There is a library down there. A private library. His library."

The pitch of Kas' voice rose. "What does she want from you? I am uncomfortable with this."

She turned toward Kas. "She wants someone to live here. If I accept...ownership is not the right word...more partnership, she will allow me to designate anyone we want as able to come here. Henton and Ryia and Douglas or anyone."

"I do not want you to be a prisoner here." Kas shook his head and drifted a step toward the door. "We should leave."

Stephenie brushed her hand against the image he projected. "I can't fit you in my head at the moment. I'm still sorting through all of the emotion—and it's powerful emotion. But I will show you. It is not a prisoner relationship Isa—that is her name—wants. But I need to think about it." She sat upright. "I need to talk to you, Henton, and the others. I don't think I could stay here forever. I'd want to go home to see Cothel again. And there is just so much snow and ice here," her words slowed and she looked around the bed room. "She said I could leave from time to time. Kervigar, as he was usually called, left often enough."

"Stephenie, it is dangerous to have highly intelligent devices in your head. This castle could take over your mind and force a change in your personality."

She looked up at him. "The castle wants a friend, not a servant or slave. But don't worry. She won't force anything on me and we can leave if we want. She just asks that I consider returning if I do leave." Stephenie smiled for Kas. She could feel his uncertainty and fear. "She's already told me that she does not know how to rebuild a body for you. However, she doesn't know what knowledge is contained in the libraries. It is possible there are books that may contain the information."

"A lure to keep you here."

"I've told her we need to return to our friends before I decide to do anything."

The guardians in front of the concealed passage rose to their feet, turned around and returned to the passage. The five by the door to the office rose and left as well.

She knew he did not want to hear her say this, but she could not lie. "Kas, I am really considering this."

"It was not able to protect the last dragon from your sire. You will be in a fixed location and vulnerable."

She nodded her head. "I know." She stood up. "I need some time to absorb everything. Tomorrow, we'll head back to Henton and the others. We'll have to take the dogs back to Alkmaar and then we can..."

"Are you okay?"

She steadied herself on the back of a chair. "I've inadvertently picked up a sense of the guardians in the castle and the city." She wiped her face. "I felt all the connections and the relays and links. I could feel myself down all those threads." Her eyes were wide. "It was too much at once, but it was also amazing. The entangled threads are scattered throughout."

Kas froze. "Is she a trap? Is she getting her powers by killing another creature?"

Stephenie felt the answer come to her before she could formulate the question. "No. There's...something called...magma...burning rock. It's full of energy. Normally it's deep under the ground, but here it is close to the surface." She grinned. "That's what causes the hot springs. Not Lami's Goddess fighting Dalkin or anything like that. No, Isa's power comes from deep in the ground and she has stored it up for centuries." Stephenie straightened, let go of the chair, and headed for the door. "She dislikes the idea of the traps as well. Kervigar thought they were an abomination. In fact, she can tell us where several traps are."

"Really?" Kas shook his head. "That is a lure to entice us. I do not trust this information."

Stephenie did not want to argue the point with Kas; her mind had shifted focus to what she thought Henton, Douglas, and Ryia would say about Isa and the prospect of living here.

Chapter 31

Although Stephenie's body ached for sleep, she found her mind racing with possibilities. There was a great deal of wealth just lying around, though money and possessions never really captivated her attention. *The libraries...* The thought of all the knowledge waiting for someone to read did intrigue her.

She tried to focus on what she should do, but Kas' constant pacing about the room kept distracting her. "If you don't settle down, how am I to get any sleep?"

"Your mind has not quieted, therefore you are not about to fall asleep. Have you continued to speak with it?"

Stephenie shook her head. Isa remained outside her thoughts, but Stephenie was now very much aware of the castle's presence all around them. "Kas, I said I won't make a decision until we all talk... but, I can't help but weigh the decision in my head. I am trying to think about what I should do logically. I want to take the emotion out of it."

He luminesced an opaque form. "Then by all means, please consider this logical conclusion: there has to be some drawback if it is trying so hard to sell you on bonding with it."

Stephenie's eyes narrowed. "She is lonely and has been for some time. She was not designed to exist without a companion." She sat up slowly. "Yes, one very big negative is she would want me to live up here for more time than we are away. She also wants the city to be repopulated at some point. The trouble is I don't want to rule anyone. I don't want to be a queen. I don't want the responsibility."

"Then you should decline the offer. It is not safe to allow a magical intelligence too much access to your mind."

Stephenie patted the bed in front of her and waited for Kas to join her. "Isa wants companionship. She needs someone with a strong mind who won't cave to her. She wants a friend."

"You did not grow up with magical devices. They have motivations you may not understand."

"Isa was constructed by a dragon. He's not going to have built something that could take over his mind."

"But Stephenie, he could have built something with a strong personality that he could control, yet you are unable to. Or, perhaps the castle has evolved."

Stephenie considered the possibility. "Perhaps, but that doesn't mean it is the case. However, if I turn her down and we simply walk away, what happens when someone else who has enough raw potential comes here? What about the Senzar mage? If she decides to offer Yreka the chance and the bitch accepts the offer." She held up her hand to keep Kas from speaking. "Granted, a large part of her decision to not kill us stemmed from our treatment of the dead and a desire not to loot, which means she wouldn't pick just anyone, but if we don't accept her, there is still a chance someone who could cause great harm might."

Kas bowed his head to her. "That is a valid concern. However, if you do assume this role and you draw a following, it is likely you will draw enemies as well. Likely powerful enemies such as the Senzar who were chasing you. As well, perhaps your sire."

"I know. That scares me a lot. I think the Senzar we could handle, but the red-haired bastard...he would be another story."

Kas floated up and took a standing position. "Then please consider that possibility in your deliberations."

"Kas, I said I would not decide until we all had a chance to talk."

"I know." His words said he already knew she had decided. He drifted to the door. "I will let you sleep. You'll need your rest before we fly back tomorrow."

Stephenie laid down wishing Kas was wrong in his assumption, but she really did want to accept Isa. *Only, I don't want to be a queen. I don't want to be tied down. But even in Cothel, Josh had grown so*

*distrustful of me. The people there fearing me and thinking the worst...
and there is the library here...* She rocked her head back and forth.
"This is hard." She sighed. She knew if it was not for Kas and the
others, she would have already accepted the offer, even if it meant she
must become a queen over a country full of people.

Stephenie did not know when she fell asleep, but she knew it was
not yet morning when she felt Isa's insistent urging that she wake.
What is it? Stephenie asked of the castle, uncertain she should trust
the sudden intrusion.

Isa showed her a young woman standing at the doors of the castle
and Stephenie gathered an impression the woman had appeared
suddenly, having flown into the city. She did not have to ask about
Kas' location, Isa overlaid her vision yet again with Kas in the library
and a guardian working to get his attention.

Stephenie grabbed her sword belt and strapped it on as she jogged
to the stairs going down. Through Isa, she saw the woman walk into
the entrance hall as well as Kas following the guardian down another
set of stairs toward the first level.

Stephenie rushed ahead. If this was Yreka, she would not let Kas
face the woman alone. Flying down the stairs herself, she moved
through one of the grand hallways and came out the side door of the
throne room just as the woman entered. Something slammed into the
threads that emanated from Stephenie's mind, blocking all of her
mental sense of the room and the woman. She felt as if she was
standing in a thick fog and the suddenness of the change caused her
to stumble. Even her connection to Isa was hazy. She knew the castle
was still there, but her vision of Kas had disappeared.

The tall woman growled. She had no visible weapons on her
person, just a simple gown in a pale translucent green that gave hint
at the firm body under the thin cloth. It provided no protection from
the elements.

The sound of the door opening and a stone guardian coming into
the throne room startled Stephenie because she had not sensed the
change before hearing the sounds. *Damn it,* she swore, trying to fight

against whatever had blocked her mind. She still could draw power and that gave her hope to protect herself and Kas against the woman.

"His smell is on you," the woman said in the language of the dragons, though it took Stephenie a moment for the meaning to register. "Why are you here?"

"I don't know what you mean? Who's smell?" Stephenie said slowly, the language still raw in her ability to speak it fluidly. She assumed the guardian had brought Kas into the room, but he was not visible and if he had entered, she hoped he would not attack on his own.

"Your father's."

"My father was the King of Cothel and he—"

"Your father is Duvargintik," the woman snarled.

"I don't know the name of my sire."

"Do not insult me with stupid word games. Duvargintik fathered you on your worthless mother. His stink makes me sick."

Stephenie swallowed. This woman was not a Senzar mage, this woman was something far worse. "By any chance is your name Caridelis?"

The tall woman moved toward Stephenie, a grace and power in her movements that caused Stephenie to take a step backwards.

I am here, can you hear me?

Kas, this woman is a dragon, she replied, sensing Kas partially enveloping her. *She's done something to block my senses.*

"Why are you here?" the woman demanded again, stopping five feet away from Stephenie. "And tell your ghost I am not amused with the Dalish language."

"Ma'am, we've meant no harm. My sire—father, had sent people to kill me and we tracked the origin of the weapons he provided to Ista. I had come here hoping to beg peace with him so he would stop harming my friends and people. We had no idea what he was or what he had done here." Stephenie carefully removed the dagger and held the handle toward the woman. "This dagger and a staff were to be used to kill me."

The woman glanced at the dagger, but gave it no interest. "Are you that foolish?"

Stephenie swallowed, but continued to hold the dagger's handle toward the woman. "I had no idea what happened here until we arrived a couple days ago. I...If you are Caridelis, I want to let you know that Kervigar had written a letter to you, but had never had the chance to have it sent."

"And you tell me that, why?"

"In some small way to try to make amends for what, Duvar..."

"Duvargintik. The man would slay you the moment he saw you just for having the impetuousness of daring to approach him. He never acknowledges his bastards. Had he been here, you'd be dead."

"Ma'am, we did not know."

"You know now." The woman looked around the throne room and then back at Stephenie and Kas. "So what is your purpose now that you know the truth? Have you come to rob the place?"

Stephenie shook her head quickly. "I did not know anyone else came here. Isa did not tell me anything about you. She...she only warned me when you appeared in front of the castle."

The woman's eyebrows rose. "The castle has reached out to you? That is interesting." Suddenly the haze that blocked Stephenie's ability to sense the room lifted. "You may call me Caridelis, Stephenie Marn. Your ghost should refrain from speaking if he does not know my language."

Stephenie quickly relayed the conversation to Kas and allowed him into her head so he would have a sense of what was happening. She felt Isa's sense of deficiency in not knowing who the woman was. "Ma'am, if Isa is yours..."

"These lands belonged to Kervigar. He's dead. The castle can do what she wants. This is not my home. However, I had left a device to let me know if someone intruded upon Kervigar's home. I do not particularly like looters."

"We have no intention of robbing this place."

"Obviously, if Isa has reached out to you and had not killed you, you were not someone she considers a threat." The dragon looked at the back of her hand. "Though it shows a lack of reason for the castle to send you to deal with me. Neither of you would be able to stop me if I decided to wreak havoc."

Stephenie's lips thinned ever so slightly. Her sire had not managed to damage much of the castle's structure, even though he had managed to kill everyone present. She wondered if this dragon was even more powerful.

"Enough pleasantries. It would seem I do not have to kill you after all."

"Ma'am, if I might ask, is there anything I can do to stop Duvargintik from trying to kill me? He's caused so many people to die."

"Stop with the ma'am. I told you to call me Caridelis. However, it is likely your father will lose interest in trying to kill you as soon as there is not anyone he can manipulate to the task that is powerful enough to do it."

"Won't he then come after me himself?"

Caridelis turned toward the door behind the dais. "Let's retire to his office. If you insist on making this a lengthy conversation, I would rather sit." Without waiting for Stephenie's reply, she moved toward the door.

Stephenie hesitated a moment, not sure how Caridelis might react to Kervigar's body. However, the dragon had not slowed and Stephenie had to hasten to catch up. She followed the dragon into the smashed office, but Caridelis walked passed the bones without a glance. Though Stephenie knew someone with that kind of power would not use only her eyes to see.

Stephenie passed Kervigar's skull and once again wished her sire had not killed such a being, but there was nothing she could do about it. So she followed Caridelis into the office. The dragon walked around the desk and sat down in the chair. She scanned the papers and quickly saw the letter that Stephenie had left where Kervigar had laid it.

"I never came past his body before." Caridelis opened the letter and quickly read it before tossing it back onto the desk. "Your father is a dragon, Stephenie. He could crush you like a slug under the hoof of a draft horse that itself was crushed under a mountain that exploded and rained down boulders." She smiled. "Of course I know about what you did in the Grey Mountains, all of us felt that explosion."

"If I'm so easy to kill, then why send others to do it. If he wants me dead, it would be easier to do it himself. I'd rather he leave my family and country alone and just get on with it."

Caridelis shook her head and chuckled. "If you sought him out and confronted him that is exactly what he would do. You would die the moment he saw you. However, for him to seek you out would mean that he would have to acknowledge you were a threat—not to him, because no one would think that—but to his plans. That would show weakness and he would never do that. Plus, there would be no sport in that."

Stephenie stepped closer. "Sport? Is this a game?" she asked, amazed.

Caridelis truly laughed. "How little you understand. Of course it is a game."

Stephenie stepped back and sat in the chair opposite the desk. "You're right. I don't understand. Are you some kind of god? Is he really Elrin? Are you just playing with our lives?"

"No, no, and yes." Caridelis leaned back in the chair. "We are no gods. Dragons never have been and never will be. We simply exist. The closest thing to gods that we know of is the balance of nature, though we often work against it. But," she leaned forward, "imagine a being that does not die of old age. A being that lives for as long as it can stand. A being with so much power that only another of its kind can kill it. A being with money and control. Now imagine what can hold that being's interest after a thousand years of life, or two, or ten."

"So," Stephenie said slowly, "to amuse yourselves, you torment people. And Duvargintik is not Elrin?"

She shrugged and sat back in the chair again. "Some torment, others don't." She used her hands to indicate the desk between them. "Kervigar was far more benevolent to his offspring and the humans and elves he liked to protect than Duvargintik. Your father is quite malicious. But a god? No. He would love to claim he created the legend of Elrin, but in truth, it was you humans that invented that stupidity. Though your father likes to use that fear to motivate people."

Stephenie bit her lip. "Great, more evidence I am nothing more than some half-breed monster."

Caridelis picked up a crystal from the desk and looked at it. "You are whatever you want to be. Isa would appear to like you, so for now, you at least have more in common with Kervigar than your father." She tossed the crystal into the air and caught it, then set it down on the desk.

"But why even create me? I don't understand. Why make me, then try to kill me."

Caridelis leaned forward. "I cannot say specifically what your father's game was, but most certainly it was to destabilize the region. Kervigar wanted stability in these lands west of Tet, Duvargintik wanted chaos and war. He, and other dragons competing with each other, started the Elven Wars that led to the fall of the Elven Empire. It is like a giant strategy game where the rulers are pieces to move about the board."

"So, my purpose was to cause more death."

"If you were revealed as a witch and your mother executed, then Kynto and Cothel would go to war, yes?"

Stephenie nodded her head. "So he wanted someone to discover what I was, burn me and my mother. He wanted me dead from the start."

"He cares nothing for his bastards. I've told you that. Because his plans did not work out and you've actually stabilized the region, he likely wanted to have you removed." Caridelis shrugged. "If he continues to throw people at you, he will look weak. More than likely he will simply wait a few centuries and try again to destabilize the region."

"I hate this. I just wish I was human. I don't know how to deal with being part dragon. I worry all the time about harming someone without intending to. I get these possessive rages."

"So you want to live without magic?"

"What do you mean?"

"Girl, you really don't understand. Anyone who has magic, human, elf, saln, or whatever, they all have the blood of a dragon running through them. Where do you think magic comes from?"

"You mean you've mated with all kinds of creatures?"

Caridelis leaned forward. "You may be squeamish about sex, but we will do what gives us pleasure and breeding with another dragon is not usually pleasant. All of that possessiveness you hate, it is stronger in us."

Stephenie shook her head. "If you don't have children—is that the word for it? Then you'll die out."

"What can I say, we've existed long enough that we no longer have the biological imperative to keep the species alive." She shrugged. "Sure, every now and then you'll find a dragon that has a child, which is the correct term, even if they might hatch from an egg. It is just not that often because if a handful of us can cause this much damage, what would happen if we overran the world?" Caridelis leaned back. "So yes, we mate with other creatures. Elves tended to retain more of our genes longer, but generally the first generation offspring is the most powerful and the traits drop off with each subsequent generation. A half-breed, as you choose to call it, born to a female dragon in form will be more dragon than human, but otherwise you will have normal species traits." She flicked her head toward Kas, "Even he had dragon blood when he had a body."

Stephenie exhaled. "This is a lot to take in."

"So, what is it you really want to ask me? Your mind is practically sweating from anticipation and fear."

Stephenie glanced over at Kas and suggested he make himself opaque. After he did, she looked back at Caridelis. "I have been trying to learn how to do transformative magic. I want to rebuild a body for Kas, but it is not something I have been able to find much about in books."

The dragon glanced at Kas and shook her head. "He has no body to transform. It is not just transformative magic, but translocative magic."

"What kind?" Stephenie asked, sensing Kas was not exactly familiar with what she was speaking about.

"Translocative magic is the power to leave your body and travel far beyond your physical form. It is seldom used because it is just as likely to kill you as otherwise. If you lose your body or someone destroys your physical form, you cannot easily go back and will end up like him, what people refer to as ghosts."

"So without a body, he is stuck?"

"If a mage is powerful enough, they could recreate a body from raw materials for themselves. Though it is much easier if you already have a body, otherwise death is far more probable."

"His body died a long time ago in—"

"Arkani," Caridelis interrupted. "I am aware of the city under Antar. I am aware of what happened there. I actually spent some time examining the walls after the Denarians left the Dalish city sealed away." She smiled at Kas. "It was quite an amazing accident, though I imagine you were not quite as thrilled with it as I was interested in it." She raised her hand to prevent him from responding. "Don't speak to me in your mundane tongue, I already know your thoughts on it."

"Can you help me learn how to rebuild his body?"

Caridelis raised her eyebrows. She glanced again at Kas and then stared at Stephenie for what became an uncomfortable amount of time. "At best, assuming he remains near you and benefits from your powers extending his life, he has perhaps one hundred to one hundred and twenty years of life in him. He does not appear to have been someone of great power. You on the other hand, have at least eight hundred years before you'll start to grow old. Assuming of course you are not killed by something before then."

Stephenie closed her eyes and bit her lip. "Why is it every time I talk with someone new, they keep extending my lifespan?"

"How should I know? Has anyone so far ever had the real measure of who you are? If they do not know your father's power and potential, they would have no way to make an accurate guess."

Kas, I don't want to lose you.

Nor I, you.

"However, even in his current state, I would expect he will last for perhaps another two hundred, maybe two hundred and fifty years at most. Without the field that preserved his state, he, like the others ghosts in Arkani, will decompose. In two hundred years, he will likely no longer be functional. More of a presence floating about and unaware of his surroundings until one day nothing will be left to hold his energy together."

"Damn it."

"Now you are beginning to understand. Dragons seldom make attachments. Human or elf or otherwise, you all die quickly. And dragons...well, we are far too territorial and possessive to get along with each other for very long."

Stephenie did not want to think about losing Kas. She knew intellectually that one person in a partnership often outlived the other, but for the difference to be so great was like poking a stick in her eye. Forcing a change in the conversation, she asked another question she wanted an answer to. "Why did you all disappear?"

"Well, around seventeen hundred years ago, too many of us were killing each other and wiping out large numbers of humans and elves. A handful of elders decided we would disappear and hide our existence. So, instead of being slaughtered by the elders, we did as commanded." She looked down at the desk in front of her. "There were always people who knew, but Kervigar may have stretched the bounds of propriety with regard to letting humans and elves know what he was."

"Is that why he was killed?"

Stephenie felt the temperature in the room drop. "Your father is not an elder. He's old, but not an elder." Caridelis' jaw softened. "No, Kervigar had beat your father one too many times. Duvargintik did not like being made the fool, so he destroyed my friend and those that lived here."

"I am sorry."

"Do not insult me. You have nothing to do with it and could not even fathom the politics involved."

"I can still express my sympathy for your loss," Stephenie growled and then immediately thought better of her response.

Caridelis smiled. "Not so much the coward after all. A word of warning though, never mistake my actions for having human motivations. I am driven by my own needs."

Stephenie nodded her head. She returned to her previous question. "Is rebuilding a body for Kas possible?"

"You still want to do that? Knowing what you know? Knowing that you are as likely to kill him in the process as to succeed?"

Kas, this impacts you, so I will not make the decision for you.

Even if we survive the process, I will die many years before you. I fear you will be forced to live alone regardless.

I would rather spend a year with you, if that was all we had, then to never have tried. But it sounds like there is a lot of risk and if you don't want to take the risk, we can find a way to make what we have now work.

She felt his acceptance and love. *I would rather try than continue like this.*

Stephenie turned her attention back to the dragon, "Yes, we want to try."

Caridelis' eyes lit up. "Excellent."

"What is your cost?" Kas asked in Dalish. "I will not have Stephenie sacrifice herself in trade."

Caridelis growled. "I will only speak my language." The dragon turned back to Stephenie. "I have no specific cost."

"You have an unspecified cost?" Stephenie asked.

"I have no cost to show you how this is done. It suits my whim to do it, that is all." Caridelis pushed the chair back and stood up. "If you must know, you may just end up living long enough to make knowing you interesting. Neither so long that I'd grow tired of you, nor so short there is no point to it."

"I will not be someone's pet," Stephenie blurted out.

Caridelis grinned. "My dear, you can be nothing but a pet to me. Do you imagine that I would ever consider you an equal? What you are to an average human, I am a hundred times to you. My power and ability is nothing you can ever hope to achieve." Caridelis softened her expression. "However, that does not mean I intend to treat you as an animal. Do you treat other humans badly because you are superior to them?"

"No. But, I won't be owned."

"I have no intention of owning you or anyone else. If you don't want me around, just say so and I'll leave. I am merely offering you friendship and guidance as you might offer it to a beloved dog or cat or horse. You crap in my house and I will discipline you, you treat me respectfully and I'll look out for you and give you advice."

"I think I understand your point."

She has some agenda, Stephenie. Be careful.

"Of course I have an agenda, Ghost. But my motivation to help the two of you does not mean it has anything to do with you nor does it mean it will harm you." Caridelis turned her attention back to Stephenie. "You will have to teach him to speak our language and improve your abilities as well, otherwise our friendship may have to wait until he is dead."

Stephenie swallowed. She knew it was not a threat on Kas' life, simply a statement of fact from a being with a limited amount of patience. "I will teach him."

"Good. Now let's find something to practice on. I imagine you learn best by watching."

Chapter 32

Caridelis led Stephenie and Kas outside and into one of the fields of wild grasses. The sun was just coming up and drifts of snow were blowing over the eastern ridge of the valley, only to melt as the ice particles hit the invisible dome of warmth that Isa maintain around the city.

Caridelis meandered through the swaying plants, not saying anything and Stephenie was not inclined to challenge the dragon. Outside the castle, the woman seemed taller and more powerful, though Stephenie could not see any specific difference. After a time, Caridelis stopped and the ground exploded in front of them, sending soil and plants into the air, but none of it hit her or Stephenie, who stood slightly behind the woman.

Out of the small explosion, two rodents the size of large rats flew into the air. They squirmed and squeaked as they hovered in front of Caridelis. "These are not people, but they have sufficient life-force that you should be able to observe what happens." Caridelis turned her head toward Stephenie. "I highly suggest you try this on other animals before you try it on Kas or another person. Unless you don't like the person."

"You're not going to harm them, are you?"

"I won't, but you may not be as successful." She looked down into the small hole in the ground and Stephenie felt there were at least three more animals in the burrow. The ground ruptured and two more lifted into the air. "Perhaps a couple of spares in case this doesn't go well."

Stephenie's face fell. She did not want to harm these rodents. However, she felt Kas' connection to her and she steeled herself to the task. She forced herself to be pragmatic, "We can always eat it if I accidentally kill it. Then if won't be a waste."

Caridelis raised her eyebrows. "Suit yourself. If you are ready, pay very close attention to the fields I create. I will do it slowly." Stephenie nodded her head and one of the four rodents moved between the two of them while the other three struggled in midair off to the side. "We have to pull the energy that makes the animal actually be the animal from its physical form. We are not trying to freeze the body, that damages the cells, we just want to break the connections between the physical body and the energy in the creature."

Stephenie focused her attention on the animal, even closing her eyes and pushing Kas from her head as to avoid any distractions. The field Caridelis created held a pattern Stephenie had never seen before. It looked disruptive and jarring. Not elegant. Not a field that would conserve energy. Slowly, Caridelis pulled the field though the animal and it started to panic and fight against the invisible bonds of gravity that held it in the air. As soon as the field passed through the animal's head, the body went limp. However, Caridelis did not release her field, instead, she changed it, building more of a trap that held the energy pattern together, locking it in place.

"The trap keeps the animal's energy together. Your Kas and the others of Arkani ended up having this happen as a side effect to all those mages trying to strengthen the fields around the city. Those on the inside trying to block out those who they thought wanted in and those on the outside who simply wanted the Dalish people inside to never escape." Caridelis moved the contained energy around in the air and then pushed it back into the animal. She created the disrupting field again, but it always remained just ahead of the animal's energy as she laid it back down in its flesh. When she finished, the animal gasped for air and twitched several times before it resumed its struggles.

Caridelis smiled and released the animal back into the ground. "Now you try."

Stephenie inhaled as she looked to Kas, but he only shrugged. She turned back to the rodent that Caridelis had moved between them. Carefully, Stephenie tried to reproduce the field she had seen.

"No, more like this," the dragon said, bending the pattern of Stephenie's field. "Good, you have it, now draw it through the animal. Good, a little more slowly. Quick, wrap the energy. Yes."

Stephenie stared at the limp form and the contained ball of energy. She had never thought it would be that easy to extract the essence of a person from their body.

"Do not get cocky," Caridelis said. "Put the animal back before you lose control over the binding field. Unlike Kas, who has natural ability to adjust energy and maintain the field that holds him together, the rodent does not."

Stephenie felt her hands shake as she worked to reverse the process. Her jaw tightened and her heart raced. But the first time through, she could not get the energy back into the body. Caridelis took over the field for a moment to prevent the animal from dying.

"Try again. I will give it back."

Stephenie bit her lip and closed her eyes. She concentrated on reproducing what the dragon had done. Slowly and methodically, she drew the disrupting field through the animal as she laid down its energy. When she was done, she could hardly believe the animal was again struggling in Caridelis' gravity field. "Is this as easy to do to a person?"

"Not someone with even the slightest hint of magic. This field that allows you to break the bonds between their physical form and their energy is extremely easy to disturb. Anything with power will instinctively fight against it."

Caridelis looked into the rodent's eyes and then suddenly it stopped moving.

"You killed it!"

"Its life is less than a blink of my eye. The body will now serve a purpose. If you want to rebuild a body for Kas, you need matter to use as a base. I recommend a recently dead body for this, that way you have to change less of it to match what Kas still has subconsciously programmed into his field. If you were powerful enough, you could convert other matter to be what you need, but that takes much more energy and control. Much safer to start with something mostly there and manipulate it. Of course, you may be squeamish about killing someone or using a dead body, so perhaps you should use a large animal."

Caridelis pulled another rodent around to hover between them. "Extract this one's energy and hold it. This one is a female."

Stephenie nodded her head and repeated the process to extract the animal's energy. This time it was easier than the last and she needed no assistance.

Caridelis held up a hand. "Now, I will guide you through the process of taking the raw matter and building a new body for that lemming."

Stephenie felt Caridelis' mind hit hers. The intensity of the dragon's personality overwhelmed her and even if she had wanted to resist, she would not have been able to hold back the tide of power. The dragon had such a vastness to her consciousness that Stephenie felt herself growing lost in its depths. She knew the dragon could rummage through every aspect of her being and there was nothing she could do to stop it. However, Caridelis did not seem to dig in her memories.

One thing Stephenie did realize was Caridelis' intelligence was not human. It was not as different as a human to a cat, but there was an alien quality that Stephenie sometimes felt traces of in herself.

"Concentrate. This task requires a great deal of attention. You have to feel the lemming's energy, all of it and translate the map to the physical form. It will take some practice. If the animal's energy pattern is not complete, you will need to invent the missing details, which I can tell will be necessary in Kas' case."

How bad is he? She asked across the mental link.

It grows worse with time and eventually there will be too much damage to build a body. As it is, you will need to study human forms. Examine the minute details with your mind's eye. "Now watch what I do."

Stephenie felt Caridelis take over her body and lead her in using her powers. She watched as the energy that made up the lemming was examined bit-by-bit, piece-by-piece. Initially she was not sure what she felt or learned from the tiny particles and states of energy, but

Caridelis took each piece of the information and walked through the body of the lemming. Caridelis used fields similar to those that Stephenie had used to liquefy stone and metal, breaking apart the tiny structures of the body and rearranged things. It almost seemed more instinct than actual thought, as though Caridelis had an intuition of how the parts needed to be reassembled.

The process seemed to go on forever and Stephenie began to feel the toll of the energy on herself, but Caridelis did not relent. The dragon simply continued the work, slowly shifting every aspect of the animal's body, converting what had been the body of a juvenile male into a young female body.

The longer they worked at it, the more Stephenie began to understand. The more she saw of the fields, the easier they became to craft and control and even easier for her to see.

By the time they were done rebuilding the tiny body, Stephenie's legs trembled with fatigue. Her body ached and she realized her stomach had been growling for food. However, the animal's energy had to be put into the new body. With care, Caridelis guided Stephenie in repeating the disruptive field and they slowly laid the animal's consciousness into the new body. When the animal jerked and squirmed with life, Stephenie opened her eyes. Night had fallen and the air had grown cool.

Caridelis released the animal back into the hole in the ground. It scrambled away on unsteady legs, but it seemed healthy enough. The one remaining lemming appeared to have been released earlier in the day without Stephenie's notice.

"Is the process that long?"

Caridelis laughed. "You did well for your first time. You have to rebuild everything in Kas' case. It takes time, though you did improve your speed as you progressed." The dragon looked at the mountains to the south and west. "Even people who come back to their own bodies need to make physical modifications, otherwise there will be no memory of the time away and problems will occur, even death. It is why it is seldom done."

Stephenie nodded her head as she stretched her shoulders and back. She had stood outside for an entire day to rebuild the body of one rodent. She thought she could do it again, but would definitely have to practice more before she ever thought to do that to Kas. *I could end up killing innocent animals in the process.* The fact that she knew she would take the risk frightened her.

"If you need a way to justify it, then I would suggest practicing on larger livestock. The humans raise several large animals for food. Do it on one they plan to slaughter. If you fail, it's dinner for someone."

She knew the dragon had left her mind, but it was unsettling just how easily Caridelis knew what she was thinking. "It would take days to do something that large."

"You'll need to be good enough to do something Kas' size. And depending on the size of the body you choose, you may have extra matter, or may even need to combine more than one body."

Stephenie looked over to Kas whom she knew had watched the events, but had said nothing so far. *Can you live with this?*

I will not condone killing someone just to provide me with a body. I would never be able to feel right about that.

Caridelis shook her head. "Get yourselves straight on what you want to do. I already said the body does not have to be human. There is plenty of raw material in those large deer." The dragon took a step away.

"I still don't understand why you want to help," Stephenie said. "I am very appreciative, but..."

"I've warned you already not to attribute human motivations to my actions. You intrigue me enough to keep me from killing you, therefore, I will make you my little project." The dragon glanced around the area and then dusted her hands against each other. "Things are changing. Perhaps one day I will be free to fly the skies again as I choose."

"Thank you. Thank you for everything."

The dragon nodded her head and turned away. "I will leave you now. However, when I feel like it, I will return. Do not come looking for me on your own."

The bloom of energy Stephenie felt inside of Caridelis blinded her for a moment, then suddenly the woman's body shimmered as it elongated and stretched. Power and energy surged as a long lizard took shape in the matter of two heartbeats. Only two feet away from her stood a dragon. The creature was beauty itself. Iridescent blue-green scales covered the thirty foot length from the tip of her snout to the end of her spiked tail. Her whole body was lean and muscular.

Stephenie looked into the dragon's emerald eyes as Caridelis turned her head on her long neck and Stephenie found she could not look away. Even the long row of spiked teeth could not pull her attention. Then suddenly the dragon was in the air. Its massive wings thrust outward, pushing down a blast of air against the ground.

Stephenie sensed the gravity fields around the creature, but seeing the pulsing wings and sinewy undulation of Caridelis' tail left her desperate to fly. *She's the most elegant being I've ever seen,* she told Kas.

And the most deadly we have ever met.

Chapter 33

Lami had risen from his bed and the noise woke Henton, though he was not certain he had actually been asleep. He instinctively sat up and checked on Ryia as he had done countless times through the night. She continued to sleep and he let her. She had awoken once the evening before and she cried in pain before realizing the extent of her injury and her tears turned to despair. *Please don't give up, Ryia.*

"She live," Lami declared. "I sense."

Henton nodded his head. "I didn't get to apologize yesterday, but I am sorry we caused Perain to become angry with you."

Lami smiled. "Dogs not bad as Perain think. You push, but careful."

It had been hard for Henton to balance his fear for Ryia's life and pushing the dogs too far. If he had driven them to injury or death, then it would have taken even longer to get her to Lami. *I managed to do it,* he thought to himself. *But what state have I left her in?*

Lami pulled on a fresh shirt and started putting together a morning meal. Henton glanced to the front door and wondered how he would be able to continue to deflect questions about Stephenie. The rumor that she had gone into Ista had spread quickly and he knew too many people in Alkmaar were talking about the ghost sled. *And when Stephenie does show up, coming from the waste on foot or flying, doing in a day, what would take a dog team two days, it will be unsettling for the locals. I just hope she grabs the food we left for her.*

"She awake?" Douglas asked in Cothish from where he was laying.

Henton shook his head. He did not think Ryia would be able to ignore the pain and pretend to sleep. Lami had managed to get her to drink a syrupy beverage before she passed out, but the look in her eyes spoke of total desolation. *Stay strong, Ryia. We can get you through this.*

"It's not your fault, Sarge."

Henton turned to face Douglas. "But it is. I could have insisted she remain in Antar. I could have prevented this."

"And she would have run off and possibly been burned as a witch. She was at risk if she came with us or not. At least here, we can wait for Steph. Steph might be able to do something. If she ever figures out how to build a body for Kas, what's an arm for Ryia?"

Henton wanted to believe it would be true, but first Ryia had to not give up on life and second, Stephenie had to do what might be impossible, *she has to escape her father's grasp.* He turned away and pushed himself to his feet. He needed to do something. "Lami, do you need any help?"

"Do you not care about your friend?" Perain demanded yet again. "At least confirm where you left her." Perain shook his head and spoke a few words to Lami who said nothing as he fixed a mid-day meal.

After several moments of silence, Henton finally spoke. "I care for Stephenie very much. I just don't want your people to come to harm in going after her."

"I am guessing she's at the border camp. To walk a hundred-fifty miles in the snow will take her twenty days. She could never carry that much food and supplies."

"Perain, Chosen," Lami said, then spoke at length in their language. Eventually, the two of them stopped speaking and Perain turned to Henton.

A moan of anguish came from Ryia and Henton crossed the room in a single bound. "Ryia, try not to move." She sobbed and tried to roll to her left, but Henton held her shoulders down. "Ryia, the healing of your arm is fragile. Lami's been working on you. You have to take it easy."

"It hurts!"

Henton brushed her dirty hair out of her face and gently stroked her cheek. "Ryia. Lami's coming."

"Keep him out of my mind. I want to die. I..." She sobbed as tears leaked from her tightly closed eyes. "It hurts so much."

"Ryia, listen to me. Stephenie will be here soon to help you. She'll find a way to fix this."

She opened her eyes. Pain filled her expression, but Henton did not know how much was physical and how much was the knowledge her arm was missing. Every time he looked at the wrapped stump of her arm all he could see was the shredded bits of muscle and skin he had to cut away from the exposed bone.

"Ryia, drink this," Henton said, taking a mug from Lami's hand. Carefully he put one arm under her shoulders and lifted her body. She moved both arms to try and grasp the cup and suddenly turned away. "Ryia, you need to drink and eat. You need to keep up your strength. You need to use your powers to heal yourself until Stephenie can come back and do more."

"I'm useless."

"No you're not. I'm not going anywhere. If you don't drink this willingly, I'll force it down your throat. I'm not going to let you give up on me. Got that!"

Ryia turned her head back to him. Tears still fell from her face. "You didn't want me before, now I'm even less of a person."

Henton set the mug down and turned her chin to look at him. "Don't make me force you to run laps around this house. You get your head straight and quit whining. No one here cares about your arm and Steph will make you better, but if you give up before she gets here, then you really are worthless. Now act like a soldier and fight." He released her chin, picked up the mug, and held it out to her.

Slowly she raised her left hand and took the mug from him. She wrinkled her nose at the smell of the thick liquid, but she forced it down and then handed the mug back to him.

"I want you to survive, Ryia. I will make sure you get better."

She nodded her head. "Thank you."

"Yeah, Ryia," Douglas said as he knelt on her other side while Henton eased her back down onto the fur rugs. "You think I can run a tailor shop on my own? I need someone to stand around and use her wise-ass mouth to chase off the deadbeats. You need to get your strength back. I need your sassy mouth."

A hint of a smile passed over her lips as her eyes started to droop. Henton rubbed her forehead and caressed her hair until her eyes closed all the way.

"She sleep," Lami said. "Rest."

Henton did not know if he had the strength to deal with her injury. Early in his career, he had a promising soldier named Vikden who had lost a hand. The eighteen year-old simply gave up on life and despite the healers, he never recovered. He died a few weeks later from drink and the look in Ryia's eyes reminded him too much of Vikden.

"She'll pull through," Douglas said. "Ryia's a fighter, even if she moans about things a bit. She's always fought on even when things have been tough."

Henton nodded his head. Douglas had never known Vikden. He got up and walked back across the room to sit down in one of Lami's chairs. "You're right, Douglas. She's strong and when Steph gets here, she'll make sure Ryia makes a full recovery.

Perain cleared his throat. "I've never seen anyone get a finger back, let alone an arm. But even if Stephenie is favored by the Goddess or what your people would call a witch, that's no reason to leave her out there."

"I expect her to be here in a couple of days," Henton said.

Lami looked to the door just as it opened. A woman with long blond hair stepped down into the room. "I did not catch what you had said," the woman's sweet voice came in accented Pandar. "Were you talking about Stephenie?"

Henton felt his mind start to cloud and he pushed back on what he knew to be an intrusion into his thoughts. He stood. His hands itched for the staff that was laying under the blankets at Ryia's side. He was a dozen feet away and knew he'd never make it to the weapon. Douglas was closer. *I just need to keep her—*

"Busy?" The woman finished for him. She pulled off her gloves and tossed them across the room and onto the fur rugs. "What a small building. It is positively horrid, but I am sure Islet would prefer this to standing out in the cold."

Almost on demand, Islet stumbled into the building, followed by Sir Walter, a heavily bundled Jerylin, and a black-haired man Henton did not recognize. The man pulled the door shut behind himself.

"I don't know what your problem is, woman," Henton growled, hoping anger could push her out of his mind, "but you can leave. You've not been invited into this home."

The woman chuckled. "You think I am some kind of..." she looked to the slender man who had removed his coat and dropped it to the floor. "What did those people call us? Ah yes," she turned back to Henton. "Vampire I believe was the word those people in Elk Valley thought I was." She shrugged as she shed her coat. "They thought there was some protection they had that prevented me from entering their house without an invitation. Really, what an absurd concept. First, I'm not some undead monster—really, I'm not. Second, I will do as I please."

"Stephenie will kill you, Yreka!" Douglas shouted with some difficulty.

"That is the hope of this desperate sister of hers." Yreka turned to Islet, "Is it not?"

Islet's glare held so much hate and contempt that Henton found himself hoping again. "She's not here. So you can leave."

"No," Yreka growled. "You've killed two of my associates. I worried that something had happened when I could not contact them, but I see it clearly in your head. You let that sniveling little girl talk you into going outside and you stumbled upon them. Olena would have left you alone. Now she is dead with her face burned from her skull and for that, you will pay." A cold smile rose to her lips. "But do not worry yet, you will live until after I have dealt with your precious Stephenie." Yreka turned to Perain. "You are not needed. Though, Henton is likely right, I expect that she'll come here without the need for your sleds. Islet had seen Stephenie fly plenty of times and I have a fair idea of her skill. The question is, how long can she keep the flight up?"

Henton moved a step toward Yreka, hoping to give Douglas a chance to get the staff. "Leave these people alone, they have nothing to do with this."

Yreka frowned at Henton. "I already told Perain to leave. I have no intention of harming the locals, I am only here to deal with the people who murdered my relatives." She turned toward Perain. "You heard me say it, I will not harm you if you leave me alone. Tell the others." She motioned to Lami with her head. "However, I would also never ask the owner of his home to leave his own property. He'll come to no harm if he stays and continues to heal Ryia. I would hate for the girl to die before I deal with Stephenie." Yreka looked toward the other man, "Werha, why don't you go bring me the staff so these two can stop getting all excited. They might wet themselves."

Douglas leaped forward but then hung in the air. Henton felt himself trapped by an invisible barrier. It pressed on him uncomfortably, but not painfully. Yreka's companion walked passed Henton, nearly brushing his shoulder, but Henton could not move his body. The man removed the staff from under the blankets and walked it back to Yreka.

"Mistress," he said as he handed it to her.

"Thank you, Werha." She held up the steel capped weapon and examined it carefully as Douglas fell to the floor and Henton found himself able to move again. "Interesting. So Stephenie's father gave this—and a dagger you say—to the priests of Mertor with the intent that they kill her." Yreka looked around the room and walked over to the ledge of stone that ran along the inside of the building's foundation. She pushed aside some jars and sat down before looking back at Henton. "That one does not think anyone going to Ista will ever return. However, Lami is not so certain Ista means death, since it is possible her father is from there."

"Stay out of our heads," Henton demanded.

"Make me," Yreka said with a gleam in her eyes. "Stephenie tells you it is hard for her to read your thoughts. Either she is rather poorly skilled with that talent, or she is intentionally holding back. But the more you struggle, the more fun it is for me."

"Henton, don't try to fight it," Islet said. She had loosened her own coat and came over to his side. "We both know what Stephenie can do and Yreka will be sorry for pressing this."

Yreka chuckled. "Let me ruin her happy delusion, Henton, please." Yreka stood up and held the staff out in front of her so everyone could see. "You see, between Henton's and Douglas' minds, I have learned that I have the weapon that Stephenie used to kill Daeri and Henton used to kill Olena and Tibva. Stephenie has been teaching this weapon how to defend itself against all the attacks she knows." Yreka smiled. "Thank you for that."

Yreka turned back to Werha. "I'm done with them, they can stay unbound if they cooperate. Otherwise, we'll tie them up." She glanced at Henton. "And just for you, any attempt to escape will cause these three girls to all lose an arm. Since your Ryia is down to one, you might not want to risk her last one."

Henton's jaw tightened. He knew they did not have many options and that he should remain silent, but the woman had walked so easily through his mind that he doubted it would make any difference. "You can gloat for now, but Stephenie has gone to find her father, the man who owns those weapons. Do you think he'd leave her without a way to defeat the weapons?"

Yreka looked at the staff. "Perhaps, but he did ask people to kill her, so I'm thinking they may not be on the best of terms. But even if she comes back with some knowledge her father imparted, well, we always have your safety to distract her with. Werha and I both were fond of Olena and we will not let her death pass unpunished." She looked to Lami. "Why don't you finish fixing lunch while I let Islet remind Henton that trying to kill himself won't work because I can gut his mind just like Stephenie did to Favian? Then Islet and Walter can cuddle some more."

Chapter 34

Stephenie and Kas had talked well into the night about what Caridelis had revealed to them as well as the prospect of rebuilding Kas' body. When morning came, she was exhausted and it took her longer than she had desired before she climbed out of the bed. However, once she had risen, she took a bath to help wake her mind, gathered a couple of books, several maps, and assembled the rest of her gear. She reconfirmed with Isa that she could not commit to the castle's offer without speaking to her friends and then she and Kas took to the air and headed south toward the border.

At first, as she flew, she simply allowed her tired mind to wander. She looked at the sky and the clouds and the snow covered land. But always her mind continued to circle around Isa, the offer, her sire, what she was, and what the others would say when she told them.

The sun had crossed the sky and despite the deliberations, she still had not come to a solid decision. She knew what she wanted, but she did not know if it was the correct choice. She wanted the others to agree with her, *but would they?*

Kas had said they would not leave her for being part dragon, but the knowledge of what she was frightened even her. Some of the traits she fought against, such as the possessiveness and protectiveness she felt, had been very obvious in Caridelis' mind. If she let those traits free, she could be a danger to those she loved the most. And while Kas would not leave her, the fact that dragons still existed and appeared to have an interest in her, frightened him more than he would admit. *And then Isa has made it worse for him. He doesn't trust her,* she thought to herself. *What am I to do? The others won't believe any of this. And should I even tell them?*

Stephenie, Kas' voice intruded on her private musings.

She pulled herself out of her pensive state and looked in Kas' direction. *What is it?* She asked, sensing his concern.

We are almost there. Do you sense the dogs?

Stephenie looked ahead. The sun had set and the encampment was in view. The monotony of the landscape had caused her to completely lose track of the passing of time. Reaching out with her senses, she looked for any signs of the others. *Nothing,* she swore as her speed increased.

I don't sense any of them, she said flying over the buildings. *The dogs, all of them are gone!* A cloud of snow flew into the air as she impacted the ground.

The sleds are gone as well, Kas said, so they must have left for some reason.

Stephenie rushed into the building they had been using. The fire in the pit had long ago burned itself out. Most of their supplies were still stacked up, but their personal gear was gone. She moved about the dark room, using her magic to feel the space, and then as her chest tightened and her breathing turned shallow, she pushed energy into an oil lamp that had been left.

Light spread out, but it was not enough to brighten the whole room. She went to grab the lamp and noticed a piece of paper under it. She read the Cothish words aloud, moving toward the door before she had finished.

> *Lami.*
> *No one dead.*
> *Two Senzar bodies east, only two here.*

She rushed out the door, dropping the lamp into the snow the moment she was outside the building. After two steps, she leapt into the air. She raced to the east, flying fast until she noticed two dark masses on the ground. It was easy to see they were bodies. She landed next to the farther of them.

"Based on the energy coming from them, they appear to be frozen solid," Kas said cautiously as he joined her side. "They are near the same energy state as the snow, so I expect this occurred a while ago."

Stephenie knelt down and examined the woman. "Henton wrote the letter; I recognize his hand. And this one was hit with lightning. Her chest and face are burned up. Was Douglas hurt? Why did they go to Lami?"

Kas drifted toward the other body. "I would conclude the same of this one."

"How did they get here? How did they know to come here?"

"I am uncertain, though I must now consider that perhaps this Yreka had managed to gain the information from your sister."

Stephenie performed a quick search of the woman's possessions, but found only a few coins, a long dagger, and an eating knife. "They must have had a camp around here. But why again just some of their group? Are these the people Jerylin reported with Yreka or not?"

Kas came closer. "Can you even be certain they are Senzar? Could Henton have mistook them?"

Stephenie tossed a coin in Kas' direction, though he made no move to intercept it and it fell into the snow. "It is a Senzar marker. I saw the symbol for fourth generation on it."

Stephenie lifted herself into the air again. She continued east, flying higher to get a wider field of view, though it made it hard to sense details on the ground. Out on the sea ice, she noticed something dark and headed toward the object. When she got close, it was obviously a sled concealed under a pile of white furs, some of which had been blown back to reveal the wooden frame under it.

Stephenie landed next to the sled. A small tent had also blown over. She pulled the furs from the sled and narrowed her eyes. "There are no harnesses for dogs."

Kas floated above the supplies still on the sled. "There is also no dog food. Could they perhaps have gone light and used gravity to propel the sled?"

Stephenie nodded her head. "It would be tiring if done for long periods, but I've found with more and more practice, that manipulating gravity is one of the least taxing things I can do."

"That is true for many mages."

Stephenie looked around the snow covered ice. "The sled came here, but I don't see any other sled tracks, although the wind could have erased them. However, this one sled and tent are not big enough for more than two." She picked up the tent and forced her way into the collapsed structure. Kas followed her through the thick side. "Two bed rolls. Food. Clothing." Stephenie fought with the tent to keep it held upright and when it would not cooperate, she flung a gravity wave upward, ripping the top of the tent in two and throwing the halves to the side.

Standing again in the open air, she started tossing aside the mundane possessions the dead Senzar had left. When she found a satchel, she opened it up and dumped the contents onto the blankets where she stood. Two journals, a small box, a bag of what sounded like coins, and a pair of small oval stones fell out. She picked up the journals and thumbed thought them quickly. It was written in the language of the dragons and Stephenie quickly scanned some of the last entries. "They've been following us, but...it looks like the word distance." She frowned. "They've been reporting to Yreka somehow. She's still trailing behind us, but getting close."

Kas pointed to the stones. "We had similar items in my time. They likely allow communication over distances."

Stephenie opened the box and found powder for ink, quills, and a couple of small jars where the ink could be mixed. The pouch contained more coins. She gathered the items from the satchel and put them back into the leather bag. "If Henton and the others went to Lami, then they could be in danger from Yreka. We have to get back to Alkmaar in case she is getting close."

"If they are hiding there, perhaps they will be concealed."

Stephenie frowned. "I don't like Henton's second statement about no one being dead." Stephenie lifted back into the air and stayed lower to the ground as she returned to the bodies. From there, she moved slowly toward the buildings. *If these two died here, Ryia would have had to been fairly close to use the staff.*

It is a reasonable assumption.

Stephenie slowed when she spotted another dark spot in the snow. The wind had drifted a thin layer of powder over the top, partially concealing what had happened. She landed and knelt down. In the darkness, it took her a moment to realize someone had bled significantly. She stood up and looked around. A long line had been melted into the ice near the blood.

Stephenie, please remember that Henton said no one had died.

Stephenie whirred about and rushed over to where Kas hovered. At his feet was a frozen hand. The forearm was shredded. *Ryia!* The size of the bluish hand left no doubt.

"Henton said she lived."

"In time to get to Lami?" Stephenie launched into the air, the snow below her crushed down under the force that pushed her from the ground. She flew at the buildings and smashed through the door, not bothering to touch the ground. Her pack and supplies leapt into her hand. She flew back out of the building and rocketed north. She crossed the border and flew toward the guardians positioned half a mile from the border and concealed by a rise in the ground.

She reached out to the guardian. *Isa, can you hear me?*

"Stephenie, what are you doing?" Kas demanded.

Isa, if I live, I will return. But, if a woman named Yreka comes in my stead, she has killed me and my friends and I ask that you destroy her.

Stephenie sensed a vague impression of the castle. These guardians were linked to her, but not as tightly as those that were in Isa Fields. After a moment, she felt Isa's acceptance and eight of the stone cats stood, turned toward the south, and started tearing through the snow like charging bears.

"Stephenie?"

Kas, I am sorry, but I was going to accept Isa anyway. I think you know that.

I did, My Love.

She let him know how much she appreciated his understanding. *If we don't survive, I want to make sure Yreka dies. Isa is sending these to help us, but we can't wait for them. We'll follow the road in case Henton and the others are not yet to Lami's, the guardians will head straight to Alkmaar, though I think we will still arrive first.* Without another word, she launched herself into the bitter air and flew south as fast as she could.

Chapter 35

The sun rose, brightening the horizon when Stephenie came upon Alkmaar. The lack of sleep and constant draw of energy for the extended flight had left her with a throbbing headache. Her body hurt and she knew that she was close to overextending herself. The fact that she had not found any signs of Henton, Douglas, or Ryia along the road left her numb. She did not want them to be suffering on the ice, but she wanted to know where they were. She kept hoping they were safe at Lami's, but not knowing with certainty brought her physical pain.

She appreciated Kas not trying to console her. Words would not fix what had happened and she knew herself well enough to know she would start yelling and Kas did not deserve that.

A mile from the city, she landed on the road and trudged through the snow on foot. There were already people about the streets of Alkmaar and she did not want to let anyone see her in the air. The likelihood that people would overact and impede her was too great. Kas had remained beside her, but he asked, *do you want me to search ahead?*

"No. Yreka may be there. I don't want you to confront her without me."

Are you in any condition to confront her yourself?

Stephenie did not respond. Instead, she pushed herself into a jog as she neared the city gates. Her breath came in gulps and filled the air with clouds that quickly dispersed in the wind. She ran through the open gates and continued jogging down the snow packed streets toward Lami's home. *Please be okay,* she told the others as her possessive rage continued to build.

The few people she passed watched her hurried pace, but no one said anything, possibly because none of them spoke her language. However, she felt a sense of concern coming from them. It was not panic, but a feeling that something was wrong mixed with a bit of fear.

When she was still several buildings from Lami's home, she slowed her pace, partially to catch her breath, but also so she could extend her senses and look for potential threats as well as signs of her friends. Fatigued, the effort to use her mental powers hurt and she stopped and put a hand on the stacked stone building beside her. She closed her eyes against the pain and took a long, deep breath. There were people in the building next to her, but the other buildings between her and Lami's house were empty, as they had been when she was here last.

With Lami's house at the edge of her ability to sense, she walked slowly forward. Each step brought her closer and allowed her mind to see further into Lami's home. After eight steps, she sensed a person whose mind she did not recognize. It took a moment to discern more, but she became certain it was a man. Five more steps and she felt a very agitated Lami and a shadow of a presence that was so muted it almost did not exist in her mind. Six more steps and she felt Douglas, another man, and—*Islet!*

Stephenie's pace increased as she drew energy into her tired body. The burning of her insides hurt, but the pain fell to the back of her mind as the first man and the shadow presence reacted. The man moved away while the shadow—*a woman*—moved toward the door.

Kas, they have Islet here. Damn it, they took Islet from Antar!

I will try to protect the others, Kas said, moving to her left and above the last empty building between them and Lami's home.

Stephenie stopped at the edge of the empty building as the door to Lami's house opened and a small woman walked up the steps. The woman wore light garments for the frigid weather and her long blond hair swayed gracefully in the wind. It moved almost as a single mass and Stephenie saw the energy fields moving among the strands to keep her hair under control. Stephenie could also see the large draw of energy into the woman.

"We finally meet, Princess," the woman said in accented Pandar.

Stephenie noted the steel-capped staff in the woman's right hand and felt her confidence waver. She had only beaten the High Priest of Mertor because she had used a bundle of poison dust to penetrate the staff's field. She had not retained any of the deadly poison because of the risk to herself and the others. *What has the bitch done to them?*

"Are you shy? You have nothing to say?"

Stephenie felt Henton and several others being escorted toward the door and her heart skipped a beat. *They're alive!* The woman came up to the ground level and stepped aside as Lami, Henton, Douglas, Sir Walter, Jerylin, and Islet were ushered out by a man dressed in heavy clothing. Her friends were lightly dressed and immediately huddled together as they began to shiver in the biting wind. Stephenie pushed her senses and felt the muted presence of Ryia still in the back of Lami's home. "You've harmed my family and friends," Stephenie growled as she slid her pack off her back and dropped it to the ground.

"And you've killed mine," came Yreka's icy response. "It is against our laws to kill the protected members of a family."

Stephenie moved forward, past the edge of the building and into the street that ran in front of Lami's home. "I know nothing of your families, but your people killed my father and took Islet and harmed thousands of my people first."

"None of them are protected," Yreka said simply. "And you lie to my face. My people have not killed your father. The King of Cothel sure, but I have not met your father." Yreka looked at that staff and picked her long nail against the steel cap. "I really had hoped to find out who would breed such an insolent child, but I understand he's been trying to kill you." She raised the staff toward Stephenie, "Well, perhaps he realized your crimes would extend my wrath to him and he wanted to avoid the punishment."

Stephenie's mind shifted her strategy. If her sire had not sent this woman to kill her, hopefully it meant she did not have any additional weapons from him to use against her. "The King was my father for everything that matters."

Yreka laughed and shook her head. "Someone without power is insignificant. The important man is the one who gifted you your powers." Yreka's eyes narrowed. "I see you have managed a much better control of your thoughts than your sister and the others. Tell me, did you meet him? I am here to judge you and a failed attempt to kill you will not absolve him of your crimes."

Stephenie felt the subtle brush of Yreka's power, but the woman had not tried to enter her mind. "Your people attacked my family first. I merely defended myself. Now let my friends go, Yreka. Leave this place."

Yreka smiled. "No. You had a chance to declare yourself to Favian, but instead you chose to kill him. I do not care if you were ignorant of our laws or not, you will die for your crimes."

"He was holding my sister hostage!"

"Irrelevant. He was seventh generation and a protected member of my family. If you had a grievance with him, proper protocol is for you to come to me over it. I decide what is to be done. You failed to do that, so after I execute you, I will execute your friends."

Stephenie felt Kas move toward the bundled man that had ushered everyone out of Lami's home. Yreka's hand moved and a blinding blast of energy smashed into Kas.

Stephenie screamed as energy flowed from her hands and smashed into the shield that instantly formed around Yreka.

Stephenie reached out and searched for Kas, but could not sense him. Her search and hesitation stopped as Jerylin screamed in pain. The bundled man had struck her with a gravity wave that ripped through the woman's chest. Blood and flesh sprayed over Islet and the outside of Lami's house

Stephenie felt an energy thread form between her head and the staff. Instinct drove her to link the staff's thread back to a control thread that came from Yreka a heartbeat before lightning filled the air.

The blinding flash arced around, looped back, slammed into the surface of the shield the staff generated, and then bounced into Lami's house, blowing snow and sod into the air. As the thunder dissipated into the air, Yreka could not mask the surprise on her face.

Stephenie failed to take advantage of the surprise. Instead, she focused on the channels coming from the bundled man that connected with Henton. A cry of pain escaped her lips as she built her own field to deflect the gravitational energy away from her friends. Her fatigue and the distance left her hands trembling.

Pain exploded through her body and Stephenie staggered back a step as she realized another blast of lightning burned a hole into her side. She had automatically absorbed the energy, pulling it into herself as fast as the staff unleashed it, but her ribs were blackened around the three inch hole in her gut.

Stephenie rammed all that power, plus what she pulled from the ground, at the bundled man even as another lightning bold struck her side. She tasted the man's fear and a momentary spike of emotion from Yreka as the field protecting the man collapsed.

The man's defenses failed before Yreka could react and the chaotic streams of energy flying from Stephenie's hands incinerated the man's head and chest before slamming into Lami's house. The ground shook, stones in the wall of the house exploded, and a large section of snow and sod on the roof vaporized.

Yreka screamed in rage, sending a gravity wave slamming into Stephenie. Her instincts cushioned her body as she hit the building behind her, knocking in a section of the building's wall.

Stephenie felt lightning strike her chest. The electricity made her heart stop as every muscle in her body contracted. However, her mind pulled the energy inward. She opened the void in her as wide as she ever had before. Her bones burned from the inside out as energy ripped through her. She did not know how to beat the staff. She had worked with Ryia to teach it how to defend itself against everything she knew how to throw at it. *Kas,* Stephenie pleaded, but she could not sense him.

She had a vague idea that Henton was fleeing around the other side of Lami's home. Her body trembled as energy struck it again and again.

"You're not dead yet?"

Stephenie could not open her eyes. She hurt so much she had no idea if Yreka was still hitting her with lightning or not. Her flesh cooked from within. Desperation pulled at her and she hoped Isa would destroy this woman. With half a thought, she reached out to the staff. *Please, you know me. I will take you home.*

"You killed Werha. You will suffer for that. I will kill your friends, then I will go find your father and kill...what did you do?" Yreka tossed aside the staff. "Clever girl, it would appear you knew more about the staff then you told the others. But I don't need the staff to destroy you."

Stephenie's senses cleared slightly as the web of energy channels in the air diminished. Through the pain, she reached out to search for Kas, but he was gone. *Without warning, just gone. I was so close!* The possessive rage billowed up within her. The others were now far enough away and Stephenie wanted nothing more than to burn this woman to the ground.

Instead of fighting against the pain, Stephenie turned toward it and continued to rip energy from the ground and her surroundings. Her entire body exploded in flames as a gout of raw energy erupted from her and slammed into Yreka.

The energy blinded Stephenie and it was gone in an instant. She whimpered with pain. Her mind felt nothing and her muscles trembled uncontrollably from the cold. She forced open her eyes, they burned as she tried to see. *No,* Stephenie cried. Yreka had been knocked back, but she still stood unscathed in the middle of a small circle of snowy ice that was surrounded by scorched stones. *Damn you!*

The woman stared at Stephenie. Then ever so slightly, Yreka tilted her head. Stephenie felt energy flowing into the woman.

Naked and freezing on the ground, Stephenie whimpered again. *Why won't you die?* Blood ran from her nose, mouth, and ears. Her flesh was blistered and raw. Her muscles had no strength and she could not even raise her arms. Her senses were blinded and she could not feel anyone, but that was fine because she did not want to feel. Jerylin was dead, Kas was gone, and she knew Ryia was severely injured.

She tried to speak, but blood poured from her lungs and she could not breathe. *No more.* Throwing away her last hesitations, Stephenie opened herself to the energy and gorged herself on it. She pulled it from the ground, the air, the buildings, and she even tried to pull it from Yreka. Death would release her, but first she would kill Yreka and the only way she could think to bring down the mage was to remove all the energy the woman could use. Without power, the woman could not attack her.

Stephenie let out a gurgled attempt at a scream as white-hot power flowed into her body. The ground iced over and snow formed in the air as the temperature plummeted, freezing out the last of the moisture. Stephenie's body cooked, but she did not stop the draw, nor did she let the energy escape. She held it in, trying to bleed away anything left that the woman could use to defend herself, then Stephenie would destroy her.

The energy ate its way through her flesh. Her body just could not handle that much power. She felt herself changing and no matter how much she wanted to avoid it, she could not resist.

She knew she would die and so she stopped fighting the pain. Suddenly a wave of energy surged into her body as her flesh changed. She opened her throat to scream, but there was no air in her chest. Another shift occurred and the pain was gone. Her skin and muscle and bone were different. Now, instead of burning, her flesh sucked up the energy, greedy for the power, it held it like a sponge.

Power continued to flow inward faster than it had before. She opened her eyes and saw the frost that covered Yreka's body.

"Wait!" the woman's hoarse voice choked out in the air so dry it brought blood to her lips.

Stephenie's eyes took in everything. Yreka still held much power within her body, but the ground, the building behind her, the front of Lami's house, and the air itself held almost no potential energy. Her own body had transformed. She still had arms and legs and hair as normal, but her skin had scaled over and cast with an iridescent glow like it had never before. Kas' dark hand print still remained over her left breast, glinting like obsidian in the sun. *I truly am a half-breed.* The simmering anger and rage inside perched to erupt and Stephenie no longer cared if it got out.

"Stop your draw of energy!" Yreka raised her hands. "I sense your anger, but Kas is not destroyed. You do not want to be the one to kill him!" As the temperature continue to drop, Yreka wrapped her arms around herself. "I had no idea you were a prime. This is incredible. I don't want to harm you. Please, stop your draw of power. I will not attack you anymore. I will not harm your friends."

Stephenie picked herself up from the ground and rolled her shoulders. The movement felt good. She felt strong. The wounds on her body had all healed. She felt her fingers ending in sharp points and took a moment to look at them. Remembering Yreka's words, she reached out and searched for Kas but could not feel him. She felt Henton and the others, they were several buildings away. Ryia slept in Lami's home, though the temperature in the building had dropped dangerously low. She felt other residents of Alkmaar coming out of their homes. Some fled while others approached to investigate the disturbance. *Let them fear the monster I am.*

"Please, Stephenie. I had no idea what you are. Did you even know? Do you understand what that means?" Yreka forced her hands to her side, though her shoulders were hunched against the cold. "It means the sources are not dead. We had feared for so long that they were all gone. But your existences means that is not true."

Stephenie narrowed her eyes as her lip curled. "You mean dragons."

"Yes. Dragons are the source of our power. I am a fourth generation descendant. But you are obviously a first generation. Only a first generation could do what you just did."

"I will rip your heart from your chest for what you've done," Stephenie growled.

Yreka shook her head and a field unlike any Stephenie had seen before sprung into existence. "You are young. Stop your draw of power. I disrupted Kas, but if you want to have any hope of him recoalescing his presence, there needs to be energy in the area."

Her anger wanted more power, but a distant part of Stephenie's mind spoke up and she slowed her draw of energy. *If he's not dead...* she did not want to let herself hope.

"Stephenie. I know you are confused. You've not had someone to teach you. I can help you learn. I can show you things that even Kas has never seen. I have lived three-hundred and sixty-two years. My mother taught me and her father taught her. I have centuries of learning I can share with you." Yreka held out a hand to Stephenie.

"You cannot hurt me, Stephenie. And I don't want to hurt you. Let me help you rebuild a body for Kas."

Stephenie could not sense anything from the woman. The field around Yreka hid her emotions and seemed to protect Yreka's store of energy. She searched again for Kas, but could not find him. She needed more time to understand the field. "Why? I thought you planned to kill me."

Yreka shook her head. "That was when I thought you were without a family and just some sixth or seventh generation cast off. You are a first generation. A prime. You are a family unto yourself. That makes you protected. I can help you and together we can set a new order in place." Yreka let out a laugh of pleasure. "You are proof the dragons are not gone! You want to stop the witch burnings? I see no purpose in them myself. My people do not do anything so stupid. I can help you bring order to your people. Your lands do not have to suffer any more."

"Your people have been cruel and have killed just as indiscriminately as any priest," Stephenie roared.

"We did not know Cothel was your land. Had we known; had you declared yourself to Favian, we would have instead sought an alliance, not a conquest. After all, my family was not after Cothel or the lands. We were after some lost artifacts you destroyed. But together," Yreka said in a hoarse whisper as she took a step closer, "we can defeat my foes and you can set the laws of your country to suit your desires." Yreka continued to hold out her hand. "Let me help you. We can find a way to rebuild a body for Kas. I can teach you skills you have not yet begun to dream of."

Stephenie's mind raced. She did not trust Yreka at all. The Senzar would use her and Caridelis had already shown her how to build a body for Kas. *But I was too late to do that,* she heard the rage inside her growl. Stephenie pushed back against the instinct to kill, she did not want to be the cause of chaos. She did not want to be the pawn her father may have intended. *And Kas may recover.*

Stephenie sensed Henton and Douglas returning along the back side of Lami's home and she suddenly felt very naked in her changed state. "Ignorance is no excuse," she spit out at Yreka. "That's what you said."

Yreka smiled. "I do not want to hurt you. The laws of our people," Yreka said, pointed between herself and Stephenie, "are such that seniority of generation established rank. There are only a handful of fourth generation people like myself left. There is one third-gen, but he is useless and has aged greatly in recent years. The law is held with the elder. No one will kill a protected member of someone else's family. If one of my family does wrong, I will punish them appropriately. If I fail to do so, then war might ensue. That ensures we do not recklessly kill each other off."

"So that makes me your master?" Stephenie asked, her rage still crying out for the woman's blood. The tip of her tongue caught on what felt like pointed teeth. The fact that Henton and Douglas could see her kept her from snarling and baring what must be rows of fangs.

Yreka smiled again. "Not exactly. There is so much for you to learn. Stephenie, please come with me. I swear, I will not harm your friends. We have both lost people under our protection, let us call it even and forget the past. Let me help you. Let our families not be at war."

Stephenie watched as Yreka's field continued to modulate. She was beginning to understand what the Senzar was doing and how the field might shield her. *A little more time and I'll burn her alive,* the possessive rage swore. However, Stephenie also saw another pattern in the energy-starved environment: tiny particles bonding and linking together. She pushed back against the rage she had so willingly let take over. A more subtle way to kill the Senzar came to her and she kept her face expressionless as she started to gather these tiny particles. Having seen how the particles entangled themselves, she began forcing others to do so, building a small, nearly undetectable cloud in the air.

"I don't want your help," Stephenie said to Yreka as she continued to link the particles to each other. She kept one half of each pair near herself and blew the other half toward Yreka. Just like the poison she used on the High Priest of Mertor, these tiny particles passed through Yreka's field as fresh air did.

Yreka's lips contracted into a thin line and her tone began to change. "Stephenie, you may live six hundred years or more, assuming someone does not kill you. While I am reluctant to harm you as long as you do not attack me, you may be certain that I can kill you if I should choose to do so. There are others that could as well."

Stephenie did not bother to correct her estimate of how long she might live. "And if I join you? If you are not lying to me and you teach me, then one day I will be more powerful than you. What then?"

Yreka shrugged. "You are more powerful than me right now. But power without skill is a waste. My hope is that we'd become friends. Then there would be no need for either of us to be a threat to the other. I am friends with the leaders of several other families and allies with more. I am a reasonable person."

Stephenie continued to generate the pairs of particles and separate them. The ones near her, she scattered around her body to hide them from Yreka. The others she could sense through Yreka's field and many of them had landed on the woman or had gone into her mouth and nose and were now in her sinuses and lungs. "There is something in this for you. You would not want to mentor someone who could later kill you."

Yreka shivered. "Think of Kas. Stop your draw and allow the energy to balance here." Stephenie did not respond, forcing the woman to stand up straight. "I am growing older. I have perhaps another hundred years before I start to become feeble. I do not want my family to be left without a strong leader and all of my children are dead. I have sixth and seventh generation descendants to rely upon, which means I have no one to turn over my empire to. Instead of allowing it to collapse into ruin, I would rather name you as my successor. Together we could make it the most powerful of the empires and once I die, it would all be yours. You could rule the whole world. If you refuse, then when I am gone, chaos will rule. No one will control my family and wars unlike anyone has seen for a thousand years will spread across the land. I have many people in my family, more than all the others."

Stephenie felt the mass of particles inside of Yreka had grown sufficient enough. *If I strike fast...* Stephenie's eyes widened; off to her left and just outside her area of draw, she felt an echo of Kas slowly coming back. She stopped her draw of power. Kas was not whole, but the hint of his presence meant he might recover. He had survived a similar attack in the Grey Mountains and she had failed to kill a ghost in Arkani simply by hitting it with energy. *Perhaps Yreka's field was not as disruptive as I thought.*

The hope that he might recover stayed her hand and allowed her a moment to think without the rage driving her. If the woman had spoken the truth, then killing her would not benefit Cothel or anyone she cared about. *However, I will not be anyone's toy.* Her scaled jaw tightened. "Yreka, I will not join you. You've harmed those I love. Far too many people have died because of you." Stephenie glanced at Jerylin's body and it pained her to continue. "However, I will not kill you either." She forced her hands to remain relaxed. "Instead, I want you to leave this place, leave Cothel, and take your armies with you. Return to wherever you came from and leave me and mine alone. Use your time to make sure your family stays in check."

Yreka bowed her head. "I can understand your anger. We all become very possessive. It is something we inherit with the power, but don't let it blind you. You need someone to guide you, not use and control you. Don't dismiss my offer so quickly." She raised her head and stared at Stephenie.

"You want to prove your good faith, then do as I said, leave. Perhaps one day I'll reach out to you."

Yreka rubbed her fingers against themselves. "You may hold out hope that your father will teach you, but that is seldom the case. Dragons abandon their offspring. They are far above us and our lives matter little to them. Don't expect help from that quarter. If the stories are true, expect death instead."

Stephenie exhaled slowly, her breath freezing in the air. "I have no such expectation. But I will not be bullied into obedience. Leave."

"Foolish girl. You may feel powerful, but you are vulnerable. I could kill you as you stand there gloating. And if you will not join me, do you think I could risk someone else coming and taking control of you? You lack skill. Without—"

Stephenie pushed energy into the particles near her and Yreka's eyes bulged. She bent over and gasped; blood sprayed from her mouth and nose as her exposed skin and clothing smoldered.

Stephenie had pushed only a little energy. The back of her mind screamed to flood Yreka's body with power and burn her through and through. And yet, Stephenie kept her rage under control. "That was a taste of what I can do to you. A sip of the power coursing through my body. I could unleash a lot more."

Yreka coughed. She wiped the blood from her face on the back of her hand as she slowly straightened, though she did not stand fully erect. "What is it you want?" Yreka's voice was hoarse as more blood rose to her lips.

"I told you. I want you and your family to leave me and mine alone. I want you out of Cothel." Stephenie stepped closer, the hardened tips of her fingers tapping softly against the palm of her hands as she struggled not to kill this woman. "I don't want a war. I don't want chaos. But, I will never be someone's puppet. Never." A low growl escaped her throat and rumbled through the ground. "If others must know of me, tell them I will rend them into pieces and spit their carcasses at the feet of their children before consuming their offspring as well. I am not a prize to own."

Yreka swallowed and nodded her head. The damage on her skin had already healed. She dropped the energy field that had been protecting her and bowed her head to Stephenie. "You are indeed a prime. Forgive me."

Stephenie felt Kas' presence had grown a little stronger, but there was no certainty he would actually recover. "Too many have died for me to have forgiveness." She knew the number of people watching her had grown. "I won't kill you if you do as I demand, but we are linked now. I can push energy into your body from as far away as I like."

"Mistress," Yreka said with her eyes still lowered. "Please understand that I can only answer for my family. I will warn my allies and any others that will listen, but there will be some that are certain they can control you. They will come for you. Do not kill me because of them. That will cause my family to break apart and you will see war. My family knows everything I have learned from your friends and they would seek revenge upon you and yours."

"I understand."

"Mistress?"

"Yes.

"I know that you are not ready to accept my offer. I swear it has been honestly given. I still hold hope that one day you may change your mind as time may dull your anger." Yreka nodded her head toward Stephenie's pack that sat several feet away. "I know you took a pair of oval stones from Olena's body. They can be used to contact me. Simply hold one of the stones, reach out with your thoughts to the device, and ask it to make contact with me. I have one like it. It will allow us to communicate over great distances." Stephenie did not reply and Yreka stood up straighter. "I will leave your lands and honor your request. Respect for another's domain is a tenet of our laws. I would like to explain them to you, even if you never take up my offer to rule over my family when I die." Yreka grinned and a small level of confidence returned to her face. "I am still amazed that the sources are still alive."

Stephenie understood the implied threat. Yreka would start a search for someone more malleable then she was. *Kill her,* the voice in the back of her head screamed. She felt the personal affront this woman had unleashed upon her and her friends, but a part of her still considered the consequences. Stephenie believed what Yreka had said and war would only harm more people. *I will not be your pawn either,* she said to the idea of her father. To Yreka, she said, "I will consider your offer, but it will be on my own terms."

"I understand." Yreka looked back to Lami's home. She had stopped showing any signs of being cold. Now that Stephenie had stopped her draw of energy, the potentials in the air had almost equalized with the surrounding environment as the wind blew warmer air through the city. The ground and the buildings had more thermal mass and would take longer to return to the temperature of the surroundings. "May I be allowed to get my things before I leave this city? For one thing, my communication stone is in my possessions and I would need it if I am to hope you might contact me."

Stephenie wanted to snarl, but instead nodded her head.

"I'll get it for her," Henton said as he slowly walked around the edge of Lami's house, a borrowed coat covering him.

Yreka bowed her head to him, but kept one eye on Stephenie. "Princess, you are amazing, if you are not already aware. You are a true wonder."

A few moments later, Henton came out carrying two large satchels and a pair of saddle bags. He placed them on the ground near Yreka and then backed away.

"Go," Stephenie said. "Keep your promise. Leave my friends, family, and people alone. If you do, I may change my mind and may contact you. If not, I will burn your corpse away and bring war to your children's children."

Yreka bowed her head to Stephenie. "Keep yourself alive until then. Word will spread about you even if I say nothing." Yreka looked toward the bodies on the ground. "If I may ask, please bury Werha. He was a good man and was simply following my orders. The same for Olena and Tibva, if their bodies are available. They deserve respect."

Stephenie watched the woman turn and walk away, heading toward the building where Argat was staying. "My protection extends to my horses and the people here," Stephenie called out. She felt the people of Alkmaar staring at her. There were more than a dozen close enough to see and hear what had been said, though Stephenie hoped many did not speak Pandar.

Stephenie monitored Yreka with her senses well after she was out of sight. As she was now, Stephenie could feel things nearly to the city walls, though not with as much detail as she could the areas closer to her.

Fear filled the air from almost everyone except Henton. The locals, Lami especially, mixed their fear with a sense of worshipful awe. She wanted to tell everyone it would be alright, but even Douglas and Islet were apprehensive.

She closed her eyes and searched for Kas. He was still far from regaining consciousness. *If no one kills us, I'll live to see all these people dead from old age long before I even start to look old. Absolutely everyone I love will die while I am still young. If I live that long...I don't want to live without Kas.*

She bit her lower lip with her pointed teeth. The pain made her open her eyes. *I still have a duty to my friends.* The moment she said it, she knew she would carry on and protect them with everything she had.

"Steph?" Henton asked, breaking through her train of thoughts.

She turned toward Henton. Douglas, Sir Walter and even Islet and Lami huddled together near the side of his house, a couple of blankets wrapped around them. She pushed a small amount of energy into their bodies to keep them from freezing. However, she did not release too much energy into the surrounding area for fear of harming Kas.

"What about Kas? Is he with you?" Henton asked, concern for her in his voice and mind, but he still had no fear of her.

"Yreka hurt him, but...he will survive." *If I say it, it will be true.*

"Ryia?"

"She lost her right arm at the elbow, but she lives." He looked back at bodies outside Lami's home.

Islet, Douglas, and Sir Walter continued to stare as she stood naked in the wind, though her finely scaled iridescent skin did not register the cold. She extended her senses again and felt Yreka leaving with a pair of horses, neither of which she recognized. Behind her, she felt the dagger from Ista. The sheath had been burned away, but the weapon appeared unharmed. She reached out a hand and the dagger, staff, and her backpack flew to her. The staff greeted her the moment she contacted it. However, she gently pushed it out of her mind.

She gathered together the entangled particles that floated near her, then used her mind to pull a small stone from the damaged wall of the abandon building. With the rock floating in the air, she broke the bonds of stone, turning it into a floating mass of liquid with far more ease than she ever had before. She placed the particles into the center of the fluid with care to avoid breaking the entanglement, then she drew the stone around the particles and allowed the stone to harden into a smooth oval mass. She left a small hole in the stone suitable for a chain or a cord and on one side, she left a slight indention that resembled the hand print Kas' had left on her chest.

She grabbed the stone out of the air and turned back toward Lami's damaged home. She did not want to look at the bloody remains of Jerylin's body. The woman's skin had turned an ugly hue as it was now frozen solid because of her draw of power. "I failed Jerylin," Stephenie said.

"What are you?" Islet finally asked. "Why didn't you kill her?"

Stephenie exhaled as she slowly released a little energy into the ground. She knew that to change back she would have to reduce the power left in her body, otherwise she would simply burn up as she returned to normal. "I will explain. I have a lot to tell everyone."

Chapter 36

The transformation from what she had become back to her normal form was more painful than Stephenie had expected, but with careful management of the energy in her body, she managed to come out of the process without feeling as if she had been trampled by a horse. She had performed the change outside in case she had misjudged the power inside of her and she had to expel it quickly. That had not happened and now the cold wind immediately made itself known, leaving her shivering. Henton came up and wrapped his arms around her and led her into Lami's damaged house.

He helped her to the fire pit where Ryia slept and draped a fur blanket over her shoulders. The energy she had stolen from the building left the room icy cold and the fire had died down to embers. Lami and Douglas immediately started stoking the fire, adding coal and kindling to bring back the warmth while Henton checked on Ryia.

"Is she okay? Why is she asleep?"

"She's not taking the loss of her arm well and Yreka tormented her mind. Lami's been giving her medicine to keep her asleep so she can rebuild her strength."

"Steph, what are you?" demanded Islet again, a sense of foreboding in her words. Her sister stood behind her, halfway across the room. "Tell me!"

Stephenie did not turn around. She simply pulled the blanket around herself, trying to be modest around so many people who had never previously seen her naked. She extended her senses and looked for Kas. His energy existed just outside the building. He felt stronger, but not yet conscious. She reached out and touched Ryia's mind, even asleep, the girl was in pain. *Ryia, can you bear to wake?*

The girl pushed her away at first and then became more aware of what was going on, she reached back to Stephenie even as she dreamed. *Is that you? I should never have come. My arm...*

Stephenie placed a hand on Ryia's chest. The girl was still partially asleep, but Stephenie wanted her awake when she started her explanations. *Ryia, wake,* Stephenie said as she pushed energy into Ryia's injured arm. Ryia screamed as she came awake, but Stephenie continued to direct Ryia's body to heal the damage. She concentrated on mending and rebuilding the flesh as Ryia's body knew it should exist, just as Stephenie's own body had mended when it transformed.

Lami came over and Stephenie pulled her mind back from Ryia. Perain and several other locals stood in the small home, their weapons were drawn, but none of them looked confident. Stephenie turned to face them, the fur blanket doing a bad job of covering her body as it hung loosely over her shoulders.

"No, Perain," Lami said, then he took a step away from Stephenie and bowed deeply to her. "Goddess." Perain and the other locals looked uncertain, but two of the men with Perain also bowed.

Stephenie looked down at Ryia. Tears flowed from Ryia's eyes, but her mind did not radiate pain as it had a moment ago. Ryia was as naked as Stephenie, but she was wrapped more tightly in blankets so her body was concealed. Stephenie pulled the bandages off the stump of her arm. The end was covered in what appeared to be healthy skin. Although Stephenie had not seen the damage with her eyes, she had sensed it and knew that was a great improvement. "It will take time," Stephenie said, "but I will make sure your arm comes back."

"Steph?" several people said at once.

She pulled the blanket around herself again and used her head to indicate everyone should gather in front of her. She sat down next to Ryia who was carefully touching the stump of her arm. *What am I doing?* She asked herself and then cleared her throat. The dry air and exhaustion made her voice hoarse.

Everyone stood before her, looking down with expressions ranging from awe to concern to fear. Islet and Sir Walter huddled together, the knight trying to shield Islet with his body.

"Everyone sit. This is going to take some time."

More people streamed into Lami's home and Lami spoke quickly in his native language. The people spread out in the back, making room for others to join, but all of them staring at her and whispering among themselves.

Stephenie.

She trembled as she heard Kas' faint voice in her head. *Here, my love!*

I...do not...feel well.

She felt her chest tighten. *Can I do anything to help? I feared Yreka killed you.*

Several moments passed and Kas came in through the open door as more people shuffled in. Invisible, he floated across the room and hovered next to her. His form was not yet as substantial as he normally was, but she could sense him continuing to strengthen. *I...I do not know. What transpired? I...I have no memory of arriving in Alkmaar. The last I can recall is finding Ryia's hand.*

Stephenie fought to contain her fear. She did not want to frighten Kas. With great care, she slowly replayed her memories since they found Ryia's hand. *Does that help?*

I think it is likely I will recover as I did in the Grey Mountains when the Senzar used a similar attack on me there. It took some time. Do not worry.

She could not help but worry. However, the crowd was growing more agitated. She kept her link to him open, as though she held his hand, then she turned her focus back to the crowd before her. She looked at Islet. "I did not find the man who sired me, but I have learned more about him than I ever expected to know." She saw Henton's expression and knew that he supported her, even as she was.

Stephenie looked back at the locals. "Lami, Perain, everyone else here, let me apologize for the damage done to your homes. I will make it right."

Perain and a couple other people started to translate for those in the room who did not speak Pandar. A few other people worked to cover the hole in Lami's home with thick hides.

Sir Walter still kept himself between Islet and Stephenie. "I heard the woman say your father was a dragon," Sir Walter challenged in Cothish. "You're some kind of demon aren't you? You are the spawn of Elrin."

"I am not a demon," Stephenie replied in Cothish as well, keeping her tone neutral and without the anger she instinctively felt at the accusation. "I am a person, just like anyone else with magic, or powers. Priest, witch, mage, whatever you want to call us, we are all the same. The source of our power is the same. It would seem we inherited these powers because somewhere in our past, one of our ancestors was a dragon." She took a deep breath. Admitting it aloud to those she loved and cared for made her stomach tight and she continued to look in their eyes for their reaction.

Ryia shifted so she could move closer to Stephenie. "I have dragon blood in me as well?"

"Yes, Ryia, you do."

"Steph, you are still the same person," Henton offered. "Kind, caring, and willing to do anything for us. It means nothing."

Islet slowly nodded her head. "We knew the man who had attacked our mother was not a typical man. I never would have guessed this, but Henton is right, you've risked yourself time and again to save me and the people of Cothel. I will continue to support you." She turned to Sir Walter and put a hand on his shoulder, slowly pulling him back so they would sit side by side.

"There are implications," Stephenie said. "People will learn of this and there will be powerful enemies that emerge. One such enemy just left."

Islet's expression hardened. "I promised Jerylin you'd save us. Why did you let Yreka leave? She killed Tain and Wilson, and Carac. She's a monster."

Stephenie did not touch Islet's mind, but she could feel the panic of confinement, just like Islet had when she was in the Senzar prison. "I let Yreka go because she has a large family of people who could wreak havoc on our countries if she does not keep them in line. I don't know how much you heard, but I actually believe everything she told me. She may be ruthless and deserve death a hundred times over, but allowing her to live seemed like the best course of action for Cothel."

"Steph," Henton said with a tone so devoid of emotion that she knew he objected. "Yreka may use this as an opportunity to muster a stronger attack upon you."

"Not for a while. I've been to Isa Fields and I saw the city and learned things. I entangled some particles and embedded them in her body. I have the other half of those particles with me." She held up the stone she formed. "Just like an augmentation device, I can kill her at any time." She knew Henton, Islet, Ryia, and Douglas would realize that distance would reduce the amount of energy she could channel into Yreka. *And time is likely to cause those particles to flush from her body, but hopefully it will keep Yreka in-line long enough for me to establish my own base of power.*

"Goddess," Perain said, bowing his head and speaking in Pandar. "I know that you have been away from your people for several days, but many people here want to express their devotion to you. Only the Goddess could drive an evil one like that woman from our land."

Stephenie knew she had been rude to speak in Cothish when the others would not be able to understand. She switched to Pandar, "I am not your Goddess. I am...I am the daughter of a woman and... and...a dragon." Stephenie waited for the locals to hear the translation, since they had not understood Sir Walter's statement. A wave of disbelief filled the room. "I don't have all the answers. I don't even know what it truly means. As more people learn of it, I think it will cause more people to come after me." She raised her hand to silence the people who started to ask questions. "I had originally wanted to wait to make this decision, but once I found Yreka's people had harmed Ryia, and perhaps others, I knew I would make a home for myself in Isa Fields."

Stephenie felt Kas' reluctance. The people in the room who heard the translation started talking between themselves. *I know Kas, but Yreka was right about one other thing. There are likely others like myself out there. If Yreka, or other heads of families, find them and decide to start using them as weapons, we could see a lot more death and destruction. I don't think we have a choice except to establish a base of power. A place where Caridelis might come and teach me more.*

I understand. I just do not fully trust the castle or that dragon

I know. I have no intention of being dominated by them. I just need you to trust me.

I will.

"As many of you likely suspected, Ista and Isa Fields had died. The people who lived there were slaughtered about twenty years ago. However, I can lead those who may wish to go there past the guardians. The city is beautiful and I will welcome any who want to make it their home, though if you do come, respect must be given to those who have died there."

"What happened?" Perain asked on behalf of several people.

Stephenie fought the yawn building in her. Her body was beginning to ache from lack of sleep and the energy that had passed through it. The transformation had renewed much of her strength, but she still wanted some rest. However, these people and her friends were not going to wait. "I will tell you what I know."

Chapter 37

The telling of their stories, from when the Senzar first invaded their lands, up to the point where Stephenie drove Yreka from Alkmaar, took a long time and Lami had taken it upon himself to fix Stephenie and Ryia something to eat well before she had finished. Stephenie left out many of the more personal details and avoided any mention of Caridelis and Kas. However, she did not conceal details such as the fact she took her own mother's head as punishment for the treason her mother had committed.

In the middle of her story, four of the stone guardians that Isa sent south pushed their way into Lami's home, causing a short wave of hysteria until Stephenie was able to calm everyone down. The four other guardians had taken up positions around the building.

The interruption led Stephenie to explain the truth about magic, the southern gods that these people in Alkmaar did not believe in, and the struggles that existed between the people who were considered priests and those who were called witches or warlocks. She demanded that any who ever wanted to enter Ista would give up their augmentation devices, but otherwise, she would not restrict anyone from worshiping the Goddess or any other deity they chose.

The questions continued to come well past nightfall and it was Henton and Lami who finally called an end to the discussions so that Stephenie and Ryia could rest. Everyone obliged them save for Perain, and since it was Lami's home and Lami had not demanded the man to leave, neither did anyone else.

As the others readied themselves for bed, Stephenie rubbed Ryia's hair and she watched as Ryia's eyes grew heavy. Her own eyes were dry, but she had two more things she wanted to clear up before she went to sleep. She switched to Cothish to keep this information between her closest friends. "I didn't say it to everyone else, but I want to tell all of you two things. First, there is a castle in Isa Fields and she is alive. Her name is Isa and she's the one that directs the guardians. She's the one that controls the weather in the city. She protects the country. She is Isa Fields and she decided to offer me the opportunity to be her companion."

Stephenie noticed the drowsiness disappeared from Ryia's eyes. She had their attention and no one wanted to say anything. "I mentioned it earlier, but I had planned to discuss my decision with all of you before I finalized it. I know it impacts all of us, but when I saw Ryia's hand in the snow," she continued to rub Ryia's hair, "I decided to accept her offer. It was partially selfish of me to do so, but I also knew without someplace I could feel safe, I would always be running."

"What does that mean?" Islet asked. "Companion? What of Kas? What of us?"

Stephenie smiled. "Kas isn't exactly happy with me, but I've been able to share more of what Isa showed me as I've been talking this evening and he's coming around. But really, Isa wants someone to talk with and look after. She was built to care for a city and a city needs people and people need a leader. It is not a dominant and subordinate relationship. I won't be a prisoner and I can come and go as I please, but it does mean she will want me to live in the city more years than not."

Henton cleared his throat. "You absolutely refused to take over ruling Cothel when I asked you to."

"And for good reason. They'd have burned me at the stake if I had. Plus, my brother is the rightful ruler, not I." She looked at the others. "It does mean that I will be making this place a home for myself. I would love for all of you to join me, but only if you want to. If you don't, come next summer, I will take you anywhere you want to go and make sure you are set up for life."

Henton frowned. "The city's stuck out in the middle of a vast wasteland. You sure the weather there is nice?"

"Like a cool spring day. I believe summer is nicer. There are even trees and fields."

"You wouldn't live there all the time, you'd still want to travel?" Henton asked.

"Yes. And no one has to decide right now. Go there and see what it is like. Live there until next year, or for five years, or however long you want. I will never force anyone to stay longer than they want."

Douglas and Henton shared a couple looks and Stephenie made sure she stayed out of their thoughts. She noticed Ryia anxiously watching Henton and so she continued to rub Ryia's hair. "Let me tell everyone the second item. When we were in Isa Fields, we met a dragon. Not the one that had lived there. And not my...father. My father is a dragon named Duvargintik. He killed the ruler of Ista twenty years ago. The ruler was a dragon named Kervigar. Duvargintik then slaughtered everyone else there." Stephenie held her breath. "When Kas and I were exploring the city, a third dragon came to investigate our intrusion. This was a woman named Caridelis."

"Damn," Douglas swore. "For a dead race, that is a lot of dragons."

Stephenie's head moved in agreement. "I have no idea how many actually exist and I don't think they want their presence talked about too much."

"What did she look like?" Ryia asked. She was sitting up to better hear what Stephenie had to say.

"When I first saw her, she was just a beautiful woman. She was tall and her body was thin and muscular, but her mental presence was unlike any I had ever seen. It was like looking at the sun. But she was also rather normal. We talked at length. She told me much about dragons and why most people have not seen any for more than seventeen-hundred years. She told me about Duvargintik." Stephenie chose not to tell them about how long Caridelis thought she might live. "I will tell everyone more about her later, but it is possible she may seek me out again. I do not know that any of you would want to meet her or she you. Her power is terrifying and she has little in the way of patience. However, I am hopeful if I do speak with her again, I may be able to close the gaps in my skills compared to Yreka and others like her." Stephenie could not keep the smile from her face. "But most importantly, she did show me a way to rebuild Kas' body."

"Really?" Henton and Ryia asked together.

Stephenie nodded her head and she felt her eyes moisten from the hope that saying that aloud brought to her. "It will take me a little time and practice, but after my transformation today, or yesterday depending on the time, I really think I can do it."

Stephenie felt Kas' love of her and his own hope at having a body. *I love you.*

And I you.

Stephenie looked over to Islet and Walter. A stiffness in their movement drew her attention. "This is probably the hardest for you, Walter. You're hearing some of these things for the first time."

He shook his head. "Islet filled me in on much of this after we were taken by Yreka. But, I am having a hard time dealing with the ideas of dragons. It is my job to protect Islet and..."

"We lost everyone who came with us," Islet said for Walter. "All of them have died because we came. Because I insisted we try to reach you."

"How did Yreka get you?" Stephenie asked. "How'd she know you knew where I was going?"

Islet leaned against Walter and he held her. "She confronted Will in Antar. She learned about the priests of Mertor from him, but he didn't know about your other plans. She left him alive, saying she had to judge you first before she could kill everyone else. He warned us that she was after you, so I decided I had to warn you. Josh was livid with me. But Rebecca and Will helped to convince him it was the best course of action." Islet wiped tears from her eyes. "Jerylin used one of the holy symbols to follow you. Then you destroyed the trap when we were still a few days behind you and we had to guess your route. Unfortunately, we were slower than you and Yreka came upon us in a tavern while we stopped along Lake Seon." Islet shook her head. "I've wanted to die so many times as she pushed us north. I...I failed you. I failed the others. I led her to you instead of warning you about her coming."

Stephenie left Ryia's side on the furs, moved to Islet, and put her arms around her older sister. "It is not your fault. I tried to outrun my problems and I'm the one that failed. I should have been able to protect Jerylin. I wasn't fast enough."

Stephenie held Islet for a long time, then finally, she gathered the blanket around herself and went back to sitting next to Ryia again. "Anyone have any clothing I can wear?"

Henton chuckled, got up, and walked to their gear that was near the outer wall of Lami's home. "I wondered how long you'd sit naked. Though, I've always said you enjoy taking off your clothes in the most spectacular of fashions. I think showing your scaly hide to twenty or thirty people is a new record."

She smiled at him as she slowly shook her head. "I'll make you pay for that one of these days. I will."

He brought over a bundle of clothing and dropped it in Stephenie's outstretched hand. "You won't because you need to keep me around to make sure you always stay clothed." He turned and dropped the second bundle into Ryia's hand. "You don't want to get like Stephenie and start running around naked all the time either."

Ryia looked up at him and nodded her head. She instinctively moved her right arm and then froze. She blinked back some tears. "I...I don't..."

"I'll help you, Ryia," Stephenie said. "And, I promise, we'll rebuild your arm."

Ryia looked up at Stephenie. "Like you will for Kas?"

"No. You have a living body to start with. We can get your arm to regrow slowly. For Kas, we need to create a full body for him all at once. Or at least most of body."

I am not going to exist with nothing more than stumps for arms and legs. You will have to find a way to make a whole body for me.

I will, My Love.

Stephenie shook her shoulders, moving the fur blanket draped over her back and glanced at Henton. He huffed and came over to take the blanket off her shoulders and held it up to shield her and Ryia from the others' sight. "Like you really care about modesty."

"Ryia does not need everyone ogling her," Stephenie said as she helped Ryia out of the blanket and then helped to slide pants onto her legs.

"I will live in Isa Fields with you, Steph," Ryia said softly. "You're the only family I have."

Stephenie smiled at Ryia and leaned over to give her a hug and a kiss.

"Hey, put some clothes on if you're going to do that," Ryia said, shouldering Stephenie away.

Stephenie ruffled Ryia's hair and pulled a shirt over her own head as Ryia wiggled her pants the rest of the way up.

"Steph," Henton said from the other side of the blanket. "I think we are all in agreement that we'll see what Ista has to offer."

"As long as we can travel," Douglas said. "I assume you'll need a tailor. You've burned up almost all of your clothing."

Stephenie helped Ryia pull a shirt over her head and then quickly pulled on her own pants. Once they were modestly clothed, she reached up and pulled the blanket down. "Of course, Douglas. Though, I'll expect you to make something flame proof."

"Good luck with that," he replied as he spread a blanket out to sleep on.

She let her mind open up again. She felt the hesitation from Walter and she knew Islet had not fully accepted what she was, but Henton, Douglas, Ryia, and Kas had taken everything she said in stride. "I love you guys."

Chapter 38

The next morning, Stephenie oversaw the burial of Jerylin and Werha, though his grave was unmarked and away from where Jerylin was buried. Jerylin was given a place of honor with other prominent residents of Alkmaar. Stephenie took the time to form a cairn from a mass of stone into a solid grave marker that bore Jerylin's name.

That afternoon, eighty-six out of the four-hundred and seventeen people that called Alkmaar home informed Stephenie they wanted to travel with her to Ista Fields. That number included Lami and Perain, though not all of those going had decided if they would live there permanently. Almost a third simply wanted to see what the fabled city had to offer and would make a final decision later. Of those that had already decided, many still considered her a messenger from their Goddess, if not their Goddess.

Stephenie did not bother to argue her status with them. She would let them believe as they liked, but she did hope many of those undecided people would stay and if they did not, she hoped they would return and tell others about the city. She knew Isa Fields could easily support four or five thousand people and if she only started with forty or fifty to seed the population, it would be a long time before it was fully populated. *Perhaps long enough that I will die of old age first.*

Alkmaar buzzed with activity as the whole city worked to get those leaving ready for the journey that could take up to twenty days depending on the weather since Stephenie would not leave the horses.

In addition to the supplies they needed for the trip, they also needed supplies to live on in Isa Field until food could be gathered from the fields and a large enough herd of animals established to support their wool, milk, and meat needs.

While preparations for the journey continued, Stephenie split her time between working on Ryia's arm, which had to be done slowly to avoid draining Ryia's body of nutrients, and her practicing transformative and translocative magic to create a new body for Kas.

To perfect her skill and not risk Kas' life, every other day Stephenie went to the butcher and asked for two animals he planned to slaughter. She led the animals to a remote part of Alkmaar and into an abandoned building. Being careful to avoid harming the animals, she drew in energy forcing her own body to transform. Only then did she attempt to take the energy from animal and rebuild the opposite animal's body in an effort swap their bodies. She hoped if she could manage to hold two animals in stasis while transforming their raw forms, she could succeed with Kas.

In her modified form, she found she could store a much larger reservoir of energy, her senses were sharper, and the process became much quicker. Unfortunately, her first attempt left both animals dead and she simply returned the bodies to the butcher to be used as food. However, both the second and third attempts were successful. The third one, due to the differences in sizes of the animals, required her to transfer the excess mass from one animal to the other as she rebuilt their bodies.

After subjecting the animals to her experiments, she asked the butcher to sell her the four animals so that they could be allowed to live out the rest of their lives. The butcher agreed quickly because of what she was, even though he felt the request to be odd.

The automatic deference to her request reminded her just how lucky she was, having Henton, Douglas, and Ryia as friends. She hoped that in time, others who intended to follow her to Isa Fields would become willing to question her requests, but she knew it would not completely fade from the majority of people.

As the time to make the journey arrived, Stephenie led everyone from the city. No longer having to conceal her abilities, she used her powers to clear the road of large drifts, making it possible for Argat and the other horses to more easily travel north. Six of the eight stone guardians that had followed her around the city were hooked up to three large sleds overloaded with the supplies she had purchased. The other two guardians continued to stand watch over her and her friends.

It took seven days to reach the border and the locals were understandably nervous. To their knowledge, no one had ever crossed into Ista and returned. The eight massive stone cats that followed Stephenie around Alkmaar put an image to the unknown, which helped to reduce their fear. However, at the crossing, more than two dozen winged guardians lined the sides of the road, giving hint that Ista still possessed a significant threat. Stephenie knew the guardians were taking a measure of each person, remembering them and asking for her confirmation that they be given the protection of Ista.

Once they completed the border crossing without incident, those from Alkmaar began to relax and the tension in the air faded. It also allowed for a handful of the locals to start jockeying for position as leaders among the people. So far Henton continued to use Perain as his primary contact, allowing Perain to manage each night's camp while Henton kept a protective eye on Ryia, Douglas, Islet, Walter, and the horses. Stephenie found that arrangement quite satisfactory and hoped Henton would continue to help her grow into her role as their Queen and Isa companion.

A day before they reached the way station, Isa informed Stephenie through one of the guardians that a large deer had died out in the snow fields. A pair of guardians had brought the carcass to the way station if she should want to make use of the animal.

She immediately took Henton and the others to the side. "Douglas, may I borrow a set of your clothes?"

"You planning to burn up what you're wearing?" He asked.

"No," she could not keep the grin from her face.

"I'll get them," he said with a knowing smile.

"We're about a day out from a small group of buildings. If all goes well..."

"We'll meet you there," Henton finished. "Just stay safe and take as much time as you need to do what needs to be done."

"Thank you," she said as she took the bundle of clothing from Douglas. "I'll leave the guardians with you. They understand rank and priority. So effectively, I've made all of you Dukes and Duchesses, including you Sir Walter. Thank you for taking care of my sister." She grinned at them. "Just don't let it go to your heads."

Sir Walter bowed his head, but said nothing.

"I'll have to commission some new clothes for myself," Douglas said. "And it sure beats waiting for your brother to knight me."

"Go," Henton said, shooing her away, "the sun's starting to come up."

She smiled at them, turned, and took to the sky with a cloud of fresh snow sucked into the air behind her. She flew faster than she thought possible, with Kas keeping pace beside her.

I have faith in you, Stephenie. Even if this does not work this time, we will make it work eventually.

Shush, she told him. *It will work and we will make Isa Field our home and we will make it live again and we will be surrounded by our friends.*

Shush, yourself. Just fly.

The morning was still young when they arrived at the way station. The anticipation of what she was about to do had driven Stephenie to keep pulling energy into herself as she flew and by the time she saw the buildings, she radiated power. She landed in front of the building they had slept in on their first journey north. Two guardians stood over the body of an aged deer whose coat was specked with grey hair.

She started stripping out of her clothing and handed them off to Kas to carry inside the building. "I'll transform here, then bring the deer inside."

He nodded his head and disappeared into the building. She took a deep breath to banish away the nagging doubt that still plagued her. She would not consider the possibility that Kas could die at her own hand just as she tried to bring life back to him. Instead, she gorged herself on energy from the ground and pushed her shivering body into the transformation.

Each time she did it, there was less pain and the change came easier. She continued to pull in energy until she felt the power tingling throughout her scale-covered form. Then she used her power to lift the frozen deer and bring it into the building.

Kas stood fully opaque next to the fire-less cooking pit. He smiled at her and his clothing faded away to reveal his naked body. "I have been trying to remember as much as I could about myself. I realized some days ago I have never visualized myself without clothing since I died. I do not remember what my feet look like at all."

She looked over his body and noticed several parts of him that were too smooth and without natural definition. His shoulders and legs were the worst. The degradation of Kas' memory of himself was her biggest worry. She had not told anyone, including Kas; however, since she had returned to Alkmaar and had other people around her to observe, she had been using her powers to carefully look over their physical bodies. It had felt wrong at first, but once she started, she found it hard not to use her mind's eye to see what was hidden under their clothing. She studied the surface textures of their skin and deep into their bodies, looking at the muscles and bones.

"I think I can compensate for gaps," she told Kas. She did not want to admit to him that she would essentially be comparing him to all of the other men.

"Well, if you plan to augment me..."

"Really?" She asked, looking halfway down his body. "You're worried about that?"

He shrugged and grinned. "I may have been dead for a thousand years, but I am a man. And you might benefit..."

She shook her head. "I love you. No matter what happens, I love you."

"And I love you as well. Do you think it will hurt?"

She shook her head. "The animals find themselves confused and scared, but I do not sense they find any pain when I bind their energy. I don't think they are aware anything is happening at that point. Like they are simply asleep."

He nodded his head. "Then please start, My Love."

Stephenie threw her field around him as quickly as she could, wanting to make sure he did not panic and try to fight her. The animals had never had the ability to challenge her, but Kas might react instinctively. However, the field snapped closed too quickly for him to react and his essence remained frozen in place. The feeling of holding his life in her control sent terror down her spine, but she pushed through the fear. She needed her head clear so that she could read every bit of him and transform the dead deer's raw material into a new human body.

Please don't screw this up, she told herself as she settled down to sit cross-legged in front of the deer. She closed her eyes and started slowly and carefully repeating the process she had now done only a handful of times. She pushed aside the desire that Caridelis was present to guide her. She would succeed or fail on her own and wishing for something different would not make it happen.

She found Kas' mind to be whole and without any obvious gaps. For his body, however, she had to adjust her process. She had to take the underlying map of what his body said it should be and use that map to expand the areas he had lost over time. The work she had done to rebuild several inches of Ryia's arm helped in the process.

The sun moved across the sky and she continued the effort. Sweat formed on her scaled body as the concentration took its toll on her, but as she had done with the lemmings the first time, she did not stop, she did not pause. The concerns of her physical body faded away.

She had no idea what time it was when she finished rebuilding Kas' physical form. She opened her eyes and looked down at his brown hair and brown eyes that stared lifelessly upward. Not only had she held Kas' energy in a frozen state, she had held the body in a similar field, keeping it from decaying as she worked.

"Did I do everything correctly?" She asked; a sob just barely detectable in her words. She considered waiting, trying again later when she might be more skilled. The memory of his skeleton laying in his home under Antar came back to her. She could not lose him. However, she also knew living without a body was slowly killing Kas emotionally. She bit her lower lip with her pointed teeth and drew blood.

She closed her eyes and generated the disruption field so she could merge Kas' energy into his newly created body. She went slowly, having to adjust his energy to match the areas she had extrapolated from his genetics and combined with what she had seen of the other men.

As she finished, she released the fields that had held him in stasis. Her own breath caught in her throat as nothing happened. Kas' new body did not move and his presence faded. She snarled and hit his chest as she contemplated trying to reverse the process and extract Kas from the body.

Suddenly he gasped and his body convulsed. He struggled to move, but he simply rolled from side to side.

"Kas, I'm here!" She reached out to him mentally and found his presence growing stronger. She felt his heart beating erratically and sensed the pain. She closed her eyes and entered his mind, this time with the intent to heal the body and whatever she had gotten wrong.

Time seemed to stand still as it stretched on. She knew stars had traveled across the night sky while she continued to work on Kas, but she had no real memory of everything she had done. Now, she found herself draped across his chest as she listened to his heart beat steadily.

"Stephenie," his slightly strange voice slowly emerged as his fingers found her left hand and entwined themselves with hers.

She let the tears fall from her eyes as she felt his mind become fully conscious. "Kas, oh Kas, I did it."

I feel strange, he said mentally. *My voice is odd. I am having to remember how to have a body.*

She lifted her head and looked into his bright eyes. "Does anything hurt or feel wrong? Can you move everything?"

He took a deep breath and slowly sat up. "Your skin. I never thought it would feel like that. Soft and silky."

"Unless you rub it the wrong direction," she said. She stood up and helped him to his feet. He wobbled at first, but then stood on his own.

"Damn, this feels good." He started to shake. "I never thought I would live again."

She stepped forward and wrapped her scaly arms and legs around him and tucked her head under his chin. "Just hold me," she told him.

Stephenie opened her eyes. She sensed someone speaking to her and realized Isa was telling her the others were near the way station. Stephenie breathed in Kas' scent and drew her hardened fingers across his chest. She had been so mentally exhausted that she had not bothered to return to her more human form. She had simply collapsed next to him and drank in the pleasure of his physical contact.

"What time is it?" Kas asked.

"I don't care," she replied, her head resting on his shoulder. A shoulder she crafted from what she knew of her own body and that of the other men. *I think I understand how dragons can so easily shift form.*

"Thank you. Thank you for doing this. I had not allowed myself to believe this might happen."

"You are welcome. But I would be lying if I said I did it solely for you. A lot of this was for me too."

He lifted his head and kissed her forehead. "Do you want to see if everything works correctly?"

She chuckled and rolled on top of him. "I would, but Isa awoke me to say the others are almost here. I'd rather wait for a little more privacy." She leaned forward and kissed him passionately. "And, you don't mind me looking like this?"

"Not at all. I think it suits you well."

She reached out to Isa to see just how close the others were and then swore. "They are really almost here. I better change back. My looking like this will take some time for the others to get used to." She kissed him again and then rolled off him. Still lying on the floor, she channeled the excess energy in her body into the stone, warming the floor until the room was almost too hot. A moment later, the iridescent scales that covered her body faded and her form shifted back to her normal appearance.

"You are beautiful," Kas said, having rolled onto his side to look at her. "It is so different to see with eyes instead of simply interpreting the light as it hits my energy field." His stomach rumbled and his eyes widened. "I forgot being hungry."

She stuck her tongue out at him. "There will be a lot you have to remember. But for now, get dressed." She reached out with her powers and pulled their clothing from the side of the room over and hit him in the gut with what she borrowed from Douglas. Then she rolled into him and wrapped her arms around his body and squeezed as she smashed her lips into his. She finally let go when she heard the dogs barking next to the building.

"Henton should have taken his time," Kas complained.

"I rather think they did. It's past mid-day." She pushed herself to her feet and quickly dressed, laughing at Kas as he struggled to get used to his body. He then used his own magic to try and push her over, which she let him do.

"Hey, you made the others dukes and duchesses, what title will I get?"

"You only in this for the power?"

"Why do you think I kept you around, Stephenie?" He said as he crawled over to her and kissed her.

"Don't get any ideas. Prince Consort is all you get. I am the Queen."

He smiled. "You could make me the court librarian or cook for all I care. I am just happy to have you."

She kissed him again and sighed. With her shirt in her hand, she sat up and slipped it over her head just as Henton opened the door.

"Steph? Oh, sorry."

She giggled from where she sat and waved him inside. "Henton, I would like to formally introduce Kas."

Henton stepped inside, followed by Ryia, Douglas, Islet, and Sir Walter. "It is a pleasure to finally meet you," Henton said with a bow.

"Stop," Kas said, Douglas' shirt was still in his hand. Kas moved forward, pulled on the shirt as he approached Henton, and wrapped his arms around the bigger man. "I never thought I'd live to see this day. Thank you."

Douglas, Ryia, and Islet stepped forward to join the hug, all of them talking at once and even squealing with glee. Stephenie smiled. For the first time in her life, her happiness and pleasure far exceeded her concerns and worries. It was not perfect, and if what she had been told was true, everyone she loved would die long before she showed any age, but she would hold on to this moment as long as she could make it last and would not allow herself to fear the future. *I will make this my home.*

www.ingramcontent.com/pod-product-compliance
Lightning Source LLC
Chambersburg PA
CBHW050541260626
47157CB00002B/391